HOOP DRAMA

a novel

Andy Silvers

Hoop Drama

Copyright 2024 Andrew Silvers
All rights reserved.

This book represents a work of fiction and is purely a work of the author's imagination. Any similarity to real persons, places, or events is strictly coincidental.
Exception: Any reference to living politicians is used exclusively for the purpose of realism and does not serve as a reprimand or endorsement of any candidate, position, party, or slogan.
No part of this book may be copied, sold, or distributed in any form including written, verbal, and electronic without express written permission by the author. Brief excerpts may be used for critical reviews or articles.
The views and opinions expressed in this novel do not necessarily represent those of the author or publisher.

Follow **regency_publishing_usa** on Instagram.

Cover design and photo by Andy Silvers
Cover model: Kwanise Crenshaw

ISBN (Paperback): 979-8-3303-6769-6
ISBN (eBook): 978-1-304-06885-9

HOOP DRAMA
a novel

3

○4○

THURSDAY, APRIL 5ᵀᴴ

The red hat was everywhere. *MAGA*. Wheeling, West Virginia was a wash of red and white. 91% white, to be accurate. As such, there were pimped up Chevys with Confederate flags that darted past gun stores owned by Baptist families of the nuclear variety. Still, some things were universal. Citizens used social media, watched Netflix, and ate too much fast food. The uneven roads were cracked, and the sky was marred by the haphazard crisscrossing of electrical wires connected to aging wooden poles. 'Nail City' was also home to the Capital Theater, the Nailers hockey team, and Wheeling Jesuit University.

A small blue building sat at the corner of Wheeling Hospital Road and Ledger Avenue—Tag & Treat Pet Shop. As a family-owned pet store for over six years, it was the source of nearly every cat, dog, fish, and lizard in that side of town. Rachael Reye and her second husband Allen Redding were not only a staple of their beloved pet store but also Wheeling Methodist Church. Their store proudly hung Mathew 13:23 on a dark wooden board.

Next to the pet store stood a modest gas station with only six pumps. It had been there for eight years and had traded owners more times than an alleged rapist has been elected president. Currently, Erik Li owned the joint, but before him a couple from Pakistan owned it. Erik was kind and quiet—really nothing to write

Andy Silvers

home about. It's his cashier Angela Torres whose name caused the residents to fear. She had been hired after a year stint in prison—and the whole city knew it. Furthermore, she tended to glare at customers who seemed too 'normal.' Once, a man with no tattoos, piercings, or disabilities walked into the store and had the temerity to spend more than sixty seconds picking a snack. Angela let him know about it without uttering a single word. She just stared, judging him silently while glancing at her razer-sharp nails.

But the weirdness locomotive had many cars. The thing about Angela was that she had a few boyfriends 'disappear' before she had even graduated community college. Martin was last seen getting a beer with her (and her fake ID) at a bar on Wheeling Island. Her next boyfriend, who was thirteen years older than her, was last seen leaving his parents' house for a date on a fateful Friday night. Rumor has it he reappeared back in Brookings, Oregon, but that didn't stop allegations from flying. Despite the few tall tales, nothing special or mysterious could really be said of Wheeling.

Across the cracked asphalt of Ledger Avenue stood a classic of senior eating. Mary's Diner.

The maroon and black painted diner had a lot full of cars from the shiny new sedan of a wealthy retiree to the rusted pickup of a local laborer. Its facade featured a plethora of smudgy windows except one—it had been smashed and replaced—looking strangely clean next to the wooden entrance door. A piece of yellow gum still stuck to the side of the door frame two months after Sarah Martin—a new employee at the time—had placed it there. She had put it below eye level, but that didn't mean no one saw it.

Inside, guests munched on classic American meals like cheeseburgers and hot dogs. Beer was served to nearly every guest as nearly every guest could drink. Bob and Masie Woodley occupied their usual seat in the corner of the restaurant near a painting of an ivory tusk being carried across the African plain. Bob's white mustache seemed to glow under the strong halogen light dangling above, and Masie's sequin blouse sparkled once more.

For three years they had made the trip to Mary's Diner. Every Thursday, except for five rare misses, they succeeded at snatching their spot and enjoying a handmade meal. This story was not unique since nearly every couple over the age of fifty had done the same. Jackie and Adrian Revis had the booth near the restroom (since Jackie had a weak bladder), likewise Kevin and his spouse of over fifty-two years occupied the seat by the entrance.

Everyone knew Carol Plush. She was the manager of the restaurant and a resident of Wheeling since she could say *Mama* and *Dada*. At the fresh age of forty-two, Carol was quick on her feet and mighty fast with orders, especially for repeat customers who hadn't tried a new dish in three years.

She was generally skinny, except for her wide hips, but an hourglass figure and dark hair made her seem a decade younger than she was. She had dark red lipstick and a ponytail during work hours. Plus, she had a tattoo of AC/DC guitarist Angus Young on her left bicep that disappeared and reappeared under her short-sleeve collared shirt. She ran a tight ship, but on days off, her ship had another captain—Robin Chapel.

Robin had supple skin, silky hair, and a narrow nose. At only twenty-three years old, she had secured the role of assistant manager (not that it paid much). After college, she had applied to nearly forty jobs in her chosen field—graphic design—but received only one call back and a failed interview. For now, she was stuck at the diner where her commute was minimal, and her pay could be consistent enough to help with rent.

Andy Silvers

Robin awaited a more fitting job but was grateful for the chance to work. After all, her college roommate Sarah Willis had applied for job after job as a piano repairman and finally landed as the director of a childcare center. She spent $47,690 and garnered $32,000 a year corralling tiny demons. Yeesh.

Robin rung up Mr. and Mrs. Wilkerson, who were not regulars but had met Robin at the grocery store a week prior, until Sarah Martin ran over to her. She didn't say anything, instead shifting weight from foot to foot and awkwardly staring at her boss. Her eyes darted to and froe, and she licked her lips repeatedly.

"Just one moment, Sarah," Robin said, handing the couple their change.

"I'll be here," Sarah mumbled so quickly Robin didn't understand a word of it.

When Robin had finished, she swiveled to Sarah, ready to solve issue number 4,871 of the day.

"Hey, Robin," Sarah said, crossing her arms. "I mean, Mrs. Chapel. Sorry. I think there's a small problem. So…um…the drawer is a little short."

"Are you sure?" Robin asked. "Let me check it." Sarah waited while Robin counted the drawer. Sarah's shift was over in ten minutes, and she had no desire to tell Carol of her mistake. "Yeesh, thirty-seven dollars."

"Damn it," Sarah said, checking under the cash drawer. "I probably gave back too much change."

Robin placed the money into stacks of twenty using paperclips to hold them together. "It looks more like you gave back too much change a few times."

"I know," Sarah said, keeping an eye out for Carol. "I really don't get it. I feel like I may have given the Flanders an extra five, but I don't quite remember. Also, these new bills stick together so maybe that's what happened. I just don't know, but I really don't want to get fired. This job is the only reason my grandma isn't kicking me out."

"I thought it was your grampa." Robin spoke softly and clearly like the best audiobook narrator.

"Oh yeah. It's both."

Robin put the money in a leather pouch and set the empty drawer on the counter. "I don't know what to tell you, Sarah. You really can't make mistakes like this."

"I know," Sarah cried. "I'm not a great cashier, but I really tried. Just let me ask my grandma for the money tonight. I bet she'd help me." Sarah wiped her eyes and stood within ten inches of Robin. She found her captive audience, and her sniffles were the orchestra's tune.

Robin sighed. "We are going to find the money."

Sarah turned around. "But we can't. We both counted the drawer and—"

"Sarah, I *promise* we're going to find it." Robin walked over to register one and counted it up. It was only five cents short. She reached back into the leather pouch and did a second count of the money. It was still thirty-seven dollars short. Next, she checked under the register and behind a dusty sign holder.

"I give up," Sarah said. "Just tell Carol I'm a dumbass and get it over with."

"Sarah, sweetie," Robin said, articulating the slightest of agitation. "I promised we'd find it, and we're going to." Robin kept the pouch in her left hand and searched with her right. After a minute that felt like an eternity, she stood back next to Sarah at register two. "I've got it." Robin pulled forty dollars from her pocketbook and put them in the pouch. She pulled out three ones for herself.

"What," Sarah exclaimed. "You can't do that. I mean…is that okay?"

"I *told you* we'd find the money. Clock out please. Carol doesn't like overtime."

Sarah gave Robin a quick smile and wiped her eyes once more. She fled to the kitchen where she grabbed her belongings before heading to her car.

Robin shook her head. "What are we gonna do with that girl?" After zipping up the pouch, she went to the manager's office to place the cash in the safe.

"Did Sarah leave?" Carol asked.

"Yes ma'am," Robin said, watching Carol fumble through a pile of papers. "Are you lookin' for something?"

"Yeah. I'm tryin' to find another menu. The one I gave the Wilson's fell apart like my career at Hooters." Carol snorted. She often laughed at her own jokes and Robin wasn't expected to care. Carol lived in her own mind palace.

"I can make something new," Robin said softly. "I think we need it. These menus haven't changed since the place opened."

"Yeah, I thought the same thing. I just ain't got the time to fix it."

"I think it's cardstock that's been laminated."

"Card-what that's been who what?"

"I can redo the menus at my apartment and have them ready by tomorrow morning."

"Oh yeah, that's right." She grinned widely. "You're an *artist*." Carol wiggled her fingers in the air as if the magic of art would sprinkle out like a saltshaker.

Robin smiled. "I'm not really an artist. I guess design is a form of art, but you're free to see it however."

"Just tell me if you can redo the menus."

"Yes ma'am."

"Good."

Robin peeked over at the register and saw a couple waiting. It was the Woodley's who left their usual eighteen percent gratuity. A group of young kids caught Robin's eye in the corner of the restaurant. One kid was the most that typically accompanied the adults at Mary's. Four was an odd sight.

Mr. Woodley shoved his wallet into his corduroy back pocket. "Thank you again, Mrs. Chapel. I hope you have a great evening."

"You as well, sir," Robin said, smiling.

Mr. and Mrs. Woodley shuffled out, with Mr. Woodley holding the door for his lovely wife. Robin grinned briefly at the sight, imagining Ray doing the same for her.

Robin took the opportunity to slide over to the table in the corner to see whose grandkids were in town this month. Low and behold, they weren't grandkids at all, but the direct children of a new family in Wheeling. The father had on jeans and a black t-shirt and his wife, sitting across from him, had on a simple white dress and bright yellow tennis shoes. Their three kids sat with them, notably in every position except their bottoms. They were all under the age of ten and all staring at a smart phone.

Robin, noticing that none of the kids had finished their food, took some initiative. "Hello, y'all. Are we thinking about any to-go boxes for the little ones today?"

"Yes, please," the mother responded, pulling her youngest back into his seat from which he was nearly standing. "They practically live on air these days."

"I'm impressed they ate this much. It's a real compliment to the cooking." The dad grabbed his phone back from the oldest child.

"Well, thank you so much. I'm glad you liked it. May I take

your plates?" Robin pointed to the barren wasteland that described the parents' plates. She literally couldn't have guessed what they ordered.

"Don't be shy," the mother said, handing her plate to Robin. "I'm sorry, miss. My kids saw the QD code—"

"QR code, Mom!" the oldest child yelled.

"Heaven forbid. QR code. Yeah, my kids saw that and had to know what it did."

"They can't help it," the father added. "They're little tech wizards. It's pretty cool that it teaches you a bit about history. I had no idea that George Handel wrote *Music for the Royal Fireworks.*"

"He's really old like you and Daddy," the youngest one chirped, squealing from laughter like he had just invented comedy.

"Oh, hush," the mother said, gently covering his mouth. "We love any opportunity to learn. We're new here. We just bought a house over off McColloch Street."

"Oh, really," Robin said. "Where did you move from?"

"Champaign, Illinois," the father said. "We're here for my job."

"Gotcha," Robin said. "I'll be back in just a moment with those boxes, and as soon as you get those, we'll take care of you at the register."

"Okay," the man replied.

Robin bustled to the kitchen past Jerry, Maisie, and Presley, who worked the afternoon shift on weekdays and were well-acquainted with each other. Under the microwave were three Styrofoam trays that Robin brought over to the waiting family.

While ringing up the only family she had seen all day, Robin had an epiphany. QR codes were a kid-magnet. Seldom had the aging clientele of the popular diner noticed or ever used the QR codes. Half the customers used flip phones and the ones who had smartphones fidgeted with the touchscreen like it was a piece of alien technology engineered to make the elderly meet an early grave.

The restaurant stayed reasonably busy, but it was never 'full.' Not really. That meant money was being left on the table. Profits were stagnating for no good reason.

Wait—the menus!

Robin could fix them that night. Just add some QR codes that families can enjoy and kaboom—double the customers.

Carol would like that. The restaurant NEEDED that.

Fifteen minutes before closing, Robin approached Carol after handling her myriad responsibilities as assistant manager. Robin needed a clean conscience before asking for a favor. "Hey, Carol. I have a menu recommendation."

"Oh, good Lord," Carol said, counting the contents of register one. "We can't add a salad or remove a side item. Last time we did that, Gerald thought the restaurant was under new management and only ordered a coffee. I basically gave him a heart attack when he paid for his drink."

"Uh…no," Robin said, smiling awkwardly. "I know we put QR codes in the menus that our customers don't use, and I saw some kids earlier that know how to use them and…"

"And what?"

"And no one is gonna want to match the…never mind. The point is that I was thinking about updating the QR codes to be a tad bigger and lead to fluffy animals or something kids like."

"What?" Carol carried the leather pouch to the office with Robin following behind. "You can do that in a night? You gotta work for NASA."

"Oh, thanks," Robin said. "But it's pretty easy. I just want

Andy Silvers

your permission before changing them."

"Yeah, sure. Just don't link any pictures that could make our guests uncomfortable."

"Thanks. I won't let you down."

"You ain't holding me up."

Robin tried to fake laugh, but Carol wouldn't have heard it anyway since she moved like a teenager seeing an ice cream truck and was halfway to the kitchen. That was still an answer.

Robin had really felt underused at the restaurant given her design degree. She offered to update the signage but was turned down. She offered to create a website for the diner but was told that she'd have to pay for it. And she even offered to post the menu to Facebook in a digital format, but Carol opted to take a picture of the menu herself and post it despite it being blurry and far too magenta. Robin created the digital version but never mentioned the subject again to avoid rocking the boat.

But now her voice would be heard, and her talent would be seen…in a limited capacity.

The lights flashed on Robin's 2009 Honda Fit. The little blue hatchback had been Robin's first car after her parents took back their Toyota Camry. The Fit had a squeaky passenger door and a coffee stain interior color that Robin had grown accustomed to in her car and her husband's. She threw her name badge into the empty plastic holder to the left of the steering wheel. The back seat was full of junk from her last fast-food cup to the book she promised to read but never did (and never will).

Most of the junk was just clothes. Not her clothes. Raymond's clothes. Her husband, Ray, was just a year older than her at twenty-four, but he had the cleanliness of a boy half his age. Every time Robin hopped in her car and saw another jacket Ray was too lazy to take inside, she reminded herself of a key truth. *Great cook and cute butt.* Just remember, *great cook and cute butt.* Unfortunately, the newlywed ambiance had faded far sooner than Robin expected. Perhaps that's the problem with reading a dozen romance novels by a writer who had been remarried three times.

Pulling into the nearly full lot, Robin approached her apartment complex. She hoped that Ray had gotten the mail after arriving home since she was on a mission and had no time left.

Their apartment was small with two bedrooms. The second bedroom had proven to be completely useless as a second room for renters. In her last semester at Ohio University, she had rented a room with an off-campus friend and only paid $525 a month. Not to mention she and her friend were best buddies until Regina got married and moved to South Korea. Now, they messaged each other once or twice a month and no more. Life had gotten away from them, but Robin was happy she found the 'one.' The man of her dreams.

Ray's brother, Carter, had been attending OU when Robin was a junior. He met her in an optional art appreciation class that allowed her to escape an English course she dreaded. Carter was cute, but Ray was cuter. Ray picked up his brother after class nearly every day as their parents couldn't afford a car for both of them.

Ray had darker skin than Robin and lovely blue eyes. He asked her out the second time they met because his confidence was exploding out of his chest.

"Hey, so…" he said, scooching closer to Robin on the KFC booth they shared. "I don't know a lot about you, but I know if I don't ask you out now, a richer, taller guy will, and I'll never forgive myself."

Okay, Fabio, Robin thought. *What class is he taking?*

"Um," Robin stuttered. "I need time to think about it."

Andy Silvers

"Really? 'Cause you have until my brother gets back from the restroom."

"Seriously? You can probably ask when he gets back. What's the deadline?"

"The deadline is I've got the keys and I'm thinking about taking you somewhere where I can sweep you off your feet."

Crap nuggets, Robin screamed internally. *Has his bicep always been that big?* "You got one chance to sweep me."

"Deal." Ray grabbed his keys off the table, snatched up his soda, and ran for the door.

Was Ray still that romantic? Sort of. But working full time at an auto shop and smelling like oil just wasn't quite as sexy as it would seem.

Robin buckled down at her desk. She opened InDesign again for the first time since senior year. She pulled out the menu from the restaurant and began copying it starting with breakfast. She played around with fonts until she decided on Tahoma. Next, she added a splash of color and some zig zags that scream *modern*. She began searching for images of fluffy animals when something touched her foot.

It was Geppetto on the floor, a robot vacuum they'd gotten as a wedding gift, bumping her. Atop Geppetto was a plate of homemade Salisbury steak and mashed potatoes. Ray had been cooking and it smelled great.

Robin smiled. She finished typing FLUFFY ANIMALS and reached down to grab her meal. If only Ray could clean as well as he cooked. If only.

Ray peeked around the corner, his short black hair being his dead giveaway. He had a single piercing on his right ear of just a black dot. His dark skin made it almost impossible to see but he liked it anyway. Ray slid closer to Robin and bashfully held the remote behind his back. He tilted his head and rocked back and forth asking, "What 'cha doin'?"

Robin giggled at his high-pitched vocal inflection. "I'm finally doing some graphic design. These are going on the menu at the restaurant."

Ray took this as his queue to get as close as he wanted. Sliding behind Robin's chair, he leaned over her shoulder to take a peek at her work.

While Robin spoke, he snuck a kiss on her left cheek. "I'm using QR codes to make the menus more inviting for kids. We have empty seats most days and our large booth is never full. Families are here in Wheeling. I know it."

"Wow. You are just so smart, and I understood all that stuff about the UR codes and I'm glad you are using that expensive degree."

"Honey," Robin said. "Don't you use the ignorant card on me. I know you know what a QR code is."

Ray sighed. "Awe. You caught me." Ray wrapped his muscular arms around his wife's chest to embrace her in a hug. "We got a slight situation."

"What's that?"

"So, we owe $1,260 this month for rent and seventy for cable…"

"Okay, my billfold's on the table. You can get it while I work."

"Uh…" Ray chuckled, sighing again. "We sorta have to pick one. I was sick last week and that means I won't have my full paycheck for this week. Sadly, since we need a place to sleep, we're gonna have to skip this week's episode of *Teen Daddies*."

"Serious?"

"Yeah, sadly."

Andy Silvers

"Alright. This is the life we live I guess." Robin spent her brain power using software to remove an animal from its background habitat. She started with a cuddly Koala and next picked a red fox.

"Yeah," Ray said, heading to the door. "I'll leave you be. I just don't wanna surprise you."

"I'll be there in less than an hour. Just let me finish these designs."

"Alright." Ray left the room, directing Geppetto into the hallway.

Robin actually worked for nearly an hour and a half finishing her masterpiece. She completed seven different images by choosing a famous historical event in American history. Then, she took the cute animal and photoshopped them into the photo like a Where's Waldo puzzle.

At 10:38 PM, she fell onto her bed next to Ray, neglecting to pull the covers over herself, then, she fell asleep.

FRIDAY, APRIL 6TH

Sleeping beauty awoke the next morning to a simulated rooster call. Ray had already gone to work, but he left his dearly beloved a plate of eggs and sizzling bacon.

Robin smiled upon seeing the work of her hand…or computer. The new menus looked excellent. The opportunity was scant to do something original and creative; Robin glowed at the chance to impress.

She printed two copies of the four-page menu and put them into a manilla folder that would be safe from dust, ketchup, and coffee stains until they were safely copied and laminated at work. Indeed, they made it safely. Robin had the morning shift today since Carol wouldn't be there. Truly, the success of the new menus would be in her hands.

She prioritized putting the required $140 into register one and two as the morning crew arrived. Afterword, glee exploded from her mind while she gathered up all the old menus she could find. She took them to the manager's office and placed them next to the laminator. After copying the new menu thirty times, she began the long process of laminating.

Just then, Markus poked his head in. "Hey, Robin," he said. "Is Sarah gonna be here today?"

"I don't believe so," she said, waiting for the laminator to heat

Andy Silvers

up.

"Thank god," he responded impassively before heading out the door.

"Hey, Markus. Could you—" Robin looked up to a vacancy where Markus once stood. She needed someone to do the lamination for her as the process would take more time than she imagined. Lucky for her, Mira came in right on time and was willing to help. Robin could ask her for impromptu favors without any backtalk. Even though she was assistant manager, giving orders was tough. Carol could bark them like a German Shephard on ecstasy. Robin, however, didn't want to be impolite or bossy. Women at her college who talked back or made a scene had trouble getting partners, romantic or otherwise.

Obviously, being polite would pay off one day. There's no reason to make a fuss. Robin's mother, Shanice, could also bark with the best of them. She just wasn't afraid. Robin definitely took more after her father. He was a shy man of short stature, but he could befriend anyone. A legacy of many friends and few enemies was desirable. Still, she found directing her staff difficult, so she often pulled the 'mom' trick on them. She'd tell them if they didn't behave, she would tell Carol. That often worked, and to her credit, Robin did tell Carol.

The age differences helped Robin too. Some of her workers, like Mira, were older, but others were high school students who could hardly care less. The oldest employee, Leonard Rask, could always be counted on to keep order in his personal domain—the kitchen. He had white hair and a goatee. He dressed in the same two pairs of black pants every day but did a good job of keeping himself clean. The palest goth band couldn't compete with the whiteness of his teeth.

While Mira handled the menus; Robin made sure the lights

were on, the restrooms were clean, the tables were ready for the breakfast rush, and much more that was committed to memory. Occasionally, she checked her smartphone for texts from Ray. Her phone dinged loudly whenever she received a message, but like most millennials, she worried she would miss something important if she didn't check regularly.

The restaurant was set to open in less than three minutes by the time Mira finished laminating the menus. A monumental task it certainly was, but the final design was excellent. This gave Robin the confidence to throw away the old menus with an audible, "Goodbye."

"These look great," Mira said, straitening the pile.

"I guess." Robin was dancing inside but collected outside.

"Really," Mira said. "You have a natural talent."

Since Mira had been preoccupied, her preparation of the bacon had been delayed. Luckily it was slower than expected as the first customer didn't even arrive until 8:17.

Once the cooking started, the building filled like a balloon with the smells of an all-American breakfast.

Eggs, bacon, and coffee. Oh my.

Grease popped off the bacon as it buckled and curled, controlled by the likes of Mira Hollister. The scent wafted throughout the kitchen stronger than any other (including Markus' new Sage cologne).

Eggs were made to perfection by Leonard. He scrambled, tossed, and fried them with ease. His eyes were often looking ahead to the next task and his left ear was usually occupied by a red earbud playing a variety of jazzy tunes.

Customers gobbled up their food at their own pace but one thing that was consistent was the lack of talking until the whole plate was clean. Quiet yet occasional noises included the clink of

Andy Silvers

ceramic mugs, the sniff of people's noses, the slurp of hot coffee, and the scraping of forks across near-empty plates. All was going well…until.

"Mrs. Robin," an older man said, holding his right hand above his head and wiggling his pointer finger.

"Yes, Mr. Cottingham," Robin responded, bustling over to him at the booth closest the restrooms.

He scratched his chin and licked his lips. "Miss, I must just be old, but I can't find the muffins. Do y'all still sell those?"

Robin smiled and gently grabbed the menu from his hand. "Yes sir. The menus have been redesigned, but all the items are still there. See here, sir? The muffins are on the bottom of page one."

"Oh, yeah," he mumbled. "Carol must not got nuthin' better to do." The man chuckled and turned to his wife who smiled. "All right, Mrs. Robin, I'll take a blueberry muffin. Vivian, you want anything?" His wife shook no.

"Okay."

Things were off to an awkward start. It's not that Robin hadn't planned for this, but the immediate backlash, however miniscule, made her question her plan. What happened if Carol got a long list of complaints the next day? She sanctioned the redesign, but Robin still made them. Yeesh.

The only thing to do was wait. The lunch crowd would come and then the QR codes could be put to the test.

But wait! No kids came to the restaurant; how would Robin even get families to come by in the first place? She began to panic, pacing back and forth and not even hearing an older lady calling for her.

"Ma'am! I spilled my coffee." She called out, debating getting out of her seat by sliding back and forth.

Hoop Drama

Finally, Robin heard. "Oh dear. Let me help." She leaned down and picked up the cup. "I'll make you a fresh cup." Using her hand towel, she soaked up the spill and raced off to the kitchen.

"Robin," Mira called from across the way. "Here's your muffin. We don't usually sell those. Maybe your menus are already a hit."

They sold muffins all the time. The menus were certainly not a hit...for now. Several hours went by so the confused older patrons left, making way for just the people Mary's needed. Families.

A blond woman with two kids and her Hispanic husband Chris, whom Robin knew, floated inside. The last time they had eaten there was when Robin had literally started as assistant manager the week before and managed to completely botch up their order.

"Good—what is it? —afternoon, Robin," the lady said. "Do you remember us?"

"Yes. I remember when you were just a tiny chubby-cheeks." Robin looked at Preston whose body had gotten thinner since being there months earlier. Robin guided them to a spot near the center of the restaurant, close to the air conditioning.

"You remember me too, right?" Leah asked, hugging her mother's right arm in the booth.

"Yes," Robin replied. "How could I forget about you?"

"I see the new menus," Chris stated, smiling widely. Chris was the nicest guy in the state. He was friends with Ray back when he worked at the auto repair shop and now, he sold insurance down in Moundsville. When Ray lost his first job soon after Robin's graduation, he helped get Ray the gig at the auto shop. That's largely the reason for the move from Ohio to West Virginia.

"Yes. I redid them a bit." Robin smiled but looked away as if

23

in shame. It was hard to take credit for redesigning something that already worked. *Just be proud of yourself,* she thought. *You did it.*

"*Get out.* Look here," he said, showing the menu to his oldest. "Sweetie, you know how old and wrinkly your daddy is. Can you show me on my phone how these QR codes work."

He had not a single wrinkle. Either way, Leah gently grabbed Dad's phone with both hands and began scanning the codes.

"It says free ice cream if we find all the animals," Chris teased. "Does that include children at heart?"

"Unfortunately, no." The menu specified one ice cream bowl for kids twelve and under.

"Stop yakkin,' babe," Angie, whose name Robin finally remembered, said. "She's got stuff to do."

Robin left the table feeling a sense of accomplishment and a bit of a plan materializing.

Gotta spread the word, she thought. *Gotta teach the community about our new menus. But who cares anyway? —no! Can't think negative. The work has been done and families clearly enjoy it. Just figure out how to spread the word.*

Chris is nice. He'll tell other people.

CRAP! Robin came to a grinding halt and returned to Chris' table. "I forgot to take your drink order. I am so sorry." Robin genuinely was embarrassed, and her smooth skin turned red.

"It's okay," Chris giggled. "I just want a root beer. The kids will have lemonade or something—just make sure it doesn't have aspartame. And you?" He pointed at Angie.

"Um…black coffee with two creams."

"Got it." Robin smiled big to overcompensate for her mistake and sped off to the kitchen. Luckily, two other servers had arrived, so Robin saw fit to focus on the business aspects of her job.

She prepared a tray with all the drinks as ordered and gave it to Megan, who was generally responsible for tables nine through fifteen. The rest of the day was like any other, except when families arrived. Robin personally visited each table to explain the rules of the new menus. She encouraged parents to tell other parents about the free ice cream, praying that it would make any difference.

Progress was slow but steady. For instance, a middle-aged mom came by the restaurant at 2:00 after her shift. Her nametag said JENETTE. She clearly worked at a bank of some sort.

"I need coffee—lots of it—with two or three sugars," she spoke speedily, but Robin kept up just fine. "I already know what I want to eat so don't leave yet. I'll take the Mary's Burger special medium rare with no onions. It would be nice to swap out fries for onion rings if you have them, and I could use a bowl of ketchup too. It doesn't literally have to be a bowl; just as long as it isn't touching the rest of the food, it'll be fine."

"Okay," Robin said, still hurriedly writing down the order. "We actually don't have onion rings. I'm really sorry, but will our fries do?"

"They will."

"All right," Robin was a bit scared. This lady talked quickly and firmly. She knew what she wanted and had a plan for everything. For instance, she brought her own coaster in case the restaurant didn't have any and she brought her own pen to sign the receipt to avoid spreading germs. She was tough and confident—everything Robin dreamed of. But it was hard for the young wife to speak her mind. She only felt comfortable doing so with Ray. Even there, it took months of marriage to soften her up.

Plus, Robin's mother made it clear that she had to lay down the law with Ray if she wanted an orderly household. Robin only believed her because her father was exhibit A of a husband who

Andy Silvers

knew the rules (until five years ago).

She didn't feel comfortable mentioning the new menu to Jenette. As Robin offered to take the menus, Jenette raised her eyebrows. "Are these new menus? What do these codes do?"

Robin momentarily stumbled for an answer. "Yes…these are our new menus—same food but different design. The codes are for kids twelve and under. They scan them to open famous pictures and then find the hidden animals. Free ice cream for kids who find all ten."

Jenette finally turned over her menu. "Interesting," she said, not the least bit of enthusiasm in her inflection. "My kids would like that."

"Sure. You know, I designed the new menus myself…" Robin let her voice drift off, expecting another question. She hoped to reflect her customers' energy back at them, and she did. There was usually more.

The rest of the day was fairly mundane. Jenette tipped well but never mentioned the menu again. Unfortunately, she accidently took the menu home with her. Robin showed the menu to every customer under forty but couldn't really be sure of how successful her 'marketing campaign' would be until several weeks went by. She crossed her fingers, toes, and anything else she could, ready to see her degree make a difference.

She handed the final bowl of ice cream to an eight-year-old boy named Riley at table thirteen.

"Do you have sprinkles?" Riley asked.

"No sir," Robin responded. "Sorry about that. But I might have some whipped cream if you want any."

The boy shook his head yes.

"Megan!" Robin called. "Can you bring the whipped topping?"

Hoop Drama

"This is a cool new feature you're offering," Riley's mother said. "Wheeling Wagon has a game room for kids, but I really don't like that because it just encourages kids to leave the table. Then they shout and fight and bicker. This is so much calmer and parent-friendly."

"I like the game room."

"Oh, I know, Riley," his mother said, rubbing his shoulder. "I *know.*"

Megan returned with the whipped cream. Robin swirled a nice spiral right on top and left the table to refill some drinks. At the end of the night, the registers were roughly the same for a Friday, but hope was in the air.

Robin knew the QR codes weren't revolutionary. They were evolutionary. But that was the point. If she could change the clientele of the restaurant from grandpa and grandma to families of two or more kids, business could boom. That's all she really wanted: to make a difference, and one day get a high paying job.

She hadn't the time to tell Ray about her success as she laid down next to him. He had a long day too and she felt guilty for not asking about his job. But what could she do? He was fast asleep by the time she finished her shower.

The next few weeks were the litmus test. Could a menu really change an established restaurant? Did Robin really want to take ownership for that kind of change? It was clear more would need to change than a piece of paper.

Only time would tell. And if things worked out, then she'd have quite the story to tell Ray anyway.

FRIDAY, APRIL 20TH

After two weeks, the restaurant was DIFFERENT.

"Robin!" Carol called out over the indistinct chatter of families. "What's the Wi-Fi password? This lady can't pull up the image without it."

"Yes ma'am," Robin said, bustling over. She leaned in close where the customers wouldn't hear. "I had to change it from *CrackPOTJerry13* to avoid problems." She turned to the customers. "Try *Mary33* with a capital M."

The customers in this case were a family of five—yes five! — who were all seated for the lunchtime rush. Robin's plan had worked, and she had done more than just a menu revision. She started with the aprons. Seriously. The aprons were always black with either a black or white shirt. The shirts stayed the same, but Robin purchased new aprons. Two of the aprons were checkerboard pattern for the managers and the others were solid blue. This shade of blue, called azure, gave the aprons a sense of fun childlike charm. This greatly brightened up the feel of the restaurant making it more family friendly. Furthermore, the chosen shade of blue matched the new menus perfectly—not a credit to foresight but it worked out well.

Robin wanted to brighten up the entire restaurant but couldn't necessarily change *everything*. The paint had to stay, the floors

28

Hoop Drama

remained dark gray, and the light fixtures couldn't be removed. However, that didn't inhibit the plan. First off, she added white tablecloths to the dark wooden tables to brighten them up. Then, she saw the lights dangling over the table had a saturated, warm color that screamed 'log cabin' instead of 'family restaurant.' After a bit of research, she changed every light bulb from a halogen bulb to new LED bulbs that appeared much brighter. These lights bounced off the tablecloths making the whole area seem new.

She discovered there was no place to write the ten animals down on the menus themselves—not that the menus would've been a good place—so she bought colored paper and cut it down the middle to allow the kids to write their answers. Yet again, 'normal' simply wouldn't do. The paper was tinted a light blue color to match the energy of the rest of Robin's design. The paper was a lighter shade that was easy to write on, and Robin made sure that colored pencils were available at every table.

The total charge for all these updates was nearly $200, but this made itself up after a single day. Speaking of costs, one free update were the songs. The speaker now played more current music from artists whom pre-teens would recognize. She still had to keep the volume low to avoid Carol having a conniption, but new music was a big hit. Robin heard several kids and even parents humming along to their favorite radio hits. All the old, mangled posters and pictures on the wall had to go. One such poster advertised an event from four years ago.

It was an incredible change, and one that didn't go unnoticed. The younger clientele showed up, largely due to word of mouth, and brought fresh dollars with them.

This didn't go problem free as Carol was caught off guard by the additional technology; but the tips were larger and the bills were bigger, so she didn't complain much.

At table three, a seven-year-old boy named Charlie showed his siblings how to use the new menus. "See, Morgan. Just hold up the camera and click the link. You don't gotta take a picture. You just need to point the camera."

Charlie's siblings learned quickly, and the parents enjoyed watching their children discover the animals inside the famous paintings. The correct answers were Koala, red fox, cat, hummingbird, bunny, lion cub, Dalmatian, dolphin, deer, and meerkat. Meerkat proved to be the hardest one, but kids were allowed to phone a friend (their parents) if need be.

Suffice it to say, Mary's Diner went from buying a tub or two of ice cream a month to three tubs a week. Robin also ensured the constant supply of sprinkles, chocolate syrup, whipped cream, and caramel syrup too. Robin carried out her plan carefully with thoughtful deliberation on every idea.

For instance, vanilla ice cream wasn't even on the dessert menu. In order to get it, customers must have kids under thirteen and they must correctly find the animals. This meant that when children saw a delicious bowl of ice cream walk by, they'd ask their parents to order it just to discover they could have it only *one* way. This ensured every family knew about the QR codes. It was akin to keeping up with the Joneses but for pipsqueaks.

In a corner of the restaurant set aside for quick-grab items like silverware, cups, and to-go containers, Carol found Robin throwing away a discarded napkin. "Thank goodness you changed the Wi-Fi password. I wouldn't have thought to do that."

"You're welcome, Carol," Robin said, admiring her handiwork across the restaurant. "The last thing we need is controversy." Robin kept her hands close to her chest. Her confidence rarely extended to her body language.

"Exactly. I thought that you just get Wi-Fi on your phone

wherever you are, but apparently not."

"Uh…it depends. I think if they have data on their phone, they don't have to use our Wi-Fi, but otherwise no."

"I'll pretend I understood all that mumbo pambo and move on." Carol gave Robin a friendly bump on the arm when Mr. Dealey walked over from his table to get their attention.

He motioned his arm up to wave as if Robin or Carol hadn't already seen him. "Hey ladies, what's this music you got playing here? It sounds like somebody is crying into a synthesizer."

Robin chuckled. "Yes sir. Some of it is weird, but the families like it. We keep the volume down to avoid disturbing our older guests."

"Older?" Mr. Dealey joked. "I'm seventy-three and going strong. I don't mind new music, but I can't understand what they're saying. You know, I had to decipher messages in Vietnam easier than this technobabble."

"I understand, sir," Robin laughed. "It's not for everyone. Is there anything I can get you, sir?"

"Oh yeah," he said, pointing at his table. "I dropped my straw when I was trying to open it, so I need a new one. And the worst thing; my wife's in the restroom, so I can't blame it on her."

"Here you go." Carol handed the gentleman a straw. "I agree, mister. This new aged music sounds like it comes straight outta Satan's asshole." Yet again, Carol laughed even though no one else did. After Mr. Dealey left, she turned to Robin. "Hey, I need you to go find Sarah for me. You take her crap more, and her break was over five minutes ago. Good luck."

Robin went into the kitchen area first looking for Sarah. The restaurant didn't really have a proper break room, but employees often sat in an empty booth near the back corner. However, since there were only two empty booths, Robin checked around back and found Sarah listening to music and leaning up against the wall. She hadn't updated to the new apron and her hair now featured a bright green streak.

"Hey, Sarah," Robin began. "We were wondering where you were. If you can just watch tables one through six, that'd be great. Markus and Riley will probably be fine. I just need you hanging around and helping them keep up the pace." Robin finished her final word before noticing that Sarah hadn't heard a thing. She waved her arms at the teen, finally getting her attention.

"Yes," Sarah scoffed, pausing her music.

Robin repeated her earlier statement.

"My break isn't over yet."

"I thought you started a while ago."

"No. I was in the kitchen…working. Then I came out here like just now."

"Okay." Robin grew angry but didn't think harsh words or loud voices would improve the situation. "When you're done, be inside near table one. Okay, sweetie?"

"Yeah."

Robin returned inside, hoping to get Carol to follow up on Sarah's whereabouts in about five minutes.

Robin headed to the kitchen where Mira burst forth with two bowls of ice cream. "Hey there, Robin. Look here. Another scoop of ice cream for some kids. I do have one concern, though," she said.

"I'll walk with you," Robin responded, following her to the table and grabbing the second bowl to lighten the load.

"So, what happens if kids come more than once? That's free ice cream with no work. Also, we can't really keep the same menu for over a year, right?"

"Good point. I have a plan for that. Every month, I will redo

Hoop Drama

the menus. I haven't exactly got Carol on board with that yet, but I'll work something out." Robin handed a bowl to a seven-year-old girl with blond hair.

"There you go, pumpkin," Mira said with a melodic sound to her voice. The kids' parents made sure they thanked their servers. "I just don't think you'll *work* anything out."

Robin waved at the kids and followed Mira back toward the kitchen. "What…I don't understand."

"Girl, you just don't have it in you to argue a costly menu change every month."

"Okay…well the paper is pretty cheap, and we already have the laminator so—" Robin started rubbing her hands together in erratic fashion.

"Robin, I just don't think it's a winnable battle. Carol is proud of you, but she thinks this'll be really simple. She thinks all the work is done. But changing the restaurant like this has consequences." Mira whispered, "Like the older patrons leaving for good."

Robin smiled as though they were on the same page. "I don't know. I just don't know."

"You need to talk to Carol about it. Not to argue or anything; just find out if she's in it for the long haul." Mira made sure the conversation ended there by walking away.

It was clear what Mira meant but her message seemed implausible. Did she think the older customers would just leave? Where else were they going to go? Robin repressed this thought and continued doing her work. That made her happy. The kids had big smiles and the parents did too.

She had nearly memorized the names of her customers up until the redesign. Now, she hardly knew anyone. But that was what she wanted. She wanted to meet new people and grow the business.

Andy Silvers

The same job now allowed her to use technology. What changed was that she finally saw the glass ceiling above her.

One reality she often ignored was that she could have gotten a job out of college in graphic design. She loved art and making clients happy, but the thought of working at a studio was daunting. The corporate world of major studios was a mountain too high to climb. Answering to clients in an email was one thing but looking a corporate suit in his eyes was another.

The online job forums had several listings for larger companies, but Robin couldn't do it. She buckled and cramped under the pressure, sometimes refusing to hit SUBMIT and other times not even getting past the offer screen. College taught her everything she needed to know about the color wheel and ethical design philosophy. But it couldn't prepare her for the real world. Nothing could.

Now she was working a dead-end job with the hope of utilizing her skills in a productive way. That's why she refused to talk to Carol about the changes. The truth (a double-edged sword) was that she had reached her limit as assistant manager and if she wanted to go anywhere meaningful, she would need to brave the world. The diner morphed from steppingstone to chain-link fence.

Until her shift ended around 4 PM, she kept happy, comforting thoughts swirling around in her mind.

Cute husband. Successful restaurant. Happy customers.

She was pleasantly surprised counting the drawers so Sarah could leave. It appeared to be about $200 higher than normal, and the night wasn't even over. Furthermore, Sarah's drawer wasn't short, an important victory as Robin had no interest in dealing with that mess again.

Once in the manager's office to deposit the cash from register one, Carol entered the room and shut the door behind her. SOS.

Hoop Drama

Robin hated feeling trapped. She took a huge deep breath as quietly as possible, but it didn't have the effect of calming her nerves.

"Good evening, Mrs. Chapel. I'm gonna miss you for the rest of the day."

Oh goodness. Why was she using Robin's last name? She truly had the subtlety of a sledgehammer. Robin gripped the empty leather pouch like her life depended on it and mumbled, "I'm going to miss you as well."

"What am I saying?" Carol said, returning to her less intimidating self. "I'll see you tomorrow—morning shift, right?"

"Yes ma'am."

"That's right. And then you're off Monday, I think."

"Yes."

Just get to the point.

"Okay...good." Carol sat down in her leather chair and leaned back slightly. "I wanna say thanks. I checked the books and we're up nearly twenty percent over last Friday. I thought that could be a fluke or something, but the last time we had sales like that on Friday was eight months ago."

Robin smiled slightly, allowing her pride to escape then quickly restraining it.

"Mr. and Mrs. Woodley didn't come for lunch yesterday. I know why."

Robin shoved her hands in her pockets, allowing her to nervously fiddle with a quarter without Carol noticing.

"We—well, actually *you* have made this restaurant into a family eatery nearly over night. We transformed like freakin' Optimus Prime." Carol snorted again.

"I can change it back," Robin said, anticipating Carol's next request. It would be easy to remove the tablecloths and have employees wear their old aprons. That's what she planned to

Andy Silvers

do…until.

"I like it," Carol spoke upon deaf ears.

"What?"

"I like it. Mary's Diner needs a change and I'm liking this one. It kinda makes me feel young again seeing all the tiny kids. By the way, you and Raymond better get on that, you know."

Too awkward. Ray wasn't even as mature as a tween.

"I'm kidding. Relax, okay. If you'll be the captain, I'll help you guide the ship. I don't understand the techno jargon, but I understand more money in my pocket." Carol pushed around a stack of papers on her desk and grabbed a pamphlet. It had a picture of a group of children on the front and a young boy inside whose image was circled. She handed the pamphlet to Robin. "That's Sereda. I forgot his last name."

The pamphlet was from a group called *Ready Set Go* and the boy was a Ukrainian citizen who needed food desperately. He was ten years old. There was one logical conclusion. "Are you adopting him?"

"No. Not quite. I'm sponsoring him. See where it says, '$79 A MONTH COULD CHANGE A LIFE'? Until now, I just didn't have the means to do that, but I feel confident now to do what I've wanted to for two years."

Robin smiled. "This is very nice. I had no idea you were so charitable."

"Ha! There's a lot you don't know." Carol got up and opened the door, allowing Robin to take her left hand out of her pocket. "You're not in trouble, dear. I think we should get those extra-small kid utensils soon." Carol left the room.

Robin tried to place the pamphlet back into the pile but forgot where it came from. She was at a loss for words. Thoughts too. One switch was flipped in her mind. For once, she saw Carol as a

Hoop Drama

type of mentor, someone who knew what she wanted to do and led by example. That was the real ceiling Robin was so worried about. How could she ever be more than a woman with her words trapped on the tip of her tongue and her beliefs buried behind her quiet façade?

She worked at a brisk pace, hoping to get to her car and think over her five-year plan. On the way out the door, however, a gentleman called out her name.

"Hello," she said, looking around for the man. She saw him approaching her. He was a middle-aged guy with light skin and pronounced stubble. He had dark brown hair and wore a black collared shirt. On the shirt was the name C.E. Proctor. Knowing he was a customer, Robin said, "Sorry, mister. I just clocked off, but my staff would be happy to help you."

With confidence he replied, "I actually wanted to speak with you real quick if you have a moment."

He followed her out the door. She definitely wasn't going to go to the parking lot alone with him, so she intentionally stopped in front of one of the restaurant windows, hoping to make this a quick conversation.

His confidence remained high. "I work for Charles Proctor Creative. We're an ad agency located near Independence Hall. Sorry. My name is Dexter Brennan." He reached out for a handshake. "A friend of mine noticed your work and referred me to you."

"My work?"

"Yes ma'am. It's my understanding that you're responsible for the new menu design here, and I can say confidently that customers have noticed. I am speaking to the right person, correct?"

"Yes."

Andy Silvers

"All right, well, I know you're busy so here's my card." Dexter handed her a premium business card with a matte finish and a QR code on one side. On it was the name of the business, C.E. Proctor Creative. "Are you available for an interview this Monday the 23rd?"

"An interview?" Robin was caught off guard to put it mildly. She really didn't want anyone to hear what was being said so she looked around and quieted her voice. "What are you offering me?"

"A chance to work at our agency. You clearly have an eye for sales and my boss told me to speak to you in person."

Robin's heart raced; she adjusted her grip on her purse as the pool of sweat made holding it difficult. She hoped to have a peaceful evening, so she wanted to say 'no.' "Yes. I'm interested." CRAP. How did she say one thing after thinking another?

"Great! Are you available at 9 AM?"

"On Monday?"

"Be there at 9 sharp. We'll be done in under thirty minutes."

"Okay. What's the position exactly?"

"We can discuss all that and more on Monday. In the meantime, have a great weekend and email us if you need to reschedule." He strutted across the lot to his dark blue sedan.

She bended his card back and forth unconsciously. She was in a type of shock, not sure why *anyone* would approach her with a job opportunity. Especially one that didn't seem to have anything to do with graphic design. She shoved the card into her purse and got into her car. Finally, able to breathe, she let out an audible, "Wow."

She checked her phone and noticed that Ray had asked her about dinner that Sunday night. Shanice was coming over and Robin had asked Ray to prepare something special. She texted back to make a burger and fries (common at the diner). That wasn't

38

what she had planned to tell him, but her mind was elsewhere.

She drove home in a mild daze, unsure how to tell her beloved about the day's last-minute surprise.

SUNDAY, APRIL 22ND

No grease tonight. Shanice was coming over for dinner. Chef Ray prepared a tasty, yet healthy, meal of chicken and rice soup with a side of fruit salad. Luckily, after Robin got her head screwed on right (and Ray texted back *WTF*), she asked Ray to make the agreed upon meal.

He removed a navy-green soup pot from the lower cabinets of his small kitchen and placed his ingredients on the counter—diced celery, brown rice, dried parsley, white salt, black pepper, evaporated milk, and minced garlic among a few other things. The Chapel's ate fairly healthy, and they ate especially healthy when Robin's mother came over for dinner.

Ray effortlessly added onions, carrots, and celery to his heated pot. Upon seeing the onions turn golden, he added parsley, garlic, and thyme. His plan for the salad was much simpler. Just take the bag he bought from Kacey Khel's and place its contents into bowls topped with shredded cheese.

Ah voila. Black Emeril.

Robin walked over, smelling the delicious aroma, and gave Ray a side hug.

"You'll be all right," he said, slightly reducing the heat of the stove.

"Thanks." Robin left her man to cook while she prepared the

Hoop Drama

apartment. Few guests ever came over and the handful that did were family members. Shanice ventured over once a month and Ray's brother, Carter, came over on rare occasion.

Carter missed his brother once Robin 'stole' him. They used to be the kind of brothers who slept in the same room, knew each other's phone passwords, and shared a few dirty jokes. Then, Carter went off to school to study radiology, causing the first rift between him and Ray. The rift wasn't one of anger, but of isolation. Next, Ray married Robin, leaving Carter without a sense of family or community. They often joked about his single status when he visited. Since then, Carter had found a sense of community at West Forest Medical Center, but it was clear that he longed for that special someone.

During the forty-seven minutes it took Ray to cook his dish, Robin vacuumed, swept, and cleaned off the kitchen table. Her mother had taught her well. She threw the couch pillows back into their spots and finally went off to change from her work attire.

She donned a classy short sleeve dashiki dress and small hoop earrings. Her mother loved seeing her daughter be unapologetically black. She adored it when Ray did it too, but Ray frequently ignored her style suggestions. However, he did wear a handmade embroidered Sokoto at his wedding roughly fourteen months prior. Since then, it was more common to see Ray in a Xenomorph t-shirt than anything traditionally African. As for tonight—a plain navy-blue t-shirt.

And of course, at their wedding, Robin wore her signature piece. No, not the dress, although it was dazzling.

Her hoops.

The crowd of forty-six people gasped as Robin shuffled down the aisle. Though not the most confident person, her three-inch hoops sparkled with tiny glass crystals encased by a golden metal ring. She wore them to every important event and had a case full of hoops of various sizes. They screamed presence, attitude, and leadership; all of which Robin wasn't exactly known for. Then again, Shanice had picked them out for the special day to show Robin how beauty was done.

When emptying her purse, she rediscovered the business card. She was excited to go to the interview, but deathly afraid at the same time. To keep her nerves in line, she shoved the card to the bottom of her purse and decided not to bring up the interview to her mother.

When the food was ready, Shanice arrived, almost as though waiting for her queue. It was cloudy outside, so she had come with a large purple umbrella, only not to need it. Perhaps it was intentional though. Shanice always preferred her family to notice her when she entered a room.

"Hey, sugar baby," she called, smiling from ear to ear. She truly loved her daughter, and she had only heard the slightest of hints from Robin about the diner. "That dress is a stunner, for sure."

"Hello, Mom." Robin took her mother's umbrella and heavy leather coat and placed them over a chair that became the 'stuff' chair. Anything that needed a temporary home went on the 'stuff' chair.

Ray rushed over to give Shanice a hug. "Hey, Shanice. I've got a healthy meal for us again tonight."

"I'm not worried, Ray. My princess wouldn't let you make me no high calorie dish." Shanice ventured over to inspect the meal, liking what she saw. She wafted the scents vigorously.

Both ladies sat themselves down next to each other and waited for dinner to be served. Ray prepared two bowls for each spot.

"I tell you," Shanice began, throwing her hand up mighty

high. "I tell you Lina is just a sad little woman. She don't understand a thing I said. *No*, I *don't* want to make an appointment, but I do wanna see my family."

"Oh. Are you talking about West Forrest's front desk?" Robin asked, smiling slightly.

"Yeah, sweet pea. Don't get it twisted, I don't hate nobody, but that lady drives me mad with her comments. I don't worry about none of that at Ohio Valley. No sir."

Robin chuckled at the thought that this story was only told for Shanice to pivot to her own workplace.

"Yeah. I've been by but I've never been in," Ray said.

"Me neither."

Ray used a ladle for the soup, then grabbed both bowls one by one to serve the salad. Lastly, he made a bowl for himself, giving himself the largest portion. Before he sat down, he rushed everybody a glass of water with a dash of lemon.

"Well, maybe one day you two can meet my coworkers. Especially Brooke. You would love her." Shanice pulled up a photo of her. Her hosts nodded.

"Thank you, sweetie." His wife slid the bowl closer. Robin blew away the steam before each bite.

"Thank you," Shanice said.

Ray's cooling method involved lifting chunks of soup into the air and holding them there while he talked. "So, guess what. If you bring your car into the shop and you need new tires, what do you think is the bare minimum you should know?"

"What?" Shanice asked impassively.

"What your make and model is." Ray paused for their reaction. "I swear, this lady literally looked at me and said 'Toyota, I think.' What the hell, woman. You *think!*"

Robin laughed. She found her husband's recollection of bad

Andy Silvers

customers quite funny. Shanice didn't laugh, but she was fully engaged.

"*You* bought the car. How can you not know this? Then she remembered it was a Toyota, so I asked her what year. She pulls out her phone and spends three minutes searching around for the email from Toyota from *four* years ago."

"Is this Ramona?" Robin inquired.

"No. Ramona has more sense. But really though. I'm happy to answer questions. Just not stupid questions."

"That's funny." Robin had nearly finished her soup. "Do you remember that guy who climbed down into the pit?"

"Oh yeah," Ray said, dropping his spoon back into the bowl without eating anything. "I do. He said he wanted to watch the process, so we told him to use the giant window inside the waiting room. But this guy went full delta forces and climbs down into the pit, nearly knocking Tyler over. I wanted to scream at him, but I held my tongue like my mama taught me to do. Then, he tries to grab for a tool—"

"Hold on there, Ray." Shanice held her hand up. "We know what you do for a living. I wanna know…" She looks toward Robin and smiles. "…what my baby is doing at that diner. Take the floor, sugar."

Robin cringed, not wanting to interrupt Ray's story (even though she'd already heard it). Ray nodded ever so slightly, granting his approval. "Um…yeah. I updated the menus a bit."

"And…" Shanice leaned her head in closer.

"And I revamped the place a bit."

"A bit? No girl, you *transformed* the restaurant. I went in there when you wasn't working, because you know, I didn't wanna embarrass you or nuthin.' I walk inside and the whole place look different. I did a triple take. Tell me about that."

44

Hoop Drama

"Okay," Robin replied, briefly glancing down at her lap. She interlaced her fingers, and more notably, lost her appetite. "Carol and I felt that the restaurant needed an update. We had several empty tables every day including weekends, so we agreed to update the menus with QR codes."

"But who *actually* updated the menus?" Shanice asked, giving an exaggerated wink.

"Well…I did. I put QR codes in it with links to famous photos. But the fun thing was that there was a cute picture of an animal in each photo."

Shanice swallowed quickly so she could speak. "Oh, I didn't know that."

"Yeah. The kids love it. And as you saw, the tables were redone, and the light bulbs changed."

"Why did you update the lights?" Ray asked, slurping down the remaining broth.

"Because the color temperature and brightness weren't right. They made the place feel dark. I think it's worked too. We have way more families come."

"Awesome," Shanice said, reaching for her daughter's hand. "I'm so proud. Finally, that design jumbo is being put to good use."

Ray had now finished both his salad and soup and took the opportunity to place his dishes in the sink. "Hey Mrs. Chapel and Mrs. Baxter, I got seconds if you want it and leftover key lime pie for dessert."

"Lord," Shanice said. "That's too tempting, but these hips just don't need none of that. No thanks, Mr. Chapel. I'm good." She leaned over to Robin and whispered, "You want anything?"

"I will probably want pie, but I can get it in a minute."

"She wants you to bring it over to her!" Shanice hollered before carrying her bowls to the kitchen.

Andy Silvers

Robin stuttered before turning around to look at Ray. She shook her head no.

Ray nodded his head yes before nodding his head erratically to make Robin laugh. It worked. He smiled and began cutting another piece. "Anything for my princess."

Shanice helped Ray wash up the dishes and load the dishwasher. After the meal was eaten and the kitchen spotless, the trio migrated to the living area to watch TV. This was a regular occurrence when Shanice came over. She loved to watch late night comedy mostly to witness her daughter's reactions. It was a bit of a reversal from when Robin was little.

Kids learn a lot from watching their parents. Even brief interactions with valets, friends, and coworkers can tell a child so much about how they're *supposed* to behave. Without even realizing it, Shanice had become the child learning from Robin what to think. Robin enjoyed the comedy, but Shanice enjoyed the company.

That night, the Chapel's piddly forty-inch TV would be the conduit for the comedic stylings of Tommy Craven. He held the 8:00 PM spot on channel 271, and while he wasn't the funniest, he was a family favorite.

Tommy bore a resemblance to Jerry Stiller but with the hair of car enthusiast James May. He had a slightly gravelly voice that made him sound more serious than he actually was. He had no fear of sliding into politics, especially with black actress Rhonda Shearer, who was the night's only guest.

After sitting across from Rhonda on stage, he opened the night with a cordial greeting. "All right. Thank you for coming on tonight. I was worried you would have difficulty sitting after that *spanking* you got at the box office." The TV audience laughed, and so did Ray.

Hoop Drama

"*Okay*, Tommy," Rhonda said, laughing with the crowd. "I remember you acted on one movie. Let's see…what was it called? Oh yeah! *Piggly Gigly's Great Adventure.*"

The audience laughed again, and Tommy played a good sport. "Listen…that was animation, so I was just *voice* acting. If I had been on screen, I would've sold more tickets than Donald Trump pretends he did at his last rally."

"Hah. Slay," Shanice cheered, leaning forward in her seat.

"True that," Rhonda responded after a loud 'Oh' from the studio audience. "I could sell more tickets eating an empty taco shell than that man ever has."

After that, Shanice shot her daughter a quick glance. Robin smiled, then scooched closer to Ray on the love seat.

Tommy spoke while a photo of politician Martin Reverend appeared on screen. "So, while you're here, I'd like to turn your attention to republican Martin Reverend." The audience booed like trained seals. "Last week, he voted in the state of Florida to require voter ID for local elections, potentially limiting the number of citizens able to practice their constitutional right. But don't worry, because *he says* that anyone who doesn't have ID will be deported to *Antarctica* to steal jobs from the penguins."

Shanice chuckled. "Good point, Tommy boy."

Robin smiled and mouthed the word *penguins*. Ray read a text from his brother about selling a lawnmower online.

"I am so thankful I live in the beautiful state of Vermont," Rhonda said, shaking her head in disapproval. "Republicans always use the government as a hammer against brown people. I met a Reverend supporter in—"

"Wait!" Tommy interrupted, wiggling his jaw like a Looney Toon. "You *met* a Reverend supporter? In the wild?"

"Oh yeah. He had a long beard and blue jean overalls and

47

stuff. But anyway, I told him if it ever occurred to him that every founding father was an immigrant too?"

"Good point," Shanice said like Rhonda could hear her.

Rhonda continued, "He said that *those* immigrants had better values. I was like, what values? You mean like coming to the US to seek a better life and then working in a hotel to feed your kids while people call you a gang member!"

"Wow!" Tommy responded. "Well said." Of course, the crowd cheered again.

"Exactly." Shanice grabbed the remote to mute the TV. "I love her. She was in that drama 'bout the car thief we like."

Robin nodded, recalling the series *Red Hands* that she and her mother used to watch together.

"I'm telling you," Shanice continued. "I admire her bravery. She says whatever she wants whenever she wants. I *absolutely* would do the same. You know what I'm saying? I don't care who gets offended. The truth needs to be said."

Robin sat there, listening closely. She found the political jabs a bit confusing since she rarely watched the news, but she trusted her mom. Her mom was her fortress. But Robin wasn't cut from the same cloth—not quite. She never had the strength to say anything like that.

How could she? The world was too big and too complicated. But that's what Shanice imbued.

Confidence…one day. *I'm young*, Robin thought. *I still have time to grow. I will stand when the time comes. Just like my mother.*

Ray rubbed his chin and placed his arm over Robin's shoulder. "I mean…I got ID."

Shanice turned to him, looking at him like a disappointed parent. "*Yes*, Ray. Me too. That's not the point. What he sayin' is that white people makin' the rules. So, if minorities can finally go to college, then they make a degree mandatory. If we can finally own a house, then they say we don't got enough credit for a loan."

"Sure."

Robin wanted an end to this debate and suggested unmuting the TV.

Now, Tommy was asking Rhonda about her latest film, *The Moon in her Eye*. Robin quietly sighed in relief.

"Yeah," Rhonda explained. "I sit there waiting for filming, and a guy in a green leotard comes over and plops down next to me. It's the wolf."

The crowd laughed.

"The wolf was CGI, then?" Tommy asked.

"Yes. And he was wearing a green mask, so I didn't know who he was. Right before we start filming, he says, 'Good luck' and I realize it's John."

"It's John Willman from *Mad City*. He played the doctor with the broken foot," Ray explained.

"So, I realize that my costar, Milo, ain't doing the scene with me. I'm thinking *what the heck*. Is Milo too cool to get in the green suit? So, I ask the director. He responds, 'Well, Milo has a shred of dignity left so he refused to do it.' I'm like, 'What about John?' You saying he don't got dignity?" Rhonda held her hands up, mimicking a begging puppy. "Then John looks up and says, ' *Woof woof.*' That's when I gave up and just did the scene."

The crowd laughed uproariously. Unified once more, Mrs. Baxter and the Chapels laughed together. They, like other families, learned quite a bit about the music and film industry watching late night shows.

That night, without a cloud in the sky, Shanice grabbed her umbrella and her thick jacket and left. It had been a pleasant night,

Andy Silvers

but Robin had her worries…about the next day.

Ray put on his camo sleeping pants like he did most nights. Robin stood silently while her husband pulled back the covers and turned off the lights. "You're gonna do great tomorrow."

"I hope," Robin whispered, and she was breathing through her mouth—an action she only did under duress.

Ray tried to calm her once more. "Hey, you know that thing about imagining the other person naked? Don't do that."

Robin looked up. "Why? It doesn't really work?"

"Nah. Cause the only person you should be picturing naked is me." Ray pulled up his shirt, then rubbed his smooth stomach.

Robin got thirsty eyes. Ray – 1. Stress – 0.

"Good night," Robin giggled, climbing into bed, and turning off her lamp. If the next day didn't work out, her life wouldn't change one bit. She'd go back to her job at Mary's Diner, enjoy the new families, listen to Sarah complain, and use her design skills once in a blue moon.

But that's also what scared her. She wanted change. She just couldn't believe she was ready for it.

MONDAY, APRIL 23RD

Robin clenched her purse while waiting to be called back. She sat in the lobby of C. E. Proctor Creative, a modern two-story complex located roughly twenty minutes from her place of residence.

She sighed quietly, trying to avoid catching the attention of the front desk worker. A tall, skinny blonde lady sat at the front desk wearing a blue hair band and sparkly blue blouse. She fit right in. Then she started speaking, nearly giving Robin a heart attack. "Do you still have Mr. Brennan's business card?"

"Yes ma'am."

"Awesome. Please email your up-to-date resume to the address on the front. Thanks."

After sending her resume, titled *Chapel_Resume_ v06*, to the address, Robin continued examining the room.

Across the way were metal printed designs featuring brands Robin had never seen. She had to remind herself what the company did because the stressful drive over made her forget what she even applied for. But that's just it—she hadn't applied.

Dexter had just materialized from thin air and offered her an interview. She reminded herself that she must be confident. Then she remembered that she had no idea what position she was being offered and she gripped her purse even tighter.

The door opened, nearly giving her another heart attack. It was

Andy Silvers

Dexter Brennan, and he looked sharp. Robin wore a plain black collared shirt and khaki pants, hoping not to seem unprofessional. The hoop earrings she donned last night were gone, replaced by nothing.

"Right this way," Dexter said, guiding his terrified interviewee down the hall into a large conference room with a heavily used white board. "You want any coffee?"

Though not particularly thirsty, Robin could use the cup to steady her hands. "Yes, please. Two sugars and no cream."

"I'll assume caffeinated." Dexter smiled and prepared them both a drink.

He sat down next to her at the end seat of the twelve-person table. He had a fancy ThinkPad laptop in front of him. He held a pair of reading glasses up to his eyes. "All right. Mrs. Robin Chapel. Am I saying that right?"

Robin nodded.

"Good." The drinks were ready on the folding table.

The discussion halted completely until Dexter had gotten up, sat back down, and handed Robin her coffee.

"So," Dexter explained. "I haven't really told you a lot up until now, but that's because my boss, Mr. Proctor, has told me next to nothing. Give me a second here to peruse your resume and get with you."

"Sure," Robin said, planning to take a casual sip. It was burning hot. She lowered the cup onto the table, not letting go of it in case she needed it as a fidget toy.

"Oh. Graphic design." Dexter wasn't really talking to her, rather to himself, so Robin didn't respond. After a blazing fast two minutes, Dexter continued the interview. "This is gonna be an easy one. My boss believes you are a fit here in our creative team. They help to imagine the copy, products, logos, and much more that our

Hoop Drama

partners need. We have a team of three currently, but we prefer four like the other teams. Our teams include the accounts, creative, strategy, and digital. Our digital team includes our in-house photographer and our computer artists. See that logo there?" Dexter pointed at the wall.

"Yes."

"That's the first logo we ever designed. It was for a family-owned bakery called Unleavened Delights."

"Cool," Robin said, mustering little enthusiasm. "Are there any graphic design jobs here?"

"Yes." Dexter zoomed in on Robin's resume. Robin waited for seven seconds for a response beyond "yes," but Dexter didn't deliver. "Anyway, you're a fit with our creative team because you seem to be an idea gal. Would you say you're an idea gal?"

"I think so." Robin tried to sip her coffee, but it was still too hot.

"Great. This job isn't a solo act. You won't be raining down your genius from on high. You'll be with a team—and a great team. Right now, it's Jacob, Catherine, and Kevin. All great people when they're sober." Dexter chuckled. Robin did too, finding the sudden joke fairly amusing. "It's full time only, with remote work available in case of maternity. Any questions so far?"

Robin, rigid as a lamppost, responded, "Yes. Let's see—how do I say this? Am I the only one interviewing for this position?"

Dexter smiled as if expecting this question or something like it. "Of course. You wanna know why you. Right? Right now, there is no listing for this position online. That's because we're still working on it. But Mr. Proctor comes to me a few days ago and says that he wants you to come in. I'll be honest; your resume is a bit scant, but Charles listens to Jenette. Frankly, my wife runs my life too, so I can't blame him."

53

Andy Silvers

Jenette? That name sounded very familiar. Robin strained to remember where she had seen her. Odds are it was at the diner, but Robin also knew a Jenette who worked at Kasey Khel's.

"The point is," Dexter said. "You got first dibs here. If you feel you aren't ready, please let me know. Seriously, this is a Monday through Friday job with lots of benefits. Uh…it starts at $52,000 a year and you can start receiving benefits after three months."

Robin's jaw dropped at the sound of $52,000 a year with benefits. Her mom had gone on and on about getting health insurance through her employer. Also, Shanice was forty-four years old and only made about $43,000 a year, so Robin had seemingly lucked out. Still, it wasn't graphic design. Her heart wasn't sold yet.

"Last year our team worked on our biggest campaign yet. It's no secret that our work with *Ready Set Go* has been the most influential in our fairly short history. We produced everything from flyers to a website to a phone case. It was the whole package…"

"I'm sorry," Robin muttered, remembering a key detail. "What was the name of the organization?"

"*Ready Set Go.* They are a non-profit local to the northern part of West Virginia. They help children in need in Asia and parts of Europe."

Robin's head spun. That was the organization that Carol used to sponsor that Ukrainian kid. The world shrunk in an instant; she wanted to be a part of the action. Designs and computers were nothing until they served a higher purpose. *Family. Freedom. Advocacy.* Robin could serve a higher purpose through her work.

A job this wasn't. A career it was.

Her excitement bubbled over. She even uncrossed her legs.

Hoop Drama

"I've heard of *Ready Set Go*. I bet you work with all sorts of great organizations that do important work." She finally released her coffee.

"Yes..." Dexter paused as though confused. "We have had many important campaigns completed. Be aware that many of them are for profit. We only deal with charities sometimes."

Robin nodded. "Yes, I see. I bet that for-profit businesses also provide a great service to our state...even the country." Robin finally stopped, feeling a disconnect with her interviewer. Plus, her vernacular wasn't advanced enough to relay her message.

Dexter still smiled, nodding slightly, and said, "It sounds like you have big plans. Keep in mind that we work diligently to satisfy our clients. They lay out key goals and we deliver a campaign that suits them. Any larger message is their responsibility. Like how some companies want us to highlight their environmental awareness. Is that something you look forward to?"

Robin nodded, choosing to let Dexter do the rest of the talking. As obvious as it sounded, she hadn't considered what companies do for the community. Most of the people she knew either hated or mildly enjoyed their jobs. No one was dancing for joy to go to work. That was a privilege.

Robin never felt privileged, especially not as a woman of color. But she felt blessed. She had the husband of her dreams, and she never waited in food lines. For the first time, she saw the opportunity to do more than collect a paycheck. She had the privilege to make a difference in the world.

"Our work definitely has a broad impact. I think Catherine would agree with you. All right, let's see. You would be provided a desk and computer upstairs inside our G suite. That's where the creative team works. Our offices are very open for collaboration. No pods here. Charles is actually out of the office today, so I'll

Andy Silvers

discuss with him if he wants to move forward. Any questions?"

"No sir."

"Okay. It has been kind of a short interview, but like I say, I didn't set it up. All right. I'll guide you back to our lobby."

Dexter led Robin to the lobby, they shook hands, and Robin hopped in her car where she let out a sigh of relief. The whole morning felt like a dream. Had the interview really been that easy? Was this really the job for her? Only time could tell. Either way, Ray was ecstatic about the interview and offered to take her out for a celebratory dinner.

❀❀❀

Golden crystals affixed to a massive chandelier glistened in Robin's eye as she sat down across from Ray. The meeting of light and dark created the atmosphere of a ballroom inside the swanky restaurant. Hope for an exquisite meal made the nearly forty-minute drive worthwhile.

Ray chose Venue 45 as it offered best-in-class service combined with top-shelf liquor.

"This is lovely," Robin said, unable to hide her happiness. Special nights were Ray's bread and butter...at least until he started talking.

"Wow. This is so much nicer than that Mary's Diner shlock, huh?"

Robin rolled her eyes. She was wearing a blue dress with black heels. They were the only 'luxury' shoes she had, and they were a gift from Ray's wealthy friend Alex Cougar. The couple got quiet while Robin thought about the future. She feared the possibility of failure, and Ray could tell.

"Hey, babe. You are gonna get that job. If anyone deserves

Hoop Drama

this. It's you."

Before Robin spoke, they ordered drinks. Ray ordered a Moscato Castello, and he made sure Robin got her Sweet Pink Confetti.

"I just don't know," she said, using a straw to avoid discoloring her teeth. "I think it's a coin toss."

"No way. You said you're the only candidate. Babe, that's a sign that God's watching out for you."

"I hope so."

"I guess you can finally tell Shanice now about all this."

"Not yet. I'd like to have good news first. If I get the job, I'll call her immediately."

"Okay. This is exciting. And hot damn—fifty thousand a year. That's Birdman money!"

Robin nearly spit out her drink. "Sure. If Birdman spent ten million a week until he was shaking an empty can and yelling 'Change! You got change?' Then yes."

"Ah. Come on. Why you gotta think like that? We can start thinking about a real apartment now. Maybe even a house. Plus, you can finally pay off your college loans. That's like $22,000 right there."

"Don't remind me about that."

As the night went on, glasses were drunk, and tasty steak was eaten. By 9 PM, Ray was dipping steak into his wine just to see what it tasted like.

"Ray. Don't do that. People will think we're nuts," Robin pleaded. She tried to grab the fork from Ray's clutches, but he had a death grip. "Damnit, Ray. This is why we can't have nice things." They both laughed, trying to stay quiet, but people stared.

After settling down, Robin remembered something she wanted to say. "Hey, you know that agency, Proctor Creative, they

Andy Silvers

did the ads for *Ready Set Go*. I heard about it from Carol."

"Hold up. Ready Set what now? What's this?"

"Oh yeah. I forgot to tell you. My boss sponsors this kid from Ukraine and the program is called *Ready Set Go*. She gives money and stuff so he can eat. Turns out, the agency actually *made* their ads and stuff. That pamphlet thing Carol showed me was *their* work. That's the kind of work I really want to do."

"Oh, I see. You wanna adopt a Ukrainian. I hope you're ready to teach little Vladimir English." Ray attempted a Ukrainian accent for the last two words. It failed spectacularly.

"Raymond...be serious. What I'm saying is that these ads do more than just sell products. They change minds. It's like a conduit to the American soul. Oh jeez, that's sounds pretentious...I mean that these ads reach people everywhere. Just like Carol. I can use my skills but for more than just income. I can be the change that I wanna see."

Ray settled. He held his hands together and thought aloud. "Is this about your mother? Are you trying to make her proud?"

Robin nodded. "And *you.*"

"Hah. You're my princess. You already make me proud."

"*Really?* Princesses don't do anything. They just wear nice clothes and daydream about men."

Ray agreed. "Good point. Maybe you could be that *Enchanted* bitch that climbed out the sewer and fought the dragon. Plus, she refused her prince."

"Gosh. I forgot about her. But for real, I do think about Mom. She has taught me so much about the world. Since I was born, things are so much better but still so much the same. I stand on the shoulders of giants...like my mom."

"Robin the philosopher."

"Yeesh. I hope you know what I mean."

58

Hoop Drama

"I do. What I wanna know is when you gonna get paid at Mary's for doubling their profits."

The subject change took a second to process. "I don't think they were doubled, and it was a team effort."

"Team my butt. Shanice is right, you transformed that place. What'd you say, like twenty percent or somethin'? That's a lot, Robin. You should get a bonus check or a raise or a golden coin at least."

"I was just doing my job."

"Robin, listen. This is what you're talking about. You made that place so much better, and they say you're just doing the job. I believe this agency is the kinda place that'll give you what you earn. I bust my butt fixing cars, but I don't do more than I'm required." Ray grabbed Robin's glass. "*You are valuable.* I already knew that. It's about time you make your fair share."

Robin took her glass back. She agreed implicitly. But Ray didn't hear what Dexter said. The companies decide the message. What corporation makes the world better just because it's right? An altruistic mega-monopoly was a fantasy.

Plus, Ray was stuck thinking about everything the world owed to Robin, not what Robin owed the world. She kept her expectations quiet. Ray had spent over $100 in one night after all. No need to spoil the mood.

Robin had no interest to fight reality. Instead, she desired to live within its unfeeling boundaries, live life honestly, and do what others weren't willing to do. And yes...her mom was her primary inspiration.

TUESDAY, APRIL 24TH

Robin had stayed up a bit late—until 11 PM—thinking over her interview. To seem more engaged, she pondered asking more questions next time. On social media, that was a good interview strategy. She couldn't cure the uneasiness by just reliving the day in her mind. What was done was done.

However, the late night hadn't been a complete bust. She figured out who Jenette was…probably. The lady who had come the day Robin changed the menus was likely Charles' wife. It just made sense. *If she comes back, I'll ask for sure*, Robin thought.

Back in the real world, a child threw a tantrum at table four, prompting Robin to clean up a soda spill. To make matters worse, Sarah hadn't come in at all. Robin really needed to call her, but her focus was elsewhere. Plus, she hoped that Carol, who had clocked in before her, had already taken care of it.

Across the room, a man waved his arm. He had three kids with him, and they were all staring at her.

"Coming," she called.

"We got all ten," a boy of no older than eight said. He held up his paper. He had filled it out with crayons, so Robin struggled to read it.

"Okay. This looks right. We only have vanilla ice cream but let me know what toppings you want."

Hoop Drama

"Sprinkles and chocolate syrup and—yeah. That's it."

"I want sprinkles too; more than my brother. And I don't like chocolate syrup 'cause it's gross." The little girl of about five spoke loudly, happy to order something herself.

"I like it plain," the oldest boy said, returning to his mother's phone to play a racing game.

"Okay," their waitress replied. "I'll be back in just a few."

"Thank you," the mother said. "This is really cool."

Robin couldn't help but be proud. No matter what happened with the interview, she always had that. That feeling was like a whiff of cocaine but less addictive.

In the kitchen, she scooped out three bowls and had Mira take them out. Then she sighed heavily. At only 3 PM, the shift seemed endless. Six o'clock was a lifetime away.

It was fast for a Tuesday. There had been far more customers, particularly for the lunch rush, than in the weeks before. Plus, Robin was finally getting to know a few families. The Parker family who consisted of Mom, Dad, and two kids refused the ice cream more than once, citing cheating. That was a problem Robin knew she had to address, but *when* was the penultimate question. Robin concluded next month was the best time.

One great repeat group was the Duluth family. They consisted of five children total. All five were adopted from Russia by two parents. Two of the kids had aged out of the ice cream prize, but the three little ones smiled from ear to ear every time a sprinkle-coated dessert was laid in front of them.

Despite her success, the new customer base served as the best form of birth control Robin could ask for. Screaming was rare, but sudden, and Robin frequently saw kids as young as four just wandering around the restaurant, staring off into space. Sometimes, Robin missed the quiet old folks. Still, families were

61

Andy Silvers

a blessing, and a family like the Duluths could rack up at least $100 easily.

Increased income could mean increased hourly rates, and Robin considered asking Carol about it. As Ray pointed out, she did change the restaurant almost entirely herself. She wasn't asked to. She volunteered to after seeing an opportunity. Either way, at around 4 PM, before the dinner rush came, Robin and Carol got to talking about the changes.

"You know," Carol started. "I actually forgot we had a booster seat. That lady over there asked about it; and I assumed we didn't have one, but then Mira said we might, so I checked. It turns out we do. Crazy, huh? Although, you should've seen the dust on that thing. It took a minute to do that."

"I'm sorry to hear that." Robin began to mouth breathe again fearing the question she planned to ask. *Do I get anything for all my work?* To ease in, Robin started with a mundane question, hoping to build up her confidence. "So, you'd say the restaurant is doing better?"

"Hell yeah. Actually, I checked the books. It's about twenty to twenty-five percent up over last month. It's mostly on weekends but we broke some records last Wednesday." Carol began taking clean utensils and packing them neatly into fresh napkins. Robin helped.

"Okay. Well, that's good."

"Yup."

Robin almost froze, then remembered Carol was watching. "So, do you think we'll be able to do anything about it?"

"What the heck does that mean?"

Sweat began to creep onto Robin's forehead. "Like maybe since we have more money, we could get a benefit."

"Like a bonus check?"

"Kinda. I think it could be nice to reward our employees for their work."

Carol stopped completely, swiveled to Robin, and placed her left hand on her hip. "I see. Listen, honey. I've been working here for years and only get a raise when inflation requires it. Life is hard out there, particularly for a lady like us."

None of Carol's rambling was answering the question.

"You can be the best employee in the world, and you never get any credit. If I was paid fair and square, I'd have a lake house. Maybe two. You know what I mean? This old life ain't the life of glamour and *pizazz*. It's a long hard race to the finish line where your kids throw you in a cheap coffin and pretend you never existed. It's just the world and the sooner you accept it, the better."

Robin tried to speak while rapidly tapping her finger against the table. "I…well…"

Her voice drifted off. Carol had a point about life being unfair, but that didn't stop her from giving Robin something. If anything, that attitude merely perpetuated the cycle of unfairness. But Robin certainly didn't say any of that. She just said, "It's a thought."

"I agree," Carol said, returning to wrapping utensils. "I will think about it. Understand I don't know how long this will last. Maybe the families will disappear after a few months. I don't know. What I do know is that if you want big bonusses or a pink Cadillac, you're in the wrong business."

That's what Ray had said. Robin began to hope that her interview had been a smashing success. Though she had never felt remotely cheated before, she suddenly had butterflies in her stomach. She calmed herself, remembering that Carol was a friend.

"I'm proud of you," Carol said, although it hit different than it would have an hour earlier. "Let's get ready for the five o'clock rush."

Andy Silvers

Robin gave up, not ready to disrupt her friendship. And a *rush* it certainly was. By 6:30, every single table had at least one customer. Plus, families were everywhere. Every employee had to be on their A-game, and several had to wear many hats. Robin herself flew back and forth from the register to the kitchen to the office. For the first Tuesday ever, register one was so full of cash, it needed to be deposited early. Robin handled it herself while Carol ran register two.

"There you are," Megan said, out of breath. "Where's Sarah. I could really use her lazy butt at tables one through five."

"Um," Robin responded, trying to write down the deposit notes. "You'll have to ask Carol because I have no idea." Megan sped away completely unnoticed.

Finally, after what felt like an hour, she brought the required $140 to register one and shoved it in.

Immediately after doing so, a blonde woman appeared and asked, "Can you break this twenty into fives, please?"

Exacerbated, Robin took the money and exchanged the bills, all without saying a word. She wiped her brow. It was so much easier when guests just left their card on the edge of the table atop the receipt.

Across the way, a family sat down in a table that had just been cleaned up. Yeesh. Robin looked across the room, seeing that Megan was very busy rushing out orders. Taking initiative, she sped over with a pad and pen.

"Good evening," Robin said, mustering up energy after a deep breath. "I'll get you started today with some drinks."

The mother, who had blond hair and green eyes, did all the talking. "Yes. We would like two Sprites for the parents and lemonade for the kids. I know what I want but these rascals can't make up their minds."

Hoop Drama

"Are you talking about Dad?" the middle child asked. Mom didn't answer.

"Okay. I can give you—"

"Robin!" Carol yelled from afar. "Do we have a second booster seat…maybe under the floorboards or something?"

"No! I doubt it."

"Copy that."

Robin returned her attention to the family. "I can give you more time if you need it."

The mom collected menus from her family to hand to Robin. "No. We should order now. I want a bowl of the chicken and rice soup, and Xander wants the steak and fries. Medium rare. My daughter will have the kid's spaghetti with meatballs, and my sons can split the—let's see here—the adult chicken alfredo. And you will get the free ice creams *only* if you eat *all* your food, got it?"

"Yes ma'am." The children spoke in near unison, like an unenthusiastic choir whose cohesion was limited to the presence of free snacks.

Robin chuckled. "All right. I'll get that out to you right away." She bustled over to the kitchen to hand the order to Mr. Rask. Just then, her phone buzzed. She immediately worried it was Ray, so she excused herself answering it during the rush. It wasn't Ray, but she had already swiped to accept the call. "Hello. Robin speaking."

"Hello, Mrs. Chapel. This is Dexter from Proctor Creative."

Robin had to close her jaw after it popped open. "Yes. I remember…I mean nice to hear from you."

"Yes, it is. I'm calling because I spoke with Mr. Proctor, and he wants you. He's gonna give it a try, so I guess you got the job."

Yeesh. *Why did he sound so bummed?* "Wow. That's amazing. I am crazy shocked; I can assure you." She really was. She had so many questions: When do I start? What do I do next?

Andy Silvers

Why me? Can you at least pretend to be happy?

Dexter continued. "It's certainly an exciting time. So, listen. He needs you to start next week on the 30th. So be aware of that. We will have a computer for you but bring your own paper since we are out right now. Actually, don't worry about that yet. I'll send Jacob to do that. Be here at 8:30. That's about it. I've gotta go. See you then." He was on speaker phone, so he hung up immediately after his last word.

"Um…okay. Thanks." Robin was caught rather off guard by his phone call. So much so that she forgot that Dexter left her unable to submit a two-week notice. That was a conversation she had no interest in having. Then again, if she ever wanted to receive credit for her work, or do important work, she needed to leave. She had the degree, and now she had the job.

Her shift was a blur from then on—a gaussian blur. She had hoped that maybe she would have longer to ponder the job. But no. Dexter called her in less than twenty-four hours. Crazy would be too subtle a word, particularly for someone with a less than stellar resume. Either way, Carol needed to know ASAP.

Before closing, and after seeing the astounding amount of cash in both registers, she did what an adult ought to do. "Hey, Carol. I really have to talk to you before we go."

"I know," she said, pulling out a rare cigarette for the road. "You want a gold star and matching Rolex. I'll think about it. I promise."

She had totally forgotten about that conversation despite how recent it was. "Uh, well…" Robin breathed through her mouth. "Actually, I got a call."

Carol waited.

Robin kicked herself for doing that again. Fear had to die a slow, painful death. "I got a job at an ad agency. It's full time."

Hoop Drama

Carol looked at Robin with a shocked expression. That quickly changed to agitated as she pulled out her lighter. "Lord. So, I'm losing another gal."

"What? Who?"

"I had to fire Sarah already. Her lying ass was stealing from the drawers."

Robin gasped. "You saw her?"

"The camera saw her. I shouldn't have hired her, but I bought her story about her achy breaky heart."

Robin went silent. Her heart raced. A bit of guilt creeped into her mind. Would a good manager have fired her earlier? It was all getting to be too much to handle. She held out her hand. "I start on the 30th, and I'm happy to work every day until then."

"Hmm," Carol muttered, taking a puff. She held out her hand too, giving a firm handshake. "We're gonna miss you."

"Likewise."

❄❄❄

A wine cork flew through the kitchen. Neither Ray nor Robin cared to pick it up. A white wine called Golden Coast Chardonnay served as the couple's celebratory drink as they drank to Robin's success. Two glasses clanged together, and two butts fell onto the love seat.

"My baby did it. You did it." Ray sat forward with a large grin pasted on his face.

"Yeah. I don't know what I did, but it was it."

"Baby, get hype. You earned the job no one else could. I would be takin' you out, but we sorta ran out of food money."

Robin laughed. "That's fine. We really don't need to eat fancy. I'm glad to be here with you."

"Yeah, but you know what you have to do now. Call Shanice."

Andy Silvers

"*Mmsh*. I knew you would say that." She dropped her head against his shoulder.

"Yeah. So, call her. You said you would. Don't worry. If she gives you lip, I'll grab the phone and hang up so you don't have to."

Robin laid down her glass. "Okay. Here goes."

She dialed the number while Ray took a sip.

[Hey, baby. What's my only girl up to?] Shanice's voice was familiar but not quite comforting.

"Hello, Mom," Robin said, putting the phone on speaker. Ray gave her a wink. "I have some news for you. I hope you're sitting down."

[Oh, good Lord! He done got you pregnant, didn't he?]

Ray laughed his ass off making it hard for Robin to hear herself think.

"Um," Robin began, smacking Ray's arm. "No. That's funny, Mom. Actually, I got a new job. I'm starting at an ad agency next week."

[Why, that's great, sweetie. They make you the CEO?]

"Yes!" Ray blurted. "Now, she's making Birdman money. I can retire and go cruising."

[Uh, no you ain't,] Shanice responded. [You gonna stay home and change diapers.]

"The cruise ship probably got childcare."

Robin retook control of the discussion. "Listen, Mom. I got a job in the creative team. I guess I'll be coming up with ad ideas and stuff. It'll be fun I think."

[Well, now. You have fun. That's the kinda job that'll use your skills. I remember when you was seven, you made a chart showing me the sales of some jewelry company. I think you had it makin' a billion dollars a year or something. Baby, you dream big. You dream big.]

"Ha," Ray said. "That's funny."

"Absolutely," Robin responded. "I think it'll be a good step for me. I can use some design skills and create cool products, I think. I'm not really sure, but I'll have a team who I'm sure will show me what to do." That was the plan anyway. Surely, her bosses didn't think she could jump into an ad campaign with complete confidence. Right?

[I hope so, baby. I hope so. But listen, it's a tough world out there. Your boss Carol understands you and respects you, but these men aren't gonna. Please promise me you'll be careful. I don't want to hear they ate you up.]

That's true, Robin thought. Business was mostly a male endeavor. For a woman of color to jump in without any experience could be a challenge. But Robin didn't sweat. She looked to her fortress for advice. "Absolutely, Mom. What did you do? I mean, what advice do you have for me?"

Shanice spoke after a brief pause. [Honey, listen. I believe in the wisdom of the ages. Let me share something with you I heard at an event from my idol, Laura Myer. She said that we are shaped by our institutions, but that we also shape them. One voice in a sea of hundreds ain't gonna be heard. But, one voice can reach another voice and then another and create a cry so loud it can't be ignored. You don't always win by going to the brass. Sometimes, you win by reaching the girl next to you. Be smart.]

"Thanks, Mom." Robin sniffled. She nearly cried but held back the tears. The advice was strong, but her emotions were stirred by her love for her mother. She felt like she stood on the shoulders of giants. No, not the people on the news, but someone closer. Someone who carried her burdens with grace…and a bit of sass.

"I need to go to bed early."

"What?" Ray asked, perhaps slightly tipsy. "Tonight was gonna be our boom-boom in the bedroom, baby."

Robin rolled her eyes. "The Horn-dog Express is closed for maintenance. I gotta be at work at 7:00. Goodnight."

Carol had updated the schedule to give her the Sunday off before the 30th. That could give her time to purchase some new shoes. She had a rarely-used pantsuit in the closet. She also had her hoops. Her large mighty hoops. Perhaps Dexter hadn't seen her as 'professional' in the interview. A collared shirt was like pajamas and bunny slippers in the corporate world.

And she finally had a good reason to buy some dark gray loafers she'd seen online. Certainly, on Monday, whatever happened, 'unprofessional' would not be on Dexter's mind.

MONDAY, APRIL 30TH

The pulsating beat of Robin's heart could be heard in Mexico. She rifled to find some gum to chew hoping to calm her nerves. The parking lot of C.E. Proctor Creative lay before her eight minutes before she had to clock in.

At least Ray had made her a tasty breakfast, knowing she'd be too nervous to cook. She would have stuffed a sausage and egg biscuit loaded with calories down her throat if not for her husband's never-ending love.

The days both past and future disappeared as she reentered the familiar lobby. There were many things she hadn't noticed before. There was a MAGA hat sitting on the table behind the receptionist. The same blonde lady sat there, unaffected by Robin's entry.

When the primary door opened, Robin noticed another detail for the first time. Before the door opened and Dexter walked out, there was a click. Clearly the thick wooden door had a serious lock on it. The reality was that the world was growing more dangerous. Anyone could own a firearm and bring it into any building. Robin appreciated the security even if the clang reminded her briefly of her own mortality.

"Welcome, Mrs. Chapel," Dexter said, holding the door open.

"Thank you," Robin responded, entering the same hallway from before. The space was actually cramped, a far cry from the

Andy Silvers

rest of the building. As Dexter led her through the hallway, the building really opened up. Partial walls were everywhere, allowing light from large windows to beam across the room.

Furthermore, the walls were rarely white. Instead, subtle pastel colors greeted the eye with a modern sophistication that reminded workers to 'think different.' The floor was not the cold concrete of Mary's Diner. It was authentic white oak, and it was shiny. Obviously, the office had been built in the past eight years.

Dexter stopped at a picture on the wall. It was a twenty by thirty glossy of him with Evan Hafer, the founder of Black Rifle Coffee. "See that. I got a pic with him last year. That's the kind of gun-loving dude that'd make any blue-haired feminist shrivel up and cry. No, we didn't do their campaign, but it was a treat to meet him." Dexter kept walking. "I just want you to understand that you may meet some cool people including CEO's, models, and more while working here. It's one of the many pleasures of this business."

"Okay." Robin didn't really know what the point of the 'blue-haired feminist' comment was, but it was beginning to worry her that Dexter wouldn't really see eye-to-eye on many things.

Dexter continued, "We're going to do a tour first. This is a collaborative space, so no one works in a tiny cubicle." They came to an elevator with the company's logo on it. It was very simple, yet effective. The letter C was designed so that it also appeared like a capital E was nestled inside. The font was reminiscent of a Greco-Roman style. It looked odd on the burgundy elevator but not so in most settings. Upon stepping out of the elevator, the drastic difference in temperature became apparent. Downstairs was fairly warm, and upstairs was easily seven degrees cooler.

Dexter opened a large door, easily as wide as it was tall. The tiny window was covered with black cloth, and it became clear

Hoop Drama

why once they'd stepped inside. "This is our photography studio. We do shoots for clients here. Our full-time videographer isn't here it looks like, but he's a swell guy."

It was clear the upstairs was designed like a plus sign with two hallways meeting in the middle surrounded by rooms of various sizes. Next, they entered a room full of Apple desktops. Two people were there, working on designs. The room was far bigger than it needed to be. This allowed workspaces to be large. Each desktop computer got its own table adjoined by a second drafting table.

Despite the cool tech, Robin took notice of the workers. Mainly, she saw their outfits, which were quite simple compared to Dexter's button-up silk shirt and black pants. Both workers wore t-shirts and shorts. A brunette man in the back even had a cartoon character on his dark blue shirt. Robin also noticed the smell of chocolate, though she couldn't find the source.

"This is our design team—well—some of them. These people kinda hip hop from place to place." Dexter led Robin to the next room, which was quite small and contained a microphone. The microphone looked like one Robin had seen on a behind-the-scenes of an Aretha Franklin album. It was the real deal.

"This is our audio suite. We can do podcasts here but mostly we use it for voiceover work." In the hallway, a short man with blond hair walked by. "There he is. Robin, this is Xavier. He is part of the design team technically, but he's also our full-time photo guy."

"Ciao," Xavier said, choosing to offer Robin a fist bump instead of a handshake. He seemed to have a Euro persona, but his dress was classic American. A white collared shirt blended in with beige pants and a brown belt. He also had distinctive red hair, like if David Bowie had starred in Grease. Robin wasn't sure what to

Andy Silvers

say, and luckily, he walked off, freeing her of any obligation to socialize.

Next on their journey was a large conference room. Robin assumed the room in which her interview took place was the only one, or at least the biggest one. However, this room had all the bells and whistles so that clients could share ideas on the interactive white board with their choice of four colored markers. The room was spotless save for a laptop at the end seat of the glass-topped table.

"You won't be here any," Dexter assured her. "This is for clients only. We meet and discuss ideas. Those ideas, the brief, are turned into a task list that we hand off to each department. Campaigns can take anywhere from two weeks to six months as needed."

Robin didn't really have any interest in working in that room...at least until Dexter said she wouldn't. His tone was antagonistic, as if he was talking down to her. Certainly, Robin wouldn't ever work in the photo studio either, but Dexter made it seem not that she *shouldn't* need to enter the conference room, but that she *couldn't* ever hope to. Still, her positive side won over, leading her to believe that Dexter simply wanted to overcompensate for the importance of the room to preserve the grandeur of business clients. It was akin to a coach explaining the importance of the benches the team sat upon or a politician explaining the history of these famous steps.

Next, Dexter showed Robin an electronic time clock attached to the wall. It had the current time and the company logo. "So, this is where you'll clock in. I doubt you're in the system yet, but you'll hit this blue button and type in your four-digit code here. We'll email you the code soon."

The duo walked quietly past a corridor featuring a dark metal

Hoop Drama

door. What caught Robin's attention was the sign saying CHARLES PROCTOR.

The boss's office.

"Is Mr. Proctor here today?" Robin asked as softly as possible.

"Yes."

Well…guess that means they're skipping his office. He must be busy anyway. There would be plenty of chances to meet the boss later.

Finally, Robin walked into a bright, colorful room with a sign reading 'The Skwad.' Standing up, as if waiting for Robin's entry, was a thirty-something man in blue jeans and a navy green shirt. Robin quickly noticed that no one except Dexter and the receptionist downstairs had nametags. That would make learning names a challenge to put it mildly.

"Good morning, ma'am," the gentleman said, giving a handshake that made Robin a bit sore. "My name is Jacob Alan Bradley. It is a pleasure to meet you."

"Oh yes," Robin said, excited by the attention she received. None of Jacob's coworkers were watching them, so he must be behaving normally. "It's great to meet you too."

Jacob continued speaking, his posture perfect by any measure. "I look forward to collaboration. You already have a desk preassigned. No password has been chosen, so be sure to do that. Also, we will catch you up to speed on our latest campaign for Major Collins University. I'll try to show you that stuff." Once finished, he sat back down to return to work.

Robin didn't really know what to say, so she said nothing.

"Kevin," Dexter said, looking toward a shorter man with dirty blond hair. "Kevin."

After a few seconds of apparent confusion, Kevin looked up. After seeing Robin, he walked over and shook her hand. "Good morning. You heard my name already, so I guess that ruins the surprise. I work here...duh. It's nice to meet you."

"You as well," Robin responded. She smiled at his quirky humor.

The man's voice was easily two octaves higher than her. Like Ray, he had a small piercing. It was difficult to tell what it was, but it looked like an orange cat sitting behind a plate of yellow cake. He also had very skinny legs, but his torso was wide, pushing his shirt tightly against his body.

Yet again, Robin saw that no one had on a collared shirt, pantsuit, tie, or even loafers. She was the only one, and it was starting to become awkward.

Kevin turned to Dexter. "Is she gonna need to be updated on MCU? I think we're doing an Idea Blitz soon."

"Yes, but Jacob has volunteered for that."

"Of course. Works for me."

Lastly, Dexter called over a lady sitting at her desk, drinking from a large energy drink. She had no wedding band, and her black hair was cut short, looking like Olivia Wilde from *Tron: Legacy*.

"Good morning," she said. "I'm Catherine. Welcome to the Skwad. We goof off, drink coffee, and occasionally get work done. So, if you know how to intensely stare at an email like your job depends on it, that's because it does." Up close, her earrings were identifiable as tiny coffins.

"Noted."

"All right, Miss," Dexter said, leading her back to the door. "So, we are doing the MCU campaign right now, but I trust Jacob to catch you up. You can start by setting up your desk area if you brought anything from home. Do you have any questions?"

Robin had a lot of questions, but they were the kind that people figure out on the job. None of them were yes or no

Hoop Drama

questions. So, she shook her head.

"Alright, well, I'm gonna go downstairs to…" His voice drifted off when she finally heard her co-workers talking amongst themselves.

Unfortunately, it sounded like they were talking about her.

"Goodness gracious," Jacob whispered. "I could fly a paper airplane through her hoops."

"Nah," Kevin teased. "You could fly an actual airplane through those hoops." Both men snickered.

Robin clenched her fist. Did adults in the advertising industry really act like that? She graduated middle school a long time ago. Now it seemed she was right back in Mrs. Owen's classroom.

"Will that work?" Dexter asked.

Robin snapped back to attention. "Uh, what was that, sir?"

"I asked if you needed to see the employee lounge. I forgot to show it to you but it's just down the hall at the end."

"Um…no. I'm sure I can find it. Thank you. Actually, what's downstairs?"

Dexter crossed his arms. "That's the accounts and finances teams. You won't really be down there unless your direct deposit messes up or something."

"Gotcha. Thanks."

"Okay." Dexter returned to the elevator.

Realizing she had stuff to get from her car, Robin joined him for a silent ride down to the first floor.

Her trunk was home to a purple duffel bag with office supplies. Back upstairs, she began placing them at her desk. The desk was tan with white trim. A silver all-in-one computer stood centered in front of her. Robin was relieved as she didn't want her coworkers to see her shabby laptop. At least, not after they complained about her earrings.

77

Andy Silvers

Out of her duffel bag came a treasure trove of items. They included a picture of Ray from her honeymoon, a gaggle of pens and pencils, and a brand-new planner which she intended to use exclusively for work purposes.

The air conditioner incited goose bumps as it turned on with a sudden whoosh.

"The breath of God." Kevin commented, prompting the trio to smile.

She placed a tall turquoise bottle on her desk, then fiddled with its lid. She truly had no idea what to do. For the first time in her life, she felt an out-of-body experience. She was there but not really. She was an employee, but only in theory.

Plus, where was Jacob to help her learn the ropes? He was just sitting there, typing away. Robin couldn't help but notice that he had large biceps like Ray did. And it seemed like he may have a tattoo on his wrist, but his hands moved too rapidly to tell. Catherine and Kevin had found ways to lean slump in their chairs. Jacob must have seen videos about perfect spinal alignment (or he was a cyborg).

Robin's computer was placed such that she could easily see her coworkers (except Jacob) without twisting her neck, but not so she could see their screens.

To do something resembling work, she turned on her desktop. It fired on with a loud whoosh of the fans. Not a head turned or an eye glared.

Robin was greeted by a lion sitting within the grassy plain, blending in well with his surroundings. She was reminded of her new menus. As stressful as that work could be, she did enjoy the feeling of knowing what to do next. There was only so much a day at Mary's could throw at her. Proctor Creative was a real company, spanning over two floors of air-conditioned office space.

Hoop Drama

After clicking ENTER, the device booted into the home screen. She did as she was told and set a password. She used the same password that she used for her social media accounts—MaximumQueen57. For other accounts, she added the occasional $ or #.

Her phone buzzed. She hoped it was Ray wishing her good luck, but it was her personal email. Dexter had sent her some information. It included her four-digit code, 2907, and her new company email—*robincwv@cepc.com*. She was told to sign into her company account and use the temporary password CEPC100. There was a link in the bottom of the email to a Smartsheet collaborative page, but she thought it was an ad.

With ease, she completed the task and updated her email with a custom password. She had two emails in the inbox. One stating that her password had been changed and another from Dexter saying that her employee ID was 2907.

Remembering what she learned from college, she checked the task manager window on her new desktop. Goodness gracious! Six cores and thirty-two gigabytes of RAM. That was rather impressive for someone who supposedly wouldn't need to design anything herself. But companies liked that sort of thing. Purchasing expensive hardware with extra bells and whistles kept employees happy while also negating the need to update (and pay handsomely) for many years. At least, that's what she heard in college. She had never been one to check the specs or run any benchmarks, but her geeky classmates made sure she knew what her university had afforded its students.

Before she had time to waste away looking at more stationary pixels, Dexter poked his head in.

"Hey, Mrs. Chapel. Come here a moment."

In the hallway, he handed her a Windows tablet.

Andy Silvers

"I forgot to have you do your I9. It has to be finished within three days of your hiring, so I'm glad Lindsay reminded me. Here, I'll wait while you sign stuff."

Because signing the i9 had actually become an escape from the lonely monotony of sitting at her desk, the process was almost fun. Dexter took the tablet without a word and returned to the elevator. Robin strolled back into the room and sat at the edge of her rolling seat. Nearly as fast as she sat down, her teammates stood up. They all ran over to a large screen and Jacob grabbed a black marker.

"Come on over, Robin," Jacob said, clearing the board with a plastic digitizer in the shape of an eraser.

"One moment." He didn't seem to hear her. How did he remember her name so fast? Robin touched her chest, knowing there was no nametag there, but still wanting to be sure.

Everyone stood around Jacob while he began drawing rectangles on the board.

Catherine spoke up first, holding up her personal smartphone. "So, we know that the new building is under construction, so we're going to lean into that to show how new students can expand their business credentials."

"Well, I wouldn't put it quite like that," Jacob said. "It's clear that students will receive one of fifteen different degrees. I think we should start with this." Jacob wrote the word ANYONE on the board. "The brief states that they want the sense that anyone can be a business pro highlighted here. So that will be one of our bricks."

Robin discovered quickly that Jacob was in charge. Maybe that's why he carried himself in such a rigid fashion. *Dress for the job you want,* she thought.

"They don't need a website for this campaign, but merch is

Hoop Drama

high on the list, and they'll need brochures for their main building." Kevin pitched in next. He was holding a two-inch binder with lots of paper inside.

"So, this will definitely be a campaign with pics needed. We'll probably want to use stock photos unless they specify that the school has to be in the shots." Catherine wrote the word photoshoot off to the side with the red marker.

"They did specify. The client wants new photos made to show real students in front of the new building," Jacob said, pointing to the binder.

Kevin quickly cycled through the pages. "What's the deadline for that? They may need to wait until the construction is complete."

"No," Jacob said. "Not if the outside is finished. I checked the school's Facebook account. It looks like the exterior is mostly done." Jacob looked over at Robin who was staring blankly at everyone. "Kevin, can you hand the brief to Robin please? Robin, sit down and take a look through there. That has all the notes from the client meeting."

"Yes, sir," Robin said, hoping to impress the boss.

She took the binder to her desk and shoved the keyboard out of the way. Indeed, the brief was rather brief. It featured multi-colored pages with various charts and graphs. The binder looked thick as many pages were empty or nearly so. They had blank lines where information could be written and charts with close-to-nothing entered.

The market strategy featured West Virginia colleges that also had business schools. She also realized that the handwritten text wasn't exactly 'handwritten.' It had been digitally scribbled, likely with the tablet Robin signed her name on earlier.

Good Lord, Robin thought. *I hope there won't be a quiz.*

Luckily, no quiz materialized, but she did sit and read the

81

Andy Silvers

binder for hours. For her half hour lunch break, she purchased a salad and ate it in her car. She did discover the break room at around 2:00 PM, but she refused to eat anything in there. Plus, the cookies were store bought. Yuck! The rest of the day was largely a blur. She read the binder, listened to banter, and completed a harassment training module.

Her coworkers were too busy to make small talk or invite her into the discussion. So, in order to fit in, Robin would have to learn the ropes sooner rather than later.

※❀※

While Ray prepared a sub sandwich for the couple to split, Robin explained the mirage of the day, complete with run-on sentences and mumbled word salad.

"Slow down," Ray cautioned. "I can't speak black woman. What did you say about the earrings?"

Robin rolled her eyes. "Well, suffice it to say, I thought I'd returned to middle school. I mean, they literally joked about my hoops like I wasn't two yards away."

She tore open a bag of chips. Though she never stress-ate, the day had been quite the load.

"I guess they're just not used to hoops."

"What!" Robin exclaimed, a chip falling from her mouth. "Women everywhere wear them...it's...they can't be that insensitive."

"Hm." Ray brought her a ham and turkey sub. He took her chips. "How long have they known you?"

That seemed like a stupid question. "A day."

"How long have you known them?"

"A day."

Hoop Drama

"I think you just have to give it time. I know you're awesome, so show them that. I have an idea. I'll make chocolate chip cookies that you can take tomorrow."

"Chocolate. Why?"

Ray sighed. "Because this is what they need. A little homemade love as Shanice calls it. Also, ditch the pantsuit."

"You ain't gotta tell me twice."

"Awesome. We got a plan…now have a great day tomorrow."

Robin looked up. Ray had the biggest smile on his face. How could her biggest fan also be the sexiest guy she knew? If she weren't so stressed, she might've asked him to bed.

TUESDAY, MAY 1ST

Dark jeans and a gray collared shirt. No hoops and no loafers. She felt a bit guilty giving up her professional style but so much better when she walked around in her navy-blue tennis shoes. They carried over from Mary's to serve as consolation at her new job.

The scent of chocolate filled the car as she pulled into the lot. She even snuck a cookie from the pile…just to be sure they were safe.

She still wore earrings, but they were small lilacs instead of large hoops. Robin wanted to seem confident, so she strutted into the building making sure to say "Hi" to the lady at the desk.

Twenty minutes before her shift began, she placed the cookies on a plate in the breakroom and made a cup of coffee with a large machine. In fact, that room felt the most corporate out of all of them. It had tile flooring, white walls (a rarity), and no windows for natural light. Plus, one of the circuit breakers was in the room, so occasionally a beep would go off. She took her piping hot coffee back to her desk.

Jacob had also come in early, but he wasn't doing what Robin expected. He was doing pushups next to his desk. More impressively, they were one-legged pushups, resting his right leg over his left. Then, he shoved his feet under a lower part of his desk, using it to do sit-ups. He must've done at least fifteen, but

Hoop Drama

she didn't count exactly. When he was done, he finally acknowledged her presence. "Are you ready for today's assignments?"

"Um," she mumbled. "I hope so. I brought some cookies from home if anyone wants any."

He raised his eyebrow. "Charlie pays for that stuff. It'll get expensive if you do that every day."

"Sure. I'm…I thought it would be nice to have some homemade goodies." Robin began to feel tired. She had gotten the same workout as Jacob without the pushups.

"Whatever."

Just then, Catherine walked in. She threw her purse on the desk and rushed out the door. Robin decided to go to the time clock, and apparently Catherine had the same idea. She watched to learn the right methodology.

Kevin walked down the hall, a sway to his hips, and punched in too. "Hm, there are cookies in the lounge. Like, real cookies. Those yours?"

Robin smiled. "Yeah. I hope you like them. I made them for our team."

"We already have cookies in there." Catherine didn't wait for a reply and walked away.

Robin wanted to say that those peanut butter 'cookies' were stale trash, but she withheld her bitterness. "Those are good too."

"I appreciate it," Kevin said. "Thank you."

Robin smiled again. "You're welcome." Perhaps Ray had been right. Her coworkers just needed time to get to know her. Furthermore, her fish-out-of-water status was ending. No one made any off-handed comments about her outfit.

Still, that didn't mean she knew the job. Back at her desk, the smiles ceased.

85

Andy Silvers

Jacob stood up. "Dexter is meeting with Rover Callum today. They sell men's hygiene products and such. In other words, everything Kevin refuses to use."

Kevin was hardly fazed. "At least I—nope! I'm not gonna say anything that would make you feel small. Heaven knows your doctor has said enough of that."

When Robin could speak like that, then she'd know she had become one of the guys. But that day would be long away since she didn't even know what kind of research to do, much less what to say to the team leader.

"Are we doing the works?" Catherine inquired, gulping down an energy drink.

"No. They are only releasing one new thing, and I'm pretty sure it's shampoo, which we've done before. But we'll get the brief probably by 11:00 AM or so."

"What should Robin do?" Kevin asked.

It was a good question, but it made everyone stare at her which was the last thing she wanted.

Jacob crossed his arms. "Do you remember the brief saying that the school needed photos in front of the building?"

Robin nodded.

"Research what kind of poses are popular on other websites and give us an idea of how many we actually need. I know they want to use real students for the website, even though that's ridiculous, so we'll need to pick them and bring them here for the high-key shoot."

Robin nodded.

Jacob could see confusion through her eyes. "In other words, research a bunch of stuff about what images we need and how many. Some of them will be in front of the school but on the website and ads, they typically won't."

Hoop Drama

"Got it."

Everything quieted down as the work truly began. For fun, Robin started with her alma mater, Ohio University. They had a business school with diverse pictures, both racially and environmentally. Furthermore, students had backpacks and briefcases. They also looked relaxed, sporting headphones and even a skateboard. Robin nearly asked Catherine about whether indoor shoots would also be necessary but hesitated. Best not to disturb a working woman.

Other West Virginia schools told the same story. The idea of anyone being a business graduate was very compelling. Then again, it wasn't exactly an altruistic message. Of course, business schools want everyone. That helps the bottom line.

Robin created a document with notes. She added different poses, locations, and styles to the list. The job almost seemed too easy. Every decision was subjective. It would be like listing several ingredients, handing it to the cook, then having the cook make up something for the customer to judge.

It created a sense of panic because there was no way to gauge when the job was 'done.' She couldn't even use her design skills to make anything. That was another team's job.

After a few hours of work, Dexter walked in with the next brief. Jacob gladly got up to take the binder. It was interesting how Dexter printed out every page, despite taking all his notes digitally. Perhaps there was something beneficial to the physical copy.

Dexter peeked over Kevin's shoulder at his work. "Is this for the MCU campaign?"

"Yes," Kevin replied. "They want a brochure ASAP, so these elements would be good for that. I think we should just use stock for these until we get our models."

"No. They want a real photo of the school on the front."

Andy Silvers

"Could we take a picture and add a stock photo over it?"

Dexter thought for a moment. "We'll see. It needs to feel cohesive, but that might be necessary."

Next, Dexter walked over to Robin. Her heart raced and she began hyperventilating.

"What 'cha got for me, Mrs. Chapel?"

She quickly pulled up her notes sheet. "So, I have these notes. This is...um...these are ideas for the pictures. I researched other schools. They—hold on. They have a couple poses for their students. Plus, we can do a slideshow with voice-over for—"

"*Diverse?*"Dexter leaned in, looking at Robin's notes.

"Um...yes. It's just a thought from what I've seen."

"*Interesting.*" A whisper sounded like a scream with the wrong inflexion.

Dexter checked out what Catherine was up to for a few minutes. Robin wanted to resume work but found that Dexter's presence was giving her anxiety. She drew several large gulps from her thermos.

"So," Dexter began. "Rover Callum wants the advanced package. Their product is called Husk and it's a new shampoo. We'll do a quick thirty-second video with motion graphics and design the product wrapping. I think a wood finish is their goal, so research what woods look dark."

"Is that ad for TV?" Jacob asked.

"No. Internet only. So, it'll be vertical."

"Got it. What's the time frame?"

"The client returns in ten days for review."

When Dexter left, Robin took a breath of fresh air. She saved her notes, then got up to check out the brief. Jacob was perusing it and writing the letter J next to certain paragraphs.

"Robin," Jacob said, handing her the binder. "Can you work

Hoop Drama

on the website. They need a scrolling webpage that lists all the features and sorta tells a story. Start with that."

"Yes, sir," Robin replied.

Kevin scoffed. "Don't say 'yes sir.' It just boosts his inflated ego."

"I like it," Jacob remarked.

It was awkward with the office being so casual to say things like 'yes sir,' but if Jacob was in charge, respect for authority was warranted. Especially for the new girl.

"It's fine. I'm glad to do it." Robin rolled up to her desk, signaling an end to the conversation. She started to peruse the brief. There were many pages, but a third were blank.

Then she noticed the company's message.

Use Husk Shampoo. Get Hot Chicks.

While that message wasn't intended for the viewers eyes, it said a lot about the industry. Several more words stood out too. *Sex. Wild. Manly.*

"...*tells a story*," Jacob had said. Hopefully he didn't mean that any guy could put on some fancy shampoo then sleep with anyone he wanted. Robin nearly asked Catherine (the only other woman) about it, but hesitated, opting to think it through first.

She would sound like some 80-year-old church lady with clacking teeth and absolutely *no cleavage*—but she wasn't.

She had seen many ads throughout her life with sexual undertones and hot guys. Maybe even liked some. Plus, she had a bit of cleavage under her shirt. Hardly any, but certainly more than yesterday.

With her fingers on the mouse, she hoped to solve the issue quickly. She wasn't a snob but making the ads herself was a different story. Plus, it's safe to say that 'ugly guy gets hot girl' wasn't the story that she imagined telling after learning about the

Andy Silvers

Ready Set Go campain.

But honestly, she was new. The world of business and advertising was not her forte. She had taken the job on the promise of pay. Anything else she expected was her overly hopeful brain boosting her ego. Her frontal lobe a reservoir for hubris.

Just do your job, Robin thought.

She put together quickly that the webpage needed a story of a nerdy loner using Husk and becoming hot. Maybe Rover Callum at least had the decency to use the same model twice for the before and after. Then, the only change would be non-greasy hair. That could be a quasi-positive message. Men who clean up get higher caliber women.

But no.

The brief clearly stated that the man's appearance would change completely. So, despite her unspoken gripes, she began working.

At the top of the page, she imagined the product being prominently displayed on a wooden table, but then got confused about what kind of page she was making. Since Jacob seemed the most aware, she asked him.

"Hey, Jacob," she called, trying to be quiet but failing spectacularly. "I have a question."

Jacob walked over to her desk. He stood behind her, laying his hand to the right of her keyboard. She had to scooch over to avoid touching his bicep. "Is this a product page or an info page?"

"So, do what Apple does. The page we're designing tells a story, but the bottom will link to the product. Don't add endless crap. Just add a before, during, and after. Even though everyone with a functioning brain knows how to shampoo, highlight how to use it somewhere."

"Okay. Um…can I ask the design people to draw stuff for

me?" Robin worried that was a forbidden question.

"Well, you probably shouldn't. Can *you* draw any?"

"Yes, sir. I have a graphic design degree."

"That's it then. Use the skills you got." Jacob patted her shoulder and returned to his desk.

Good news. If Robin could draw, she could create. Unfortunately, she got a bit too confident. "Hey, Jacob. Does the ad seem sexist to you?"

Jacob stood up and thought for a moment. Kevin scoffed again and Catherine smiled to herself. These close quarters desks were really becoming a problem.

"If you mean that the ad is like every other ad ever made, then yes. But really, Robin? Have you been living in a monastery?"

Her pounding heart could be heard in Brazil. She spoke up to cover the noise. "Yes. Of course, I was joking. Will we do a photoshoot for this webpage?"

"Yes," Jacob said, sitting back down.

"Got it."

Oh, how she wished she could teleport. She wanted to David Copperfield herself out of the room onto a beach with someone's signed card.

But she couldn't.

That moment forward, Robin would speak to group members individually rather than yell over the desks. Either way, a job's a job, and she sketched up some ideas that she knew Dexter would like.

After her lunch break, where she ate alone in her car, she finally came up with an idea for the ad that would win over consumers. Not for a second did she consider sharing it with Jacob, but that night, Ray got an earful.

Andy Silvers

❀❀❀

"So, you asked that *out loud?* Savage. You're lucky that wasn't gym class with dodge balls." Ray chuckled and slurped his linguini noodles.

"Not funny, Ray." She could say that to Ray, but in truth, her frank question was a moment of ignorant bliss. "I know. I know. I can't believe I said that. I just felt that maybe Jacob would work with me, but it's not like that. The client tells us what they want, and we do it."

Robin laid her head on her hands, causing her hair to fall past her shoulders. She had a beautiful silk press framing her round face. That's why it took her up to half an hour to stylize her hair every morning. But of course, it was worth it.

Ray gently pushed the hair back over her shoulder. "Sweetie, this is a whole new career. You did better than I would've."

"Really?"

"Yeah. But you gotta know where they're coming from. Men only shampoo for women. I got no hair and even I shampoo for you."

Robin smiled but she frowned internally. He didn't get it.

"It's a confidence thing. Guys like to look good for girls."

Robin sat up and pushed her hair back. "Sure. So, here's my idea. What if you made the ad less gendered and marketed toward men *and* women?"

"But it's men's shampoo—"

Robin grabbed his hand. "Hold up. Shampoo does the same thing for men and women. So maybe, the ad should have the girlfriend want to try the shampoo because it's so nice. Then, she's not an object who just likes him cause he's magically hot now. You know? She likes sexy hair, and he has what she needs to get it."

92

Hoop Drama

Robin sat there for several seconds. Ray ate several more bites, so God only knows if he caught the whole thing.

He got the gist. "I don't know. It seems like a simple boy gets girl story."

"Yes," Robin sighed. "But that's what everyone does. The lady has no personality or anything. And maybe it'd be fine if he didn't magically become some six-pack hunk after, but—"

"Honey...don't overthink it." Ray smiled the same way a classmate named Greg had back in high school. It was a smirk that said, 'come back to reality,' and it was a feeling that couldn't be reasoned away.

Robin licked her lips and looked away. She didn't quite have the vocabulary or energy to explain the point clearly. But she knew what she meant. The story was simple because it was easy. It was easy because it took no effort to appeal to men's desire for hot women.

"All right. What if I let you shampoo my hair tonight, huh? You can even use that lavender goop you like." He winked seductively, but she wouldn't take the bait.

She shook her head. "Never mind. I give up, but I love you."

"Love you too."

Maybe asking a guy with more hair under his arms than his head was a bad idea. Or perhaps, it was just the start of a trend.

WEDNESDAY, MAY 2ND

Kevin ate the last cookie, so Robin planned to bring a batch of ginger snaps on Thursday. No one can resist the Shanice recipe. Also, wearing her tennis shoes worked great. Her feet were never sore at the end of her shift, and she could get groceries without looking like she walked out of Dr. Jameson's Sunday school class.

Unfortunately, her coworkers still didn't see the problem with the ad. Ray didn't need to understand, but if Catherine didn't even care, how could anything change? The plan was to acclimate quickly, to help the team accept her, then she could speak, and they would listen.

Hopefully.

Step one was to bring a drawing pad to work. Another word for ad agency is creative agency, after all. She whipped out her three-sided pencils and large pink eraser. Jacob said to prioritize the Husk webpage in the morning and save the college campain for the afternoons.

She set it up so that each page was the next sequence in the scrolling webpage. The very top was a simple image of the shampoo on a dark oak plank surrounded by a fancy log cabin bathroom. Earth tones were a priority. When the user scrolled down, they would meet Caleb, an average dude with scrawny arms and no facial hair.

The text would read; CALEB STILL USES DOLLAR STORE SHAMPOO LIKE A CAVEMAN. DID WE MENTION HE'S SINGLE?

When the user scrolled down again, they'd see Caleb on a couch with his arm over the backrest. A movie played, but no one sat with him as he munched his popcorn.

Next, the user would see him showering (from the waist up) using some generic white bottle and looking miserable. The text would read; WHEN YOU USE CHEMICALS, YOUR HAIR DOESN'T GET THE NUTRIENTS IT NEEDS TO THRIVE.

Next, the user would see him use a stepladder to reach a tall shelf featuring a bottle of Husk. The text read; GET A SHAMPOO THAT BRINGS YOU BACK TO YOUR MANLY ROOTS.

Finally, after scrolling further, a tall sexy man would hold the shampoo where the viewer could see the product label. The text simply read; GET YOURSELF THE GIFT OF HUSK.

The next shower shot featured the sexy man holding the bottle with one hand and applying the shampoo with the other. The text read; BE THE MAN YOU ARE INSIDE WITH A SHAMPOO THAT GETS YOU THE GIRLS YOU WANT.

The next shot showed the man answering the door with the bottle still in his hand. At the door stood a group of stereotypically hot women with (of course) perfect hair.

The same scene of the movie would be featured again, but this time, the couch is full of women, including one with Caleb's arm over her. The text read; NOW CALEB LOOKS HOW HE FEELS, AND THAT GIRL UNDER HIS ARM LOOKS GOOD TOO.

Robin needed to add a section that highlighted the product itself. Luckily, the job was fairly easy because the data was all laid out in the brief.

The final shot showed the bottle sitting atop a wood plank

Andy Silvers

covered in a thin mist of water. The text read, HUSK IS MADE WITH NATURAL INGREDIENTS INCLUDING SHEA BUTTER, AVACODO OIL, AND JOJOBA SEED OIL TO BRING THE EARTH TO YOU.

Again, Robin observed how perfect that would be for women's hair too. Finally, at the bottom of the page, she added a closing image and a space for the soon-to-be-decided discount code. The bottom of the page had to feature the sexy man with all three of the girls. Robin drew this scene from the waist up, sure to leave room for the BUY NOW button.

Robin felt the urge to smile. She was proud of her work and also upset that she'd produced something so vain. Still, she knew Jacob would like it, and at that moment that's all that counted. If she could win over the leader, she could win the followers.

She stood up, shoving her chair back in one smooth motion while grabbing her drawing pad. She didn't begin to breathe through her mouth because she was confident in her work.

On her way toward Jacob, she spotted a nice photo on Catherine's desk. There were two young children, likely between five and eight, standing in front of a field of bluebonnets. The boy and girl wore white collared shirts and jeans. It was a highly professional photo. The lighting. The posing. All perfect. What stopped Robin in her tracks was a peculiar detail—the flowers. Bluebonnets were native to Texas, so the picture must've been taken prior to moving to West Virginia. The thought occurred that maybe it was a vacation picture, but the children both had blonde hair, a feature Catherine certainly did not possess.

Before Robin could continue playing CSI: Wheeling, Catherine noticed her poking around. "You got something done already?" she asked.

"Um…yes. I drew the website layout."

Hoop Drama

Catherine hit SAVE on her work and jumped up. She guided Robin to a table positioned along the far wall. Its location next to the window meant everything was bathed in light; even the white paper appeared to glow. At the beginning of the design, Catherine carefully reviewed the images. Robin felt indifferent until Catherine removed a red pen from her pocket.

"So…this is a good start, but this first question makes it sound like the viewer should find Caleb attractive…"

"Yeah," Robin said. "I can see that."

"Instead, put this." Catherine changed the question to WHY DO YOU THINK HE'S STILL SINGLE? "That's not the only option but it better sets up the story for later."

"Okay. Thank you so much for your help."

"That's how campaigns get done. Collaboration. All of our desks are open. That's why they face each other." She was matter of fact, not cordial or inviting.

"Really? That's good to know."

"Yup. We could never do our jobs in tiny, isolated pods. That's not the Proctor way. Anyway, this next page is fine, but I'd adjust this sentence here."

She pointed to the 'gift of Husk' sentence. She altered it to read; TRANSFORM YOUR LIFE WITH HUSK SHAMPOO BY ROVER CALLUM. "Companies want you to remind the viewer who they are. Also, this guy doesn't have any nipples."

Both ladies grinned.

"Uh-oh. I forgot to draw those." Robin didn't just smile at the joke. She smiled at the chance to make Catherine an ally.

Catherine turned the page twice more. "I like how he answers the door in a towel. That's a good call. She added one final note on the last page. "So, I wouldn't reuse the same image. Just make the background a solid oak texture and replace the BUY NOW button.

Andy Silvers

That's too aggressive. I'd put TRY HUSK." With the lid placed back on the pen, she returned the drawing pad to its owner.

"Maybe I could help you later with the college campaign," Robin smiled, hoping for an equally warm response.

"Uh, no. You need more experience first, my girl. My desk is open." She returned to her desk.

So much for making Catherine an ally.

Luckily, Jacob liked what he saw. "Looks like you already got some notes. It's good to collaborate. Until you get the hang of things, I'd let one of us review your stuff."

"Yes, sir."

"So, the model here will be hired by us, but we will use stock photos for the backgrounds. Please go to several stock websites, use your company email, and find several options for the background images. Don't buy anything. Just create a PDF with a look book for our design team. Be sure to submit it."

"Copy, sir." That almost sounded weirder than 'yes sir.'

Robin spent the next several hours working on stock image searching. At around 12 PM, the entire crew made their way out the door, ready for a lunch break. It was clear that punching out was required.

Luckily, Jacob spoke up to give Robin the info she needed. "You get an unpaid thirty-minute lunch and a paid fifteen, but we all just combine them into a forty-five. Got it?"

"Yes," Robin said, testing out a response without 'sir' in it. Actually, she was still confused, but admitting it would make her seem more out of touch. If the lunch was only thirty minutes and she had to clock back in, then how did they take forty-five minutes for lunch? Maybe they just lost fifteen minutes of pay every day. Robin was not going to do that. Perhaps they clocked back in and finished their lunch at the office. The confusion led to stress: stress

Robin really couldn't afford that day.

She texted Ray that she was learning the ropes. He responded with a smiley face.

The closest fast-food place was a chicken place. The grilled chicken salad was about as healthy as Robin could find, but there was a purpose in mind. It only took eight minutes to grab lunch, meaning she could eat with her coworkers in the break room. As she entered, her heart rate increased. There were several people in the room eating including Xavier. But she didn't really *know* Xavier. The only person she knew was Catherine, who was eating a sub sandwich by herself. This was a great opportunity to make an ally.

After setting her bag down, Catherine glared at her without uttering a word. Robin became so tense, she forgot to ask if she could sit there. Instead, she just said, "I grabbed a salad." *Crap*, she thought. *That is probably the dumbest thing to say*.

"Okay," Catherine said as though caring would cost her money.

Robin sat down. The seat was cold like a park bench. The crinkling of the paper bag sounded like a barrage of gunfire compared to the silence just moments before. She finished half her salad before saying anything, just to let Catherine recover from her unannounced entrance.

The silence gave her the chance to examine her meal partner. She didn't want to admit it, but making friends was much easier at Mary's. Perhaps it was because the assistant manager always had an excuse to talk to people.

Nevertheless, detective Robin noticed that Catherine didn't have a wedding ring and that she was left-handed. Her fingernails were beautiful. A thin line of yellow polish lined the tips of her fingers, and the rest was a shiny clear coat. Before Robin could make any more insightful discoveries, Catherine spoke up.

"Are you friends with Dexter?"

"Not really. I met him at my workplace, and he offered me an interview."

Catherine could play Texas hold 'em because she kept her reaction entirely internal. This made Robin unsure what to say next. She watched as Xavier left the room.

She spoke up again, trying to say something nice. "You have two beautiful children."

Catherine smiled without making eye contact. "Do you have kids?"

"No. Not yet. I've only been married a year, so I've got time. But I love the photo on your desk. The flowers are a great choice."

Catherine worked quickly to get salsa off her fingernails. "Those aren't my kids, you know. They're from a stock website."

Crap. That came out of left field. It was a bit creepy to have that photo on her desk, but instead of hasty judgment, Robin opted to nod casually and hope there was a logical explanation.

Indeed, there was. "That picture shows the life I *will* have. But I can't get there. You probably understand. No man wants a working woman. Heaven forbid you out-earn him."

Oh. A familiar tale. "I totally do. My husband, Raymond, is a great guy. He encouraged me to apply here even when I wanted to quit. I guess he's the kind of guy who can handle a working woman. I definitely make more than him now."

Catherine was listening closely, but still presented a poker face. She balled up her trash and got up. "Must be nice."

Poor gal. She could be happy. She really could. Robin knew there were men like Ray who not only tolerated but admired a hard-working woman. If Ray could sip martinis on the beaches of Maui while Robin made millions selling artwork, he would. But in truth, Catherine had her work cut out for her.

First, she must find a guy. Pretty easy. Then she must find a single guy who's ready to mingle. Harder. Next, she must find a guy who doesn't have the strongest career aspirations and is ready to have kids. Hard. Finally, she must find a guy who would enjoy staying at home with the kids while his wife worked forty hours a week. Hardest.

Yeesh. But it could be done. And Robin was no matchmaker, but a project she did enjoy; so starting May 2nd, she made it her mission to help Catherine have the life she dreamed of.

Thankfully, Catherine stopped by the table one last time before leaving. "We usually clock back in and hang out in the room, except Jacob who might go blab to Dexter about the Dodgers or something."

After shoving the rest of her salad into her mouth, Robin returned to the time clock, then to the Skwad.

Turns out, everyone was there, including Jacob, and he had begun a discussion about the illusive Charles. "Do you think he used the wrench because my money's on that?"

"Bitch please," Kevin retorted. "He'd use a candle stick just to make it more of a challenge. Unfortunately, ad agency isn't in the list of rooms."

"We got a lounge." Jacob laughed a hearty chuckle as he signed back into his desktop.

"True." Kevin giggled.

Robin wasn't entirely sure who they were going on about until Catherine pitched in.

"He's got a Mercedes though, and I think with his bad eyesight, anyone could be a victim tonight."

"Crap," Kevin said. "That'd definitely be me. Charlie would see me walking to my shotty car and think, *target acquired.* Fatty on the move."

Jacob sat on his desk. "Now don't think so negative. With how everything is going woke, fat is the new thin. I'd be surprised if Rover Callum didn't use you as the sexy hunk in their ad."

Kevin posed like a bodybuilder. It was clear why Dexter and Jacob got along so well. They were basically the same person.

However, it was also clear they were joking about Mr. Proctor. If Robin had known this was coming, she would've stayed in the hall. Since everyone else was facing each other, she carefully sat in her chair to avoid eye contact, slowly flipping through her drawing pad. If she wanted to stay hired for more than a week, joking about the chief executive was a bad strategy.

Luckily, her full thermos was now empty, giving her an excuse to leave the room. She decided to try the lounge cookies, even though they looked cheap and undesirable. It smelled good though, a surprising twist. As expected, they were gross.

Upon returning to her desk, the joking had stopped. Catherine was filing her nails, Jacob was reading something on his phone, and Kevin was vacuuming under his desk with one of those silent vacuums used in classrooms.

Robin knew that Catherine wouldn't accept her dating advice (even though Ray was perfect) until she knew the job. While waiting for the last seven minutes to end, she devised a loose plan to visit Xavier after work, hoping his input about the photography process could help her plan better ideas.

Then, Dexter entered the room. Robin noticed quickly that his shirt was untucked. He also stretched upon reaching Jacob's desk. "You got the email, right?"

"Yes, sir," Jacob said, checking his computer. "I'll leave tomorrow at 9:30 or so."

"Awesome. Major Collins has the students meeting you in the

Hoop Drama

Felton building. Room 114."

Jacob nodded, then Dexter leaned in close to whisper something in his ear. A brief, silent conversation ensued. Finally, Dexter made his way to Robin's desk.

"How's your first week going?" Dexter smiled a plastic grin.

"Pretty good. Are we doing the Major Collins campaign now?"

"Indeed. Jacob tells me you did pretty good on the webpage design. I'm excited to hear you contribute."

"Of course, sir. I'm willing to learn. Catherine has been a big help."

Catherine rolled her eyes over at Dexter, but she had nothing to say.

"Okay," Dexter replied. "Well, we're going to be doing merch for them, but it should be pretty easy. They just want shirts and coasters and stuff. However, they need a video testimonial. So, I'd like you to watch testimonials from other colleges to better help our team tomorrow."

"Okay. So, you want me to see what kind of questions are asked?"

"*Yes*, Robin."

If condescending had a face…

"Yes sir," Robin replied. "I'll get on that."

Dexter spoke to Catherine as well, but Robin decided not to eavesdrop. But *wow* did that guy dislike her. She read the brief and was fully aware of the video ad, but he acted like she had the IQ of a sheep.

Either way, a paycheck was a great motivator, so she put mouse to screen and began watching testimonials. The process was interesting but still unnerving. Yet again, she found herself doing something with no clear endpoint, no obvious objective, and no

Andy Silvers

way to track her progress. She *really* needed to speak with Xavier.

That evening, after clocking out, she went straight to the design team's room. The guy who had worn the cartoon character was packing up.

"Hey," Robin inquired. "Do you know where Xavier might be?"

"Uh…he left this room a few minutes ago," the man said. "He might be in the video suite."

"Okay. Thanks."

She bustled to the video room. The door was unlocked, but every light was out. He wasn't there. She decided to try again the next day. As she entered the elevator, Ray texted her saying that lasagna was in the oven.

She slung her bag back over her shoulder and entered the hall. It was pretty clear that the videos she'd help plan weren't pure testimonials. Instead, they were interviews supporting the theme of anyone being a business professional. A few candidates would be filmed talking about their backgrounds and what they hope to get out of a business degree. The fact the Dexter couldn't imagine her comprehension still left her irritated, but the plan didn't change.

Learn the job. Make allies.

Down the hall, an echoing sniffle caught Robin's attention. Curiosity did the walking for her as she made her way to a small corner near the bathrooms. It was Kevin, and he was sketching and listening to music.

The new girl waved, assuming he hadn't even noticed her, then turned away.

"Hey," Kevin said, removing his left earplug. "Do you have any more cookies?"

"Um…yes. Not the chocolate ones, but I was gonna bring

Hoop Drama

ginger snaps tomorrow. Does that sound good?"

"Yes. I'll eat some in the morning."

Her thoughts became words as she asked about his presence downstairs.

He thought carefully about his response. "I like to be here. It's relaxing. My art isn't any good, but it gives me something to do."

He seemed in a chipper mood, but his eyes told a more complicated story. He planned to stay for a while. A bag of Chinese chicken delivered to the agency revealed that story.

"Your home must be far away." Robin was unsure what to say, but if she didn't say anything, her coworkers would remain a mystery. In that case, she'd always be the black sheep of the lot.

"No," Kevin said. "It's not far."

"See you tomorrow," Robin said, not even smiling. It wasn't worth the energy, plus Kevin had begun to insert his earplug before finishing his sentence.

She shuffled to her car. Across the way, Charles climbed into his Mercedes. "Good night, Mr. Proctor!" Her words echoed across the lot, but Charles ignored the sound.

THURSDAY, MAY 3RD
Part One

Sleep granted relief no amount of wine could have. She prepared her cookies, knowing that she'd receive no thanks, and headed off to work. Changing hearts started with changing minds.

After dropping off the cookies in the lounge, she ran into the squad room right as Catherine ran out. No one was there, but perhaps they needed to clock in first.

Despite the abnormal situation, the peace and quiet made for a great distraction. She booted up her computer, reopened her sketchbook, and checked her emails.

A message about the Major Collins campaign appeared unread. The email explained the planned visit for a man named Brody to stop by the next day. Apparently, the client would visit more than twice at the start and finish of the ad campaign. Robin scoffed quietly, remembering what Dexter had said about the large meeting room upstairs and how she would never be in there.

She revisited her work on the scrolling webpage, adding nipples to any drawing without them. But soon came the stress. The PDF Dexter had wanted only had three images. That wouldn't cut it if the boss asked for her progress. She immediately opened up two stock websites and continued looking for backgrounds. One site had a prefect shower image without people. She had found great images before, but there was always a model standing there.

Hoop Drama

Luckily, this image was over 5,000 pixels across and had the right color scheme to match the wooden aesthetic. Her curser was dangerously close to the CLOSE button when Melanie startled her.

"Hello," Melanie said. "Robin, come downstairs for the meeting in 112. You're late."

Late? Drat. What was happening down there? Not knowing where 112 was, Robin quickly jumped up to follow Melanie downstairs. It turned out, 112 was the conference room where her terrifying interview had occurred. However, because she was late, coffee couldn't be used as a fidget toy.

Eight people attended the meeting. No one wanted to sit at the opposite end across from Dexter, so Robin sat down next to a man with brown hair. She didn't know his name, but she recognized him as the guy with the cartoon shirt (today's character was a blue frog). Next to him was a skinny man with frosted tips who Robin only remembered existed upon seeing him again today.

Dexter waited for the ninth member to sit down. "Thank you for joining us. I thought Jacob had told you about the Idea Blitz but apparently not."

Jacob sat forward. "I thought Kevin told her."

Kevin scoffed like a child accused of eating the last cookie. "I thought Catherine told her."

Catherine responded like she usually did—stoically.

"It's fine," Dexter commented. "We can just begin again."

A moment of guilt sunk in until Robin remembered how no one had told her about the meeting. Catherine had walked out last, so she was the most culpable, but it was clear that no one *wanted* to tell her. And no apologies were uttered, rest assured.

"So…this is our entire design team," Dexter began. He pointed to Xavier. "You know Xavier, our photographer and resident ginger. That guy with the frog is Henry Brooks. The lovely

Andy Silvers

blond across from you is Melanie, and last but least is Percy Osterholm. He's a Virgo."

Kevin and Jacob laughed. Then, Kevin threw an entire ginger snap into his mouth.

"So, we are hard at work on the Major Collins and the Rover Callum campaigns. Since Jacob refused to strip for the shower photos, we have asked Tony to return for us." Dexter smiled, then so did everyone.

"Yes," Jacob responded. "Tony is perfect for that."

"Wait a minute," Kevin noted. "Is Tony playing the skinny guy or the buff guy?"

"Buff," Dexter answered.

"What?" Catherine laughed. "Get Melanie ready with the Photoshop brush."

Everyone laughed. Robin smiled.

"I'm telling you; Tony has been working out. And yes, if we gotta add a little digital magic, we will." Dexter made the room howl. "Anyway, some guy named Brent from Rover will be our skinny guy. I'll email you when he comes in."

"The next order of business is Major Collins," Jacob said, staring at Robin. "Robin and I will go by around 9:30 and we'll get our students. Robin, you did check out some video testimonials for us?"

Robin was under the gun, but she was ready. As long as they didn't ask her about Rover Callum, she had quite a lot to say about colleges opening new schools. "Yes sir. I found a plethora of info for us." Big words sounded mature, so she tried to use several. "Our intent is to showcase how anyone can be a business professional. We will ask about their upbringing and focus them on the idea of personal growth. College is a chance to put your ideas to the test, so we want them to talk about how a degree can

Hoop Drama

elevate their potential. Um...so basically, they talk about their childhood—the ordinary. Then they talk about their future—the extraordinary."

Melanie began a slow clap that everyone soon followed.

"Wow, Mrs. Chapel," Dexter said. "Good job. Maybe you should be employee of the month."

Jacob rolled his eyes.

Dexter leaned to his left. "Jacob, what 'cha got for the Rover Callum thing?"

"So, I sent the webpage to Henry to design—"

Dexter interjected. "I saw. It's good."

"...and I've been working on the product packing. Rover wants to sell Husk as a bundle, and 68% of the market does the same so we'll do a Nature's Body set with 12 fluid ounces per bottle. No plans for a larger size yet so... For a single bottle it's eighteen dollars, but shoppers will save ten percent with the bundle. We're putting their Rover dog mascot at the top of the wrapping and using a Mango wood finish to give it an international appeal. That lighter color will work well with a walnut background. That'll be stock."

"Wait," Dexter halted. "Is it selling overseas?"

"No," Jacob replied. "The Mango is for the perception of the product as imported. Surveys seem to suggest that Americans like specialty soaps with ingredients from foreign markets. All the bottles will be white plastic and opaque. That seems to be popular. My belief is that that fits more with the female market, but Rover has their color palette, and we can't mess with it."

"Are you an expert of the female market?" Catherine asked in jest.

"Well...I'm an expert on men's haircare for those under fifty in the Eastern United States."

Andy Silvers

"You should listen to him," Kevin suggested. "He has a doctorate in receding hairlines."

Jacob smiled wide like the Grinch and pushed his hair to one side. "Good morning, Catherine. Dr. Jacob Balding at your service." He offered a cordial handshake.

Even Robin laughed as the whole room chuckled.

None of these people were particularly classy, but they had a comradery on par with a family—and Robin wanted in.

Robin spoke up. "I also worked on the images for Rover Callum."

Crap! That was the *one thing* not to mention.

"Oh," Dexter said. "How's that going?"

She had heard that honesty was the best policy, and the last thing she needed was to seem sneaky or mischievous. "I found roughly three images that I put into a PDF. Until this meeting, I was a bit unsure what the pictures had to be. I heard you say that we're hiring the models to do the poses so that helps a lot."

Her heart danced a familiar *ba-bum ba-bum ba-bum.*

"Okay," Dexter replied. "That's good. You've only had one morning to find images and I'd say that's a good start. Awesome."

Finally—something positive.

"Thank you, sir. I'll continue it after we meet."

Dexter shot a coy smile. "Didn't you hear? You're going with Jacob at 9:30."

Actually, Robin *did* hear. But it was a strange feeling. Sometimes, she heard something, but it didn't fully process until it was mentioned again. Jacob said it less than thirty minutes prior, but leaving the building to go on a trip was new, and therefore, slipped her memory.

"Yes sir. I forgot."

Melanie thankfully changed the subject to something

familiar—color theory. "I'd recommend a red towel for the Rover Callum images. When the hot guy answers the door—red towel. When he sits with the pretty ladies—red blanket, or red popcorn bowl if desired. I think that the manly aesthetic should be purposely broken up with something that evokes pleasure and heightens awareness. The part where Husk shows up is particularly where viewers must be engaged."

"I like it," Dexter noted. "We'll run it by Rover and see what they think."

The collaboration was exciting, but the idea was a scooch misguided. The grounded visual language of the ad would be mangled by the sudden appearance of red, particularly of high saturation. The undertones of sexuality were a clever thought, but a distracting color collided with the organic imagery. But of course, Robin didn't say any of that.

Melanie was well-spoken, and indeed she amended her statement as if by listening to Robin's thoughts. "If nothing else, a darker red can work; something like carmine."

"Absolutely." Dexter smiled and threw open the MCU brief once more. He had his tablet, but Jacob had brought him both binders for his review.

The team spent roughly fifteen minutes discussing search engine optimization and market segmentation. Robin found herself tuning in and out based on who was talking. Melanie and Jacob always held her attention. Dexter, Kevin, and Catherine rarely did. Perhaps it was because they seemed less authoritative. Maybe they were just the most annoying. Either way, time flew by and when Robin regained attention, the team was standing up.

Jacob walked around to the side opposite Robin. "All right. Get yourself ready."

She nodded but didn't stand up right away to think it through.

Andy Silvers

When she got up, she rushed to the elevator, then jammed everything on her desk into her purse. Finally, she applied a layer of lipstick to clear up any missed spots. Jacob simply grabbed the brief and his phone. Men.

Jacob had a large navy-blue truck; the largest truck Robin had ever seen. It sat high off the ground and featured six wheels. The interior cab was shockingly clean, the opposite of Ray's, and the radio instantly boomed with country hits. The music was quickly muted and both passengers buckled up.

"Do you want me to pull up GPS?" Robin asked, smiling kindly.

"I can get there." His stoic attitude was enough to facilitate a silent trip.

Major Collins had a bustling student body who were eager to get to classes quickly. Many students bopped to music, others skateboarded on the sidewalks, and some sat around chatting. Images flashed of Ohio University where Robin had met several of her closest friends. Sarah Willis popped into her head. Sarah wore matching jewelry every day and had a collection of boots only a queen could dream of.

Above the passenger seat, a garage door opener was clipped to the sun shade. The back window had a rectangular sticker that was illegible from the inside. On the floor was a wrapper for a stick of gum. However, on closer inspection, she noticed it was nicotine gum. Not a whiff of cigarette smoke was present in the car. Perhaps Jacob had quit.

They parked in the guest spot. Jacob circumvented the welcome center even though it seemed like the best place to start. After checking his phone, he guided his 'assistant' to the Felton building which required a brisk walk past the library.

Inside, Jacob avoided the front desk, opting to waltz right into room 114. The room was clearly designed for presentations. The walls were littered with information about scholarships and financing options. A group of about thirteen students sat talking amongst themselves until Jacob entered.

He plopped the brief right onto the front podium and spoke in a clear voice. "Good morning. My name is Jacob Bradley. We're here to conduct interviews for our ad agency. If selected, you will appear briefly in a Major Collins ad discussing the new business school. We will not be filming today. Instead, please wait patiently over here and leave the room when our interview concludes."

A tall skinny man with dark hair raised his hand. "Will we need to sign a waiver or something?"

"Good question," Jacob responded. "There will be no waiver. Instead, you will sign a talent release the morning of the interview. Only three of you will be selected so don't get too excited. You will need to keep talking to a *quiet* whisper while we do our work. If you cause a disruption, I will be forced to call your mom and tattle on you."

That got a soft laugh.

Jacob then grabbed the binder and lightly tapped Robin's arm with his fist. They set up shop on the far side of the room while the students relocated to the other.

The students were a unique bunch. There was an even split of men and women, but a very representative split of races. There were six white students, three black, two obviously Hispanic, one potentially middle eastern, and one Asian student. It was a great opportunity to do something important for Wheeling and West Virginia more broadly. This was the kind of work Robin could gladly put on her resume.

Jacob pointed to a white female with blonde hair. "You first, sweetie."

Andy Silvers

She strutted over, her blue heels clanking with every step. "What's your name?" She looked to Robin.

"I'm Robin Chapel. I'm helping select candidates." She made herself sound confident, but she wasn't. But she took steady breaths, opting to treat this like a job interview. She had interviewed a few people as assistant manager. Never had she felt stressed. In truth, Carol always had the final say with new hires, so it would be easy to let Jacob lead here.

Jacob sat perfectly rigid with his legs spread wide. "So, I take it you're a sophomore?"

"Yes, mister. I transfer to the business school next semester. I'm very excited."

"Gotcha. What opportunities do you think Major Collins has afforded you?" Without a writing utensil in hand, Jacob was all ears.

"So, I think Major Collins has given me a chance to make something of my life. I grew up in a teeny tiny town called Springdale Pennsylvania. Actually, that's where my family still lives. Anyway, my dad is the principal of Springdale Junior High School and my mother is the senior technician at Wilson Trucking. She doesn't drive them. She repairs them."

"Okay," Jacob said. "And how has MCU helped give you opportunities?"

"Yes. Okay. So, I came here on scholarship for cheerleading, but I really didn't feel being an athlete was right for me. You know, I had been told by my parents that my good looks and athleticism would give me opportunities that would bring success or whatever. But I really felt controlled. So, I found the business school because I saw them building it and felt that it would be right for me.

"My friend Leah will also be coming here so that's a plus. But I think stocks are cool and Roth IRA's and my feeling is that a

Hoop Drama

business degree can help me get any job I want because capitalism runs everything. Hopefully I won't have to start a company or something because my boyfriend Camden is really smart with computers. He's studying software development, so that'll certainly help us out."

Jacob stared at the smiling girl with a blank expression. After several seconds he asked, "So what will you do with your business degree once you graduate?"

"Um…I think I will go into management somewhere. Maybe start at my mom's place. She said she'd talk to Alex for me. If not, I might see if L'Oréal needs a business administrator. Yeah."

Jacob stared past the girl at the group chatting in the background. "Okay. Well, thank you for your time. We'll contact you soon if we decide to move forward."

"Okay, thank you so much." She got up and waved to her friend across the room. Jacob pointed to a muscular guy with wavy hair and a rocket tattoo.

On his way over, Robin whispered in Jacob's ear. "That girl was a bit privileged, don't you think?"

"Her story is fine, but she has the IQ of a bottle of Xanax."

Fine? Her story was *fine* if being coddled and given all the answers is inspiring.

The young man sat down next; his arms crossed as though *he* were interviewing them.

"So, what's your name?" Jacob led the way.

"I'm Toby. I'm a sophomore."

"And what opportunities to you think Major Collins has afforded you?"

"Well, my dad owns a bait and tackle shop, so he wants me to know the ropes of business ownin'. Um…I sorta wanna sell hunting gear probably. Like sights and ammo and stuff. I got a

115

Andy Silvers

football scholarship, so everything's covered, but classes are still hard. I swear if I find a way to use relative maxima in my life, I'll donate a kidney to science or something." He chuckled, then Jacob did too.

"You taking calculus?"

The young man uncrossed his arms, relaxing like it were his home. "Yeah. It's about a bitch. I mean, I just can't anymore. Anyway, MC has given me a chance to learn stuff. I like managing stuff. My dad basically makes me manager when he's not in the store. That's most Sunday's. Those are his drinkin' days." The man threw his arms behind his head and leaned the chair back on two legs. "I just know I'm gonna have to understand business stuff. I guess the Small Business Management degree would work. I'll start that next semester."

"Wow," Jacob said, leaning forward. "You've got a great story. We'll definitely reach out to you. Thank you for your time."

"Yeah, man." Jacob accepted a fist bump. Robin also bumped him but only because Toby offered. "We'll contact you."

The morning was beginning to drag on and on. Both students had stories that would be about as inspirational as foot fungus. They both only knew what they wanted because they were handed it. Shanice never gave Robin anything just because she was her daughter besides food and water. She got one single scholarship to Ohio University, and it only amounted to $1,800. That left her with almost $23,000 in debt. Yes, she lucked into the job at C. E. Proctor, but 'luck' wasn't her middle name.

Jacob pointed to a tall white guy with a big gut. As he walked over, Robin rolled her eyes subtly. *Maybe by tomorrow, he'll interview the black students*, Robin thought. Irritated by the thought of listening to another story of heartbreaking privilege, she spoke up. "Hey, Jacob. What if we split up to interview people. I

Hoop Drama

bet that'd be a lot faster."

Jacob nodded. "I was planning on doing that after I showed you the ropes. Go on then. Meet over there." He pointed to a corner inlet in the wall with two cushy chairs. Then he gave her the brief.

Robin made the best of the opportunity. She found a pretty black girl with a dazzling afro puff, motioned her to sit down, and drew a deep breath for her first solo interview.

THURSDAY, MAY 3RD
Part Two

"Good morning, ma'am," the young lady said. "My name is Tanya Kushall. I'm a sophomore here. Thank you so much for this opportunity."

"Absolutely," Robin smiled, knowing this would be a good interviewee. She was polite, attentive, and unique. She wore faded blue jeans and a button-up shirt. On her wrist was a large plastic bracelet of leopard skin pattern and her feet were covered with canvas slip-ons featuring a distinct woven style.

Robin could almost taste her bold cherry lipstick because it seemed to glow off her face. Best of all, she had two hoop earrings adorning her head, shimmering like glass in the light. They had a one-inch diameter and looked like a flower wrapped around itself. Gorgeous.

And her voice was melodic, with a deep sound that could perfect an audiobook. She sat up straight. Robin matched her posture with urgency.

"All right. Tell me a bit about how you arrived at Major Collins." Robin chose a different question than Jacob to start. She thought about how hard it was for so many youths to go to school, and if Major Collins wanted a great story, they needed to start at the beginning.

"Certainly," she began. "My parents arrived here from Kenya

Hoop Drama

when they were five. They grew up in Los Angeles where my grandparents could find work. I was born in Los Angeles a year before my father lost his job. We moved to West Virginia where we've been ever since. Coming here was not too easy. My high school offered several scholarship opportunities for myself and my sister. But my twenty-five on the ACT wasn't enough for tuition coverage. My family would have to cover $7,000 a semester for me to attend. To make that happen, I worked full time at a salon. I have a thing for nails. After a year, I finally had enough to start here. Now I'm a freshman. I rambled a bit so I hope you got something from that." She smiled awkwardly.

"Oh yes," Robin assured her. "So, what do you hope to do with a business degree?"

"Anything I can. Truthfully, I may not attend next year if I can't afford it. My advisor assures me we'll make it work but I still worry. My mother went back to work after eight years for me to go to school. Every dollar she makes goes to my tuition. She is *storge* love. If I earn a business degree, I would love to work as a social media manager."

"Did you say *story* love? I've never heard that before."

"No ma'am. I said storge. It means parental love. My mother would sell her left arm to get me through school. When I make a living one day, I will repay her every penny."

Robin smiled. Her mother was the same way. She hadn't covered tuition, but she had been there by her side. Shanice tried to figure out what to do with the house when Jesse left them. She had to deal with the mortgage and a daughter in college at the same time. When Shanice moved to Wheeling with her daughter, she had found a cheap deal on a house with fire damage.

"What else do you need for the video?"

Robin thought. "It's clear you'd make a great spokeswoman.

Andy Silvers

I'll let you go so I can get someone else, but it was an honor to meet you."

"Likewise."

Robin removed her phone to type up the student's name. A wave of the hand invited the slimmer Hispanic boy over to the chair. Smooth skin and a gelled coif made him seem years younger than he was, but a distinctive mustache helped him fit in. He sat down and gave a subtle smile, alluding to his shyness.

Perhaps he wouldn't be best for a video. Then again, he volunteered, so Robin asked his name.

"Sure. My name is Miguel Rosas. I'm a freshman here. I literally just applied for the business school and I get an email saying that I should be in their video." He crossed his legs and sat forward.

Robin nodded. "Okay. What brings you to Major Collins?"

"Good question. I can tell you're a professional," he said, blushing something fierce. "I went to school in Richmond and my parents didn't really want me to go to college. Honestly, I didn't either but my counselor said my ACT score could probably get me into any state school. So, I applied here and started last year, but I had no idea what degree to get. I thought maybe like animals or something, but I'm just not cut out for medical work. Anyway…yeah."

"Okay," Robin responded. "And what led you to choose the new business school?"

He took a deep breath and stared down at the floor. "A few days ago, my dad and mom divorced. Well—finalized the divorce. So, my dad never really wanted me to go here and he really thought I'd just work at our local bakery and take care of my siblings. I have four siblings and I'm the oldest. But he moved out finally and my mom's been saying I should get a degree. I'd actually be the

Hoop Drama

first to do it in my family other than my uncle."

His report seemed contradictory so Robin asked, "Did you say your parents didn't want you to go to college? I thought I heard that."

"Oh. My parents both didn't want me to go so I can watch my siblings, but my mom talked to Ryan—our pastor, and he says that God might be opening a door. My dad probably doesn't even know I'm here, but it's hard for my mom by herself."

"All right."

"Sometimes...I feel guilty for leaving my family alone." He wiped a tear from his eyes. "I'm sorry. A sob story will make a crappy ad."

Robin chuckled, then laid her hand on his knee. "Don't worry, Miguel. Your mom loves you. I can tell."

"Yeah. And I mean, it's like really cool that I can be here." He regained his composure but crossed his arms. "I mean, very cool. I just don't wanna leave her alone."

"It sounds like your mother has storge love."

"Say what now?"

"It means parental love. You're not hurting your family, sweetheart. And you're not letting your mom down. Wanna know why?"

"Why?"

"Because you were never holding her up. She's holding you up and sometimes it's really tough, but in four years, you'll be a degree holder, and from the sound of things, the man of the house."

"Oh wow. I guess you're right." He breathed heavily to avoid crying anew. "Thanks ma'am. You're pretty cool."

"Well, I wouldn't—"

"Robin!" Jacob hollered. "When you finish up, we can go."

Robin peered over at the students left without an interview.

Andy Silvers

Mostly people of color, and now, all confused. "Are you sure. Will we come back later?" She quickly checked her phone. It was 10:57. They should have had at least until lunch break.

"No. Probably not."

"Hey," Miguel interjected. "I'm good. Just don't have me cry in the video."

"Of course. Thank you for your time."

Jacob stood up, putting back a seat he had moved while checking his emails.

After strolling over, Robin pointed to the confused students. "Are we telling them to leave? Are the interviews over?"

"Yes. We have our three students. Toby, Maisie, and that girl who left."

"The one you said was like Xanax?"

"No. A brunette with a father that teaches here."

"Okay. But what about—"

Interrupting Robin's question was Tanya. She walked over quietly, but Jacob saw her. "Hey. Do you two need my name or number for future reference?"

"No," Jacob replied. "We found our people. Thanks."

Robin couldn't hide her surprise and Tanya didn't hide her confusion. "So, she said I would be good for the video. I felt I should talk to you too. Are you in charge?"

"No. I'm not really in charge, but I've been doing this for a long time. Thank you for your interest, but we're good for now."

WHAT THE HELL! *Not in charge.*

Then why does he think he can make all the decisions? If Robin were white, Jacob would've seen her skin turn red and her pupils grow like a full moon. If she were white, Jacob would have cared what she thought, instead, with her face frozen, he strolled out of the room.

Hoop Drama

"I'm so sorry," Robin muttered to Tanya while scurrying. She issued a "thank you for your time" to the remaining students waiting patiently.

Unable to catch up to Jacob until she had yanked the truck door open, she nearly laid into him with a giant piece of her mind…but he spoke first.

"We don't really need to be back soon, so let's get lunch out. What'cha down for?"

"I…I just wanna know what happened."

Jacob got buckled, reminding an angry Robin to do the same. "We interviewed some students. Splitting up definitely made things go faster."

What the actual hell, Robin thought. Despite not being in charge, it was still crucial that Jacob become an ally. After all, many more days (or more likely years) were ahead for Robin and her senses came back in full. But that didn't stop her from calmly asking a few questions while she still had time.

"What about the students I interviewed?"

Jacob cracked his knuckles while exiting the parking lot. "We just need three good ones."

"But you only picked white ones. And one of them—never mind. The point is that Tanya and Miguel are awesome. They should be able to represent." She was sure to speak calmly, not raising her voice more than ten percent.

"Um…we only had three slots available."

"But the university is so diverse and great stories will be missed."

"Decide now. Cavernous Chicken or Mary's Diner. You ever been to Mary's?"

"Cavernous is fine, but what about the great stories?"

"Look, I got you a diverse group. There's two girls and one

Andy Silvers

boy. Plus, the girl at the end was a foster child."

"That's wonderful, but…" Her voice trailed off. She lost not her energy, but her hope. Jacob clearly lived in a bubble. But how could he? Certainly, an ad agency would allow him access to every corner of society. Maybe he was a devotee of the red had collective. Either way, Robin never expected this from him.

She leaned her head against the door until they reached the restaurant.

He tried to cheer her up but in the wrong way. "Don't be so pouty. I'll buy your lunch. How's that for a business trip? Granted, I'm handing the bill to Chuck, but still."

Robin ate a chicken salad. She purposely sat down before Jacob, and luckily for her, he didn't insist on sitting with her.

Back at the office, Robin flew back inside and ran upstairs. Across the way, she saw an unfamiliar face.

It was Charles.

She bustled down the hall hoping to get his attention. "Sir! Mr. Proctor!" He was in his own world. When he turned a corner, Robin lost her chance, his door shut and a lock clicked. She stood next to his door, but every second that passed came with the feeling another person was judging her. In mere seconds, she gave up.

However, the sound of Dexter's voice caught her attention. He was in the room 'she would never need to be in.' The window glass had a frosted finish, limiting visibility, but it was clear he was pitching ideas to someone.

Ultimately, she made her way back to her desk.

"So…" Kevin teased. "How was riding in the Jake-mobile?"

"It was fine." Robin sat down, unloading a mass of stuff from her faux-leather purse.

"I sign a waiver every time—no, the only time I rode with him. He treats Wheeling like his own demolition derby." Catherine checked Jacob's reaction. He shook his head in silent disagreement.

His driving wasn't the problem.

From then on, things would be different. It really had seemed that Jacob was the department head. He carried himself with a military-like stoicism that seemed fit for a leader. But he was more akin to a tyrant. Perhaps 'tyrant' was a bit hyperbolic. But his demeanor seemed to change in a mere hour.

What could those other students have said that was so awe-inspiring that Jacob felt no need to interview anyone else?

"Robin," Jacob chirped from his desk. "Dexter emailed you what he wants you to work on. Get on it."

"Okay." An email from eight minutes ago revealed her assignment. Despite her lack of progress on the Rover Callum images, the MCU campaign took precedence as the execs were to arrive tomorrow morning bright and early. To prepare for Friday, Dexter wanted a script of exactly what questions the three students would be asked, what their student IDs were, and what day the studio would conduct the interviews.

All of these seemed like Jacob questions. So, Robin allowed him to do most of the work by emailing Jacob precisely that.

His response was as follows:

Names are Toby Albo (74993108), Maisie L. Richards (10552963), and Penelope Hafford (90035518).

Question 1: What's one thing about you that's most unique?

Question 2: What will you do with a business degree from Major Collins?

Question 3: How is the world changing and how has Major Collins prepared you for the future?

The best day would be Wednesday, May 16th.

"Jacob totally should have just done this himself." Robin

Andy Silvers

whispered then looked up to see if anyone noticed. No one did.

Immediately after hitting SEND, Catherine squealed and covered her mouth. Robin got up but then slammed her rear back on the chair, noticing how erratic her behavior seemed. This could be a great time to get the quiet Catherine to speak.

Yet again, Robin got up. Casually, she strolled over to Catherine's station where she was reading a webpage for an event called Friday Night Fright. "Hey, Catherine. What's this?"

"This is Friday Night Fright at the Necrosis." Her voice was much peppier than normal. Clearly this fright stuff struck a nerve. Robin listened extra carefully. "It used to be a hospital or actually a clinic. Now, it's being used for one night to screen a movie by Klein Hearst. It'll have costumes and lights and such. Sorta like a haunted house." She worked diligently to create an account in order to purchase a ticket.

"Wow," Robin said with just the right amount of manufactured excitement. "Fun. Is it gonna be like *Friday the 13th* or Elm Street?"

"No. Scarier. They're playing *Post Mortem Prison*. It's so scary, but hell if I'm not going."

"Okay. So, what's the—"

"Hey, I'm about to type in my credit card info, so I'll need you to walk over there." Catherine dug through her purse past a bat keychain to get her pocket book. It had a red X imprinted on it designed presumably to look like blood. Robin obliged.

Twenty minutes before clocking out, she remembered that she was supposed to visit Xavier's photo studio. However, at nearly the same time, she received two text messages. One from Shanice said she'd be over that night for dinner and one from Ray said Shanice will visit that night for dinner.

THURSDAY, MAY 3RD
Part Three

Robin was a tad hyperactive. That's because not only did she have no time to prepare for her mom's visit, but she also withheld the craziest story of the day for when everyone could hear it at once.

Luckily, Ray was on top of things with a tasty yet healthy meal. While he cooked, his sweetheart snuck another kiss on the cheek and a snuggle. She'd missed her babe while at work. A romantic date within the next week was certainly needed.

"You think she'll like these sandwiches?" Ray gave her a smooch back.

"Oh yeah. Is this Napa almond?"

"Yes ma'am. It'll be a quick meal since Shanice didn't tell me until after I got home. Hey, at least she told me."

"Yeah. Maybe she likes you now that you cook for her."

"I hope so."

The meal was indeed simple. Napa almond chicken salad sandwiches were the main course with scalloped potatoes on the side. Ray's cooking was like an art. He had already set out a tray of almonds on a baking sheet that was still piping hot. He created the dressing by mixing lemon juice, apple cider, dry ground mustard, dried basil, dried crushed rosemary, and ground pepper into a bowl. Robin assisted with cutting over two dozen seedless red grapes into halves. Truly, Ray could've worked at Mary's, but

Andy Silvers

it just wasn't in the cards for him. Plus, he wanted to do something special just for Robin. If he cooked for half of Wheeling, the luster would dissolve.

Everything sat within fresh sourdough bread creating an aroma powerful enough to attract the whole complex. Robin went to get her famed hoop earrings when the guest of honor arrived.

"Shanice! Hey! Welcome..." Ray greeted his mother-in-law with the vigor she required.

"Hey, sugar. Where's my sweet Robin?" She threw her purse and a white vest on the 'stuff' chair. The scent hit her hard in the best way. "Hm. Wow, is that chicken?"

"Yes ma'am. It's Napa almond chicken sandwiches. And scalloped potatoes that I need to grab *now* before they burn." Ray rushed over to the oven and removed the baking pan. Behind the aluminum sheet sat golden potatoes seasoned with thyme and parsley to perfection. Shanice had found black Emeril.

"Wow. You got a gift. I'll give you that." After a deserved compliment from Shanice, Robin strolled in with her size nine knitted flats.

They were a bold golden color that may have clashed slightly with her navy green skirt, but she made it work. Ray wore a black shirt with Megatron on it. Typical.

"Hey, honey. Give me a hug." A warm embrace preceded a hectic rush to the restroom. "Sorry, girl. I'll be right back."

"Your mom's a riot," Ray joked, preparing the plates.

"That she is." Robin helped with the meal so that by the time her mom returned, the table would be set.

Shanice arrived in the most Shanice way possible. "Baby, that cracked vase in the little girl's room gonna make people think you're poor."

"We *are* poor," Robin replied.

Hoop Drama

"Not with that fancy new job you got."

Ray poked his head around a pan dangling from the cabinet. "Yeah. When you gettin' paid, honey?"

"I've been working for about a week so it'll be a while. But I should get about $2,100 or so next week maybe."

"Damn!" Shanice hollered. "Give me some of *dat!* My daughter's a rich woman after all."

Robin blushed. "That money goes to college first, Mom."

"Actually, get a new vase first. Thank you *very much.*"

Ray laughed, prompting the entire family to laugh. "Come on, people," Ray said. "Let's eat."

Shanice went right for the emotional jugular. "You gonna have to cook more food when that baby comes around."

"Yeah, honey," Ray remarked. "When dat baby coming?"

"Thanks," Robin said. "I don't know, but not anytime soon."

"*Whyyyyyyy?*" Shanice replied. "You got a good job, a good hubby, and you're still young enough to chase a child around the living room."

Robin did want children…to an extent. She wanted to feel like life was going her way first. Very few of her college friends had kids, but the ones who did recommended settling down. Even though Ray would gladly volunteer to stay home, she didn't want him to have to. Plus, deep down there was always a chance Dexter would just get sick of her and fire her. He could do that within three months if he felt like it.

"This ain't because of your job, is it? Don't let 'em beat you up, dear." Shanice had prepared herself two scoops of scalloped potatoes and was finished with those.

Robin sighed. She rimmed her plate with her fork. "I…don't always feel like I belong." Before she told her story, she wanted to gauge audience interest. If Shanice thought her situation was mundane or unavoidable, she would let it go.

"Uh oh. Did those men treat you wrong?"

"Yeah," Ray added. "You seemed upset when you got home."

They cared. "So, my teammate and I go to a school called Major Collins. It's me and Jacob. We interview some students to be in an ad for the new business school. Jacob let me conduct some interviews in the corner, but he didn't use a single one of them. And he said he chose a *diverse* group because two were women. I just…am annoyed."

Shanice put down her sandwich and swallowed back. "Baby, I'm so sorry. How many women did y'all interview?"

"No, that's just it. I interviewed two people of color and Jacob refused to interview any. This girl—Tanya—was wonderful. She taught me a new word and had a great story, but Jacob will never know. I was shocked. Plus, he's not in charge." She whispered "not in charge" like it was a secret.

Shanice nodded. "It seems to me, you gotta say it."

"Say what?" Ray asked.

Shanice pointed to everyone. "What *we've* been unable to say for *centuries.*"

Robin's jaw shook. She knew her mandate, but was unsure how to do it. Plus, how could she make allies if she was Mrs. Big Mouth? "I know, Mom. But you gotta understand—"

"Yes, sweetie. It's hard. But I didn't raise no coward. You are strong and brave and beautiful. So many women got the slings and arrows before us, and we gotta be another generation that cares."

Ray nodded.

"I wish you could take my place, Mom," Robin said, wiping away a tear. "I need a warrior."

"You are a warrior, baby. Tell her, Ray."

"Uh…yeah. I'm not gonna be mad if you choose to stay silent.

Hoop Drama

But if you choose to speak, I'll be right there with you." Ray put his smaller plate over the larger one.

"Thank you, Ray," Shanice whispered.

The next few minutes were silent minus the sound of crunching and drinking. But Shanice spoke again first. "We're gonna have fun tonight. Y'all up for Tommy Craven?"

Ray nodded. "Sure."

After a team effort to close down and scrub up the kitchen, the living room became the home of family fun night. They played the recorded episode from Sunday night.

Ray told a brief story while everyone settled down. "Well, I nearly got crushed today. So, we got one of those Atlas BP lifts and I think Lorenzo didn't set it up correctly. It had a white hatchback on it, and right when I pull off the tire, the stupid car drops like ten inches and nearly clocks my head. You know, it seems like it's on the metal arms, but it's really just two cables holding everything up. I don't even know for sure what happened. Maybe the car wasn't properly placed on the lifting points. It could've been a faulty lock release. I'm good now, so I didn't text you. But I was freaked out." He looked over at Robin who was listening with concern. "But I know that any day, I can leave and my lovely wife will be able to support me and our maybe baby."

Robin bumped his arm. She didn't say it but her heart was racing after that story.

"Shush," Shanice said. "Tommy's on. I think he'll talk about the lady who got abducted."

"Hah," Ray chuckled. "You mean that Florida lady who says an alien left her dog outside on her porch?"

"Yeah. Also, baby, now that you rich, you gotta upgrade to a big old seventy-five-inch TV."

"I'll think about it." But not seventy-five.

Andy Silvers

Tommy began with a satirical monologue about his childhood. "Good evening, everyone. When I was a child there were three TV stations. You had boring, more boring, and please kill me now. Today, we have more TV channels than porn stars to fill them. One show I recently watched was *Rex Ryan*. It's about a man who steals a car and finds a picture of himself in it with a target over it. Now, he must try to figure out whose car it is and if he's already marked for death. As you know, Peter Keller stars in this series, and I just have one question. Why is he so *damn thirsty*? I mean, you literally stole a car from a professional assassin, but the only target you're thinking of is covered by *denim* pockets. Dude—can I say dude? —please get to a safe place before trying to figure out if Jane prefers Victoria's Secret or Tom Ford!"

Robin giggled, but she could see that Shanice was confused.

"What's thirsty? Is that like a code?"

"Yes, Mom," Robin responded. "It means sexual attraction."

"Of course. Everything is sex now."

Tommy continued. "For all the car thieves out there. Take it from me. Practice safe stealing. All right. I'm nearly fifty now—" The crowd cheered.

Shanice shook her head.

Tommy responded, "Yeah, I know. I'm old. Anyway, I go to the airport last month after I visit my dear old mother and her demon cat, Pouch. I'm really tired of airport security. I see why Tom Cruise flies private. Anyway, I have a knee prosthesis and I really thought that had set off the metal detector. So, this small lady with hips wider than a quarterback comes over and pulls me aside. My wife would be watching, but she was busy flirtin' with the baggage boy or something. I don't know.

"She tells me she's gonna do a simple pat down. So, I assume the basic rub your back—sorta like a massage but gayer. But no!

Hoop Drama

She practically clangs my low hangin' fruit with a metal stick. I'm a grown man, so I didn't cry…*much*. Also, she's wearing these baggy-as-hell pants. I'm thinking, 'Lady, what are *you* hiding in there?' *Really*, there could be an entire Al Qaeda unit lurking in those folds. You never know! So, with my dignity gone and my virginity guaranteed, she finally finds what was settin' off the alarm. And I'd love to tell you about it…right after these messages."

"Right now?" Shanice groaned.

"Actually," Robin noted, after laughing quite hard. "What's Carter up to these days?"

"What?" Shanice replied, trying to hear over an ad for prostate medication.

Ray muted the TV. "She wants to know about my brother."

Shanice nodded. "Yeah. Carter is doing all right. I visited him just last week. He's so proud of your new job, Robin. He knew those graphic design skills would come to use one day."

Ray hugged his wife. A proud family they would always be.

"I tell you…you and Carter both got a thing for workin' women. That never would've flew in my day. But I hope that boy gets him a workin' woman too. I know he loves his job though. A good person will find a way to him soon. I pray that."

"You think he feels alone?" Robin inquired.

"Oh yeah. I think he—I don't know. He just needs a little sugar in his life."

"What has Roxanne said?" Ray asked.

"Oh, I don't know. I haven't seen her since your wedding. She ain't left Ohio yet. She's got a great boy. Id'a been happy with Mr. Carter Chapel."

"Mom," Robin said. "Stop it. I found my forever prince."

"Maybe we could have Carter over next time you visit,

Andy Silvers

Shanice," Ray suggested.

"Yeah. Maybe we could. Oh! It's coming back on. Unmute it." Shanice swiveled back toward the TV. The intro band played the usual theme.

"Welcome back, folks," Tommy said, using his hands as much as his voice. "So, I was at the airport when I set off the alarm and they pulled me aside to rape my innocence. But I hadn't told you what they found. I wanna be clear, I had taken off my belt, removed my watch, and my wedding ring, my shoes, and even my wallet. So, I was getting ready to explain that I had a metal insert in my knee. But lo and behold, in my back pocket, the airport troll pulls out a hearing aide. A bright pink hearing aide, which proceeds to squeal something awful. 'Darn it,' I say. I've stolen my dear mama's hearing aide. Now, her Fifty Shades audiobook will sound a bit one-sided. She'll hear the spanking but won't know who did it.

"Anyway, I take out the stupid battery and the lady lets me put it through the scanner thingy. But now, I'm the worst son ever. My wife, Megan, says we can just call her and explain what happened. She says we should mail it back. But we can't do that because the plane is departing soon and the whole charade with airplane mode…and yada-ya. When we land back at LAX, I do call her, but she's too perky. She says, 'Hey, did you land safe?' I say yes. I tell her I stole her hearing aid on accident and that I must've put it in my pocket after dinner.

"She tells me she bought a new pair, and I about yell. I ask her how much that costs and she casually tells me 'Four *thousand.*' Good lord, lady! My mom is not money-bags Mom. She lives in a thousand square foot house with one TV and one record player. So, I ask how she managed that and she tells me I left my credit card on the couch. All right, Mom. We'll call it even." Tommy pauses for cheers and laughter. "All right, joining us tonight is Doctor Dale Cellario to explain why cardio isn't enough to lose weight…"

"You wanna hear that?" Robin asked her mom.

"Nah. I'm good." Shanice rose to stretch. "I'll see you two love birds soon. Keep me posted on your job."

"I will." Robin handed Shanice her personal items.

Ray took a deep sigh. "You should think about what she said."

"I know," she whispered. Robin had hoped so much to use her work to make a difference in the world. She never imagined she had to change the entire company first. "Jacob doesn't even know he did anything wrong, so I might just leave it be."

"I know you don't wanna make enemies. But maybe you're trying to befriend the wrong people. Your coworkers are just doing what they're told."

"You think I should talk to Mr. Proctor?"

"Maybe."

"That hasn't gone so well yet. I've barely seen the guy."

"I have faith in you." Ray wrapped his arms around her and breathed in her lavender scent.

"One quick thing, honey."

"Yes."

"Don't you *ever* almost die and not tell me."

"Yes ma'am."

FRIDAY, MAY 4TH

Homemade cookies were a privilege Jacob had to earn. He had gotten on Robin's bad side, so he could forget about it for the remainder of the week. Since Kevin seemed to be the biggest cookie fan, she'd bring another batch on Monday.

The irony of Robin's situation wasn't lost on her. Her problem was an ouroboros. She was upset, and if she acted as such, she would be seen as snooty or rude. But that would only exacerbate the problem, making her more upset. Women simply couldn't go into work with a chip on their shoulder unless they wanted a barrage of male coworkers trying to 'explain' life to them. It was irritating. Her only choice was to be the same pleasant Robin she always was but with fewer chocolate chips, of course.

The timeline of these campaigns was also beginning to wear on her. She imagined a pitch meeting, one week of work, and maybe one more to spice things up. But these campaigns went on for weeks. Only incremental adjustments were made, and what's worse, she couldn't see her coworkers work to get a better picture for the whole process. That reminded her to make visiting Xavier a priority.

"They're coming, boys…and Robin," Jacob stated loudly, overlooking the office. Perhaps Catherine was one of the 'boys' now. "Since Dexter will be meeting with Major Collins, we're

Hoop Drama

going to work on the Husk campaign today. We have designs for a white plastic package but we will create a black variant for Dexter to pitch."

"Good thinking," Kevin said. "That white looks nice—I mean, I like it, but it doesn't fit the extreme manly image of the Husk line."

"Yes," Jacob teased. "Of course, you prefer the white packaging. It matches your skinny jeans and soy latte lifestyle."

With a faux teenage girl voice, Kevin retorted, "*Oh my gosh, girl. Like, that is so offensive. For real.*" His nasally sound made the whole room laugh.

Robin looked down to see that Kevin was actually wearing skinny jeans. That only made it funnier.

"Robin," Jacob called out. "Check your email from me. You'll be working on a market segmentation chart today. I'd use Publisher for that. We will be printing it out. Just read the email. Catherine, I want you to…"

Upon checking her email, there was a wall of text taller than the Empire State building detailing everything Robin had to do. It wasn't design related. It was pure data-driven research. She began to mouth breathe. A mental thunderstorm.

Should I ask Jacob for more specifics?

Yes, but he hates me.

No, but I need advice.

The choices were scant and her time was limited. Maybe she could slip out really quick and ask Dexter. Instead, she stayed put and read the email slowly, line by line, until she knew where to begin.

The message tasked her with getting Dexter ready for his presentation. It included an email with a spreadsheet of Rover Callum's sales by percentage. It noted that despite Rover Callum

Andy Silvers

having several men's products, women's shampoos were by far the best selling. In total, women made up 68% of sales, but Rover wanted to make that a 50/50 split if possible. That was why Dexter advised breaking tradition and using a black plastic for the Husk bottle. Robin needed to create two primary pie charts showing the current split of sales across both demographics. These graphs would visualize which products were selling and to whom. Then, she needed to create a hypothetical future chart, showing how Husk could disrupt the formula and increase sales among male customers.

Good gravy! This was pure research and certainly not what Robin signed up for. To rub salt in the wound, she had to make two 8.5 by 11 pages that would be shown to the executives. That meant perfect grammar, spelling, and formatting. The only thing the email didn't say was when this was due.

She asked her first question. "Jacob, when is this due by?"

"The end of today would be ideal."

Robin gulped back her body weight in saliva. She checked her phone just in case Ray had gotten crushed, prompting her to leave work early. He was safe.

Luckily, Robin knew Publisher and she knew design.

For several hours, she created the most nerve-wracking two-page document she'd ever done. Rover Callum had done most of the work for chart one by spelling out in detail which products were the best sellers. She created a lovely chart with bold colors and easy-to-read text. This process required quite a bit of coffee. Her purse nearly ran out of hazelnut creamers by lunch time.

"I'm gonna get to the cookies first, Jacob," Kevin teased, stretching after hours of idle typing.

"Go for it." Jacob got up too, but only to stretch.

Kevin smiled. "Did you do coconut this week?"

Hoop Drama

Robin didn't realize he was talking to her. She hadn't made a single cookie for Friday. "Um…I didn't bring cookies in today." Jacob laughed. Catherine ignored the whole conversation. "But there should be some ginger snaps from yesterday."

Kevin giggled. "No, sweetie. I ate those."

Robin's soul glowed a bit. "I take it you liked them?"

"Oh yes. My thighs might not, but my belly did."

Jacob rolled his eyes before heading toward the time clock.

"Well…it's nice to hear you like them. I think they're better than month-old store food." That's all Robin could think to say. She was hungry after that morning project.

"Agree."

She was last to leave the Skwad room as she had to save her work and grab her purse. No one waited for her—not surprising as she was still the new girl. She headed for the elevator, not a thought in her mind.

But then, the sound of indistinct chattering grew louder as the elevator approached the second floor. When the door opened, there were suits, ties, and loafers. Executives.

A tall white man with green eyes spoke up upon seeing Robin. "Oh. Hello, ma'am. Are we in your way?"

"No, sir. I'm just going downstairs. Don't mind me."

The man guided his team of two others out of the elevator. "Aren't you the media supervisor?" he asked. "I'm Brody Pearson. I work at Major Collins. This is Roger Gates—we call him Roger That, and next to him is Zack De'Amalio. It's an honor to meet you."

She shook hands with all three. "It's an honor to meet you too. I'm helping with the campaign in the creative team." Suddenly, her nerves overtook her body. Her jaw actually shook saying "team." Her eyes darted left and right. Her only choice was to walk into the

139

Andy Silvers

elevator and smash the close button.

She tried to push past the men into the elevator, but her execution was lacking.

"Ma'am," Brody said, holding the door open. "Are you okay? Zack, see if you can get her some water."

"I'm fine." Robin saw purple splotches appear over Brody's face. She held onto the rails to maintain balance. He grabbed her hand and escorted her from the elevator. She was rarely drunk, but once during her junior year of college, she got drunk during a late-night party. This felt eerily like that.

He continued to hold her hand until she regained her senses. "That's great that you work in the creative team. How's that going?"

She was so worried about her sweaty hand making Brody uncomfortable that she spoke her mind. "It could be better."

Oh no! Maybe Brody hadn't heard that.

"Really? How so?"

He heard it. "Well," Robin continued. "I went to…to Ohio University. I was one of three black students in my class of eighty or so graphic designers. My mom only had one child, but she still couldn't get me through college. I worked in a fabric store every summer I attended school. It was the only place I could get more than $14 an hour. Never once did I feel like I was taking a free ride. I got a scholarship, actually, for being low income. My father…he left us right after I graduated high school…" Robin took a deep breath to avoid fainting.

"Oh, wow," Brody said. "That's an inspiring story. I'm so happy you got that degree."

"But there are great people of color at Major Collins who won't be in the ads." Robin regained her balance and hit the elevator button again since the door had closed. She prayed for a

140

Hoop Drama

swift escape.

"*Who* won't be in the ad? Did you meet someone in the business program?" Zack inquired.

Robin nodded. "Talk to Tanya Kushall. She's amazing."

"What's your name?" Brody asked as Robin entered the elevator.

"I'm Robin Chapel. I'm a college graduate." Despite regaining her consciousness, Zack still handed her a cup of tap water. She stared at it as the doors closed in front of her.

The familiar smell of her car welcomed her to lunch break. She drove to a sub shop nearby. They had a great turkey and provolone sandwich that was excellent. She sat silently inside the store eating her food. A large sweet tea soothed her dry throat. To her surprise, she had no regrets about what she said to the executives (her foot was still tapping rapidly).

Normally, her nerves would act up and she'd be formulating how to apologize to Brody, but not this time. Somewhere in her conscience, she wanted to see Tanya spotlighted for the first time in her life. Maybe it was revenge on Jacob, but it didn't feel that way. She felt relieved instead.

Certainly, she hadn't been rude. Not a hateful word or brazen insult was spoken. She just said what so many people before her hadn't said. She did right by Shanice, even if by accident.

Crunch. A piece of lettuce fell onto the table. Then a buzz. It was her phone. For three minutes, she refused to check it. It was probably just Dexter emailing her to stop annoying the clients. She was prepared to apologize for the sake of her job, but only after her break was over.

With a full cup, she reentered her car, enjoying the heat that had built up inside. When she plugged in her phone, there was a strange email address listed—*bpearson@MCU.edu.*

Andy Silvers

What the heck. How did he get her email? She nearly asked him but realized that Dexter had probably done it. His message made her gasp.

Robin Chapel,
It was a pleasure to meet you this morning. I hope you feel better now. Please remind me of that student's name and I'll speak with her. It sounds like you would like to spotlight people of color in our campaign. I think that's a wonderful idea. Please use this line as a direct messaging platform.
Kind regards,
Dr. Brody Pearson, PhD

Robin checked the time. He was still in his meeting with Dexter. Why would he email her during the meeting? Robin sat in stunned silence until she formulated a response. She messaged him as follows:

Dr. Brody Pearson,
It was a pleasure to meet you too. I apologize for my behavior this morning. Thank you for the water. I think POC want to be seen and heard, but not seen as the "other." We are often ignored or silenced, and I believe that your campaign that says that anyone can go to college is inspiring to people like me. I hope you meet Tanya Kushall. She's a sophomore.
Sincerely,
Robin Chapel, B.A.

She hesitated to put her college degree but felt she earned that tag alongside her name. She hit send, but didn't wait for the reply. Instead, she clicked her seatbelt into place and drove back to work. With two minutes to spare, she punched the time clock.

Hoop Drama

Curiosity guided her feet past the meeting room. Dexter was definitely still in there with the executives. Catherine showed up to clock back in. Robin scurried to the break room to make it seem like she had a plan. They had hazelnut sweetener so not all hope was lost. Her pocket bulged as she returned to her desk.

"Really," Jacob asked Kevin. "You think *Avatar* is a great movie?"

"Yeah," Kevin responded, logging back into his desktop. "It's not the greatest movie ever made, but the effects are fantastic."

"Really, dude? Those effects are in every movie now. Plus, they made the military look like idiots. Give me a machine gun and Id'a taken out half the herd of avatars in an hour."

"Hey, dummy. Those are the *good guys*. Remember?"

Jacob scoffed. "If it's got a tail, I'm shooting it."

Catherine returned and interjected. "Don't hurt that kitty outside your house, Jacob. If you shoot it; I shoot you."

"What!" Jacob exclaimed. "Did you hear that?"

"Yes, and I agree," Kevin responded. "Cats are wonderful creatures and you better leave them alone. If I could give that cat a safe home, I would."

"You can have it. I'll never understand why people keep an animal inside the house just cause it's cute. I'd consider a dog…like a shepherd or something, but it'll stay outside and guard stuff."

"Uh oh," Catherine said. "You'll need two dogs to guard that ego. Maybe three."

Robin smiled. Someone finally saw what she saw, and it was a woman. Hooray for some common sense. She ceased listening to her team to check her emails. Somehow an antivirus company had gotten her work email, but nothing from Brody. Progress on the document was slow as she prepared her apology.

Mr. Brennan. I'm so sorry for what I said. I was dehydrated and I really should have talked to you first. I hope you can forgive me.

That seemed too groveling.

Dexter, I'm sorry for what I said earlier. I was dehydrated so I didn't think through things first.

That seemed too vague.

Dexter, I'm sorry I'm a black queen who tell the whole damn truth. If my skin offends you, get a new job.

Perfect! But that was a ticket to the bread lines.

Now her nerves returned. She felt like her only hope was to go over Dexter's head. She jumped out of her seat, prompting stares from her colleagues, then headed straight to Mr. Proctor's office. Unfortunately, Dexter was leaving the meeting at the same time.

"Robin," he said. "How's progress going? Where are you headed?"

She really wanted to ignore him and claim later that she hadn't heard him, but she instead said, "One minute."

The door was shut, so she grabbed the knob, but as per the usual, it was locked.

Dexter approached her, causing her stomach to drop. "Charles is away for a wedding. If you have questions, I can answer them."

She had one. "How did the meeting go?"

Dexter frowned. "It wasn't what I expected. We'll go over it on Monday." He walked her back to the room. She sat back in her rolling chair, defeated. "Jacob," he called out. "Come see me a moment."

Jacob hit save and entered the hall. Robin had no hope in deciphering the mumbling outside the door. Page one of two reopened on her desktop, and despite her inner butterflies, she began page two.

Rover Callum needed to increase sales among men, so Husk needed to be cool, masculine, and sexy. A second pie chart showed an increase in sales among men for Husk shampoo plus a few other products. Robin tried to reiterate what the webpage had said about how men would feel sexy and get all the ladies (as if that were true). Her eye twitched at the blatantly sexist and cliché depiction of women.

She wanted to take Catherine up on her offer to proofread her work, but she just hit submit instead. Dexter hadn't provided on-the-job training, so he was to blame.

Later, she stopped by Xavier's studio. Luckily, he was in.

"Hey, it's Robin. I was wondering if you had a moment."

He gave her a side eye glance while shutting down a desktop PC. "I'm going home."

"Okay," Robin said, forcing a pleasant smile. "I was just wondering if you could teach me the ropes of creating an ad. I just want to better understand the process."

Xavier stared at her for several seconds. "…why?"

"I'm new, and I'll be the first to admit that I have very little experience in marketing. I just think your perspective would be helpful here."

Xavier gulped down a mysterious blue liquid from his anime-inspired thermos. "Can you come in like an hour—no. A half hour early tomorrow?" She nodded.

"Be here at 7:30 and I'll teach you stuff."

"Thanks." Robin tried for a handshake but the favor wasn't returned.

MONDAY, MAY 7TH

An exhausted eyelid peeled open on a rainy Monday morning. Robin groaned at the thought of leaving for work forty-five minutes early. Nevertheless, she grabbed a large yellow umbrella that once belonged to Carter and waded out to her parked Fit. She hadn't grabbed her container of peanut butter cookies, but she didn't realize that until after she entered the parking lot.

She arrived at 7:27 AM. She knew that because she franticly checked her phone while removing her seat belt. She accidently slammed the metal latch against her window. Yeesh.

You have to slow down, she thought. Indeed, her nerves were too high as of late. That wasn't a healthy way to live. A health podcast she listened to while jogging had said that the body cannot change until the mind does. One must learn to master their own thoughts by finding peace in every moment.

She started with deep breaths. Then she closed her eyes and imagined a lake with geese gently wading on the surface. She noticed that she was seated on a white wooden chair, wearing blue jeans, and sitting next to Raymond. She reached out her hand to touch his. His hand was soft, and she could swear she heard his voice whisper something indistinct.

Then, she looked back out at the lake. A subtle fog draped itself over the still waters akin to a blanket over a sleeping child.

Hoop Drama

Water striders traversed the water's surface like a skater gliding across the ice. A cool breeze felt heavenly on her forehead. Her heart rate lowered to a steady rhythm.

Just then she swiveled to Raymond, who jumped up out of his seat and turned to face away. He dropped his shorts to bear his naked rear end at Robin. Suddenly, she was thrust back into the real world of her lonely car. Presumably, the meditation gurus and monks of old would never have imagined such a sight, but it made Robin chuckle, and that's what she really needed.

The design office was open, but Robin had no idea if Xavier had arrived yet, so she ventured to the Skwad to drop off her things. At 7:38, Xavier arrived, bringing with him a large tote bag covered with stickers. Robin decided to just wait at the studio door.

When he returned, he unlocked the door silently, hardly acknowledging Robin's presence. When they'd first met, he at least had the decency to say "Ciao." Positivity had to become her calling card, so Robin guessed he must not be a morning person.

Speaking of morning people, Carter texted her, saying that Ray invited him to the next dinner.

ROBIN: *Yes. We would love to have you. I don't know the date yet, but we'll text you. Be warned we eat healthy. How's the job?*

Xavier turned on the lights, booted up a laptop, unpacked a box, and removed a large DSLR camera from a Pelican case.

CARTER: *I'll bring some cheese puffs. It's fine. I wish Leslie would just retire already. I watched a great film last night called The Dead Will Rise. It's scary so you wouldn't like it.*

Before Robin could reply, Xavier spoke up for the first time.

"So," he said with a long sigh. "You want to learn *photography?*"

"A little. I just want to understand the process from idea to

147

Andy Silvers

delivery. But we can start with photography if you want."

"Okay. This is a Nikon D500. We use it to take pictures of models and products on these backdrops." He pointed to the wall upon which a large roller held four different backdrops. The current one in place was solid white with a matte finish. It was huge as it spanned twelve feet wide by ten feet tall. The models would stand on a raised platform that Xavier explained next. "We can paint that platform any color we need or just overlay a green screen or something. Those stands you're seeing hold flashes that I synchronize to the camera to achieve optimal lighting. For Rover Callum, we'll take pictures of two models and at some point, we'll move a couch up here for that."

"A couch?"

"Yes."

"Will it fit in the elevator?"

"No, we'll push it up the staircase. Will we have to pivot? Yes, we will." Xavier smiled.

"What?"

"It's a *Friends* joke. Never mind. We'll probably just have the model sit on a cushion or something and add the couch in later. That's my job, but Melanie might do it. We don't really need the green screen for photos but our video camera requires it."

"Cool. Can I see that?"

"No. We receive the files that you create for the clients, but only after feedback is given and approved. Well—not quite. We've begun designing the product packages in software, but we won't print any until what's-his-face approves."

"Dexter?"

"No. The Rover Callum marketing lead. See. Take a look." He unlocked the laptop and opened up a file folder titled 'Rover Callum.' Inside was a series of folders and subfolders so vast it would make the national archives blush. Finally, Xavier pulled up an image of the sticker used for the Husk shampoo bottle. "We have a 3D version too so the client can really see everything."

"Wow. I wish I was doing this. I have a degree in graphic design from Ohio University, but I got put in the creative team. I think it's because I redecorated the restaurant I used to work at, but I don't know."

"Well...we don't really need any more designers. Honestly, we're a dime a dozen. But finding people willing to do market research and create charts is tough. Anyway, is that all you needed?"

Robin really wanted to ask about the personalities of her various co-workers—try to get inside their minds. However, Xavier didn't seem like he would be willing to spread gossip.

After a few seconds of silence that became two minutes, Xavier added, "The client pitches their ideas and tells us what their brand identity is. They pay for every service we do. If we design a logo, they pay for it. If we conduct a revision meeting, they pay for it. If we hire a model, they pay for it. It's gonna cost Rover Callum thousands of dollars. The more services they use, the more money we make."

That peaked Robin's curiosity. She realized that as a salaried employee, she received her check every month without fail. But C.E. Proctor doesn't bring in the same amount of money every month or every year. They seemingly relied on luck to continue financing the payroll. Unfortunately, Robin also began to realize that Xavier wouldn't really be able to teach her how to do *her* job.

But she had one final question. "Do you ever see Charles Proctor?"

Xavier thought for a moment, then he gave Robin a strange glare. "Yes. He's not my direct supervisor, but I've seen him."

Andy Silvers

He concluded his answer there and thus concluded Robin's training. As per the usual, Jacob was there early doing pushups and other exercises.

"Good morning," Robin said to Jacob but wishing not to.

"Hello. You're here early."

"Yes. I was just visiting the photo studio." No follow up question was asked. He didn't care.

Where Jacob lacked words, Kevin did not. "Good morning, Squad. Hi, Robin. Did you hear about Kayley? She's finally married and she's moving to Wisconsin."

She nearly responded until it was clear the comment was for Jacob.

"Thank god," Jacob said, signing into his desktop.

This scenario reminded Robin of how her coworkers had felt about Sarah. She had always given her the benefit of the doubt, but she learned the hard way to listen close. This time, she pitched in properly saying, "I know the type."

"Sorry, Robin," Kevin said, swiveling around. "Kayley is Chuck's daughter, but she hangs out around here sometimes and she just doesn't *shut up*—"

"And she steals from our supply room," Jacob added.

"Who's this?" Catherine inquired, entering the room with a graceful strut.

"Kayley," Kevin replied. "She's finally leaving West Virginia. She got married."

"Oh, good for her," Catherine said, logging in. "I always liked her."

"That's because she was nice to you," Jacob opined.

Catherine responded, "If you acted like gentleman, she'd be nice to you too."

Again, Catherine spoke words of wisdom. "I'm So Excited"

Hoop Drama

by The Pointer Sisters played inside Robin's mind. Robin almost roasted the two men right there, but realized that reading the tea leaves would prove advantageous in the long run. "Yeah. There was this girl at my old job who was just as lazy as could be. She also stole right out of the register. We had to fire her, but not before she gave me a sob story."

Jacob spoke after a brief silence. "Oh yeah? Where did you work before here?"

"I was a manager at Mary's Diner."

"Yes!" Kevin exclaimed. "I love Mary's, especially with the redesign they did."

Robin never bragged, but this time it slipped out. "That was my idea."

"Really?" Kevin asked.

"Kinda. I designed the new menus and changed all the lights and stuff. I mean, Carol had to approve it, but still." A bit of old Robin snuck in there at the end.

"That's nice," Jacob said. "I guess Charles noticed that."

Before more positive vibes could be emanated, Dexter walked in. He didn't really want to be noticed, but his team didn't care.

"Hey, Dexter," Catherine said. "Wanna see a movie with blood and guts?"

Dexter refused to answer. He stood brooding by the desks, staring at the team with his arms crossed. He could easily be an unnerving presence. What followed was a cold shiver, slithering like a serpent down Robin's back.

Then, Dexter spoke. "So...the photoshoot has been changed. Luckily it wasn't postponed, but we have a new directive." His voice was flat with no nuance or flare, and it was deeper than normal by just a smidgeon.

"Did you send the brief?" Jacob asked, searching through his

Andy Silvers

email.

"No," Dexter replied, still cold as an icicle. "I will in just a minute." He dropped the binder on Jacob's desk, but left his fists over top it, signaling not to touch. "I've never had a company recommend such useless changes, so I apologize in advance for the extra work you will have to do. Use today to look over the brief and make adjustments to your research. Thursday, the Rover Callum men will stop by, so finish anything you haven't done. I'll be in my office. Do not disturb unless you're bleeding."

"What if I get a papercut?" Kevin asked, breaking the tension with a machete.

"Ask Jacob to finish the job." Dexter said no more as he left the room. Jacob chuckled like a middle schooler.

Kevin asked, "What is that supposed to mean?"

Jacob replied by mimicking a slicing motion over his neck.

Whatever was happening, it was serious. So serious in fact that Robin refused to get the binder from the desk. Instead, she quietly checked her email hoping for a digital copy of the brief.

After refreshing the page three times, a new email from Dexter appeared. It contained a zipped file with the notes taken during the second briefing. She really hated getting info in these emails due to the lack of organization. Her computer's download folder was filling up quickly.

What she read astounded her. Her heart raced like a Bentley at Le Mans. Just as the engine revved with irregular rhythm, so too did her heart as she attempted to breathe quietly.

Major Collins wanted a more inclusive campaign!

It was there in the notes and clear as day. The executives liked the interview questions but wanted to add a person of color. Tanya's name was not mentioned. Furthermore, they wanted to find ways of appealing to the black community with their images, designs, and sales copy. They had only a few suggestions, but urged Proctor Creative to figure out ways of tweaking the existing material.

When Robin read her first assignment, she had to cover her mouth. In a joyful panic, she got up and made a beeline for the women's restroom. She wasn't sure if anyone was in there, but she stood before her reflection, mouth agape, and began to grin. Not only had Brody not hung her out to dry, but he had implemented her ideas into the meeting.

And wow—Dexter was *pissed*.

Robin hardly knew Dexter in a way one would deem as close, but she discovered what his angry side looked like. If she were forward-thinking, she might have considered the future ramifications of her decision, but instead Robin glowed like an ember in the mirror. She even let out a brief squeal. After grabbing a cup of coffee from the break room, she returned to her desk.

Her coworkers had started to converse about the situation, including a couple of NSFW jokes.

"Do you think he ran outta tampons?" Catherine asked.

"No," Jacob replied without a hint of humor. "Read the brief. The client suddenly asked for some diversity crap that we didn't expect."

"Yeah," Kevin added. "If they really wanted that, they should have told us from the start."

"Well, but that's not even the worst of it," Jacob continued. "I went to the school. They're *super* diverse, and it's not like they can reject black applicants anyway."

"And it's not good for business," Catherine noted.

Jacob threw up his hand. "Yes."

Once the team had quieted, Robin could collect her thoughts. They had some good points, but they missed the broader picture.

Andy Silvers

Discrimination often existed as implicit bias. So yes, the law said they had to admit black students, but that didn't mean they had to *accept* them into their culture.

By creating majority-white advertisements, they implied that education was for white students. Shanice had mentioned that in her college (before she dropped out), she had been 'educated' by her fellow students about the importance of George Washington and Thomas Jefferson for nearly twenty minutes. But not once—not once—did they mention they had owned slaves. If Ronald Reagan had owned slaves, it would have dominated the news and ended his career for sure.

Of course, Robin didn't say any of that.

Finally, she began the task that had dropped her jaw earlier. She was supposed to research black business people and include a few of their famous quotes. Next, she had to adjust the brochure with one of these quotes and add a section about the school's diversity initiative. Her job was to write the blurb so that the design team could format it. That was a lot of pressure, but she was ready. She simply paraphrased what her mother had told her two years ago about black talent having a voice in Hollywood.

Now, her job was exciting. Ray was going to get the full story with all the little bitty details when she got home.

She had gotten so excited that she ate lunch alone at a local sub shop to think about her day. She texted Shanice a brief message about how well the day was going before settling in to her seat with a toasted meatball sub. But she remembered her goal—make friends. Be a team player.

But…Catherine still needed to find love. And she forgot to stop by Kevin every night after work. It just seemed out of her comfort zone; a step too far. But how can anyone know she cared for them without giving them her most valuable asset—time.

Hoop Drama

That started to percolate in her mind until she saw a poster on the wall near the front door. It was for Friday Night Fright. Just then an epiphany sprung forth like a hare in a grassy field. She could invite Carter to the movie screening to meet Catherine! They couldn't know in advance of course that they were being 'shipped,' but the idea was rock solid. As soon as she got home, that'd be the first thing she did.

But Kevin still weighed on her mind. It seemed that he used humor to mask a deeper pain. Why else stay late at work night after night while doing nothing of consequence? No sudden solutions jumped out, but luckily her business hat returned once she clocked back in.

She handed her work to Catherine, feeling confident about it for the first time.

"Wow," Catherine said. "I can't really think of anything to fix, but then again, I don't have much experience with this. Hopefully, we'll be done with the updates and ready to send them to creative by Wednesday."

Robin just replied, "Great."

The day had been excellent, and therefore Robin had a certain spring in her step that night after work. And yes, she had remembered to wave to Kevin on the way out.

Ring. Ring. It was Shanice.

"Hello, Mom." Robin opened her car door.

[Robin? Yes. I need your help. I wrecked the car and I—]

"Wait, what? A wreck! Are you okay?"

[I'm fine. Someone hit me at a stop light. Listen, baby. I'm tired. I really need you or Ray to drive me to work for a few days. My car is impounded and they closed before I could get it back.]

"Gosh. Where are you?"

[A nice lady drove me back to my house. Please, sweetie. Do

155

Andy Silvers

you think you or Ray could drive me to work tomorrow?]

"Yes. Of course." Robin had gotten buckled. All the sounds of cars driving by and wind blowing had ceased. It was as though she were wearing noise canceling headphones. "Can you call out tomorrow? I think they'd understand."

[No, sugar. I need my paycheck. I need to be there at 8. Can you talk to Ray for me?]

"Yes, ma'am. I'll do that. What time should we get you?"

[Do you work tomorrow?]

"Yes."

[Darn. Just drop me off early at 7:30. That'll work.]

"I love you, Mom. Don't worry. When I get home, Ray and I will work it out. You just get some rest."

Robin hit the gas for the quietest ride home in years. That night, instead of telling Ray about her wonderful accomplishments, she coordinated her chauffeur schedule.

TUESDAY, MAY 8TH

"Remember you're picking her up at five." Robin hustled to get herself ready. This time, she remembered the peanut butter cookies.

"Yes, dear." Ray had the day off, but Robin wanted time to ask her mother about the accident. Curiosity and empathy were mixed together into an emotion soup.

Social media was a cavity filling, only done when needed and after several reminders. But like many Americans, she had hundreds of friends. Her mom had posted about the accident, stating that she wasn't responsible and that she hoped the insurance company (Maxwell Sawyer) got things straightened out soon. Robin liked the post, then planned to post one of her own later after picking her mother up.

Shanice had a teal Toyota Camry, but now, the front was damaged to the point where the engine didn't even run. Ride sharing services were available, but she hardly knew her way around a new-fangled app.

A cozy two-bedroom home with twenty years of wear and tear sat at the end of a cul-de-sac on Hebron Road. Now, with her husband gone (not deceased), the one-car garage was more than enough. Shanice had followed her daughter, Carter, and son-in-law to WV after selling her former home.

Andy Silvers

At 7:26, Robin pulled up the driveway, texting her mom upon her arrival. With an eye on the front door, Shanice decided to open the garage door instead (probably to make a show).

She opened the back door and threw a monstrous purse and a second makeup bag onto the back seat. Then, she plopped herself down next to Robin without a single word.

Robin looked up at the house. "Aren't you gonna shut the garage door?"

"Dagnabbit!" She threw open the door and closed the garage with a six-digit code.

"How are you?" Robin inquired, initiating an important discussion.

"You know me. Livin' the dream."

"You got *Dad* in that purse?"

"No. Jesse decided Florida was better, so Florida he can stay."

After three minutes of near silence, Robin asked, "So what happened?"

Shanice took a deep breath. "See...I was driving down twenty-five toward my favorite post office, when—well, I was in a hurry to get there before they closed, but I *ain't* break no law. Okay? I was fixin' to turn left and I had a green light, but this bitch in a Mazda runs the light. I hit the brake and she turns left to avoid me and I HIT HER! She was the one running the light, but my car was hit worse."

"So, she got hit on the side?"

"No, like on her bumper. But that's not the crazy stuff, okay? No sir. We wait for the police and she lies through her teeth. If she was a wooden puppet, her nose would've reached the Mars Rover."

Robin giggled. "What'd she say?"

"She told the officer, *some bald guy with a Hitler stache*, that

Hoop Drama

I hit her. But she drove through the light. I saw her!"

"A Hitler stache?"

"His was more curly, but you get the idea. Anyway, she claims that I tried to do a U turn in the road or something. What kinda drug-addict moron drives like that at five in the evening? Tell me."

"So, did you get your car?"

"Sorta. I paid the stupid hundred dollars to get it out of impound, but it don't drive. And insurance needs to do an investigation to determine a cause or some BS like that. Just check the cameras. I'll do it if you can't."

"I'm sorry, Mom. I wish I could help."

"Oh, baby, you are. I just need them to prove she ran the light and I'll get the car fixed, but I don't have $4000 to fix it right now."

"Me neither," Robin said, pulling into the parking lot.

"Yeah, you do, baby. You got that fancy job now. Start by getting yourself a new TV."

Robin sighed. "How do you even remember that?"

"Every momma got a memory like a cat."

"I'll think about it."

Robin parked in the guest spot.

"Hey," Shanice said, grabbing her purse. "Come inside and meet Brooke."

"Uh…"

"It'll be fast. They'd love to meet my sweet daughter."

After some glares back and forth, Robin turned off the car and walked inside. Shanice was the front desk lady along with two other people at Ohio Valley Surgery Center. They handled procedures that required a one-night stay at the most. Most patients left within four hours of waking up.

Without a second thought, Shanice exclaimed, "Hey, Brooke! Guess who this is?"

Andy Silvers

Brooke was standing there cleaning the desk with paper towels. Behind the desk was Abram Waterbrook, a slender man with a pronounced bald spot and a snake tattoo on his wrist. His hands were hairy like a bear, and his eyes were blue like the Caribbean Sea.

Brooke, a tiny girl with no tattoos who was no older than twenty-seven, smiled back. "Is this Robin?"

"Yes, it is. It looks like Gina ain't here yet, but this is Brooke. She's my favorite." Shanice laughed like a cartoon villain.

Robin smiled and shook her hand. "It's nice to meet you. I'm Robin Chapel."

"Like a church," Brooke stated. "Do you go to church near here?"

"Uh…no. My husband and I aren't really into that."

Brooke glared at Shanice. "You raising a heathen?"

Shanice laughed. "No. She's my saving grace today. Listen good, my car got hit yesterday."

"What!" Abram chimed in. "Were you speeding again?"

"No, but she ran a red light and blamed it on me."

"Yikes," Brooke said. "That sucks. Insurance will get that straightened out."

"Yeah, but they'll take their *sweet* time," Shanice rushed through a door and disappeared for roughly three minutes.

"So," Abram said, stretching behind the desk. "You think the libs will cry like babies when Trump puts a wall on our border?"

"Um…no." What was Robin supposed to say to that? Why did strangers feel the need to gab about politics without being asked?

"Yeah, they got walls around their mansions, but they get butthurt when you try to put a wall around the country. Just ridiculous." Brooke joined in. It was like a medical clinic owned by Roger Ailes.

160

Hoop Drama

Thank goodness Shanice works here to straighten these people out, Robin thought. She could give them a good dose of reality. Robin had met people with differing political views, of course. It's Wheeling, West Virginia. But the level of ignorance required to ignore the president's awful comments was quite concerning indeed.

Luckily, Shanice returned, appearing behind the desk in her work outfit.

Robin took the opportunity to change the subject. "Do you need me to bring you a snack later, dear?"

Shanice waved her hand as if swatting a fly. "No. You go ahead and go. I know you've got important designing to do."

"Oh, fancy," Brooke said.

Robin smiled and made a quick retreat to her car. She only had eleven minutes to get to work, but luckily it was a short drive. Plus, she was excited to share her homemade peanut butter cookies. Feeling a sense of optimism about how things were going at work, she took a selfie in front of the surgery center and posted a quick message about how proud she was of her mother.

At C.E. Proctor Creative, the team was their usual self.

"Hey, Kevin," Robin said with a flighty voice. "I brought peanut butter cookies if you're interested."

"Oh, darn," he said, logging into his desktop. "I usually get here after you, so I haven't seen them. I'll go later. Hey, Catherine, you better go now if you want any."

Robin smiled. She was making allies one cookie at a time.

"Oh. If they're homemade, I may try one." Catherine seemed happy, so Robin used the opportunity to take her order.

"Do you have a request for a bakery item I could bring?" Robin unlocked her desktop while standing up so Catherine could see her clearly.

161

Andy Silvers

"I like carrot cake, but I don't really need it. The snacks we have are fine."

"Okay. Well, I'll keep that in mind." Robin knew she'd change her mind. People love homemade treats.

Except maybe Jacob. But Robin still discounted his opinion. She didn't want to, despite how crucial he was to the team. Jacob simply hadn't earned her trust, but that didn't mean he had incurred her hate. Hate wasn't in Robin's dictionary. Hate can't change minds.

Dexter entered the room, a frown still pasted on his face. "All right, team. You've got your directives. The Husk execs are returning this Thursday, so we really want to put our best foot forward on that. I like the work we got, but we still need copy for the web page and Instagram ad. Robin, you did well on your two-page market segmentation charts—"

"Really?" Robin said, jaw open wide enough to catch a dove.

"…yes. That's why I said it." Dexter walked around the room while talking. "Anyway, I suspect Rover Callum will return in a few months for more marketing, so we need to give them our best. Catherine, you're in charge of the brochure's content and layout."

"You have to try Robin's cookies," Kevin noted. "They're real homemade treats."

Dexter turned to Robin. "Maybe I will." He then planted himself squarely next to Robin's desk, leaned down, then whispered, "Hey, so I've got you working on the Major Collins stuff still. What you submitted seems fine, but I sent you a few more things. I just sorta figured this post-modern stuff might appeal to you. Start using the team account." After a quick pat on the shoulder, he left the room.

Robin had indeed received an email. It listed a link to a website called Smartsheet that featured a list of options for team

Hoop Drama

coordination. The page listed 'Documents' as an open folder, along with several others. Robin checked a past email right quick, realizing this website had been linked all along.

She could've seen her coworkers' work after all.

With the 'Documents' page open in her browser, she checked the other pages, finding both the Rover Callum campain and all others going back four years. It seemed that this could teach her more about her job than Xavier ever could, and it was right at her fingertips. Luckily, she wasn't a private detective.

The documents folder listed her colleagues' work, but not her own. She immediately spent the next twenty minutes uploading her work from the Husk campaign as well as MCU. Her job, found under the 'Assigned Tasks' page, listed a few new diversity paragraphs and a new diversity section under 'Campus Life.'

Thrilled, she got to work. Each section of the campus life page had a picture of a student. It was fairly obvious the school used images of real students, but the brief called for a stock photo of a young black female between the age of eighteen and twenty-five. Robin did her best to find a lady who looked like Tanya Kushall. There was no place to directly upload the image, but she inserted the link and clicked SUBMIT.

Could any of her coworkers have told her about this? Yes. But they probably assumed she already knew.

After hours of work, and discovering that Kevin's last name was DiGeronimo, she shut down for her lunch break. As expected, Kevin was in the employee lounge.

"Hey, Mr. DiGeronimo," Robin said while Kevin piled a napkin with cookies.

"Oh," he replied, slightly stunned by her appearance. "You found out. Yes, it's Italian. And I'm impressed you pronounced it right. Girl, these cookies smell great."

163

Andy Silvers

Robin checked how many he had taken. Nearly half. "I'm glad you like them. Maybe I'll bring brownies tomorrow."

"Only if they have pot in them." Keven laughed, catching a piece of cookie that fell from his mouth.

"Okay, I'll see what I can do." He seemed so cheerful, but Robin had to know why he refused to go home. She wasn't quite sure how to phrase it. "So, you stay here at night pretty late." That wasn't even a question. She just said the first thing she thought.

Kevin's smile vanished. "I guess so."

"I hope everything is okay. I just don't want you to be lonely." That sounded better in her head. She cringed, hoping that she didn't overestimate the power of cookies.

Kevin rolled up the remaining four cookies in his napkin. He swallowed before he spoke. "I appreciate it. I...had a roommate, but he's not there anymore. I just prefer to be here. It gives me time to think."

"Did he move out?"

"Why do you wanna know?"

Robin panicked for an answer. The reality was the truth (she really wanted to make allies) wasn't going to sound like the truth. Instead, a false answer: a white lie, would sound better. "I'm just curious if you're doing a personal project or something. My dad used to create stepping stones with concrete and glass marbles. After a month, he had created a circle path in our back yard that he'd walk on nights when he needed to think."

"Oh. That sounds cool. I just draw doodles mostly. And listen to music. Do you listen to Andy Williams? Like 'Moon River' or 'Almost There'?"

Robin tended to listen to whatever was on the radio, so she knew the classic hits, but not specific albums or songs. "Um...I think that was a Frank Sinatra song, right?"

Hoop Drama

"His cover is great too, but it's Williams."

"Oh. Okay." Clearly cookies were a better way into Kevin's mind. "Well," she said, ready to leave with her dignity intact. "I am always down to talk if you need to. Yeah. That's it."

"Okay." Kevin gave an awkward smile and left the room.

Robin made her way to a sub shop, but brought her food back to the agency for fear of running out of time. Dexter stayed away for the remainder of her shift; plus, the work was great, so she left that night with a sense of hope and optimism unlike any day before.

☙❀❧

"Baby, that's wonderful!" Ray said, eating the rest of his homemade baked chicken with bread crumbs. Robin ate the unfinished half of her sub, though she left room for a piece of chicken.

"Yes!" she exclaimed. "They reworked the campaign. I never thought—in Wheeling, it couldn't happen—that they'd make diversity a focus for their campaign."

"I thought every college was doing that."

Robin nodded. "I sorta did too. But apparently some only pay lip service."

"How do you know they really mean it?"

"I guess I don't, but you should've seen Dexter. He's *not* happy."

"Why?"

"I don't think he likes the new campaign. He calls it *woke*."

"If treating black people like humans is woke, I think he's in the wrong country. Try moving to…somewhere else."

Robin chuckled. "Exactly. Oh, and I should tell you about my plan."

Andy Silvers

"Uh oh," Ray said, covering his face. "Where's my fire extinguisher."

"No. No." Robin threw her rapping in the trash, then stood next to Ray. "I wanna try to hook Carter up with a pretty lady."

Ray gasped. "Hah. Really?"

"Yeah. My coworker, Catherine, is perfect. She wants a man who can stay at home and likes horror films."

"Wait," Ray pulled out his phone. "What's her full name?"

"Actually, I don't remember. But I'm gonna ask Carter to go see that Friday Night Fright movie thing and bring Catherine."

"Yikes. You're gonna *hate* it."

"But think about *love*, Ray. You know Carter is lonely." Robin walked behind his chair, putting her arms around him. "I'm not gonna have time to invite him tomorrow, so I'll do it tonight."

Ray gobbled up his last bite. "I wanna listen too."

"No. You'll speak and make jokes. Plus, I'm not gonna mention Catherine anyway, so there's nothing to hear."

"Fine. *Pfft*. Be that way." Ray smiled and began doing the dishes. Robin loved a man who cleaned.

After moving to the bedroom, Robin made the call. She was nervous, but too excited to put the phone down. "Hey, Carter. How are you?"

[Good. Is Raymond home?] Carter sounded a bit distorted. He was likely using his earpiece.

"Are you out?"

[Yeah. I'm at Kasey Khel's getting some cereal.]

"What? It's after seven."

[I'm sorry, princess preachy. I don't get to choose my schedule.]

"Nah. I'm just kidding. I was wondering if you'd be interested in seeing a scary movie in like a week or something."

Hoop Drama

[Uh…what movie?]

"It's about a prison, I think. It's at Friday Night Fright."

[Oh yeah. I know Friday Night Fright. You wanna go to that?]

"Well, it won't be my favorite, but I think it could be fun. Kinda like Halloween in May." Robin waited several seconds for Carter to answer. She quickly searched it while on speaker phone. "Oh. It's called Post Mortem Prison."

[Oh, really? That's a classic. You know, the FBI investigated the director for that one.]

Oh lord. Maybe Robin should've stayed in her lane. "Wow. That's pleasant."

[Yeah. It was fine, but they thought he was using real corpses since it looked so real and he ain't got permits and stuff. I'll go see it which you, I just don't want you to regret it.]

"Nope. No regrets. I'll text you the details."

[Okay. Be sure to bring a hand to hold since you sure ain't holdin' mine.]

But he would be holding someone's.

"Yup. I'll figure something out. Be sure to order a ticket."

After seven minutes of talking about Ray and the drama at West Forrest, Carter hung up and Robin did a little dance. Ray poked his head in to see if they were still talking.

"It's a date!" Robin yelled, spinning around like a Disney princess. She was nervous but optimistic as the worst that could happen is a ship that doesn't sail.

"If Carter marries her, I'll let you decide our kids' names."

"I already will do that. Anything else?"

Ray shook his head. "Just take lots of pictures at the event. I need what the Russians call *Kompromat* for the wedding."

Robin giggled. "Deal."

THURSDAY, MAY 10TH

Shanice remembered to shut her garage this time. "I saw your post."

"Oh yeah. Thanks. I just want people to know that your family has your back." Robin had complimented her mother on social media and briefly explained that her car was totaled.

"My agent is workin' on the report, so I'll get a call back today or tomorrow. Thanks for doing this." Shanice buckled up and changed the temperature to her liking.

"Absolutely. So...I wanted to tell you about my job..." Robin glanced over at Shanice at a stop sign.

"Oh good," she said. "You been promoted to manager yet?"

"No...thankfully." Robin double-checked to be sure the brownies were in the back seat. They were. "Actually, I won big this week. I talked with the executives—Dexter definitely doesn't know about that—and they mandated that the campaign be more diverse." Robin grinned from ear to ear.

"Wow. I knew you could do it, sugar. You've always been a fighter."

"Yes, but I don't think you get it. They were totally opposed to diversity and stuff before. Dexter even makes jokes about feminists for some reason. One of the execs of a college nearby called Major Collins emailed me asking for ideas. It's insane. I

Hoop Drama

just…never expected this result." Robin glowed.

Shanice paused before she responded. She wanted to gauge her daughter's reaction first. A reverse of their parent-child relationship had occurred. Shanice was now the learner. "I am thrilled, sweetie. You can't let those people silence you. America is waking up. They waking up to slavery, Jim Crowe, and prison injustice. But that don't mean every state got it figured out. No sir. Keep it up, sweet pea."

Confidence felt weird. It was extra air in her lungs, more gusto in her walk, and less shake in her voice. Today, she was going to be Robin Chapel, girl boss. Oof, maybe just confident employee.

Looking back, the road that led here was rocky, but so easy compared to those who'd come before. She may not have had the full support of her boss or coworkers, but she had half the country on her side. At least, in theory.

While approaching the surgery center, Robin recalled her conversation with the staff. Their lack of understanding had left her confused and annoyed. But Shanice was there as a light in the darkness, and Robin wanted her mom to know she was proud. "I had a strange conversation with your coworkers yesterday. Something about libs crying and a border wall."

Shanice's eyes widened. "Really? They're crazy kids. Remember how this side of the country votes. It's just a fact of life."

Robin nodded. "Yeah, but you must have a field day correcting their BS. Surely, just holding a mirror in front of them is enough…"

"Oh yeah. I've said a thing or two." Shanice peered out the window, watching people walk in and out of the facility. "Maybe one day I'll inspire change like you."

Robin chuckled. "I bet you already have. Have a great day."

Andy Silvers

Robin yawned.

"You too. Be a queen today." Shanice grabbed her giant purse and headed inside. Robin didn't wait long before heading to work.

Her nerves shot up slightly, remembering the Husk execs were coming by. She took a deep breath. Instead of allowing the day to be a crisis, she made it an opportunity. *Be who your mother knows you are*, Robin thought. What's the worst that could happen?

The brownies made their way into the employee lounge. The joke wasn't funny until it was rammed into the ground. No, they didn't contain any pot. But they contained white powder technically speaking.

"No way," Kevin joked. "You actually did it."

"Not quite," Robin rebutted. "They are drug free."

"I'll still take a few...just to be sure they're safe." He smiled. Though he didn't quite feel like an ally, he seemed like a colleague.

That reminded her—Catherine!

Robin returned to the Skwad room, keeping her target in sight. She contemplated what words should come first.

Hey, Catherine. How are you?

What up, Catherine? You should totally see the movie with me.

Hey, Cathy. I've got tickets to Post Mortem Prison. Just putting that down if you're picking up what I'm putting down.

Unfortunately, Robin had resting B face while thinking and Catherine took notice. "Do you *need* something?"

Her actual words were less cool. "Um. I was just—so I'm going...here's the thing. You told me about that Friday Night Fright thing, remember?"

"Yes..."

"Well, I got a ticket too. So, we can both enjoy the carnage. Actually, I read the killer will be there for a photo shoot."

○ 170 ○

"Are you following me or something?"

RED ALERT. RED ALERT.

Robin held her breath. Things were going horribly.

Luckily, Catherine was joking. "Just kidding. Yes, I'd love for you to go. It beats the drab monotony of this concrete block. That's for sure."

Robin's tense shoulders relaxed. And she released a blast of air. "Yes. Agree. If only the others would go."

"I know," she replied, finally pausing her work. "I told Kev and Jacob about it, but they don't seem interested. But it's way more interesting than the movies they carry on about. You know," Catherine leaned closer. "The FBI actually investigated the director. Really. They thought he was using *real* corpses."

"Wow!" Robin reacted like she was hearing it here first. "That's wild."

"Damn straight," Catherine responded, ignoring Jacob who had entered the room. "Anyway, look for me so we can sit next to each other."

The plan was working like clockwork. "Absolutely."

"Look for you where?" Jacob asked as if he was entitled to know.

"At the Friday Night Fright. Remember, I invited you?" Catherine stared at Jacob with a look of judgment that the female species had perfected.

"Oh. Pass."

"It's for more sophisticated viewers like me and Robin."

Robin smiled. She liked being 'sophisticated.'

Jacob chuckled. "If sophisticated people watch others get their intestines ripped out and used as jump ropes, then sure." Jacob laughed at his joke. Robin really wanted to but held back.

Catherine rolled her eyes.

Andy Silvers

After seeing Dexter fly by the room, she got to work. He was likely prepping for the meeting in an hour. And Robin had a plan. A simple plan but those were the best.

At exactly 8:50, Robin peered out the window after pretending to stretch. Two cars pulled into the lot. Unfamiliar cars.

She grabbed a handful of folders, shoving some random documents inside. Her nerves shot up, but so did her adrenaline. After spending far too much time picking what papers to grab, she hustled to the ground floor. There, she opened the top folder, pretending to read its contents while hiding behind the corner near the elevator.

Before zero hour, her mind flashed back to when she was seven. On her birthday, she had been taken to see the National Underground Railroad Freedom Center in Cincinnati. It was a nearly three-hour drive and certainly not what a little girl dreamed of doing on her birthday.

She was taken through the exhibits, only picking tiny nuggets of knowledge along the way until she saw the Nellie Mae Rowe exhibit. Her mother shared her knowledge of the artist, explaining that she made great strides despite great struggle. What really stuck with Robin, even a decade and a half later, was Nellie's creative spark. She hardly made art to sell. She did it for her own benefit. Sure, visitors to her 'playhouse' were wowed by her works of surreal art. But she used pencil and paper to create for fun, pulling from her life and dreams.

That memory lasted a lifetime, even serving as her inspiration to pursue art. She considered doing art as a career but was motivated (by her mother) to do something more 'relevant' that incorporated art. Nevertheless, in the years that followed, Robin could be found drawing in her room at night. She tried painting but wasn't the best at it.

Hoop Drama

Her mother would peek into the room and ask, "Are you practicing?"

She would say, "No, I'm just drawing." For Robin, her art wasn't 'professional,' but it didn't need to be. She loved to create visual tales, even abstract ones, like her hero, Nellie Rowe.

Even though Nellie's art never had a political purpose, so to speak, the young girls she inspired would, and at a time when it was needed most.

Finally, the locked door opened. Two men and one woman entered, wearing dark clothing, and murmuring about something indistinct. As they rounded the corner, Robin walked out, bumping a man who knocked the folders out of her hand.

"I am so sorry, miss," he stated, covering his mouth. "I didn't even see you."

"It's okay," Robin replied. Her heart was pounding. She had half a second to abort the plan, but she held firm. "Are you from Rover Callum?"

"Yes," the man in front answered. He had gray hair and was wearing a navy-blue suit. The first thing Robin noticed was the strong scent of cologne that radiated from him like a cloud. "We're here to meet Dexter for the Husk campaign."

"Well," Robin said, smiling. "I would *love* to try Husk."

The execs looked confused. The woman spoke. "It's intended for men."

"Yes," Robin responded, fully prepared. "And who's buying Rover Callum?"

The man replied softly. "Mostly women."

"Precisely," Robin said, moving her hands as if giving a presentation. "I work in the idea team and I just love the Husk product. The natural ingredients like avocado oil and shea butter are something I adore. Imagine an ad where the man's bottle of

Andy Silvers

Husk is empty because his wife just loves it so much. It's funny and clever."

The group still looked confused.

"You see the idea?" Robin asked. "If women are buying from you, sell *them* on the product first. Then, their men will buy it next. You can try to reach a new market, or you can use the current market to reach the new one."

The execs nodded slightly. The man asked, "What's your name?"

Robin hesitated giving it away, but she was already in too deep. "I'm Robin Chapel. I'm an artist, designer, and researcher."

"My name is Ronald Spar. I'm the lead of marketing and research at Rover Callum. We should talk later." He fumbled through his jacket to find a business card. "I've got to get upstairs. Thank you for your time."

"Absolutely," Robin replied, stepping aside, and pressing the up arrow on the elevator. "It's an honor to meet you."

"Likewise." Ronald entered the elevator and the door closed.

Then Robin released a deep sigh. She had done it…again. This time on purpose. Hopefully, the lack of words like 'race' or 'sexism' made the proposal more palatable. Either way, Robin became worried about someone seeing her downstairs, so she flew up the staircase and slipped behind the executives to reach her desk.

Before she checked her assigned tasks pages, she took a peek at Catherine's work. She made sure to memorize her last name— Graham. Then she returned to her work which had begun to seem like a distant memory. Her paragraphs needed a bit of tweaking and her next assignment required a bit of research.

She had been asked to create a plan for media buying. Which services should Husk use to advertise their new product? Robin looked up 'media buyer' first, then tried to understand where the marketing materials would be located. After doing some research; she discovered that TV channels, magazines, Google Ads, billboards, and more were used to place the media. This was self-evident, but what wasn't was how Husk should be incorporated into this plan. She hadn't the slightest clue where to start.

Suddenly, Jacob appeared behind her, causing her to click a random link on her screen. "Hey, how's it going? You got any research done for the Husk campaign?"

Robin held her tongue…at least from saying any swear words. "Not yet, but you're not in charge."

Dead silence. Catherine and Kevin both stared at her like she was an alien creature. Robin turned around slowly, seeing Jacob peer down at her with narrow eyes and tightly pressed lips. Her stomach did a little flip as she tried to speak. Eventually, she was able to say, "I appreciate that you care to check. I have to plan Husk's media buying, but I haven't started."

Her stark comment had offended his sensibilities and he spoke more frankly than normal. With a stern voice he said, "Figures. Your output has been the weakest of the team. When you can create viral content, I won't need to bug you." He sat back down at his desk.

No one said a word. Robin was embarrassed to say the least. And yes, she did need help on this assignment, but the last person she wanted to do so was Jacob. She held her tongue earlier because the last thing she wanted was conflict. Making people happy just came naturally, but Jacob was like a middle school boy. He always just showed up to say something nagging or unnecessary. The teacher didn't say anything because they never heard him speak and no one could really tell on him because he was just being *mildly* annoying. But it was day after day after day.

Andy Silvers

Eventually, Robin got up, choosing to ask Kevin to collaborate on the media buying.

"Sure," he said, pulling out his ear buds. He brought Robin over to the window where a large table stood. There, he opened a business laptop and signed in just like his desktop.

"Has this laptop always been here?" Robin inquired.

"Yeah. It's for Skwad use. We can take it around the building if need be. But we're going to go downstairs since we'll need to talk a lot." Kevin carried the laptop into the hall as Robin followed. They took the elevator. "So, you told off Jacob, huh?"

Robin rubbed her hands together. "Yeah. I didn't mean to. I just found out like a week ago that he wasn't in charge."

Kevin shook his head. "Yeah…but you gotta understand him. We just let him lead since that's what he likes. Plus, I don't think he wanted a woman talking back to him."

But he needs one talking back to him, Robin thought. Yeesh. If Jacob weren't so spoiled, he'd make a better team member, and ironically, a better leader. "Okay. Well, I didn't know."

Kevin led them to the conference room where Dexter had interviewed her. She saw the familiar *Ready Set Go* poster on the wall. She stretched, then sat down next to Kevin.

"I don't know why Jacob expects you to deliver the same as us, but let me show you sorta what Dexter wants. Can you sign in here?" He slid the laptop over to her.

"Sure." Robin signed into her account. Then she opened her ASSIGNED TASKS folder.

"So, obviously, we don't buy the ads ourselves, but we help plan the campaign. They're gonna want you to show them *everything*. We have to show them where the ads will go, what each ad will look like, and the timeline for the ad placement. When Husk is officially announced, they'll need a launch video and we

○ 176 ○

Hoop Drama

have to really sell it since it's targeting a new demographic." Kevin opened a folder in her page labeled TEMPLATES.

There, he downloaded a document with a timeline built in. "So, we want to reference the initial brief to see what they wanted. Then, we'll begin doing the outline. They'll probably want the campaign to last for two months at most. In sales, you have to move hard and fast. But this all has to be coordinated with the actual release of the product. So, you don't want the ads to go live until the product is actually for sale. Rover Callum is only available in a couple of stores in West Virginia, but they sell a lot online and in magazines."

Robin sat up straight and took a deep breath. She was so surprised she actually smiled. "Goodness that's a lot of stuff."

"For sure. That's why it's a team effort. Let's get started."

For the next two hours, they worked exclusively on the media buying strategy. Rover Callum already used certain outlets like magazines and Instagram ads, so that needed to be first. The design team had created several images that Kevin used in the PDF. She learned more in that time than any day before. Kevin was a patient teacher.

He had a kind spirit that no other employee had. Thus, she was motivated to help him in return. She asked him once more about his roommate, hoping he'd open up.

"Gosh. Do you want his number or something?"

"Sorry. I'll stop asking." Robin meant it, but hoped one day Kevin would open up. She really wasn't a nosy person either. Her tendency was toward being shy, but with her new career came a new woman.

"It's fine," Kevin sighed, closing the laptop screen. "His name was Neville Roseman. We were roommates for about two years…but he died. I got the call from Wheeling Hospital that he

Andy Silvers

had been in a car crash." Kevin stood up to make coffee. "I've left his room in our apartment for a few years. I only go in there to vacuum."

The pieces were coming together. He must have decided staying late at work was better than going home and seeing Neville's bedroom. Instead of asking for confirmation, Robin simply said, "I'm here if you need me." She grabbed her phone and sent her cell to his work email. "I sent you my number. If you need to talk, let's do."

Kevin nodded.

While cleaning up her desk area (and avoiding eye contact with Jacob) she noticed an email from Brody.

Mrs. Robin Chapel,

My team have discussed your ideas in full and would like to inquire for more info. We would like to ask you for a specific favor regarding our campaign. So as not to waste your time, please let me know if you can do coffee this Saturday the 12th. Let me know if Mugshots works for you at 9 AM. I hope to meet before our campaign proceeds.

Kind regards,

Brody Pearson, PhD

SATURDAY, MAY 12TH

"Yes. I'm sure," Ray reassured his wife while she adorned her best pantsuit. "This is a big honor. I mean, I've never been invited out for coffee by a big wig, so I'm not sure what will happen."

Robin had to reread the email to be sure it said what it did. The marketing lead at Rover Callum wanted to meet *with her*, a random agency employee. "It's just weird. I don't have a plan or anything."

"You'll be fine. You're my princess. Plus, remember what you told me. You want credit for your work, right?"

"I'm pretty sure *you* told me I should want credit for my work." Robin held her husband's hands.

"Either way, this is it." With a quick kiss on the lips, she was on her way.

Feeling overdressed at a coffee shop was easy. A young woman wore a shirt that didn't fully cover her back tattoo and a college-aged boy sported a Playboy t-shirt. Nevertheless, a warm cup of coffee with two creams made Robin a bit less nervous.

"Good morning," Brody said, approaching Robin from her left. He was wearing a white button-up dress shirt and spotless gray pants. His loafers were black and shiny. So, at the very least, Robin wasn't underdressed.

"Good morning, sir." She arose from her chair for a firm

Andy Silvers

handshake. "I appreciate this opportunity." She had no clue what 'opportunity' she was being given, but that seemed like the classy thing to say. She remained resolute, even as she wiped sweat off her hands with a napkin.

"It looks like you got a drink. What'cha having?"

Robin fought not to say 'um.' "It's a black coffee with two creams."

"Great choice. I'll get myself a latte and be right back." He suddenly had the voice of a Jeopardy host. He enunciated every syllable and stood with incredible posture. Furthermore, his teeth were sparkling white and straighter than seemed possible. After three minutes, he returned. "I hope this wasn't too sudden for you. My colleague, Mr. Roger Gates, recommended this meeting on Wednesday and I had to think about it first, but I really like his idea."

Robin tried to cross her legs but hit the center-post of the table. She scooched her chair back and tried again. "Yes sir. What's the idea?"

"Well, we've made some changes to our campaign strategy as you've probably already noticed. We do feel like diversifying could increase potential sales and market reach. Now obviously, we discussed all this with Mr. Dexter, but I'd like you to help with the campaign. We need an image for the website, but we've had some difficulty finding a lady with your...complexion to be our model. As a college graduate, you'd be perfect for the ad. And by the way, we would like to substitute Ms. Tanya in our video."

Nothing sunk in except the Tanya part. "Really? That's great."

Brody chuckled. "We thought you'd like that. And if you agree to the photoshoot, I'll let Dexter know right away."

Uh oh. Dexter.

She hadn't really thought this through. Then again, it was

Hoop Drama

sprung on her last minute. She wanted so badly to ask if Dexter knew about her interference with the campaign, but it would imply guilt to ask. She had no intention of taking over the campaign and certainly not royally screwing over her boss, but still. Something about all this felt good. After all, Dexter wasn't going to champion for black students any time soon. "I'd like to do the photoshoot."

Pride now. Ramifications later.

"Great," Brody replied. "You dress however you want. Be free to represent your community in an honest way."

Really? Did that mean a dashiki shirt and giant hoops? "Can I wear hoop earrings?"

"Sure. I don't see why not. Just avoid logos."

Suddenly, her cautious optimism shown through. "This wasn't my idea…in case Dexter asks." It was as though a good angel was on her shoulder to relay a hard truth.

"Yes," Brody responded, unsure what to say. "Our team formulated the idea after speaking to you. We can hire out a model, of course, but we thought we would ask you first."

Robin smiled externally. Her mind was racing—not with thoughts, with abstract feelings. And it never even occurred to her to ask if she should be paid for the gig. A rookie mistake.

After a big gulp of his beverage, Brody asked, "Hey, can I follow you on social media?"

"Um—" Yeesh. She tried so hard not to say that. "Yes sir. Find me on Twitter under Robin Chapel." She would've used Facebook but her high school profile picture seemed unprofessional.

He pulled out his phone immediately and did just that. When her phone buzzed, she followed him back quickly to be polite. Though, it was genuinely cool to be meeting a fancy exec. She wasn't exactly a social media butterfly.

181

Andy Silvers

To her surprise, his top post was about a Christian movie called *God's Compass*. He was most likely republican, a truth that seemed to have no bearing on the meeting.

"Please feel free to email me with any questions you have," he said, grabbing his trash off the table. "I'm sorry for the hurry, but I must be going." He offered another handshake.

"Absolutely. Pleasure to meet you."

Robin chose to get up too so it looked like she had places to be. But it was her day off, and Ray had taken Shanice to work. She was free to do anything, but top of mind was a shopping spree.

Then, Kevin called. After they hung up, she'd need to add him to her contacts. "Good morning. Robin speaking."

[Hello. Hey. So, I thought about your comments and wanted to see if you were willing to help.] His wording was just vague enough to be confusing.

"I'm always willing to try." She stopped there, hoping he'd fill in the blanks. Meanwhile, she tried to remember what exactly she had promised.

[I really don't know what to do with Neville's room. If you could stop by one day next week, maybe we could figure out what to do. I should just get another roommate. Lord knows I could use the money, but I just can't.] He paused. [I know you're not a professional therapist, but if you mean what you said, I'd really appreciate it.]

It was more than she had expected him to say, that's certain. She'd hoped that, like a therapist, she could just say some nice words over the phone or during lunch break. But that's not what Kevin needed. He needed a friend. Despite a myriad of internal objections, she said 'yes.'

Now, she had spun so many webs with so many different people—Catherine, Carter, Kevin, and Brody—that she had

Hoop Drama

caught herself inside her own handiwork. How on earth had the quiet and gentle Robin become Wheeling's Dr. Phil?

✿✿✿

Her car made loops around various buildings as she traversed the Highlands. Technically, Warwood Shopping Center was closer, but it was a tad dilapidated. Furthermore, Robin was in the mood for clothes, and since her mom kept whining, a new TV. She hit up Kohl's and JC Penny just before lunch.

A dazzling emerald pair of hoop earrings landed first in her basket. She only got a carrying basket to force herself not to spend all of Ray's money—scratch that—her money. It would be easy to get used to always making four thousand dollars a month. A purple leather belt was next followed by three shoes, one pair of slippers, and two loafers. Had Ray been able to go, he would have staked out the hats, so Robin got him a green and blue hat with a blocky face on it. She just figured Ray would like the design without realizing it was a Minecraft branded product. Videogames were like Jewish dubstep. An anathema.

In the long checkout line, she checked her phone, seeing if anyone needed her. Across the way, examining a rack of electronic doodads, a young family of color stood. They laughed and joked about the weird ways they could use the various products.

"Hey, honey," the father said. "If you ever have to plug your phone up from downstairs, you can use this cable." He pulled a ten-foot USB cable off its mount.

His wife walked around to examine the neon yellow cable, holding a toddler in her arms. Despite being no older than three, his long hair contained beads of many colors. Robin unconsciously touched her belly, rubbing it very gently. Then, she left it there

183

until it was her turn to pay.

His wife, with several beads in her braids as well, pointed to another gadget. That one appeared to be a battery pack. "This thing looks like that thing Brenda uses in her car."

"Oh yeah." The father grabbed the item, which was actually a phone mount for a car. "We don't need one."

"What about me?" A young girl grabbed her father's arm to pull his hand down lower. "I can put it on my dollhouse to watch videos about home stuff."

"Maybe when we get you a phone, pumpkin. Maybe." Her father placed the item back on the shelf.

Then it was her turn to check out. Her total was $104.26, and she hadn't even gotten a TV yet. She exchanged pleasantries with the cashier, a young blonde named Minnie; but she thought about the family. Her friends had said a strong woman puts career first, but a small part of her soul said that wasn't always true.

The Best Buy associate buzzed over like a bee in a hive to answer all of Robin's questions. She really didn't need his help since her only requirement was that it be less than $500. Unfortunately, he described every feature she could never need and handed her a protection plan packet before she knew what was happening.

"On top of the manufacturer warranty, you'll get an additional two years of protection which covers accidental damage, hardware malfunctions, and missing parts; all for a low price. And if you become a member, you can get access to exclusive prices and we'll send our team to your house if your TV needs repair. Plus, free two-day shipping." The man smiled like he had just proposed.

Robin really didn't want any of that but her no-can-do voice that worked with Ray didn't work anywhere else. By 2:17 PM, she had purchased a $400 fifty-inch TV and $199 for the membership.

Hoop Drama

She put a note on her phone to remember to cancel before it renewed.

Either way, Shanice would be happy and Ray—well, he didn't pay the bills anymore.

✳✿✳

The large box stood in front of the Chapel's crummy TV waiting to be set up.

"Do you wanna set it up tonight?" Ray asked, unplugging the old TV.

"Honestly, no," Robin replied, yawning.

Ray gave her a hug. "It sounds like someone needs to go to bed." It was only 5:45 PM.

"No, let me grab a snack." Robin went to the kitchen to find some dried raisins. That was her preferred evening snack. She had already done the unthinkable—bought dinner at a fast-food place. Sure, she ate like a teen before she was married, but times had certainly changed. Ray sat with her at the kitchen table. Only two lights were on. Cars outside acted as the soundtrack to a quiet evening.

"I gotta tell you about today." She didn't always get to tell Ray about her day due to their competing work schedules, but she had quite the story.

"Oh yeah. Tell me about the meeting."

Robin suddenly had to pause to determine what to say first. "Okay. So, I went to the coffee shop. The executive guy shows up wearing a fancy suit. Brody is his name. And he offers for me to help in the campaign. They want me to be a model in the ads."

"Don't you have to look sexy to be a model?" Ray laughed out loud.

185

Andy Silvers

Robin slapped his arm. "Not for a college, perv. Uh. Anyway, they want me to represent the black community and wear my hoop earrings." She smiled ear to ear.

"That's great. You really are going places. We gotta celebrate." Ray stood up. "Ima make you a special treat for work. What do you want?"

"I don't really need—" Suddenly, Robin recalled Catherine's request. A cake was tricky to make, but Ray could speed up the process. "I think Catherine would like a carrot cake."

"Done. I know a great recipe." Ray found his cleanest 'kiss the cook' apron and began rummaging for ingredients. He hardly knew any Shanice recipes, but his mother had taught him a few things.

Mentioning work brought back a variety of thoughts including Kevin. "Hey, Ray. So…my coworker asked me to help him at his apartment."

Ray turned around slowly, his face bearing a scowl. "Who's this?"

"My coworker, Kevin DiGeronimo. He's been sad lately and he wants me to come by his apartment this week to help him with a room. I think Thursday would work."

Ray looked confused. "A room, huh? That sounds like a recipe for disaster. Is he straight?"

Her jaw popped open. "I think so. I mean, he is slightly— never mind. It's not like that. See, his roommate died and his room is now empty, so he wants me to help him."

His eyes narrow like those of Batman in the animated series. "Pretty sure he's an adult. Let him fix it himself."

Ray was usually less disagreeable, but this did involve his most precious gift—his wife. He didn't know Kevin like she did, so she tried to explain better. "I know what you mean, but I think

186

Hoop Drama

he just needs a friend. Pretty sure we'll just brainstorm ideas for the unused space." She anticipated his next complaint and spoke first. "Yeah, I know we could brainstorm anywhere but it'd be hard to plan without me seeing it. Plus, he just needs a friend. You know…someone who cares. Listen, Ray, I really am making inroads with my coworkers in a way I thought impossible when I started." Robin walked over and squeezed his arm, squishing her face on his bicep. "I want to make allies. Not just friends."

"I'll drive you there and pick you up."

"Huh?"

"I'll drive you there and pick you up. From the apartment. You can't go until after work and I'll be free to drive you."

His mind wouldn't change. His protective instinct rode in like a prince on his steed. Robin agreed.

"I also will come by Monday to meet him…so I know his face." Ray handed Robin the bag of flour to put up.

"I have to take Mom to work on Monday."

"We'll all go together. I mean, we'll drop her off and I'll take the cake inside to meet Kevin." He was now baking on his own as Robin prepared her complaints.

"But you'll have to pick me up too. It's like—"

Ray laughed. "No, we'll use both cars. I won't embarrass you too much."

MONDAY, MAY 14TH

Ray had the honors of visiting Shanice's coworkers today. Yeesh. They were like a high school click in some ways. They hung out like they weren't at work and talked gossip of all sorts. When Ray returned, he seemed confused.

"Those people don't shut up," Ray said, plopping down into the driver seat so his wife could rest her eyes.

"Yeah...but did they talk about politics?" Instead of answering, Ray just swiveled his head to face her, eyes wide open. "I'll take that as a yes."

"I didn't need a sermon, but that one small lady told me about media bias. She was saying that democrat politicians retire to jobs on cable news and that's corrupt...I think. She apparently has never heard of Fox."

Robin chuckled. "Yeah. It's good that Shanice is here to tell them the truth."

"Um. True, I don't remember what she said to them, but I know she enjoys her work. Just like someone else I know..."

On the seat behind Ray lay a delicious carrot cake with white icing. Robin briefly pondered opening a bakery with all these treats she was making. Inside, the receptionist opened the door so Ray could carry the dessert. He admired the modern design since this was his first time seeing the office.

Hoop Drama

"I forget you haven't seen in here yet," Robin noted as she stepped into the elevator.

"If that Kevin guy gives you any trouble, just let me beat him up," Ray said, speaking tough while holding a cake.

"*Shh.* Don't mention it in there. He's a nice guy…plus he loves our treats." For five minutes, Robin was the boss.

Robin punched into the time clock.

"Oh fancy. We have one of those where I work."

"Fascinating," Robin mumbled quizzaciously, heading down the hall.

"Ours is gray with a white button."

Ray could say the most useless small talk. Men had the ability to find something to say in every situation. Usually it would be pointless, but they'd expect their partner to react as though it's of utmost relevance.

In the Skwad room, Kevin and Jacob looked up at the couple. It was sad that Catherine hadn't arrived yet since the cake was for her. Ray sat the dessert down on the drafting table near the door.

"Oh," Robin said. "We're gonna put it in the employee lounge. I'm just dropping off my things."

"Okay, but I wanna say hi to your coworkers real quick." He approached Kevin for a handshake.

Kevin rose from his chair to oblige. "Good morning. Are you Robin's husband?"

Ray used his confident 'Obama' voice. "Yes sir. I'm the lucky man. I hear that you are hanging out with Robin this week."

Robin shook her head at his impression. The level of cringe charted an eight on the Richter scale. Even Kevin froze like an icicle.

Robin muttered, "Good lord in heaven."

"Um…yes." Kevin crossed his arms and looked at Jacob who

gave him a strange look. Kevin apparently thought transparency was the best bomb defusal technique. "I've invited Robin to help me brainstorm ideas on Thursday. You're free to come if you want." Kevin sat back down.

"Are you finally getting a new tenant?" Jacob asked, awaiting a handshake.

"That will be discussed."

Robin smiled, hoping for the best.

"You are?" Ray inquired.

"Jacob Alan Bradley," he replied, perfect posture as always. "I've heard so much about you."

He had not.

"Oh," Ray replied. "Well, I hope it's all the good things. By the way everyone...we brought carrot cake. It'll be in the break room, so help yourselves."

Robin smiled. But where was Catherine?

"No way," Kevin spoke with glee. "I'll get myself a bunch for lunch. Oh, that rhymed. Thanks, Robin."

Jacob seemed to have some level of respect for Ray because he said, "Much appreciated. I'll try some too."

"You're welcome." Robin grabbed the cake to help encourage Ray to get going. As she did, Catherine finally appeared.

"Oh, Robin. What's that?"

"It's carrot cake. I'm about to put it in the lounge. I thought you'd like it. By the way, that's my husband, Ray."

The third and final handshake commenced. "It's great to meet you," Ray said, leaving the room. Robin followed suit, heading to the lounge.

There, she set down the cake, opened the clear lid, and grabbed plates from the middle drawer. "Perfect."

"You are." Ray leaned in for a kiss. Robin returned the

Hoop Drama

gesture.

"Oh, hello." The sudden appearance of Dexter startled them. They reacted as though they'd been caught in the middle school teachers' lounge.

"Good morning, Dexter. Mr. Brennan. This is my husband." Ray offered a handshake from across the room but Dexter didn't reciprocate.

"Have you clocked in?" His tone was cold. He barely cracked a smile for Ray.

"Yes sir."

"Good. We should talk after *this* is done." He pointed to the cake with his entire right hand.

"Okay." Robin gave her husband a final hug. To make it seem like she wasn't turning the office into her private friend zone, she asked Ray to leave. "All right, sweetie. Thank you for helping me carry this. I'll show you downstairs." They walked past Dexter, who still gave his icy glare.

Inside the elevator, Ray spoke again. "I see what you mean."

"*Shh.* Yes, he's not the friendliest, but what boss is?" They parted ways at the locked door. Robin forgot to give him another kiss or even a hug since she had Dexter's command on her mind. Upstairs, Dexter was waiting. He motioned her to the client meeting room.

Maybe he knew.

"Mrs. Chapel," he began. Robin refused to sit down due to the barrage of butterflies swirling inside her stomach. She also began to mouth breathe. "The Major Collins photoshoot is this Wednesday. I have been informed that they want you to be in the photoshoot. I just…don't understand when they would've had the chance to meet you."

Dexter left that open ended. He must've wanted an

191

explanation. Robin hated lying, so she told the truth.

Most of it.

"I felt dizzy, and the college execs were coming toward the elevator and offered me some water. They asked about me and I said I work on the creative team."

"Dizzy?"

"Yes sir. I stepped out of the office when they saw me."

"Uh huh. Did they *ask* you to be in the ad?"

Robin had a clever answer for that. "No, but we talked about the struggle to afford college, and I guess they felt I was right for it 'cause I'm black. Who knows?" She played ignorant so well.

He appeared to relax, swinging one foot in front of the other. "Yeah. I don't know what's up with all this woke stuff. I wanted to make sure you were comfortable with the shoot. You're *our* employee first. Are you good to do the ad?" Finally, he produced a quick smile.

Inside, she was screaming 'Hell Yes!' Outside, she said, "Yes sir. I don't mind."

He nodded, then thought for a moment. "Mr. Proctor doesn't want guests past the lobby."

"Yes sir. I should've asked." That's all she could think to say.

Dexter didn't respond. He simply opened the door, inviting her to leave first. Back at her desk, a wave of relief washed over her, cooling down her body temperature. If she was going to talk to any more execs, it wouldn't be for several months. But now, the ball was rolling in her court. She opened her Smartsheet page, checking for the week's assignments.

A lot of finalizations had to be done. The process was an assembly line that kept starting over again. First, her team came up with a plan, then the design team created it, then the finances team coordinated payment. But the execs had to have their say during

Hoop Drama

Dexter's meetings. So, the process began again with the Skwad adopting the changes and sending everything to the design team. The fact that she still wasn't on that team was irritating.

Sadly, the other campaign had been unaffected by her meddling. The conversation with the Husk execs appeared to be in vain because the updated brief had a variety of notes, none of which included appealing to women. Indeed, the sexist and predictable ad remained the same. The biggest change was that Rover Callum agreed to break the brand formula by using a black plastic bottle. Yippee.

To make herself feel better, she combed through the MCU campaign looking for anything about the diversity initiative. Finally, inside Jacob Bradley's folder, a schedule popped up. It contained the digital images C.E. Proctor would provide for MCU. Under 'Video Acquisition,' the scheduled interviews would occur. It seemed odd not to just film it at the University. There was plenty of empty space. However, Robin grinned when she realized that Tanya Kushall would be in studio the same day as her. Good things come to those who wait, indeed.

Under 'Photo Acquisition,' Robin's photoshoot was listed. Her name was actually there. The page listed a few other images, but no names were listed. Instead, it just read STUDENTS. Robin finally got to see some of the merch ideas that Jacob had come up with. They were basic items like pens, hats, keyrings, folders, and even socks. Either way, the finish line was in sight, and she was running in first.

"Hey," Catherine said, peering around her desk.

"Hey. Have you tried the cake yet?" Robin asked.

"No. But I will. Anyway, don't forget the movie is this Friday. I'm *so* ready."

Robin delighted in her optimism. She would never have

193

imagined this result even two weeks ago. Kindness had paid off and hopefully romance would ensue that Friday. "Me too. It's gonna be a bloodbath." That was the last thing Robin would normally say. Luckily, Catherine loved it.

"I know! Carnage awaits." She got back to work.

Later, Robin found Kevin in the break room (of course) eating cake. He didn't even wait to open his lunch bag.

"Good choice," a confident woman said, approaching him.

"Yes. I imagine so. It was nice to meet your husband."

He had embarrassed Kevin a bit, so Robin performed damage control. "Sorry about his bluntness. He's gonna drive me to your house and back. He's like a hawk. I guess he can't stand the idea of me getting hurt."

Kevin set down his cake. "It's good to look after those we love. One day they can be there, then the next be gone. So, I wanted to clarify really quick what we're gonna do, then I need to go to lunch."

"Okay. We can go together if you want."

"No. I've got plans. But maybe later. Anyway, Neville's room is basically untouched. I just can't bear to move anything. I need an outside opinion. Someone who never knew him, I guess. If Ray will drop you off, then I'll make coffee so we can talk about stuff."

She smiled. "Okay. I can come by at 7. Does that work?"

"Yes. I'll text you the address. All right. I'm out." Kevin took his cake and rushed out.

Robin sat in the employee lounge eating her peanut butter and banana sandwich. It was strange how much was about to change yet, alone in the lounge, she was reminded just how small a fish she was in a vast sea.

At her desk, she found working difficult. Being a professional model was a big deal, and if Xavier would be taking the pictures, she had to know what she was doing. A quick search of black models brought up thousands of images.

Some images were a bit too sexy for the college campaign, so she focused on corporate shots. The models were great at making it look like they were in deep thought. If she wasn't careful, deep thought would just look like intense stress. Their mouths were typically closed and they always had a twinkle in their eyes.

Several models had hoops just like hers. Every hair style was represented from the classic afro to Bantu knots and even box braids. Robin had mastered box braids and could create them fairly quickly. That, plus a sparkly pair of hoops, would be perfect for Wednesday. On second thought, sparkles were distracting.

Dexter had called this shoot 'woke,' but he knew nothing about black culture. Or heck—American culture in the current year. While in the media women like Beyonce, Queen Latifah, and Lupita Nyong'o ran the world. In rural America, black queens went largely unnoticed. But Robin couldn't help but feel like a champion for being celebrated for just being herself. That's what Dexter missed. He had always been celebrated, and likely Charles too. They lived in a world of white corporate elites who never even considered the people beyond their small echo chamber.

Major Collins chose to shed a spotlight on her skin, not to say that she's different, but to say that she isn't.

ANYONE.

A joyful glee overcame Robin on her ride home. She blasted Whitney Houston and Patti LaBelle off her playlist. If Tuesday was exciting, Wednesday would be an absolute riot.

WEDNESDAY, MAY 16TH
Part One

The razzle dazzle was everywhere. The Chapel's bathroom became a sauna where steam and glitter floated through the air like stars in the Milky Way. A fashion icon was in the making.

"How do I look?" Robin searched for compliments from her husband who eagerly awaited her transition to professional model. At this point, however, she was wearing a tan business skirt and no top. Just a bright yellow bra that Ray found quite fetching.

"Amazing!" He had to put on shoes to keep from slipping as Robin had gotten up three hours early to prepare.

"That's just 'cause I'm not wearing a top." Robin giggled while grabbing a black shirt to throw on under the vest.

"Maybe a little."

Ray then grabbed her shirt, pulling it up over her head. She hardly resisted as he pulled it over her arms. "What are you doing? Ray!" He walked out with her shirt.

"That's dark green. It doesn't go with the beige. And are you sure about beige? It screams ninety-year-old heiress or widow." Ray had many suggestions despite never wearing women's clothes (or watching *Say Yes to the Dress*).

"Is it? I can't tell in this lighting."

Ray found her a similar shirt that was definitely black. Robin threw it on, followed by the vest, then the jacket. She buttoned both

Hoop Drama

buttons figuring that would look the most professional. With little time to decide, she chose to wear a pants instead of the skirt. The beige went well with her visible black undershirt.

Her dazzling hoops couldn't go in until she did up her hair and makeup. She did her quickest heat-free box braids in years. It still took ninety-six minutes, meaning a section on the front had to be styled differently. When complete, her sink was a mess of hair, holding jell, and rubber bands. After her makeup was applied, including a natural burgundy red lipstick, she was ready to add the finishing touch—the hoops.

Instead of wearing the hoops from her wedding day, online images seemed to recommend a sparkly style that catches the light from every angle. She had previously chosen not to wear the sparkly ones but loved the way they looked in the mirror.

"Wow." Ray gasped when he returned from throwing on a pair of shorts from the dirty clothes bin. "That's my woman." He leaned in for a kiss but access was denied.

"Honey, I just put on lipstick and I can't afford to ruin it." It's as though he didn't understand the art of beauty.

"Okay. Sorry to try to love my wife." Ray teased while admiring her look.

Robin touched her cheek. "Here." After far too many kisses, she made her way to the kitchen.

To avoid teeth stains, she settled for a protein shake with plans to gobble up a big lunch. She hadn't found anything dashiki inspired for the occasion, but the bright colors and tight patterns might not work well on camera, so another time would have to do.

But her biggest fan saw her next—her mother.

"My lord, child. Look at you! Oh yeah. Get some!" Shanice made it clear what she thought as soon as she opened the door. "Get out. Let me get a picture."

Andy Silvers

Robin stepped out and did a quick twirl. Her mom checked the quality of her braids and was mighty impressed.

"Did you use the no-heat method I taught you?"

"Yes, Mom. I did. Thank you so much."

"Wow. I don't know what to say. When I get my car working, I'm taking you out to lunch. I'll just say that." She gave a tight hug. "For what it's worth, I wish your daddy could see you right now."

Her father, Jessie Baxter, had left the family right before she left for college. No divorce. Just gone. But on days when her mother was unavailable, he had been faithful to help his daughter braid her hair. He had helped more than 150 times over the years before heading to work. Despite the current circumstances, Papa Jessie would always have a place in her heart.

"Me too." They drove to the center, where Shanice once again invited her inside. "I've already met your coworkers."

"You're not meetin' them, baby. You're showing off that gorgeous look."

She really didn't want a speech, plus she needed to leave now to be on time. "I can't. I have to get to work. But *you* should wear braids like this. I think it'll suit you."

Shanice grabbed her giant purse. "My coworkers don't really like them."

"What. Why?"

"I don't know, but you look wonderful, darling. Go in there and show your friends how a real queen behaves, huh. I believe in you."

"Thank you, Mom. I couldn't have done it with—" Shanice slammed the door. Robin smiled. "...without you."

When the building got close, a bit of panic creeped in, making her bones feel cold. She sat in the parking lot and took a deep breath. Then, against every instinct she had, she strutted into the

Hoop Drama

building, swung the door open, and glanced at the receptionist who took notice right away.

"Oh, my goodness. Robin, is that you?" She stood up to stare. Robin couldn't remember her name at all.

"Yes. Do you like it?" She gave a little twirl followed by a flick of her hair. Fashion had just met its next star.

"Yes. It's stunning. I just don't like the lunchbox." The young lady pointed to Robin's lunchbox which clashed with her business aesthetic.

"Don't worry. The lunchbox is not part of the look."

Upstairs, she clocked in and set her stuff down. Jacob was there, of course, and he gave her a strange look. "You don't need to dress up like that for the shoot."

"I know. I wanted to." Confidence had acquired a new member. It worked too as Jacob had nothing else to say. Digging through her work files revealed that the shoot wasn't until nine, but it didn't specify if she'd go first or the college students. She wanted to squeal so bad but knew that Jacob would judge her.

"What the…" Kevin walked in. "You look great, Robin."

That was the reaction she was waiting for. Now she squealed, ignoring Jacob's face entirely. "I know. I'm doing the photoshoot. It's really exciting."

"Maybe you can be our official model. Although, those hoops are a bit big."

There's some negativity, but none of it would penetrate the shield. "No. I think they're perfect."

Jacob asked the same thing Dexter had. "How did you even meet the executives?"

"Uh…they just saw me going into the elevator and asked about my life."

He furrowed his brow. "Really? Just like that? I doubt it." He

Andy Silvers

whispered the last sentence.

Her heart had no room for panic, so she just responded, "Well, it's not my business." Meaning: *it's not your business*.

Then, Catherine walked in. She didn't seem super excited. Robin had perhaps been too quick with assuming their friendship. "Oh yeah. The photoshoot thing is today."

Robin tried to fish for a compliment. "Do you like it?"

"Box braids are a pain in the ass to do."

No luck. "Yes, that's true."

"Did you bring any sweets today?" Kevin asked.

"No. Sorry." Her outfit was sweet enough.

Jacob shook his head. "Disappointing."

As if he even cared.

"Don't worry, Kevin. I'll try tomorrow."

"No. I'll make something for you. You know, when you come over."

Robin sat down. "Okay. That'd be nice."

"So, it's a date? Go get 'em tiger," Jacob teased.

"Robin and I are not dating. She's helping with Neville's room." That seemed to stop the teasing dead.

Spending the prior shift searching through poses left her way behind in her work. A queasy feeling returned that she'd last felt on exam week in university. The sense that she was behind was a concern, but one that she'd blame on the client if Dexter asked. She opened her email. She had seven new unread messages.

Speaking of Dexter, he appeared in the hallway as Robin made her way to the photo studio. Just a few yards away, she saw Tanya Kushall and the two other students walk into the studio. Robin waved but they didn't notice.

"If I haven't already said it," Dexter began. "I'm sorry they dragged you into the shoot. Despite our jokes, we never model in

Hoop Drama

our clients' campaigns."

Robin played along. "I understand, sir. It's a sacrifice I'm willing to make." She started walking toward the studio.

The smallest sacrifice in the history of earth.

"Hey. The interviews will go first. In the meantime, you should really get some work done. I know you didn't turn in anything yesterday after lunch."

Busted. Just like in high school.

"Sure. I have a lot to catch up on, but the thing is that I'm new to all this, and I'm nervous. So, I need time to learn the ropes." She was nervous but mostly she wanted to hear Tanya's interview.

"Uh huh." Dexter waited. Maybe he could be a decent guy sometimes. "Fine, but you'll work overtime tonight if you have to get caught up."

"Absolutely." She zoomed into the photo studio like a cartoon character. Xavier hadn't come in early, so he was still setting up.

At first, Tanya didn't actually recognize Robin. So, she jogged her memory. "Hey, Tanya. Remember me?"

Tanya grew a wide smile. "Yes. Rhonda, right?" She donned a plain white blouse and blue jeans. Her hair was pulled back into a pony tail. She was still gorgeous but she picked a safe choice, even choosing simple flower earrings for the occasion.

"Robin. It's a blessing to see you again."

The two gals began a lengthy hug. They had only met once before yet somehow, they felt like sisters. "It's so cool to be chosen. I'm nervous. If I had known I had to look like you, I might not have agreed to appear in the video."

"Oh no. I'm just an overachiever." Robin pulled the young lady to the side, being sure to smile at the other two students. "Listen, you remember that guy with me at the school?"

"Yes."

201

"Well, he didn't want you to be in the shoot, but I talked to the execs and got you in." Robin smiled but Tanya just looked confused.

"He didn't like me?" Her concern was real.

Yikes. Suddenly, she remembered that careful verbal articulation wasn't her strong suit. If she could rewind the clock, she would've just said that she championed for her behind the scenes. "Actually, he didn't interview any of the women of color, but I loved your story. It was inspiring, uplifting, and honest."

"Thank you. I bet he just didn't have time."

Oh, Tanya. Beautiful. Honest. Naive.

"Well, it's great to have you here."

"All right. Shush it." Xavier finally spoke. "We're doing interviews first. Please stand in that corner while I film. Will you stay silent? Yes, you will. Robin can explain what silent means for those who need a reminder." He plugged the video camera into a monitor by the stage. It showed a large, clear image of the scene.

A wooden stool was placed in front of a green background. Overhead, a mic hung down from a long pole. Bags of sand held the stands firmly in place. The young man, named Toby, was joined by Penelope Hafford. *Oh gosh*, Robin thought. Toby was that bait and tackle guy.

She had no problem with country guys or even hunting (not that she'd ever held a gun), but Toby just seemed like a snooze fest. Penelope, however, had dressed nicely to the interview and had great posture, so perhaps she would have a great story.

Since Penelope went first, Robin didn't have to wait long for an answer. Because the student was cool and confident, she studied her work for her own shoot.

"Okay," Xavier said. "I'm gonna ask a series of questions. Just answer honestly without going on tangents. Remember, we can

Hoop Drama

always do take two so don't worry about messing up. I've put this little toy on top of the camera. That's where you look. Okay?"

Atop the camera lens was a little rainbow-colored stuffed bear. Had Xavier bought a Care Bear for professional video work? Maybe. He stood by the camera, holding his laptop to read off the questions. Robin stared at the monitor.

At first the room felt cold, but the studio lights brought sweat to everyone's brow.

"This is my first time modeling. I'm excited to—"

"Hush, please." Xavier could hear the quietest whisper. "Please take conversations outside. Robin, remind them for me. All right, Penelope, I'm going to start recording. Allow me to check focus and then ask questions."

Oops. It was the timid Robin herself leading the conversations. Back in middle school, twelve-year-old Robin had used moments the teacher left the front as an opportunity to begin yacking about stuff from cute boys to celebrity gossip. Years later, her talkative rebellion diminished until she was a wallflower who nearly disappeared in the back of the class.

As predicted, Xavier began with the question she had emailed to Jacob in the weeks prior.

"What's one thing about you that's most unique?"

Penelope smiled to stall for time. "I'd say my most unique characteristic is my musical talent. I can play the clarinet and the violin pretty well. I've been studying them since I was ten years old."

A concise answer. She was professional, but Tanya was still more interesting. Robin quickly pulled out her phone, put it on silent, and opened up her contacts to add a new one. She handed the phone to Tanya while pointing to the screen. Tanya gladly added her contact info.

203

Andy Silvers

Then for the next four minutes, she and Tanya messaged back and forth, trying to better understand each other.

TANYA: *Thanks for inviting me. I am still nervous.*

ROBIN: *Don't be. I'm here for you. Just do as many takes as you need.*

TANYA: *Thx. I had no idea you were an executive here.*

ROBIN: *LOL. I'm not an exec. I wish. I talked with your school to get you in the interview.*

TANYA: *Thx. I hope I do well.*

ROBIN: *And btw the university is making their ads more inclusive with a focus on black voices.*

TANYA: *Really? That's cool. You're very smart.*

ROBIN: *Wow. You should meet my mom. She's awesome.*

When Penelope was done, Xavier called out, "Okay, Tanya. You're next."

"Oh gosh," Tanya exclaimed. "I'm next."

Robin got up too to guide Tanya to the stool. Meanwhile, Xavier had Penelope sign the model release. It wasn't made by Proctor Creative, instead, it was sent by Major Collins.

"You can do this, Tanya. Just tell them what you told me." Robin used the monitor to try to position Tanya just right. However, she didn't really need help. She looked great wherever.

"Is my makeup smeared?"

"No. You look great."

Xavier returned to check the settings. "Okay. If you were listening to the first girl, we're gonna do the same kind of thing. Just be sure to look at the teddy please."

Tanya glanced at Robin, her mouth widening in an awkward smile.

"You *did* listen to the first interview?" Xavier asked.

Robin knew her own BS answer, but Tanya was very honest.

Hoop Drama

"No sir. I was otherwise engaged."

"Okay. Well, just relax and keep your eye on the toy." He clicked RECORD then pulled up his laptop.

There was no place for Robin to sit closer so she stood by the large monitor. Toby played on his phone in the back of the room.

"What's one thing about you that's most unique?"

"So, my life has been filled with unique moments," she smiled from embarrassment. "I would say that my most unique thing is when I lived in Los Angeles. As a kid, I was asked to be in a watch commercial. I was only three and the director put me in the background in corduroy overalls." She laughed. "It was very odd and the clip is available on the internet, though I don't recommend you watch it." She crossed her hands, signaling an end to her answer.

Her voice was less melodic than before and likely that question wouldn't even be used in the ad. It was simply an ice breaker to help nervous students relax.

But it did break the ice. The next question Tanya was ready for, and she gave the answer Robin had heard before. Finally, Xavier asked question three. Now, with his interviewee fully relaxed, she gave an answer Robin hadn't been ready for.

"How is the world changing, and how has Major Collins prepared you for the future?"

WEDNESDAY, MAY 16TH
Part Two

With a melodic tone and a candor like a US senator, Tanya spoke. "The world is evolving to accept and celebrate people of color. But with a switch of the president or a change of an executive, progress can be pushed back exponentially. Major Collins is a champion for diverse voices and peoples whose stories are just beginning to be told. Even though my family has suffered hardship, I've never wanted to tell my own story. My goal is to use my voice to uplift black creators through social media marketing and brand management. Major Collins has many classes that offer these skills and I am so grateful to attend here. I don't intend to become an entrepreneur, but I want to support the thousands of incredible people who do."

The room went silent. Xavier waited for more until finally cutting off the camera. Afterword, he stared at the monitor, but he was clearly thinking. Finally, he spoke. "That was good, but we should probably do one more take of that last question…if you're up for it."

Crap! He didn't like her answer. He wanted a generic answer about how the world is competitive which requires students to get a great education to succeed. But that wasn't the truth. It was easy to think of white American businessfolk because they were everywhere. Steve Jobs. Bill Gates. Mark Zuckerburg. George

Lucas. Elon Musk.

But how many black entrepreneurs are famous enough to be named from memory other than Oprah? Hardly any. Tanya's answer, reflected her goal of standing behind the next wave of young talent, guiding their online marketing to millions of citizens. Major Collins greenlit a diverse campaign, but Proctor Creative had ulterior interests. Xavier *couldn't* be allowed to pressure Tanya into giving a different answer.

Robin leapt into action. "Xavier, I know that Ms. Kushall is nervous. Let's do my photoshoot real quick and we can film her afterword."

Shockingly, Tanya complied. "Yes. That'd be nice."

Xavier appeared annoyed, but he acquiesced. "Fine. Be ready after Robin."

Tanya nodded. But Robin needed to get her out. She waited until Xavier was switching cameras and pulled Tanya aside, whispering firmly in her ear. "Tanya, Xavier doesn't want you to talk about diversity. He wants you to change your answer."

"I can change it if it's required."

"No. You have to be honest. Listen, you need to sign that consent form and leave."

"*Leave?*"

"Yes, so Xavier can't interview you again."

"But what if he calls me back another day?"

"Just say you already filmed and you answered every question…which is true."

"If you insist. I trust you more than him."

Xavier had already mounted the Nikon camera and was about to turn it on. Tanya quickly signed the model release form. The darkness shrouded the letters on what she was signing. Then she scurried out the door.

Andy Silvers

"Be back in fifteen." Xavier peered over as she exited the room. Robin prepared herself, checking her makeup and texting Tanya a message.

ROBIN: *Keep me up to date. Thx.*

"Okay, so you'll hold this briefcase and stare off into the distance." He picked up a navy-blue canvas briefcase for Robin to hold. It looked empty and it was. Then he sighed. "You should probably lose the hoops. They look ostentatious."

Robin nodded and took out her left hoop, then it occurred to her. The only people who hadn't liked her earrings were men. But men *like* beautiful women, so what gives?

While any woman can wear hoop earrings, they were definitely tied with black and Latino cultures, dating back to Nubia in 2500 B.C.E. That was the problem. Xavier may not have known the history of African cultures, but he knew the modern associations and refused to accept them.

Not today. Robin quietly put the hoop back in, grabbed her briefcase, and made her way to the backdrop.

Xavier didn't even seem to care at first. "Hey, I need to change the backdrop real quick." He rolled a white backdrop over the greenscreen. Then his tenor changed. "Hey, you need to take them out please."

At least he said "please."

Robin stood strong, but spoke with a slight shake in her voice. Her unconscious fear guided her lips into a subtle quiver. "I was told—Mr. Brody Pearson said I could wear whatever I like."

"When?"

"When he asked me to be here. He said I can wear hoops. I asked about hoops."

Why did she justify herself to him? He didn't care about her answer anyway. He wasn't asking a legitimate question with the

208

Hoop Drama

goal of gaining more insight or better understanding his model. Xavier was used to models doing whatever he wants.

After a long silence, Xavier finally said, "Fine." He got the camera ready and gave instructions. "Don't look at the camera. Look to the right or left and be sure that your head isn't tilted down." Awe, that meant ignoring the cuddly teddy toy.

"Got it." Outside, she was cool and calm, but inside she was a spider on a hotplate. This was her moment to shine and boy did she shine.

After a few shots, Xavier altered the strength of the hair light. Then he fiddled with the camera settings. Finally, the shoot commenced. The lights were blinding, so when Robin looked into the studio, she only saw black. She couldn't even see Toby who was still sitting there.

Robin held the briefcase with a firm grip. She posed some with her hand on her hip and some without. She looked left and right just like she was asked. Her face went from serious stares to friendly smiles. Beyonce and Oprah had been her digital tutors for this modeling session. Though she couldn't review the pictures, the final one was still on the monitor.

Wow! Her eyes looked tack sharp and her earrings reflected golden light that created star shapes. She was a star.

At the end, she was thirsty. But her plan had to be completed. She walked over to Toby and told him it was his turn. She didn't ask Xavier—she just did it.

"Go find Tanya," Xavier instructed while changing the backdrop once more.

"Okay." It seemed that he would be fine having Toby go next, so Robin left, planning to feign ignorance if anyone asked.

Her desk was left intact, and the list of emails still sat there unread. Her coworkers looked normal; the same clothes and same

Andy Silvers

emotionless stare at a computer screen. Robin took one last moment to admire her outfit, to picture herself on the MCU website, and to see Tanya speaking about her career in an ad.

Then reality hit. Her next three assignments revolved around Rover Callum. She needed to help imagine the Instagram ads featuring the Husk design. However, instead of becoming despondent or allowing her joy to be compromised by a momentary setback, she sat up straight and got to work. Life wasn't always going to hand her treats upon a silver platter; temporary circumstances couldn't dictate her mood.

But after just a few minutes of work, a cold aura seemed to crawl beneath her clothing. There was someone standing behind her.

Yikes! If Dexter had found out that fast about Tanya, he'd win investigator of the year. Or Xavier, who was due to show up any minute. But it wasn't those two. She peered over, seeing that one of her coworker's chairs was unoccupied.

Jacob.

Robin turned around slowly in her rolling chair, keeping a straight face that maintained eye contact. "Yes."

The muscular man leaned in, pressing his palms on her arm rests. He was mouth breathing like Robin would sometimes do, so perhaps he was worried. But his eyebrows told a different story. He was angry and had choice words for his colleague. "I know what you're doing."

Uh-oh.

"What am I doing?"

He stabilized himself on his feet to avoid rolling the chair. "You're messaging executives. You're also making a mockery of this company—giving ideas and having tea time with the suits. Plus, you went behind my back to get that Tanya girl into the

Hoop Drama

campaign. Who *the hell* do you think you are?"

Her heartrate increased dramatically, especially now that all eyes were on her. Though Robin wished to get up and move the discussion to another corner—or preferably another room—Jacob had placed himself in the perfect spot to box her in. Unlike with Xavier, she chose not to try to defend her actions.

"Please give me space. It's wrong to harass a coworker." Her words were strong but her cadence wobbled like Nick Wallenda. She prepared her legs for a kick, just in case. He could react in any number of ways. Luckily, he pulled back, allowing Robin to stand up.

He stared at her with fire in his eyes. "It's wrong to play God too. We work as a team to deliver what clients want. Not what we want. Hm."

Finally, he returned to his desk, not even giving her a final angry glare. The conversation was over. Robin was relieved, but also scared. Yes—scared. She stared blankly at the computer screen, rigid as a statue.

Catherine only had a few words. "You okay, Jake?"

Without fully thinking it through, her earrings were shoved into her purse. Her coworkers could never see her how she saw herself, and that wasn't okay. She briefly considered crying, as if it was a conscious choice. Sadness. It came and made a home inside her frontal lobe. It didn't stay for long.

"ROBIN! You know where Tanya is?"

Yikes. It was Xavier, and he was making a show, unintentionally of course. For a second, Robin considered asking 'who?' but realized that was a terrible idea. She was never good at making things up. That wasn't her strength, not even as a child. But with higher stakes, she wouldn't confess to anything.

"Tanya…she left." True so far.

211

"Left? Did you ask her to wait?" He gripped the door handle like Jacob had gripped her chair.

"I did." Truth gone. "She didn't want to change her answer. Sorry."

He inhaled and released the door handle. "Ridiculous. And you had *one* job! We're not making a civil rights documentary."

"Inside voice," Catherine ordered.

Robin was chomping at the bit to remind him that the client asked for more representation in the ad. However small a victory, Xavier's admission revealed that Robin's guess had been correct. He didn't want Tanya to say the truth. A white-washed answer was so much easier.

But Robin was clever, remembering what had worked earlier. "I know, it's unacceptable. So many colleges seem to be pushing for diversity quotas now. Tanya said what she wanted, and I bet the college will eat it up. I bet they'll like every word." Goodness, that felt like speaking Mandarin.

Jacob gave an audible *Pfft*.

Immediately, she decided she would *never* say anything like that again. She could handle lying (to her surprise), but not dishonest messaging. Major Collins was valid in their choice to incorporate diversity. And Robin was proud to be a part of it. Heck, she would be immortalized on the website, not just looking cool but representing black college graduates.

Xavier nodded. "Next time, just tell me so I'm not wandering around."

"Yes sir." Crap. There was that 'yes sir' again. "I've just gotta catch up on a lot of work." Truth.

A lot of work did get done. In complete silence, the squad did their tasks. While clocking in, Kevin smiled at her, which was a highlight in a day marred by stress. But she used the silence to

Hoop Drama

reflect on her accomplishment. Despite not planning anything, she managed to convince a college executive to have her appear in a photo for the ad campaign. Three weeks ago, Robin would have laughed at the idea.

She was a queen, and she knew Ray would remind her.

❧❀❧

"Yes, girl. Twirl again." Ray popped open a bottle of wine for the occasion, but he hadn't thought to grab glasses, so the first sip was straight from the lip.

"Thanks." Robin had put the earrings back in once she pulled into the parking spot. She knew Ray would like them, and heck, so did she. "I'm ready to do the thing?"

"Yeah? Spend more of my money?"

"What? It's *our* money."

"Damn straight it is. You earnin' like a boss now."

"I want to set up the TV." Robin used her car key to rip the tape off her new 4K TV box. Ray sat the bottle on the sofa. He pulled the coax cable from the wall and picked up the old feather-light TV.

"We should donate this to the less fortunate," he said, placing the TV on the couch.

"Great idea."

"Like Carter. He's less fortunate since he don't got a wife. Ha-ha!"

Robin rolled her eyes whilst rotating the box ninety degrees. "Booty on *call*...."

"Booty on—Hah!" Ray danced his way over, putting his hands on Robin's hips. He tried tickling her, but it didn't work. Too many layers.

213

Andy Silvers

"Ray. Stop and help me slide this out."

Together, they pulled the white foam from the box. Then they grabbed the accessories and promptly threw out the instruction manual. "Hey, baby. I don't think this thing comes with batteries."

"It has to."

"Well, Ms. Priss. I don't see any." He opened the remote just to be sure. Nothing.

"We'll get some later." The new TV was slim. Only about eighteen millimeters thick and the stand had a snakelike curve making it resemble a fancy monitor. Also, fifty inches looked pretty big with tiny screen bezels.

Ray plugged the new one in while Robin consolidated all the trash. She placed it into the empty box, then joined her husband. "Hey doofus, you have to screw in the stand first. See."

"Fine." He chuckled as he grabbed the included screw driver. The stand was rigid plastic that seemed useless until all six screws were in. "Now I gotta get us some batteries." Ray walked out, snickering as he headed toward the bedroom.

Robin had set the TV on its stand and gotten the coax cable screwed in. They really needed to cut cable, but Ray hated to stream sporting events. After grabbing the remote, she remembered that Ray had wandered off. But hold on, the batteries were in the box after all. They were taped to the foam.

"Ray!" she hollered. No response. "That man would fall off a cliff if I weren't here." She bustled down the hall, calling out his name. "Ray. Raymond Deon Chapel!"

A corner-turn later, her eyes grew to saucers and her hand instinctively clutched pearls that weren't there. Ray was completely naked on their bed with a heart-shaped box covering his manly bits. He posed on his side with one leg angled to ninety degrees.

○ 214 ○

Hoop Drama

Holy moly. Robin wanted to make a joke about finding the batteries, but she was distracted by his pecks that shone in the lamplight. "How long have you been planning this?"

He smiled a saucy grin. "Let's just say these chocolates are half eaten."

Robin sighed. "Well, sorry to break it to you, but the TV's broken."

"What." Ray dropped his leg down.

"Yeah. It's on but there's a giant blue line in the middle."

"For the love of Mariah Carey. Nothing ever works!" Ray jumped up, throwing the chocolates onto the bed. Robin stepped aside so that he could walk his angry ass out of the room. And yes, she admired the dark side of the moon.

Ray stared at the TV for several seconds, trying to see the problem. He even unplugged and plugged it back in. "Robin!" he shouted. "Why you gotta do a brother like that? There isn't a line or—"

One jaw was on the floor. Robin had stripped down to her yellow bra and matching briefs. She hadn't had time to remove everything, but her message was clear.

"Oh *yeah*..." Ray sat next to his wife, throwing the chocolates onto the floor. Then after lying down on his back, he used his left hand to unclip her bra and his right to turn off the lamp.

THURSDAY, MAY 17TH

Despite not getting her beauty sleep, Robin was perky and alive the next morning to take Shanice to work. It was taking far too long to get the wreck sorted out, but Robin loved the chance to spend time with her mother, and of course, tell her about her incredible photoshoot.

"I've got news," Robin teased.

"You bought me a new car?"

"No. Better. Well, sorta. I did the photoshoot yesterday and I looked amazing!"

"I know you did. Let me see the pictures."

"I don't have them...or access but I saw one and I looked great. Plus, they put Tanya in the interview."

"Who that?"

"Mom...remember Tanya Kushall? She's the college girl from Major Collins who Jacob refused to listen to." Despite not wearing any hoops or a pantsuit again today, she showed some spirit by wearing a dashiki shirt and black dress pants. Her V-neck shirt was lined with stunning gold embroidery against a patterned burgundy color.

"Oh. I'm so proud of you for speaking your mind. I honestly didn't think it'd work." She chuckled after every third word, making her comment seem more casual than it should have.

Hoop Drama

Say what? "Why not?" Robin knew why not but she wanted to hear her mom's own words.

"Well…it's tough these days to speak up for social justice. Yes, if you're a millionaire popstar, it's easy. But regular folk like us got it tough. Plus, all your coworkers are men, right?"

"Almost all. Catherine is a woman, and OH! —I should mention I'm seeing a movie with her tomorrow."

"Really? I was gonna see that *Book Club* movie too. Don't ask me what book they're reading…" Her face carried a sly grin.

Robin had no idea what movie she was referring to, so she corrected the record. "Not quite. I'm seeing a horror film at an abandoned hospital."

Shanice was a bit of a blabber mouth. If Robin conveyed why she wanted to see *Post Mortem Prison,* Shanice might spill it to Carter. Or worse, act really weird in front of him to the point where he got suspicious.

Shanice leaned in and touched Robin's forehead with her palm. "Are you ill or something, baby? Let me get you to a doctor STAT!"

Robin smiled. "It's something I'm doing as a friend with Catherine. I'll close my eyes some."

"Wait! Is that the movie Carter is seeing? At his apartment, he was yacking on about this scary movie at a haunted hospital."

Almost busted. "Yes. That's it."

"Does he know you seeing that?"

What to say. What to say. She could lie like she did to Dexter, but that didn't feel right. After three seconds that felt like 100, the decision was made to keep the future-romance under wraps. "Yes. Catherine invited me and I decided to invite Carter." Her mom couldn't have heard why Robin was going since Carter didn't even know.

217

Andy Silvers

"Okay. Whatever."

To avoid any more political lectures, Robin stayed in the car. Though, luckily her mom didn't invite her inside this time. One day she'd know what to say to those people, but not yet.

At work, her nerves shot up slightly. Maybe Jacob had told the whole office about her meddling. If he wanted to get rid of her, turning the office into an anti-Robin zone would help. At her desk, she couldn't help but wonder how Jacob had found out her secret. But a quick retrospective revealed that her email was the key.

She had left her work email open when she left for the photoshoot and Jacob had only mentioned things that were written about. He had no clue she had purposefully interrupted the Husk execs. Speaking of which, she buckled down the entire day to catch up on their unfinished campaign. She even heard her coworkers chatting, perhaps collaborating, but if she couldn't do her own job on time, allies were a fantasy.

The best news was that Dexter left her alone, suggesting he didn't know about her meddlesome antics.

You're doing the right thing, she told herself, all without a hint of irony.

❀❀❀

"I can't believe how tired I am after just sitting and clicking buttons all day." She was exhausted after work. She went home to rest straight away, but Ray rudely awoke her from her slumber. In a slightly wrinkled shirt, she rode to the address.

"We can cancel if you need. He'll understand." Ray seemed energized despite working a job that should be more demanding.

"We're *literally* at his address. I'll wake up. I'm sure." She pushed open the door only for it to close back. One good kick with

Hoop Drama

her foot and her night began. Kevin lived about twelve minutes from the Chapel's in a midrange apartment. Robin had driven past it once before when trying to use a shortcut to the passport office. She had no use for a passport, but her family had recommended it. That was the value of family. They were always there.

Ray stayed put until Robin had waived him off, even forcing an impatient Buick driver to go around him. She pushed her box braids back behind her shoulders, then walked toward building 302C. The complex sprawled over a large area, giving each apartment building space for walkways and other amenities in between. Robin strolled past a tiny park where a young girl swung back and forth on a rusty swing.

Kevin's apartment was two-stories tall, featuring a short sidewalk to the front door. Narrow red bricks surrounded the beige netted door. A black cat figure stood guard by Robin's tennis shoes. Likely, he had been too busy to remove Halloween decorations.

Then, she rang the doorbell.

He opened the secondary metal door. "Robin, hello."

She briefly considered calling him Mr. DiGeronimo, but something in her hesitated to open with a joke. Ray could do it with ease, like he was friends with everyone, but not her.

She peered around the spotless area. The first thing anyone would see was the small kitchen table. "You have a nice place."

"Thank you," he said. He seemed slightly perturbed, refusing to smile while gazing around the room as though he were seeing it for the first time.

He pulled out a chair from under his walnut table. "Take a seat. I'll get us a drink and a snack."

"Sure."

He dressed unlike he did at work. At C.E. Proctor, he never

219

wore shorts, but tonight he sported gray shorts without pockets. He wore a collared button-up shirt, something he never wore at work either. It was an Aegean blue hue with white buttons and a fake pocket over the left breast. His eyes seemed heavy, like he was tired, but his body moved swiftly, like he wasn't.

In his compact kitchen, he pulled a glass container of sugar from an off-white cabinet. Then, he placed two mugs on the counter. Both were the kind of souvenir items tourists bought at gift shops. One was from the Orlando Sea World Park and the other was a Kings Domain design featuring the Jungle Xpedition.

"I like my coffee black with one sugar, but let me know what you want."

"Sure," Robin said, remaining seated. She could still see him through an archway. "Decaf please. Two sugars and no cream."

As silent as a butler, Kevin prepared two piping hot cups. Then, he sat down, crossing his legs with his chair pulled out from under the table. "I've got muffins for us, but I'd be rude to ignore you for too long."

Robin smiled. "Thank you." She hadn't a clue what to say. The time was 7:12 PM, and mid-evening naps were bad for her sleep cycle. "What kind of muffins?"

"Oh…it's good. They're banana crumb, and girl they're excellent. Neville and I used to make them before I'd go to work. I never had the foresight to bring them to the breakroom. Perhaps we were just stingy." He grinned while stirring his coffee.

Fleetingly, Robin almost asked if Neville and Kevin were boyfriends, but then realized that was a terrible idea since not only did they have separate rooms but Kevin never used the word 'boyfriend.' Plus, it was his choice to reveal things in his own time. "I'm excited to try them."

"I've got plenty, so you can take a few home if you want."

Hoop Drama

While sipping her coffee, she examined her surroundings. The sun had set behind the trees, sending a gold cast across the room. On the wall, an indistinct record hung. Behind her was a small patio with a dirty plastic chair laying sideways next to a bag of dirt. To her right, a TV stood on a stand. Next to it was a game console of some sort. Robin had never been allowed to play videogames as they were deemed too addicting. Below the TV was a basket full of what looked like DVDs, but they were probably video games. To break the silence, she inquired about the games. "Do you play video games?"

He looked at the basket. "Oh, not really. They were Neville's. He liked games based on real places like theme parks and historic monuments. Yeah, I'd be away for hours and that's what he would do. Either that or listening to music."

"Oh, okay. I like the Halloween cat you have outside. At least...I think that's what it is."

He chuckled, spinning his empty cup around in a circle. "Yes, that was Neville's favorite Halloween decoration. Really, I couldn't put it in storage or he'd pull it back out, so it just stays there all year round. It's funny since its left eye has fallen out in the rain, but that just makes it more spooky."

"Oh, really? I didn't notice that. That's funny." After another minute or two of silence, Kevin retrieved the muffins.

A gold-rimmed plate could only hold five of them. "Be careful. They're hot. Duh." Kevin placed them on the table, removing a blue oven mitt.

With a napkin carefully held below to catch crumbs, she ate the first one. "Wow. It's awesome."

"I'm glad you like it. I tried to think of something you hadn't brought to work yet but that was a freaking challenge. You brought cookies, brownies, cake, and lord knows what else. So, here's the

Andy Silvers

best I can do."

"Well, it's great." It did taste like too much butter had been used, but who complained about that?

Once Robin finished, he prepared a plate wrapped with Seran plastic for her to take home. Then, he stood next to the table, one hand placed over the other, waiting for the night to truly begin. He hadn't eaten a muffin and his eyes seemed distant. He was in thought, but not the happiest one. "Okay."

That's all he needed to say. She got up, throwing away her napkin before following him up the stairs to the second floor. Robin liked the idea of having two floors but not for an apartment. It was just too much space to maintain.

Finally, Robin saw the mysterious Neville Roseman for the first time. His picture hung on the wall next to the restroom. He was skinny and tall—easily five inches more than Kevin—and he was overjoyed with the thought of standing next to Cinderella at what appeared to be Disney World. She got the feeling he never needed to be asked to smile for photos. His heart was filled with joy.

"Here it is." Kevin pointed to the room at the top of the steps. The door was shut with an 'Under Construction' sign taped three quarters up. But he didn't invite her in. Not really. Instead, he stood totally still, staring at the door with his hands crossed, as if at a funeral.

Robin had no idea what to do. Right across the way on the left was another bedroom. It must've been Kevin's and the door was cracked but visibility was low due to the lights being out. Without asking, she slowly turned the knob, opening the door that creaked like a haunted house. The light was off, but she quickly switched it on. However, she refused to just walk in. Instead, asking, "Are you ready?"

Hoop Drama

He only nodded.

Inside, a queen bed featured an orange comforter with large cartoon eyes and a big smile. There were two small narrow windows and a two-door closet. Another picture of Neville was on the wall to the right of his bed. He had light brown hair that was fairly curly. He wore a navy-blue shirt and baggy brown shorts. Behind him was the Washington Monument. Apparently, he had great vacation time. Out of pure curiosity, Robin asked his age.

"He was twenty-five when the accident happened. Um…"

At the end of the full bed stood a large box. However, upon closer inspection, it was more than that. It was a cat bed inside a little house. It even had a fake house number printed on it. 214. Everything became clear upon seeing Neville's dresser. He had several pictures of a little orange tabby cat. One had clearly been taken inside his bedroom.

"Awe. Was this Neville's cat?"

"Yes. That's Liz. She was his best friend. Probably more than me. I called her Lizzy too." He still seemed uncomfortable, like he was wandering through a nuclear waste site.

Robin didn't quite know what to do. As sad as things were, Neville seemed to have a good life. "Did Neville work anywhere? Maybe I met him." She knew she hadn't met him.

Kevin inhaled slowly. "Uh…he worked at a grocery store in the bakery for about nine months but that was mostly it. He did pet sit some but I was always there too. So…" Kevin placed his hand over his heart. He placed his other hand in his pocket to prevent it from shaking. "He wasn't the brightest but he was…he was my sunflower."

Robin knew enough. Solutions were the next step. That's what she had been called over for after all. "Is Liz here?"

"No. I really wanted to keep her, but I just couldn't do it. She

223

Andy Silvers

lives with a great family on Buckner Drive now. Once a month, they call me with an update."

"Okay. Well, you have all the toys and stuff here. I think you should adopt a kitten." She wiped her finger across a dust-laden dresser.

Kevin's jaw dropped open. Then he crossed his arms. "I don't think I can."

"Do you want a new tenant instead?" She spoke softly for his sake.

"I *really* can't do that. Why should I get a cat?"

"Well…it might cheer you up. Don't get an orange one, and don't name it Liz." Proving her idea, she discovered an empty litter box inside the closet. Several empty coat hangers hung above the box and the only other thing was a gray vacuum.

"It's just…not really a great idea."

Finally, Robin took charge, using her strong voice for the first time at Kevin's home. "Kevin, buddy, you need a change. A cat or maybe a kitten is perfect. It'll certainly keep you from staying at work for hours at night." She sat on the bed. Kevin was still distant but certainly pondering the idea. "I don't want you to be lonely. If you want, we'll go to the pet store next week and pick out a kitty for you. I'll even buy the first round of litter."

He smiled. Something was clicking. "Maybe if you pick it out."

"Sure."

"Maybe…"

"I'll let you think about it." She got up to walk over to him. "Can I give you a hug?"

He flinched. "A hug?"

"Never mind. Let's go downstairs. Ray should be here in ten minutes. Remember, I'm going to see that corpse movie

Hoop Drama

tomorrow." Robin left the room and stood at the top of the steps.

That snapped him out of his daze. "Oh, good heaven. I forgot about that. You and Catherine are something else." He shut the door back as they headed downstairs.

"Yeah. I'm not too excited for the blood and guts but I'm happy to make friends. You know, it's not comfortable but look how happy Catherine is."

"Yeah. That's true."

"She's excited at work. That doesn't happen much. I won't remember the movie most likely—my eyes will definitely be closed during the gory bits—but I mean, that's not the point. I'm gonna remember how excited Catherine is forever. I hope you find peace." Robin smiled.

"Yeah. I hope you do too." Kevin handed his guest her muffins. "Thanks, Robin. I'm sorry I was rude. I just don't know what I want."

"See you tomorrow."

"See you."

She walked where Ray could see her, then waited in the dark. He pulled up exactly at 8 PM. "Hey, sexy."

"Hello. I've got muffins." She waved them in his face.

"Sweet. Life coach and matchmaker. Is there anything you can't do?"

FRIDAY, MAY 18TH
Part One

Ray seemed more ecstatic about the movie than Robin. "I bet you a new pair of light-up tennis shoes you wet yourself. I'll get some adult diapers for you after you leave."

"Shut up." She gave him a gentle shove. "I'll be fine. If anything, *you'll* need to buy some condoms for the evening."

Ray laughed aloud, covering his mouth. "DAMN! You are confident. If they are that perfect for each other, I'll eat my own shoe."

"I think it's possible." Robin put on a light jacket in case it was cold inside the building; on her feet were slip-resistant tennis shoes.

"Maybe they hook up in the venue. Like, what if they sneak off to a haunted bedroom?" Ray joked.

Robin corrected him in jest. "No, they don't have bedrooms like that in a hospital. But they do have bathrooms."

"Oh really? I can just see them making out in a dark room with Pazuzu staring at them from the corner." Ray laughed so hard he had to grab the countertop for support.

"Hah! Yeah. And he'll be like, 'Sorry, ghosty. I'm trying to score here.'" She grabbed the counter as well.

"Back off demon, I'm trying to get to first base!"

"Ray. Ray. They find a Catholic priest but he's more scared

Hoop Drama

of their sinnin' than the creepy girl. HA!"

"…or they have a make out session in the spirit dimension!"

The doorbell rang, requiring them to settle quickly. It still took a full seventy seconds before Robin could open the door.

Carter arrived about five minutes late, but nothing too serious. He came inside to say hello to his brother. Robin, terrified that Ray would spoil the surprise, rushed Carter out the door.

"I've got the keys, darling," he said, wiggling the keys to his 2015 Subaru Outback.

Robin began to mouth breathe. "That's why we're taking my car. Let's go or you're staying." Obviously, he could just take his car, but luckily her plan worked.

"All right, bro," Carter said, giving a fist bump. "I'll see you soon."

Her phone's map said the destination was more than twenty-three minutes away. "Yeesh. We gotta hurry."

"So, Raymond says you got to model for the agency…" Carter buckled up and used Robin's plug to charge his phone. Since she was using GPS, she really needed that, but arguing with Carter was much harder than Ray.

"Yeah. I was asked by the execs at Major Collins to model for them. They're doing a new section to spotlight diversity—my idea—and they asked me to model. But my boss, Dexter, is *not* thrilled about it."

"Really. So, it wasn't his idea?"

"Oh no. He only did it because Major Collins wanted it. Oh, and just so you don't think I'm a narcissist, I didn't ask to be the model or something. They asked me out of the blue. I'll show you the pictures if I can. Wait! They might be on our database. I'm trying to remember the photographer's last name…"

"Don't worry. I already think you're a narcissist."

Andy Silvers

"Gee, thanks." She checked her phone. It was at 67% battery. "You know the crazy thing? I've never met my boss."

"Really? How do you know he's pissed?" Carter leaned back in the seat, spreading his legs wide enough to give birth.

Robin had to think about that for a second. "No, Dexter is my supervisor. I should have said supervisor. My real boss, Charles Proctor, I've never seen in person."

"Oh. He's probably busy." Carter clearly didn't get the seriousness of the situation.

"Crap. Let me explain. He's the CEO of the company. Right? And his office is on the same floor I work—which is odd since the other execs are downstairs but fine—and yet I've never seen his face. Like…I've tried. He just disappears."

"Oh. That's weird. Maybe he doesn't like you."

Gracious, Carter. "Never mind. You're just like Ray."

The event was packed with cars. A group climbed out of a white van wearing costumes. Robin suddenly felt underdressed. She also realized she needed to somehow find Catherine in the sea of people and darkness.

"Just do it." She tried to find Catherine's contact info in her Smartsheet account, but her password wasn't saved.

"Are you okay?" Carter kept an eye out for strangers. He was told to keep Robin safe at risk of Ray slitting his throat.

Finally, Robin felt no choice but to reveal her secret guest. "Carter. So, my friend Catherine from work might be joining us, so I'm just lookin' for her." It was becoming abundantly clear that simply having Catherine *look for her* at the event was foolhardy. There were easily a hundred people there, and while that may sound small, the parking lot and building complex were rather large. The hills also made seeing into the distance a challenge.

However, after Carter and Ray had gotten in line, Robin got a call. "Hello." It was an unknown number.

[Hi. Is this Robin? It's me, Catherine.]

"Hey! Thank God. How did you get this number?"

[Your work email includes it in the contact info.]

"Awesome. Are you here yet?"

[Hell yeah. I already got my pass. You need it at the door. Are you in line?]

"Yes. I'll wave so you can find me."

"You didn't tell me about your friend," Carter said.

Uh oh. Robin assumed he was actually upset. He was not.

"I don't care. Relax. You look like you're being possessed."

"Hey, Robin…and company." Catherine was wearing a black dress akin to Morticia from the Addams Family. She even had some serious cleavage. Good for Carter but probably uncomfortable to wear.

"Hi," Robin exclaimed. "This is Carter. He's my brother-in-law. He loves horror so he'll join us." Then she tried to make the ship happen. "He loves gory movies and he's very smart. He works at a medical center and did I tell you how much he can deadlift?"

Catherine smiled. "It's nice to meet you." It would be much easier to ship the couple when they're both excited anyway.

"Hey. I'm Carter Chapel. It's nice to meet a fellow horror fan."

She shook his hand. "Cool. That's a pretty lame costume."

He had no costume. "Yeah. I didn't dress up. Though, I'm black, and to some people that's scary enough."

"Aha!" Catherine giggled like a high school prima donna. "Do you know how the intestines were made for the movie?"

Oh no. They were about to share gross stories about the film's production. Quickly, Robin faced forward and without trying to, listened to others' conversations.

Andy Silvers

"This is gonna be lit," a man wearing a Terminator costume said. His gelled hair resembled James Dean.

A young man with strong red hair was with him. He had no costume, although his shirt appeared to feature the name of a grunge band. "Like absolutely. I love the costumes people are wearing. They always go all out for these fright nights."

"True," the first guy replied. "If this place is really haunted like they say, then Angela will show up here with her next boyfriend...and it'll be the *last time* we see him."

The ginger guy squealed. "Wait. You mean Angela *Torres?* Gosh, that bitch is insane. How many boyfriends gotta die before the police investigate her?"

"They probably did, bro. They just can't find the bodies. You know how it is—no body, no crime."

She had heard of Angela once before but totally forgot exactly what she'd heard. Wheeling wasn't exactly famous for ghosts or axe murderers, so movie nights had to suffice as the town's supernatural entertainment.

Robin had already paid for her ticket; she just needed a physical pass to enter the main building. Behind her, an angry father argued with the staff regarding his twelve-year-old daughter. What a moron. The tickets were only available to ages sixteen and up.

"Let's sit here." Carter led the way to the third row back. It was pretty clear they were in the hospital's cafeteria, and it was dressed up with spooky imagery.

Robin hadn't noticed anything odd about her chair until Catherine pointed it out. "Holy crap. These are like electric chairs. I'm getting a picture."

Indeed, the chairs for the guests, excluding the last two rows, were fake electric chairs featuring real straps. Robin saw a much

230

Hoop Drama

scarier sight when she realized that she was between Carter and Catherine. That would *not* work.

"Hey, Carter," she said. "I don't like this seat, let's switch."

"What?" Carter asked. "They're all the same."

Men just have to ask stupid questions. "I mean, I don't like this angle. Get up." Luckily, he got up, allowing Robin to place the two love birds next to each other. Since the film wouldn't start for twelve minutes, the two of them shared stories. Mission success.

Once the movie started, Robin felt a chill down her spine. She truly hated movies like this. As a girl, she had trouble even watching *The Wizard of Oz* due to the wicked witch scaring her enough to hide. However, the opening was more cheesy than scary. After the credits, the interior of the hospital was revealed.

The plot featured deadly inmates who had died but somehow were coming back to life. They couldn't be let out since they were murderers, but they couldn't be detained easily since they couldn't die. They only way to stop them was to lock them up or remove their head. Yuck.

To Robin's dismay, the next scene featured a topless female guard putting on her uniform. Then, she entered the hallway to sit at her post in the control room.

Utterly pointless nudity. That's the kind of obligatory crap that every R-rated movie seemed to have just to be edgy. Proctor Creative would definitely do nonsense like that if it were allowed to. That shot had no bearing on the plot.

When Robin's brain returned to the movie, she had a big scare. A jump scare featuring an undead strangler had her gripping her wooden chair for dear life. After four minutes, she made her escape. "Carter, I'm gonna get a soda or something. Maybe pee too. I'll be back."

"Scaredy cat." Bullseye.

231

Andy Silvers

Instead of getting a drink, she went to her car. The movie was 134 minutes, and she had no intention of having nightmares for the next month. Her car glided down the road turning left and right at random places. Then, a familiar sight graced her periphery.

Mary's Diner.

The diner closed in a half-hour, but next to the Woodley's table, Carol stood, taking a late-night order. A smile adorned Robin's face. She seated herself at table four and waited for her server. Megan was surprised to see her old boss.

"Robin? No way. You look great. Braids are totally you."

Robin flipped her hair a bit. "Thanks. How have things been?"

"Uh. For a week or two it was crazy. We didn't have another manager so Mira had to sorta be that, but now we have Seth and he's pretty cool."

Robin nodded. "Okay. I'll just do a pumpkin pie and a decaf coffee with two creams. No sugar." She was elated to see her menu still there after all that time.

"Coming up. I'll get you a scoop of ice-cream too. You look a little skinny."

When Carol saw her old coworker, she bustled right over. "Honey, hi. It's been too long." Both ladies hugged like life depended on it.

Making Robin even happier, all the employees (the two who were serving) wore her hand-picked outfits just like before. "Are y'all still seeing families a lot?"

Carol smiled. "Don't you panic, dear. We're going to get you that watch one day."

She had totally forgotten about that conversation, and sincerely had no interest in digging up old debates. She just had a soft spot for Mary's. Simple.

"Just playing," Carol continued, sitting herself down across

Hoop Drama

the table. "Yeah, business has boomed. I mean, families live here. They were just going everywhere else. Oh, can you update the menus? I mean, you don't work here no more but I sure as hell can't do it."

Robin smiled. "Yes. I'd love to. I'll start tomorrow."

"It ain't gotta be tomorrow, child. Just by the end of the month."

She should have said no, but honestly a part of her felt like working for Mary's was a bit rebellious. She had left the small-town manager role behind but her heart always belonged there. And indeed, at Mary's she was respected, remembered, and seen. Definitely seen. Though nothing could quite replace $52,000 a year with benefits. "How's that child you're sponsoring doing?"

"Oh…Sereda. Yeah, he's good. I mean, sweetie, I haven't met him, but my eighty bucks is helping a lot. Look at me. I'm too old to adopt, but I can give some money, and I'm so grateful business hasn't slowed. So…yeah. How about you?"

"Um…I've been doing some good too." Her good was marred slightly by controversy and backlash, but still. "I've had more success at Proctor Creative than I expected. I was in a photoshoot so I'll show you that…I was given…" She actually didn't know how to phrase things. She hardly felt that she was bragging. It was simply difficult to paraphrase her accomplishments.

Getting Tanya into the video. Adjusting the marketing strategy for MCU. And making allies with Kevin and Catherine. But how does one use 'making friends' as a serious accomplishment? That's basic adult life. But of course, things were not all simple. Institutional barriers made normal activities hard. Finally, she figured out how to phrase it. "I've made a positive difference in the community with my work. And my coworkers respect my talents, even though I'm new."

Andy Silvers

"Well, that's good. I knew you were talented, so it's good you're happy."

Before she could ask about Seth, Megan returned with her food. It looked excellent. "Thanks."

"I'll go. I gotta do stuff, but come back soon. We miss you." Carol tapped Robin's hand then left.

Every bite was savored, not rushed. She actually hadn't had vanilla ice-cream in months so it was like meeting an old friend. Well…eating an old friend.

After a quick drive back, she parked in her same spot, then got a soda, just to be consistent. The movie was in the final act, so Robin closed her eyes multiple times. But instead of being questioned endlessly about her disappearance, she noticed that Carter was smiling. And laughing. And whispering.

They seemed like old friends. Perfect. Who'd have thought people could bond over grotesque violence and unnecessary carnage? Goth lovebirds maybe.

"That was easily the best kill," Carter whispered to Catherine.

"Yeah. I would've been able to duck down, but you said it."

Then Robin noticed something crazy!

Carter was holding his soda cup, but Catherine was sipping out of it. Love truly works in mysterious ways.

FRIDAY, MAY 18th
Part Two

In the glow of the screen, Detective Robin checked to see if Catherine had her own drink. But no. The people behind them must've thought Robin was insane staring at her friends instead of watching the movie. Catherine was definitely sipping out of Carter's cup. Who knows what she would sip next.

"I'll get you your own drink," Carter smirked. Romance confirmed.

"No, I'll get my own," Catherine got up and scooched past four people including Robin. "Sorry. Excuse me. Thanks."

Robin really wanted to ask Carter about the sipping to see if the relationship was truly blossoming, but the movie was still playing. She tested the waters saying, "Can I try a sip."

"Hell no. You got your own."

After the film, the group made their way outside. Unfortunately, Carter insisted on seeing the credits to prove to Catherine that a random extra was indeed Jackson Elwood. A few people went to explore the hospital, but thankfully the trio went outside instead.

Once the crowd could talk, they did. Chatter abounded everywhere and some people had clearly gotten tipsy.

Catherine pointed across the lot. "Look! You can take a picture with Hector."

Andy Silvers

"Who?" Robin inquired.

"Did you watch the movie? The guy with the guard's uniform and the chain belt." Catherine had savored every minute, and was referring to the primary antagonist. Or, considering it was horror, the protagonist.

Hector was the lead character for the undead crew who guided his fellow inmates during their escape. While the other criminals wore orange jumpsuits, he had stolen a prison guard uniform. Someone dressed like him was stationed in an outdoor photobooth under an iridescent sign.

"Yes. Let's get our picture taken." Carter grabbed Catherine's hand and walked toward the booth. Robin, however, noticed the long-as-heck line to the booth.

"Guys. Maybe we should go home or…" Every word fell on deaf ears. Begrudgingly, she waited with them in line. She almost wished they just got it on in the bathroom so Robin could leave.

"Do you have your camera?" Carter asked.

"Yes. My phone. Crap, maybe Robin should take the picture. You can use my phone, right?" Catherine pulled out her phone.

"I think so."

"Yeah," Carter added. "And use my phone after."

"No. No. Just give me your number and I'll text you the photos." Catherine gave a seductive smile which had Robin lifting her eyebrows above the clouds.

Carter cheerfully gave her his number. They touched phones to transfer data wirelessly.

"I actually have *Nightmare on Elm Street* on VHS." Catherine bragged with a wiggle of the eyebrows.

"Oh. I've got the Steelbook but it's definitely better to watch the VHS." Carter got one-upped by a movie nerd.

Catherine was happy to make up for Carter's failings. "Maybe

Hoop Drama

we could watch it together sometime. I guess you can come too if you want, Robin."

"Uh, well maybe I will." Robin really wanted to address the obvious romance budding up, but didn't know how. "You two seem pretty happy together." Oh lord, was that the right way?

"Happy?"

"Together?"

"Yeah." Robin began to regret mentioning it. Plus, the line wasn't done yet.

"What you trying to say?" Carter asked, glaring at Robin like he often did to Shanice.

"Yeah," Catherine joined in.

"You two had a good time…and you're exchanging numbers…so…" Robin tried to drop a hint, but they refused to pick up what she put down.

"Are you trying to suggest that we hook up or something?" Catherine asked the question like it was a crime but at least someone got the memo.

"If you feel like you want to." Robin's answers were getting worse and worse. Yet again, she began to mouth breathe. She shoved her hands into her jacket pockets and peered around them to the line that had moved up quickly.

Thank goodness, it was their turn. Catherine and Ray happily approached the creepy man with gray skin. They got into position while Robin waited next to the photographer.

The man playing Hector was enamored with the unwilling couple. "Nice Morticia dress, ma'am. I love it." Oh wow. His voice was not what Robin expected. It sounded like a college professor or maybe a mattress salesman. It wasn't the least bit raspy like the actor, and he sounded like he had a slight lisp. He smelled like barbeque and never attempted method acting.

237

Andy Silvers

"Oh thanks. It's not even a cheap costume. I bought a real dress and modified it."

"Great. Young lady, join us for the photo." He was referring to Robin. Only now do the odd-couple realize she wasn't standing with them.

Catherine provided motivation. "Come on, Robby. Get over here. We can show Jacob what he's missing on Monday."

Robby? What the actual heck? The thought of showing up Jacob was strong enough to get Robin over there, but she had "Robby" stuck in her mind now.

From left to right, Carter stood, then Catherine, then Hector, then Robin on the right. Hector (or whoever he was) put his gloved hand over Robin and Catherine's shoulders. Then the photographer snapped the photo.

"All right. Next," the photographer said, reviewing the pictures.

"Wait," Carter demanded. "You had your hand on her shoulder. Let's retake it." Carter positioned himself next to Hecter to alter the photo.

My shoulder, Robin thought. No. It turns out he was referring to Catherine's shoulder because the photo was retaken, but Hector was still touching Robin like before.

Apparently, it was only okay to touch Robin's shoulder because Catherine was off limits. "How do we get the photos?"

The photographer checked his laptop. "We email it to everyone who bought a ticket.

"So, I'll be able to see everyone's Hector photo?"

"Yeah. You'll get a link to our Friday Night Fright webpage and then you can download the full resolution image."

A small group of guys left the building laughing their butts off, inviting the group to explore the hospital. Robin stayed outside, texting Ray about her success.

ROBIN: *It worked. They are officially in love.*

RAY HUBBY: *Prove it.*

ROBIN: *She gulped from his cup!!!*

RAY HUBBY: *Score! I gotta see that.*

ROBIN: *Yeah lol. If they don't leave the hospital by 10, I'm out of here.*

They were a strange couple. Wait a minute!

Their couple's name was *CATHETER!* Oh my gosh! How ridiculous. She had to tell them immediately. She braved the crowds to rush inside.

Some people had moved the seats around to talk, but it was clear the double doors across the room were open. They had gone all out on the creepy aesthetic adding fake webs, red lighting, and skeletons on the floor. Down the hall, an unconvincing scarecrow moved its animatronic head side to side. An elevator was covered in fake spiders, but the button didn't work. She realized that a staircase hid behind the wall to her left. Upstairs, several people in costumes stood talking. One man jumped around a corner to scare his friends.

Tiles in the ceiling were missing, and the lights were out. The only way to see were work lights added by the event hosts. The building truly hadn't been used in years. A calendar inside the first room was dated for six years ago. Instead of adding decorations upstairs, the hosts of the event relied on the natural eeriness of the building to scare people.

"Carter? Catherine?" Robin made the first noise she had in several minutes. A young woman laid on the floor as if dead while her friend took a video; a strange choice of fun.

In the next room were several hospital beds lined up next to dusty windows. Robin jumped when a woman screamed outside

Andy Silvers

the room. Now she was anxious. There were people all around her; still she felt alone.

Finally, in the next room over, she heard Carter's voice. And hot damn—he was holding Catherine's hand. "See that? We could use that at my job." He grabbed a stethoscope off the counter. He put in the nasty earpieces to check Catherine's heartrate. With doctor lovebug doing his best romancing, she probably measured 190 beats per minute.

"Carter, those ear tips are gross." Finally, Mrs. Rationality arrived to ruin the fun.

"Hey, Robin. There you are. I thought you'd died." Carter took out the device and threw it onto the dusty counter.

"Yeah. I thought she'd gotten possessed by a demon."

"Well, you're gonna die when you hear your couple name. Get this. *Catheter!* Crazy, huh? Catheter!"

"What are you saying?" Catherine asked.

"It's your couple name." Robin made herself laugh like a toddler. It must've been time for her to go to bed. They didn't seem to think it was funny.

"I never said we were a couple. We're just having fun."

Catherine seconded that. "Yeah. Adults can have fun too."

Really? When was the last time Catherine had fun with a stranger by sipping his drink and holding his freaking hand?

They were insufferable. "Fine. I give up."

"Thank you." Carter led his not-girlfriend to the next room. It was unsettling to say the least. A stark white hospital bed lay centered in a decaying area. Glass panels were missing from the window where headlights shone through. A mangled wheelchair stood ominously in the corner beside a smashed heart monitor. Carter took a step onto broken glass which caused him the least bit of concern.

Hoop Drama

"Maybe we should leave." Robin had said that twice before but they hadn't heard it. Thankfully, Catherine checked her phone.

The time was nearly 11:00 PM. "Yeah. I have to get home."

"Okay, let's go." Carter was fast when *she* asked.

With half as many cars in the lot, it was easy to find their spot. The engine revved up but the not-couple stood talking outside. Robin rolled down her window. "Hey, Carter. It's now or never."

"I think I'll let her take me home," he replied.

"What? But your car is at our house."

"Oh yeah. I'll pick it up later. Catherine wants to show me her apartment first."

For real? Maybe playing hooky with Pazuzu was more probable than she thought. "See. I knew you two were into each other."

Catherine jumped in. "Yes, but it's none of your business."

What the heck? Good gravy, these two. "Not my business?" Robin protested. "I set this whole thing up!"

A brief pause precipitated a hasty escape.

"What do you mean you set this up?"

"Yeah. You don't own the hospital," Carter noted.

The window could not go up fast enough. Robin cranked up the radio and made quick work of the peddle. Her speakers blasted pulsing EDM while the odd couple watched. When Carter returned to get his car, she was sure to lock the apartment doors.

"She did *not?*" Ray watched college football on his fancy new TV.

"I'm dead serious. They were handsy and everything. I offered to take him, but now he's at her apartment doing lord-knows what." She checked her email for the Hector photo, but it hadn't been sent out yet.

He rested a beer on his stomach. "Wow. Is he gonna get his

Andy Silvers

car tonight?"

"He's gonna get a ride. That's for sure."

Ray burst out laughing, requiring him to set his beer down on the coffee table. "Did they really get handsy? Like caressing and touching or something?"

"Um…not like that. They held hands mostly, but I wouldn't be surprised."

"How did you survive the—?"

"But guess what? I know their couple name…Catheter!"

"Cath—HA! That's hilarious."

Right then, she thanked her lucky stars God had brought Ray into her life.

MONDAY, MAY 21ST

A shiny new bracelet adorned Catherine's delicate wrist on Monday morning. It wasn't the usual attire featuring a skull with vines growing out or a black cauldron. It was just nice silver jewelry.

Carter's gift for sure. While logging in, she inquired about its origin. "Is that from a certain handsome man?"

Catherine gave a coy glance. "Yes. It's not that expensive but it was just a way to say 'thank you' for taking me out."

"Out? On a date?"

"Um…not really. We just went to the mall and checked out a new Thai restaurant. It wasn't really a date, but it felt nice."

How's going to a fancy restaurant not a date? It didn't matter. What mattered was that Catherine was happy. "Great news. You two are a great match." She pulled up Smartsheet.

"Robin…I know what you meant. You meant that you invited him to meet me. That's really sweet."

Awe. Robin nearly cried. If it weren't for her password not working, causing her mild acrimony, she'd have opened the floodgates. Turned out caps lock was on.

Then, Kevin entered. "Hey, I brought two muffins with me, but I ate one so there's only one in the break room. I guess I don't quite have the hang of it." He smiled.

It was incredible how one weekend can feel like an eternity. She had to get back to the Major Collins campaign, but it felt like a distant memory. She needed to update what she had previously started, and probably collaborate with Kevin or Catherine. That way her work would be up to company standards.

But before starting anything in earnest, and after seeing Jacob come in late, she got a call. It wasn't a number she recognized, though it was the familiar 304 area code. She hung up. They could leave a voicemail if needed.

After signing into Smartsheet, she checked on the updates. A link appeared to an unlisted version of the new MCU diversity page and NO WAY! The paragraphs Robin had created were there. The execs had asked that the diversity page not be located under 'Campus Life.' Instead, the new diversity page was listed under 'Our School' in the top header. To add to the shock of it all, Robin's picture appeared there under 'Campus Life,' just like she expected. Wow! She looked stunning. Her hoops were dazzling, her skin was flawless, and the lighting was impeccable. No, she wasn't a student like the other two people, but she didn't care. She ripped her smartphone out of her purse to snap a picture. Then, she realized a screenshot would work better. A squeal made its way into her throat but was detained from exiting her lips.

Then, Dexter appeared in the doorway. "Robin Chapel, please answer your phone. Follow me."

Thoughts flew in and out like rockets. On the way out was any semblance of joy or excitement. She wanted to text Ray the screenshot but that thought was already in the air. Then she realized that Dexter had called her—something he never did so how could Robin be at fault? Then, the final thought landed on the runway.

She was in trouble.

Hoop Drama

But it couldn't be. Either way, her teammates had gone silent. They stared at her as she rose up, except for Jacob who had better things to do. She grabbed her purse and clutched it with both hands. Dexter avoided the elevator and took the stairs.

If Robin was headed to his office, this would be the first time. Indeed, she was. She saw the strangest thing she'd seen in a while. On his wall was an 8 by 10 glossy of president Trump. It had been edited to depict him shirtless with rippling abs while riding a velociraptor. Utterly ridiculous.

Before she could study the rest of his office, he began what would be a disheartening conversation. Dexter minimized his open programs, which felt like an eternal process. "Robin, we have a problem." He stared at her like he expected a nod of agreement. She gave him nothing but an empty glare, then his voice dropped a few octaves. "We, we being Charlie and I, have noticed that you've been messaging the Husk execs without our knowledge."

He knew. But how much did he know?

"Same with the Major Collins people. I couldn't for the life of me figure out how you'd gotten into the college campaign, and then finally, I got it. You *asked* to be in it." He furled his brow as though threatening her with a sentence.

"No." Robin gave the meekest response of her life. She wasn't sure he even heard it.

"No? Then how did it happen?"

"I bumped into them by the elevator and I just told them about my life. It was hard for me to go to college…and I guess they found that inspiring."

"You guess, huh?" He stared with daggers in his eyes. Robin's chest pulsed like a bass drum. "What about this diversity nonsense? Was that your idea?"

Uh oh. A simple question with a simple answer. Yes. But it

245

Andy Silvers

was something nearly every major company did, so it wasn't like Robin invented it. Also, diversity was not nonsense. It was reality. "I've always championed for inclusion and the execs probably liked that idea, but I never made them do anything…"

He scowled for a moment, then grabbed a printed piece of paper. It was a printed email from Brody. A portion was highlighted in yellow.

Your talented artist Mrs. Chapel was instrumental in guiding our campaign in the right direction. Great ideas can come from anywhere.

Every word of that was positive, yet Dexter surmised the wrong conclusion. "Our clients shape our work. Not random employees with big mouths. This woke nonsense has to stop."

"What does *woke* mean?" That question had more purpose than she thought, giving her insight she needed while buying time as well. Time for what? Time to put together a valid excuse that was worded properly. She lacked an advanced vernacular and a gift for articulate summation.

"Woke. It's a left-wing thing. It's hard to define but you know it when you see it. Robin, the point is that our company has a hierarchy of management. Mr. Proctor and I have talked about this and it's clear that you have no experience answering to the chain."

And no training.

"We didn't hire you for your fresh take on current affairs. We wanted a team player who could learn on the job."

"Mr. Proctor…" Robin said, almost in a whisper. "Can I talk to him?"

"No. He's busy. Your behavior has—"

"He's always busy."

Dexter paused. He had (seemingly) never been interrupted by an employee before. Robin felt guilty. She saw in herself a similar defiance to Sarah or another rebellious employee. But she wasn't like that. She was kind and friendly and respectful. But somehow Dexter (and Jacob) had a way of crawling under her skin and tearing through like a parasite. They launched personal attacks in ways no one had done before and made Robin an enemy.

She wasn't defiant, but she was growing more courageous. Words had to be chosen carefully. One word of hate or dishonesty could jeopardize a month's work.

Dexter sighed. "Yes...he's the boss. Your behavior has been narcissistic and you've put yourself ahead of the company. Need I remind you that you're still in your trial period. That's three months where you can be terminated at *any* time for *any* reason."

She gulped. Was this her last day?

"Mr. Proctor wants you here, so you'll stay. But be warned. I'm counting this as strike *one* and *two*. That's all." He returned to his work, ignoring Robin completely.

A cyclone of thoughts spiraled in her mind, and she needed to get out of the office for her sanity.

She took the stairs yet again, pausing to collect herself. She was mouth breathing, but more revealingly she was crying. There was no warning; just uncontrolled emotion. A tight grasp of the railing with both hands served to steady her soul.

With a deep breath, she pondered many questions. Last of which was 'how had Dexter found out?' At first, she assumed that he had simply checked her email, but then Jacob became a suspect. Why had he been so calm during Dexter's cold entrance? He's the first employee to discover her secret, after all.

The story was now very simple. He *hated* her, so he turned her in. It was a by-the-book calculation done by an unfeeling coworker to tear down her identity. In doing so, she would become employee number four and nothing more. He nearly succeeded at erasing

Andy Silvers

Robin Chapel.

Back at her desk, her tears were gone, replaced by anger. Despite her emotional nature, rare were times when she took things personally. The excuses that worked to quell her pain before didn't work. For the first time, passion was the engine. She began work on her assignments, knowing that getting behind would make things worse. As for her allies, one had been irreparably severed.

While checking emails, a new message from Brody appeared. She read it quickly, but knew better than to respond.

Mrs. Robin Chapel:
Thank you for your work in our campaign. We have yet to see the final results, but I have seen the raw files from your shoot. We believe in you and your initiative to bring black voices to the forefront. Hopefully, we will be finished with the campaign (the agency part) by June and we can discuss further opportunities to talk. Perhaps you could speak at our Tuesday night event. I will discuss options with the board. Thank you and best of luck.
Kind regards,
Dr. Brody Pearson, PhD

Every fiber in her body wanted to reply. Like a rudder on a cruise ship, Robin wanted to direct every ad campaign and guide the ship to diversity island.

But…reality.

She reread the email slowly, ready to respond covertly. In her private email on her phone, she sent a quick response.

Dr. Brody Pearson,
Thank you for your kindness. It has meant a lot. This is Robin Chapel from C.E. Proctor Creative. Upcoming is the historic date, June 19th, also

called Juneteenth. It means a lot to our community to celebrate this date as a nation. I'd be happy to advise your team. My faith in America is restored when citizens speak, and people LISTEN. Thank you. We'll keep in touch.

Robin Chapel, B.A.

A moment was needed to process that reply before hitting send. Had she gone too far? Ultimately, Brody's original offer was a courtesy, not a reward. She hadn't earned that respect or attention. But after Dexter belittled her (at least he did so privately), she felt ready to charge into battle atop a galivanting stallion like a prince charming, ready to save herself. The worst Brody could do was say 'no.' *But that wasn't true.*

He could turn her in to Dexter. He wouldn't even know he was condemning her to termination. Frankly, that email seemed like a smoking gun claiming Robin was the orchestrator of everything. But not so. Brody was simply being nice by giving her more credit than she actually deserved. It wasn't really her 'initiative,' except in so far as C.E. Proctor Creative's social messaging. Before Robin, they'd likely never done anything like create an 'Our School' page with a diversity section.

Maybe if she was fired, he would hire her on at Major Collins, liberating her to continue her work free and clear. But life was never so easy.

Despite her anxiety, she hit SEND.

※❀※

"Should you really eat that much chocolate?"

"I'm trying to relax." Robin had opened a box of Hershey bars and eaten at least half. Ray was right (once a year) but chocolate made a girl relax. She was terrified at getting caught and angry at Jacob for ratting her out. She was in the pits of Hell while her campaign was soaring with the angels.

A gentle hand stroked her hair. "Baby, I know it'll be okay. I believe in you."

This was the one time being married to him didn't help. Of course, *he* believed in her. But what about the world? Or her friends. "I was asked by Brody for help using my work email. Is that wrong? And it's not like I carried some bitterness into work. My work *was* the problem. You know what I mean? If those stupid men weren't racist!"

"Whoa," a calm voice replied. "You don't know they're racist. I'm not allowed to fix cars *my way*. I have to do it their way. It sounded like Dexter was professional with you."

A professional douchebag. "He made a lot of assumptions. And what about Jacob? That bastard was looking at my emails a few days ago—he told me he was. Then, the day I get caught, he doesn't even look up when Dexter calls me. It's just…"

"Relax. I've got you." Ray wrapped his arms around her while gently removing the chocolate from her hands. "You know who would be proud of you? Shanice. By the way, you're taking her tomorrow because I've heard enough about whether dogs dream or why insurance companies are evil."

Robin chuckled. Shanice was her fortress. "I know."

She wanted to call her mom, but a long yawn put a pause on that. Being the gentleman he was, Ray guided her to their bedroom to sleep. He also probably enjoyed removing her shirt.

Now an exhausted haze weighed on her. She stared blankly at Geppetto as it bumped her feet. When her mind returned, she asked a question. "Where's my chocolate?"

"You ate all of it." He was smooth. "Hey," he said, hastily

Hoop Drama

turning off the lights. "Let me tell you a story. Okay. I got told on to my boss by a customer today."

In her groggy state, she looked at him from the comfort of her pillow.

"Her name is Donna, which is fitting because she's a prima donna. Anyway, we do an align and balance on her car—some sort of minivan. Then, I offer an oil change since she was due. She had a Kia I think and she said they recommended synthetic oil." He checked his spouse.

"Kia's are good."

"You paying attention? There's gonna be a quiz tomorrow."

"Yay…"

"She says that her husband trusts the dealer because they always treat her right; and I say that could work, but synthetic oil is more expensive. Yes, it lasts longer, but I just explained her options. Then, she says that I'm just trying to sell her *our* oil to make a quick buck, and I say 'no.' Not at all. But I'm not kidding when I say her face was furious. She had the biggest eyes I've ever seen and her tiny lips were pushed together so hard, I thought her Botox would be squeezed out of her ears."

"I can see that."

"Yeah, I know. Then she says she'll just get the synthetic oil from her dealer. I say 'okay.' Problem solved, but no! She still wants a quote on our oil. I give her one—it's about $65—but she doesn't know how much Kia's price is for synthetic since her husband always does it."

"Hm."

"But she knows our price is high because she's magically an expert. So, I say that's fine; we'll do it another day. Then as I ring her up, she decides to do the oil change anyway so her husband won't get mad at her. So, I ask if she wants synthetic or regular and

Andy Silvers

she's *pissed* that I didn't tell her we had synthetic. She thinks that ours is the same as Kia, but I don't know since I'm not there."

"Oh…"

"Then she says I'm giving her an ulcer by changing my story every five minutes, and she goes over to complain to my manager who literally sells her the most expensive oil we have. She's an absolute crustacean."

"…"

"Goodnight, my princess. I'm gonna finish your chocolate."

TUESDAY, MAY 22ND

The early riser disabled her alarm and plodded into her kitchen. She found the Hershey's wrapper in the trash can. The last thing she wanted to do was go to work, but she was the breadwinner.

There were no emails from Brody yet, but soon she hoped to see one. Maybe she could make her work with them off-the-record, allowing it to stay separate from the ad agency. Either way, she'd have the chance to tell Shanice about it on the way to work. A hot cup of coffee precipitated a hot oven. Despite her concerns, she made an easy-bake cookie recipe.

Kevin still wanted to find a kitten with her that week and baked goods were a great conversation starter. Though, that thought didn't occur to her until after the cookies were done. Her routine had become subconscious.

As she drove her Fit to her mother's house, she began to perk up. The only person who could understand her struggle was her mom. She had been there and done that.

Shanice was equally perky while hopping into the front seat. "Oh, baby. I tell you; miracles do happen." Shanice bore a strong perfume smell; something she rarely used. Maybe she had a secret date later. "My car is gonna be fixed! It'll take a few days because heaven forbid, but it's happening. That stupid bitch who hit me— her name is *Carol*, of course—is gonna pay up big time. Ha-ha!

Andy Silvers

Thank you, Jesus."

Her joy was infectious. "Wow, that's great. Is that why it's not in your garage?"

"Yes mam. And my record is clean. Cleaner than your car! Oh, what is that smell. Is it chocolate?"

"Yes, Mom. I made cookies for work—"

"Yeah. I forgot you do that. How's work going, by the way?"

Robin's mind focused and her grip tightened. "I actually wanted to talk about that. My boss found out. He found out about my meddling—though I wouldn't call it that, but still—he knows. Mom, he knows."

She seemed confused, but it was hard to tell while she applied lip gloss. "Oh. I knew you were having trouble. What were you doing behind his back?"

Robin hesitated to answer that. Shanice already heard some of the story, but in truth, only Robin knew all the pieces. Guilt built up for lying to her boss, but he had it coming. Plus, Xavier was the one manipulating events by discouraging Tanya's testimony. He didn't ask Dexter for permission. And Jacob refused to interview more students. He didn't ask for permission. The only one who needed her hand held was Robin. "I emailed the executives about diversity. One of them is Brody and he helped get me into the photoshoot."

"So, it was the men's idea?" Shanice didn't seem fully invested, but maybe after a few more sentences she'd get it.

"Yes, part of it. See, they asked me to be in the photoshoot. It wasn't my idea, but it was my idea to email Brody about ideas. And it was my idea to…never mind."

"What? Did you steal money?"

"Mom!" Goodness, Shanice jumped to conclusions a lot. "No. I would never. I thought—It's just that I got Tanya Kushall into

Hoop Drama

the photoshoot and then I made sure Xavier couldn't change her testimony. But I'm not sure Dexter even knows about that."

The vibration of the engine seemed loud amid an abrupt silence. She really only scratched the surface of the situation, but it was indeed a long story.

"So, you have nothing to apologize for?" Her mom was fully attentive now. What stung was that she'd asked the same question to little Robin too. She'd lie and say she didn't do something bad, but her mother would ask that simple question.

So, you have nothing to apologize for?

Robin ran out of ideas. What was the truth? Maybe a little of both good and bad. "I need to apologize for being angry and letting my feelings get the better of me. And...I guess...I need to apologize for being sneaky. I just wish I could tell the truth without—"

"What? Consequence? Honey, Martin King was assaulted and sprayed with water cannons. People who say what's true aren't given crowns on this earth. They're vilified."

Robin's jaw began to quiver. Is that what social justice looked like? Failure. Turning the other cheek. People don't change the institutions by capturing the entire entity. They change the people inside the institution one by one. On the shoulders of giants, it was so easy to see the greener grass, but in reality, the giants were just lifting people up to the next level.

"I won't get a crown in this life..." Shanice became somber as well, placing her hand over her heart.

"No...you will."

The next four minutes went by rapidly in complete silence. Robin put on a brave face, hopping out almost without trying.

"Hey," Shanice reacted. "You going in?"

"Sure. You're proud of me, right? I want to be strong, even

when it's hard."

Her mother's face was not what she expected. She raised her brows and clenched her lips together. She hadn't been there when Robin received her first political lecture, and she likely enjoyed her coworkers. She couldn't see the front desk as a warzone if she tried. But to Robin it was the first test.

"Mrs. Church!" Brooke called out, as if seeing a friend. "You're back."

"It's Chapel," Robin corrected. It felt good to be assertive. Her heart still pounded, but her mind felt alive.

"Oh gotcha. I forget you're not a Baxter." Brooke was accompanied by Gina—an older lady Robin hadn't met yet.

Gina had gray roots and blonde dye. She was likely around Shanice's age, but her skin was less smooth. She had slightly yellow teeth hiding behind crimson lipstick. She was married, and she bore a shiny cross necklace over her work shirt. If 'sweet pea' were depicted visually in the dictionary, she might be its representative.

Shanice sped into the back room behind a white door. Robin wanted to follow to avoid being alone, but a new bolder side of her took charge. *They're just medical staff,* she thought. *What could go wrong?*

"You work at the ad agency?" Gina started, typing faster than a professional novelist.

"Yes," Robin said, sliding closer to the front desk. "I work in the creative department."

"Yes. She's an artist." Brooke chimed in. Everyone seemed to know Robin better than she thought. Her mom must have given them an oral biography.

"I design things, but at C. E. Proctor, I help the team brainstorm ideas. I was even on the website." That didn't come out

Hoop Drama

quite like she meant it. Robin still lacked the skill of conciseness and careful articulation. That was something the Obamas were better at.

"Wow," Gina noted. "You worked at a restaurant then got hired at the agency? Impressive."

Maybe things would be cordial. It was indeed a huge gift, even if things hadn't quite ended how she'd like. "Thank you. I used to work at Mary's Diner."

"Yes, I saw you there. I heard you added table cloths and change lightbulbs." Gina smiled wide but she spoke with a questioning tone. It seemed she didn't believe Robin had done those things or maybe she didn't think those things were very impressive.

"That was me." Her voice broke. This conversation was going nowhere. "Our sales increased like thirty percent."

"Really?" Gina asked. Brooke didn't seem to be listening to either of them.

But Brooke was listening because she asked, "What *did* you put on your resume?"

A quick moment passed until she understood what she was asking. Gina knew she was a diner employee first, so how did she land the gig at Proctor Creative? Robin still didn't fully know, but she had no competition (if Dexter is to be believed); plus, she was chosen—possibly by Charles' wife—due to her work catching just the right person's attention. It was a classic story of hard work paying off. "I guess hard work paid off. I was asked to interview before the job was opened. It was an honor to be chosen." It didn't feel like an honor, but that was another discussion altogether.

"The job *wasn't open?* What? Does that mean you didn't submit a resume?"

Darn, these questions were way too personal. They had neither

○ 257 ○

the right nor the reason to know that information. Instead of answering, she changed the topic. "Shanice won the case. She's getting her car repaired right now."

Instead of responding, the two ladies stared at each other as if they were both thinking the same thing. But what? Did they think Robin had no work credentials? Certainly, they knew she had a four-year design degree. That was itself a major qualification. She could stick with something to the end.

With her attention toward Brooke, Gina said the sentence that became a dagger in Robin's soul. "So, she's basically an affirmative action hire."

A cold breeze made its way down Robin's spine with a serpentine crawl. "What did you say?" She wanted to swear but something in her moral compass wouldn't let her.

Brooke smiled innocently. "We just think that your company may be meeting quotas. It's not an attack." She seemed so sure of herself.

But it was certainly an attack. It was a blade pierced through her body to gut her where she stood. "I...work very hard." Robin hesitated. She meant to say 'earned my job,' but her voice wouldn't say those words.

"I know she's good with art, but they didn't put her in the art team." Gina conversed with her colleague like Robin wasn't in the room. "I mean, colleges do it. Companies do it. It's normal."

Right then, Shanice came back, fully dressed for work. Suddenly, every possible comment flew through Robin's head, but she asked a pragmatic question. "Did you tell them about my Bachelor's degree?"

Shanice had to think for a moment to see that the three ladies were chatting. "Oh yeah. I'm proud of my little artist."

"Everyone has a degree these days. Heck, I got an accounting

Hoop Drama

degree but look where I am." Brooke spoke as if she were wise beyond her years but she was dishonest in the extreme.

"Mom," Robin stated, speaking bluntly. "Did you tell them how I got my job at the agency?"

"I think so. I'm still not sure why you weren't put on the art team, but they probably will move you there after a year." She threw back a blue mint.

Gina shook her head. "I don't know. You probably just checked the right boxes."

At this point, Robin's blood was boiling, her face was sweating, and her heart was racing. How dare they suggest Robin was anything but talented. Plus, the last thing Dexter would ever do is hire someone of color...to check a box.

Shanice knew Robin well, and the visible signs of anger were all too familiar. "Baby," Shanice said. "Are you okay? Did you tell them about your trouble at work?"

Finally, she snapped. "NO! They said I'm a diversity hire. But *it's a lie!*" She hadn't called another adult a liar since college when a boy had said that Robin was pregnant. She simply had no desire to judge character. How could she know who any stranger truly was unless they revealed their heart?

Her mom's eyes grew heavy. She wasn't prepared for this discussion. But she should be. She had spent her entire adult life standing up for truth and justice. But in that moment, she only said, "I don't know why they hired you. But it's possible they just wanted to give a black girl a chance. That's not so bad."

Gina and Brooke nodded and smiled at Shanice.

WHAT THE HELL! The world turned upside down. Gina tried to pitch in, but it just made things worse. "It's not an insult, Robin. You should be happy to be given such a rare opportunity."

Brooke nodded. "Yeah. I'd take that job."

Andy Silvers

At the end of her line, a broken woman sobbed her final words. "Find your own ride tomorrow, Mom."

Before she could be seen drowning her eye liner and mascara, she fled for her car. Abram tried to say something but it sounded like mumbling in her ears. A loud click meant the doors were locked. If she could stay in that lot all day and just ignore the world, she would, but Shanice ran outside. Mom hadn't earned another word, moreover her dash said that she had a mere three minutes to punch in.

Shanice texted her something, but she didn't read it. Instead, she flew into the building, slapping away tears, and clocked in exactly four minutes late.

Jacob was there, of course, fiddling with his sock, but Robin refused to look him in the eye. Instead, she ran for the restroom, redoing her makeup as best she could.

Her fortress had crumbled, and her career was one email away from implosion. She was truly alone, and Dexter wasn't going to lift her spirits high. For the next few minutes, she fought back tears by mindlessly counting the tiles on the wall. If she broke down at her desk, she would forever be a basket case in need of sympathy or extra space. Ray worked, so she couldn't call him. However, he would be taking Shanice home, and that would be a ride he wasn't ready for. He simply had no idea that a giant had fallen.

The cookies were still in the back seat, so Robin grabbed them to explain her sudden disappearance. Because her mouth had dried like the Sahara, she took one and ate it whole.

Catherine was still happy. Love truly was the most powerful thing in the world. She gulped down an energy drink until she locked eyes with her coworker. "Robin, are you okay?"

This was not a conversation Robin was ready for. She'd hoped to be invisible once again so that she could do some work and go home. "I'm fine."

Even just saying those two words stung like a hornet. Her mother had just stabbed her between the shoulder blades. Not only did she refuse to stand on the side of justice, she refused to have her daughter's back.

"You don't seem well." Catherine paused her work. Robin realized how kind Catherine could be when she walked a broken soul out of the room. She could speak in private, without the mocking stares of anyone. Without breaking down in tears again, Robin relayed her situation in the women's restroom. "I think Dexter hates me. And my mom…my mom does too." No! Robin had to stop talking about her family to keep from crying.

It seemed strange how men felt better when they said exactly what happened and how they felt about it. The more detail, the better they felt. The more they laid into their opponent, the better. But Shanice wasn't supposed to be an adversary. She was supposed to be a friend. No, closer. She was supposed to be storge love.

Catherine put her hand over her heart. "Wow. I don't know what to say. All I can do is help you get through the day. Let's collaborate on your work. It'll make things more fun." Even though Catherine hadn't said what Robin wanted to hear, she said what she needed. Survive the day.

In the Skwad room, Kevin peeked his head over at their work. "Hey, Robin. If you aren't well, we can cancel getting the cat. I'm completely okay with that."

Good grief. Could he really read misery on her face?

That had slipped her mind during her partial breakdown, but the kitten wasn't for her. Kevin needed to go. "You should still get the cat. It'll really help you."

"I can't go without you. It's just not the same."

Andy Silvers

Anger almost filled her veins, but then the thought occurred to her. *Kevin needs a friend in his life.* Despite her current pain, Robin made up her mind, knowing she'd feel better in a few days. "Let's try this Friday. After work."

"It's up to you."

"What are you mumbling about?" Jacob asked, as if he had a right to know.

"Nun-yuh-business." Catherine was a blessing.

The rest of the shift, real work got done thanks to Catherine Graham.

※❀※

In his same spot, Kevin sat listening to music and eating Robin's cookies. She just smiled at him, knowing she had nothing important to say.

But a crazy thing occurred. Mr. Proctor was downstairs in the doorway of the finances team, talking about something. He had broad shoulders and a fancy suit, but his face was obscured. The woman in the room referred to him as 'Charles,' so it was definitely him. Robin had the chance to tell her side of the story and hear what the boss actually thought.

The CEO tapped the frame of the door and headed out. Robin began to follow him, not realizing she was quiet as a mouse. He made his way through the primary locked door, with Robin grabbing it behind him. She made her way toward him, ready to speak for the first time.

But then...

What about Shanice's remark? There's no way a MAGA company would ever hire for diversity. Plus, Robin had indeed transformed Mary's diner. She earned her place. The reason she

Hoop Drama

had no competition was just coincidence. They found her while she was making a business better, just like how the ads were better. Plus, the design team was full. There was no room on that team so Shanice was probably on to something. They started her off on the Skwad to bring her into the fold and then they move her to the design team when an opening is available. Simple.

But while Robin told herself all that and more, she still didn't say a word. After just eight seconds, Charles had entered the parking lot. He was gone. Yes, she could've simply opened the door. There was time.

But she choked. It wasn't worth it. If her mother was right, it would destroy any will to work. The only way to keep her heart intact was to let Charles walk out. Robin bowed her head in shame, but she just couldn't do it. She couldn't ask Charles for the truth because the answer could very well push her to the brink.

WEDNESDAY, MAY 23RD

She hadn't told him about Shanice, only that she had a bad day. How on earth could she wake her sleeping husband and tell him to drive her mother to work? At 5:25 AM, fear was racking her body, making it impossible to sleep.

A solution arose. She pulled out her phone, went into the living room, and opened a ride sharing app. It was called Gizbo and Shanice would certainly have no clue how to use it. After forty minutes of fiddling with it, she got it to work. She paid the full fee for a ride that morning. In order to tell her mother about it, she'd have to review her texts.

SHANICE: *I love you. I can come by tonight to explain everything. I have something to confess, but I don't want you to think I'm not on your side. Please answer.*

Robin had a hard time responding. It was like daggers piercing her fingertips with every letter. But she had to send her the ride info. It was fairly obvious what she planned to 'confess.' She wasn't the warrior Robin had expected. That much was clear. Any further detail would have to wait.

ROBIN: *I've got you a ride to work today. It's paid for. The lady's name is Lina Doherty. She'll drive you from your house to work. 7:45 in a blue sedan.*

It was a very clinical message, but that's the best she could

Hoop Drama

muster. Her mother responded within two minutes, but Robin had no interest in reading it.

She tried to fall asleep once more, but it was very hard. Her body was still, but her thoughts trampled each other like a menagerie. She was angry. Dexter had been right in his own perverse way. Companies don't want her input. Sure, that wasn't her job, but it was obvious that *no* company did. She simply didn't have the power to speak freely. Either she was preaching to the choir or she was screaming into the void.

Jacob was a rat. He had turned her in, not when he first found out, but when it was most advantageous. And she couldn't get revenge. Partially, because hate was hardly in her dictionary, but also because Dexter would certainly fire her. He was probably biting his tongue with anticipation for the chance to ditch her. And Jacob was soulless. He rarely showed compassion. Sure, he joked with Kevin, but that might just be to pass the time. Would he stand by Kevin's side if he were wrongly accused? Likely not.

But a modicum of hope snuck in. Not hope that Proctor Creative would ever change, but hope that Catherine, and maybe Kevin could be persuaded to treat Robin as a friend.

Ray plodded into the bathroom. He was a zombie walking through his morning motions. But he had information. She wanted to know what he knew. What had Shanice told him?

"Hello," Ray finally said, only to brush his teeth.

"Hi." She wanted to give him a hug but hardly felt she'd earned it. After all, he couldn't possibly understand why the knife had cut so deep.

"I'll listen when you're ready," he finally said. Those words were cold comfort in the moment.

Robin wasn't ready for a fight—a fight about who was right or wrong. He would likely defend Shanice, citing that family sticks together. But there was only one way to know for sure.

"Mom hurt me in a way that's hard to explain."

He nodded. "She was quiet last night. I knew you two had fought. I can drive her this morning, but you need to tell me now."

"No...I got a Gizbo for her..."

He stared in confusion. He didn't know her. "Okay."

"Please tell me how she feels."

Ray grabbed a pair of pants without thinking. He owned four identical pairs, which made life easy. "I don't know. She said it wasn't my business. You two really are close."

What? She hadn't told him. Now her questions could only be answered one way. "She and her coworkers called me a diversity hire. That's what I'm upset about. She refused to defend my experience or talent. I know it seems weird, but I can assure you those people are as right leaning as it gets."

He paused after buttoning up his shirt. "That hurts. I'm not gonna interfere. Shanice told me that you'd need time. And she told me one more thing." He floated closer. "She said to hug you until you know you're loved."

Robin wrapped her arms around him and finally teared up. Thankfully, she could cry in private, then go to work to be professional.

No treats accompanied Robin to work that day. She hadn't the energy to bother with it. The blonde woman at the desk was missing. Robin almost didn't even notice until she heard blabbering on the other side of the locked door.

Her pass got her in where every employee seemed to be hanging out. Room 112. It was the same room in which she had interviewed. Just one was seated. Fixated, they stared at a TV on the wall. Henry in design was doing something on a laptop while everyone watched the news. It was a local channel—channel 7.

Hoop Drama

The story was quickly discernable. A shooting had taken place.

The victim was Kenan Porter. He was just thirty-two years old. The story became crazy. It seemed based on the reporter's comments (live from the scene) that an older man had shot Kenan directly through his front door.

"That's crazy," Kevin noted. "If you can't drive a car, you shouldn't have a gun."

The reporter, a young woman with blond hair, continued. Kenan had apparently walked up to the front door of a stranger at around 4 PM that afternoon. When he had knocked on the door, the older man named Todd had shot through the door twice with a hand gun. Finally, good news. Kenan was alive! He was in the hospital, surrounded by his family.

His wife, Olivia, commented to a reporter saying that senseless acts of violence need to end. Robin, of course, agreed. Todd was white, and Kenan was black. Did that play a role? Probably. How often do Americans shoot random people who knock on the front door?

One person was missing from the conference room—Dexter. Perhaps he didn't care. More likely, the truth was too hard to hear.

"That guy's either a racist or an idiot," Henry said, closing his laptop. Suddenly, it was clear they weren't watching live TV. Instead, Henry had pulled up a video on the channel seven website.

"You think he's an idiot?" Catherine asked. "If this guy shot everyone who knocked on his door, then why is this the first we're hearing about it?"

Finally, someone with sense, and it was Robin's favorite coworker.

"It's just irritating." Uh-oh. Jacob was butting in. "The news media will now suggest that *all white* people are terrible because one white guy acted stupid."

267

It hasn't been just one, Jacob. Open a history book.

Xavier piped in. "If he's like me, he'll sue grandpa's pants off. I would."

Kevin suddenly looked at Robin, then like a horror film scene, so did everyone else. Robin actually became confused for a moment. Did they actually want her opinion? Had she been dead wrong about Proctor Creative, or at least its employees? If showing them the news would make racial justice that easy, she would've compiled a reel on day one.

"Well...I think he's probably a racist." Her voice was soft but everyone still heard. She could've heard a pin drop.

"Really?" one said. It wasn't clear who.

"Of course," another said. It sounded like Xavier but it could've been Henry. Everyone shuffled out of the room. Upstairs, Robin fiddled with the timeclock for several minutes. She hadn't clocked in and would need to adjust her timesheet. At her old job, the time could be adjusted on the machine itself.

Once she made it to her desk, everyone had already begun working. "Kevin, look!" Jacob pointed to his monitor.

"Oh my gosh. Is that *Tony?*" Kevin glowed with amusement. "He looks like if Thor took steroids but also ate nothing but Jello."

They must have been looking at the Husk ad campaign. The emails clearly showed that the job was basically finished. Robin's work at least was done. It had felt like an eternity.

It was strange too to see Jacob acting so...normal. He was having fun and being spontaneous—the opposite of his business self. The real Jacob was controlling, ignorant, and offensive.

The Husk images looked great. They incorporated the darker aesthetic of the new manly shampoo well. The themes and ideas weren't what Robin had hoped. They were almost exactly what she'd created weeks earlier. The website looked wonderful too.

What could be left for the MCU campaign? It seemed over. She pulled up her company email. There, she was hit with a surprise.

Mrs. Robin Chapel,
Thank you for your part in our campaign. We couldn't have done it without your input. I wanted to inform you that we have secured a speaker for our Juneteenth event. She is a columnist for the Atlantic with a long list of credits. I'd like to personally invite you on June 19th to join us at the event. It's free. We could arrange a full campus tour for you as well (if that'd interest you). We'll stay in touch.
Dr. Brody Pearson, PhD

Seriously? He used Robin's work email. She formulated a careful reply.

Dr. Brody Pearson,
Thank you so much for the invite. I appreciate the offer greatly. However, from this point forward, I may not conduct business activities with you on this or any other platform. All ad-related content must be handled through the C.E. Proctor Creative director, Mr. Dexter Brennan. As such, I must decline the offer, though I wish you well.
Thank you,
Mrs. Robin Chapel, B.A.

Wow. It was like a punch in the face to reply like that, but if Jacob had access to her email, then he'd tell Dexter for sure. It wasn't fair that some companies were willing to hear her story, but her boss refused to care. Shanice proved that even an older woman with nothing to lose could fall victim to social pressure.

It was over. The Robin who made the world better had died, replaced by an empty shell who only nodded along to the repeated

Andy Silvers

nostrums of the white patriarchal elite. The reason rich powerful women of color could speak truth to power was because they *were* the power, at least to some extent.

But real people need insurance. Real people need to pay rent. Unless Major Collins could offer her a job, she'd always be one of the silent majority. That didn't sit easy, but the truth never did. Honestly, it crossed her mind to put in her two-week notice that evening. But then...

"Hey, Robin," Kevin said. He seemed to understand her pain as he spoke softly. "I'm willing to give it a try. I don't want my house to be empty. You're sort of like a sister I've never had."

"Thanks." She grabbed some pills to stop a headache before it got worse. It felt like she had been working for hours but it was only 11:24.

"Dexter's meeting with our new clients now. We'll have something to work on soon. I was thinking we could go to that pet store near Mary's Diner. I know you used to work there so I don't need to send you the route. Just let me know."

"Sure." She desperately wanted to quit, but Ray would be angry if she gave up their paycheck without telling him. It was clear making allies was fun but not a substitute for social victory. The only way to change C. E. Proctor was to replace the management.

"Awesome." His joy was infectious, and without trying to, she smiled.

The world seemed to come to a standstill until lunch time. Robin left the building and went somewhere familiar—her apartment. She never did that, but her mind was so drenched in negativity that she yearned for the feeling of home.

While eating a salad, she prepared a text.

ROBIN: *Ray, I don't know if I can handle this job anymore.*

Hoop Drama

I've helped everyone but myself. Please tell me what to do.

She hit send, but only after four minutes of staring at her phone. Her lunch break would be over soon, and she hoped he responded in time for her to be free. Maybe she could watch Tommy Craven for a few hours. Or do some laundry.

Ding.

RAY HUBBY: *If everyone really hates you then leave. But if you got one friend, stay. Chapels don't quit.*

Wow. She hadn't expected that answer. To be fair, Ray wasn't the type to leave his job over arguments or drama. And Robin's main issue was outside of work—her mother.

With a breath deep enough to suck up an ocean, she hopped in her Fit to return to work. Punching back in was shockingly easy. It could have been laborious, but her coworkers made it worth it.

Pop! Jacob sent a cork flying across the room. He had gone to Kasey Khel's given the bag on his chair. "Who's ready to begin round two?"

"What was round one?" Catherine stood by her desk while Kevin read what must have been the new brief.

"Never mind. The point is we have our new project. It's a bitchin' company that makes armor plates and stuff. They need us to market a new plate for—what's it? —a backpack. Yeah. It's gonna be sweet."

Jacob seemed like he was opening Christmas presents, but a lump stayed lodged in Robin's throat.

"They've already got a video," Kevin remarked while pouring himself a glass of champaign.

"Yes. Hey guys, help yourself to the wine. You too, Robin." Free wine was still free wine. "So, anyway, I saw the video. It's great! This guy with a twirly mustache pokes his head around a corner and shoots a giant rabbit thing. It's totally Bugs Bunny even

Andy Silvers

though it's white, but I can tell. And he's facing away while the dude shoots his backpack like three times. I think it's 3A protection, but I forgot."

Catherine teased, "Are you excited? I can't tell."

The whole thing seemed a tad insensitive given recent events, but for the first time in over a week, Robin didn't have a comment. Then…

"Don't get too excited." Dexter entered the room with his familiar digital tablet. "Oh, my lord, is that wine?"

"Yeah. Try some."

Dexter shook his head at Jacob's antics. If only he reacted so casually to Robin's. "Anyway, we are nearly done with Rover Callum and Major Collins. I'll remain in contact to discuss ad effectiveness. Thanks, team, as usual. But the truth is we're a bit low on revenue. This Justin Cavalry company needs a pretty standard package. They've got product designs and manufacturing. They just want a uniform website overhaul and media buying for the new product."

"I'm not worried." Jacob gulped the Chardonnet.

"I don't care. Point is, I'll be on the lookout for new clients. Higher paying clients. Please don't get drunk. See y'all later."

"He sounds happy," Jacob teased without guilt or fear.

"Who gets drunk off one bottle anyway? This is lighter than old grape juice."

Catherine sipped some wine. "His tampon might be a bit tight."

Everyone howled. It was funny, but Robin feared laughing would just put her on the chopping block. The wine was good, but the fun was just beginning.

"Okay, guys. Let's think." Jacob took charge and opened up the existing website. Yikes. It looked like it was made in 2005.

Hoop Drama

"So, we need to update their UI and design themes. We want modern, yet masculine. Their brief states that nearly sixty percent of sales come from men."

Kevin used the whiteboard to draw a rounded shape that curved like the letter U. Then he drew two smaller circles next to it. "This will represent the masculine themes." Once Jacob chuckled, it was clear he had drawn a phallus.

Catherine quickly erased it. "Grow up, kids. One thing we should add in the store is updated popularity data next to each product."

"Explain," Jacob requested.

"So, next to each add-to-cart button it tells you how many of that item have been sold in the week. It'll say like '14 units sold this week'."

"Oh, that'll be a new thing for our website specialist to try."

Kevin smiled and wiped wine from his chin. "Robin, what do you think?"

She had been caught off guard, but it's as if she could say nothing wrong. Oddly, her coworkers all seemed to value her. Maybe they didn't, least of all Jacob, but their stares made it seem as though her opinion would be considered equal. "I think they have to get rid of their second landing page."

FRIDAY, MAY 25TH

She didn't quit. The job had gotten fun. She still had reservations about advertising body armor in a world where innocent people were shot through a front door. But in a strange way, Proctor Creative felt like a real job. She forced all her worries into the pit of her stomach in order to be the woman Ray knew she was.

"We'll get the backpack in a few days to use in our photo studio." Kevin held the brief while standing next to the whiteboard. By this point, the board was filled with ideas, including some from Robin herself.

"I thought they had photos." Catherine seemed more joyful than in weeks past. Maybe it was her new man that was causing it. When Robin had just married Raymond, they were on cloud nine. They spent money they didn't have, played music they shouldn't listen to, and ignored all world events for at least a month.

"No," Jacob corrected, still acting like the boss. "They have a great video ad, but no professional product photos. We offered to do it so we could get paid more."

"Oh."

She had no interest in posting about her work (or anything personal) online anytime soon. In truth, Ray also rarely posted anything from his shop on Instagram or Twitter. His coworkers occasionally did, but overall, the boys just did their jobs. Despite this, she really wanted to post something to show solidarity for the Porter family. She worried that perhaps Dexter would see it. There was really no reason to worry about her private political speech and yet, she did. He had successfully scared her into staying quiet. Though she told herself she wasn't scared.

The brief was filled with interesting notes. Apparently, Justin Cavalry had done ballistics testing for their new plate and needed the charts on the website. Robin knew companies had outside facilities test products but never really felt the need to read about the tests in depth. These tests, done by a ballistics laboratory, showed the type of weapon used, the testing parameters, and the result for each shot. The new backpack plate passed with flying colors.

The product was estimated to cost consumers roughly $500 for one or $900 for two. It was a foreign world; one with numbers, labels, and designations Robin had never seen. A true anathema.

"We'll run Instagram ads, Facebook, Snapchat, and certainly Google." Jacob summarized the white board. The team had to split up (just a few feet) to research the target audience, ad placement, and other logistics. Robin had been tasked with brainstorming for the new website. She checked out other websites, though not firearm sites to absolve her search history. They almost all used a clean white background with simple academic text and full-screen images. She got stuck wondering how to implement the vertical video on a horizontal webpage. She asked Kevin for help.

"Good question. I think it'll be fine on the mobile site since most people use phones anyway, but on the desktop version it'll need to be placed next to some content."

She was still confused, but knowing Kevin was a kind man deep down, she risked embarrassment by asking for more details. "Sure," he started. "On the mobile version the video will fill the

Andy Silvers

screen, but on the desktop site, the video will have some paragraphs of info next to it. But there's a chance they'll tell us they don't want the video there at all. Who knows."

The campaign needed this: one website overhaul, up to six photos for the product page, some copy describing the new product, and social media buying to round it off. That seemed like a large campaign but Catherine assured her that some companies ask the ad agency to do nearly everything.

"No way," Jacob suddenly said.

"What is it?" Catherine inquired.

"We had another deal fall through. Dexter said he talked with a protein shake company about doing a full campaign with ads and such, but it fell through. They couldn't haggle out a good price and abandoned ship. It sucks because smaller companies think they can do everything themselves. They get Bob from manufacturing to put together the photoshoot and Karen from HR to handle the website, and you know what? It always looks like crap."

He had a point, but it was interesting to hear. It sounded like the ad agency needed to hire an ad agency. Hopefully, hours wouldn't need to be cut. That'd be a last resort.

At the end of her shift, she followed Kevin to the pet store. She thought she'd be exhausted after a long day, but her excitement kept her energized. Finally, she remembered what the store was called. It was called Tag & Treat Pet Shop. They closed in roughly two hours, so they had to hurry.

She knew he would be prepared. "You know which cat we're getting, right?"

"Uh...no. I got distracted looking at the dogs since there was this tiny little lab that was as cuddly as a stuffed animal." Hm...*men.*

"Great. You want a dog now." They popped in and heard

○ 276 ○

Hoop Drama

several birds squawking. The smell of mulch and fur filled their noses.

"No. I just get distracted easy. Look at that. This dog is half white and half black. It's a domino."

In a cage on the concrete floor sat two small puppies with tags. One was indeed di-colored. Cruella would adore him, though she shan't be granted access.

"Can I help you today?" the young lady at the counter asked. She looked like she was sixteen so perhaps she was the owner's daughter. She had lovely blond highlights that Robin took notice of immediately.

"No thanks. We'll let you know." In the back, there were cats. For some reason, they weren't in cages like the dogs. They were in a special play area behind a wooden door. Plexiglass stood between a fluffy Chartreux and a giddy smile.

Though not exactly a pet person, Robin briefly had a cat when she lived with her parents in Ohio. It was a mix between domestic longhair and a Snowshoe. They named it Randolf after their mailman (long story). It had died when Robin turned eight, and Mr. Baxter had no interest in getting another.

"What about that one?" She pointed to a white one who was the only one looking to play.

Thud. "Crap. The door's locked."

"I'll go ask the lady."

The employee, named Cassie, opened the door to help her customers. "Yeah, that white one is called Mello. She's very friendly unless you grab her tail."

"Okay." Kevin was looking elsewhere. He didn't want that one. He kicked a rubber ball that made two kittens chase after it.

"So, we have several breeds and ages. They have all been spayed or neutered as far as I know. We also provide nail trimming

277

Andy Silvers

services if you become a member."

"How much is that?"

"It's free—well, the membership is—and we charge $25 per trim. But you also get coupons, bonus offers, giveaways, and more. So, it's definitely worth it."

Finally, Robin had found the perfect one. She was white and brown, probably a year old so no litterbox training needed. Plus, she was extremely friendly. Robin put them in her lap and they laid just like it was a bed. "This one is great."

"Yes. That's Peach. She doesn't look much like a peach but we found that she likes peaches so there you go. Her previous owner left her when they moved."

"Awe. That's sad. You like this one, Kevin?"

All the cats had now gathered near the three of them, competing for treats and attention. Two had even started a fluffy fight. But Kevin found one in the corner. It was a black cat, likely about two years old, hiding under a plastic case. It appeared nervous when Kevin picked up the plastic, but then perked up at his gentle voice.

"That's Jell-O," the employee stated. "He's been here for over eight months; much longer than any of these other little fur balls. We'll give you that one for a discount."

Kevin lifted an eyebrow in confusion. "Why? Is he violent?"

"No sir. Look closely at his left eye. He's blind in that eye. Someone actually left him in a garbage can."

"Wow," Robin said. "People suck."

Jell-O quickly grew comfortable with his new friend. Robin still preferred Peach, but it was Kevin's choice. "I'll take him."

"Awesome. Leave him here for a moment, and let's do the paperwork at the counter."

"Perfect." Kevin showed his ID and signed several forms.

278

Hoop Drama

Robin checked out the puppies until Kevin spoke again. She was tempted to bring a puppy home just to see Ray's reaction, but that wouldn't be fair to the dog.

"That'll be $25 plus the usual $20 adoption fee."

"Is that a discounted price?"

"Yes. Jell-O has been difficult to home so he's fifty percent off. We're glad you're taking him."

Kevin looked distraught. Maybe he had changed his mind. "Are any of the other cats on discount?"

"Um…no. We cut the price to $50 if they are over a year old and charge $100 if they're under a year."

Kevin looked at Robin, though she was unsure why. "Actually, I'd rather pay $50. He's still a cat, right?"

"You don't need to. We offer the special when it's required."

"I have to."

After it was clear Kevin was sticking to his plan, the young cashier walked around the counter. "I'll ask my mom."

In about two minutes, the store owner, Rachael, walked over to assist. "Hello, sir. Thanks for visiting us today. Did I hear correctly that you want to pay the full $50 price for Jell-O?"

"Yes, ma'am."

"Okay. Well, I'm not really sure how to do that without changing the system, so I'd recommend paying $25 for the cat and donating another $25 to resources for the store."

Kevin thought for a moment. Since he was an adult, Robin just waited patiently. "Okay. That'll do."

"Awesome."

Luckily, Kevin had brought a cat carrier since Robin totally forgot. Unfortunately, Kevin remembered that she had promised to pay for the first bag of litter. Oops.

But it was totally worth it. He smiled like a kid at Christmas,

Andy Silvers

and Robin went home to crash.

She made herself a salad dinner using some chicken Ray had left in the fridge. He walked out to give her a hug right at 7:02 PM. "Hey. How'd it go?"

"Pretty good. He got a cat who's half blind, but he's sweet, so I'm happy."

"That's good."

"I'm glad you didn't feel the need to pick me up like my private security."

He scoffed. "You were in a public place. That's safer."

"Thanks, bodyguard. How was work?"

"It was fine." He stole a piece of chicken off her plate. "We did inventory today, so that was fun—not really. They're thinking about changing my hours which I'd be pissed off about if you weren't at that job...which reminds me. I hope you don't think about quitting. You know what they say. When the going gets tough, the tough get—"

"...going. I know. I know. I think I've changed my mind. It's...I still have issues with our new campaign, but I think maybe I could enjoy my work."

"That's good. A lot of people would kill for your job."

Ray had always been positive about the job, so *sulky* wasn't an option. Drama at his job would never make him quit; the exception being if his boss lied about him. Maybe there was some truth to men being less emotional. But only some. "I know."

"But you gotta talk to your mom." Ray gave his serious face. This involved leaning in close and raising his eyebrows up to his hairline.

Really? Last time she discussed Shanice with him, he had implied it was a private matter. Now, he was acting as a mediator. "I will."

Hoop Drama

"Hm," he said, relaxing slightly. He had something to say. She could tell after a year of marriage when he was prepared with a comment. "You know what happened today?"

"With Mom?"

"Yup. She got her car fixed."

"That's good." Although that meant that Robin had paid for a Gizbo ride for nothing.

"Yeah. But you didn't know because she didn't tell you. She called *you* first when she had her accident. Now, you two are practically strangers. If I can say, you and your dad are not on good terms. Please don't leave her too."

"I didn't leave my dad. He left me…us."

Ray nodded. "You can't control other people's lives, but you can choose not to leave her. You're off tomorrow. Consider calling her. Please." The twinkle in his eyes nearly caused Robin to sniffle.

He was right. She hadn't had a major disagreement with her mom in years. The problem wasn't that Shanice couldn't be forgiven. The problem was that her fortress had been torn down; and now, she had to find another one or build her own from scratch.

SATURDAY, MAY 26TH

A text popped onto her smartphone bright and early.

KEVIN: *Say hello to Jon.*

He had sent a photo with his message showing the cat laying on his bed. Jell-O was a funnier name, but undoubtedly, Kevin had his reasons for naming the cat Jon. It was precious and hopefully now Kevin would have some joy in his non-work life.

This hadn't been the result Robin expected, but it was a positive result nonetheless. Her heart was hopeful…until. Her mom texted her back.

SHANICE: *Of course, I'll get lunch with you. You will always be my baby girl. See you around 11:30.*

She spoke like nothing was wrong. It hurt just a little, but it would hurt more if Ray returned from work only for Robin to confess that she hadn't even tried. She wore her casual clothes—meaning extremely casual. She literally had on blue and white pajama pants and a gray shirt. At least she had a bra.

They met up at a local BBQ joint called Westing House Eatery. She couldn't imagine going to Mary's because her mom would remind her how much she missed it.

SHANICE: *Be there in five. Dropped a hoop in the toilet.*

Robin smiled. Though, inside she was frightened. She predicted where the conversation would go. Her mom would

Hoop Drama

apologize, act like their relationship was fine, and discourage Robin from speaking the truth. She would admit that standing up for people of color was only a privilege of the rich, then they'd laugh about stupid things politicians had said.

That was the forecast. Shanice wasn't a fortress. She was a doormat. *No, don't think negative.*

"Hello," she said, wearing a wild coat that was completely inappropriate for the weather. It was leopard print and had giant tooth-shaped buttons. Her velvet pants seemed understated by comparison. She didn't smile, but she was upbeat. She had hoop earrings that made Robin wonder when she would ever get to wear them again.

"Hi, Mom." They were led to table seven by a young brunette server.

RAY HUBBY: *Tell your mom I said hi. Tell her we got a new TV.*

That was his no-effort surveillance tactic. If she claimed she forgot about lunch, he could say, "No, I reminded you."

"I'm so happy my car is fixed." Shanice used half the booth to throw her coat. Underneath was a pastel purple blouse.

"That's good. Ray told me." It was like two Robins were fighting to speak. One knew her mother well and was happy to talk while the other wanted to escape. An invisible hour glass ran in her mind until the moment she'd have to mention her job. One thing was certain; she would never speak to Mom's coworkers again.

"Yup. Carol got the bitch-slap for lying to the police. I'm Scott-free and back in action."

The server appeared. "What would you two like to drink this fine day?" He was pretty cute. He looked somewhat like Ryan Reynolds when he was in his twenties.

"I'll have a cherry Coke and I'd like to get one ticket please."

283

Andy Silvers

"Certainly."

Robin gave her mother a look. Maybe she'd claim Robin 'owed' her after this free meal. "I'll have coffee with two sugars. No cream." Her throat suddenly became dry. "And a water with lemon."

"Sure thing."

"You don't have to cover my meal, Mom."

"I know, baby. I don't gotta do a lot of things, but I want to. I want to start by apologizing to you…"

Here it goes…and before she had her water. Maybe she should have ordered wine or hard seltzer.

"…we didn't mean nothing negative that day—actually, let me skip that. I did lie, Robin, and as a woman of integrity, that's not what I want to do. I want to lead by example, so I slipped up." She sighed. "As parents, we tell our kids to do all the things we know they should. Don't lie. Don't get divorced. Don't get in jail—or at least caught. Anyway, I told you to stand up for blackness because that is what you *should* do…"

"Are you two ready to order?" The waiter returned.

"Yes," Shanice said, followed by a detailed instruction set for her cheese burger. Robin got a BBQ pork platter with green beans. Plus, the waiter had her drinks.

After he left, Shanice continued. "I told you what you better do, and I ain't lie about that. I lied about me. My whole life has been a battle in my mind. I wanna say the right thing, but I never had the fire to do it."

"You lied about me too." Robin felt compelled to speak. "I'm not a diversity hire. That's the last possible thing."

Shanice nodded. Like a therapist, she took her client seriously, acknowledging her troubles with grace. "Yes, ma'am. I did. I took my coworkers ideas too serious. They planted that seed, but I let it grow. I really apologize for that. You *earned* that job."

Yeesh. The second she said that, the veins in her back turned to icy water. She still didn't feel the job was 'earned.' After all, Dexter made it clear he had no idea why he was even interviewing her, then later he said Charles wants her there. It was all so strange, and it made her want to speak to Charles first thing on Monday. "Thank you."

"You probably already guessed it, but my coworkers are mega MAGA super-duper MAGA folks who vote republican like their *damn* salary depends on it. And yeah, I don't speak up like I should. I don't remember where I was going with that…"

"It's fine. I get it." Robin gulped down her water first. "We can't make a change in this world; not without power. I shouldn't have even tried at work. Unlimited hubris."

Shanice frowned fearfully. "No, honey. You did good."

She was pushing her luck. Her apology seemed empty if she just doubled down on the tactic that nearly lost Robin her job. "No. You were right not to even try. I'm just upset that you gave me bad advice that could've been a disaster."

Shanice nodded again. "I don't think it was bad advice. Parents tell their kids to do all the things good people do."

"Then I'm not good people, or maybe I am. I don't know. I told Ray I wanted to do more than a nine to five, but I had no idea I had chosen the wrong field. You pushed me to do something that you knew I couldn't." She had become rather accusatory. She decided without clarifying it to stop beginning sentences with 'you.'

"No, baby. That ain't my heart. I thought you done won."

"What?"

"You sounded like you victorious. You got in the photo thing, you helped that Tanya girl, and you got Major Cannons to change

Andy Silvers

their vision. I saw the website. Don't think I didn't. You look stunning in those hoops and my friends agree."

"Your work friends?"

"My other friends."

It was true. She had made some progress at Proctor Creative, but it was short-lived. "I did succeed a little. I agree, but that's the furthest I can go. My coworker Jacob ratted me out. He read my emails and sent them to Dexter. So, my success is done."

"Or maybe it's just beginning." She glowed with joy.

Robin wanted to glow, but the truth was like a blanket covering her shine. "No. Major Collins has their clients. Plus, you should see the current campaign. It's crazy in light of the Kenan Porter shooting."

"Yes, I saw that. Poor thing, and his poor kids. But that's why you gotta stand up. My job don't change nobody mind, but yours can. *Oh yeah.* You got this."

For a moment, she cracked a smile, but then it faded. "Maybe at my next job."

"If you don't start now, you won't start ever."

"Here we go," the waiter said, delivering fresh food. It smelled heavenly, though it could only hope to match Ray's best dish.

After a few moments of silence including a few bites, Shanice said, "It's your choice. I just want you to know I'm there with you."

"I appreciate it."

"No, really. I've told off my coworkers good and hard. You know what they called me? A lib. Ha-ha. Can you believe it?"

Robin was stunned. "What did you say?"

"I told them that I vote democrat, that my daughter *ain't no* diversity hire, and that Mexico will never pay for that wall."

Robin chuckled. "All right. I'm proud of you."

Hoop Drama

"And I'm proud of *you!* Just don't stop. Keep pushing."

Robin nearly said 'I can't' but knew Shanice wouldn't accept that. Instead, she replied meagerly. "I'll try."

"Do or do not. There is no try." Shanice spoke with a funny voice that Robin found confusing. "Come on. You know Dad's favorite film is *Star Wars*. How's your food?"

"It's good." She had eaten half of it. "Um…we got a new TV. Ray really wants you to know that."

"Finally. Your days of poverty television are over. I hope you can forgive me enough to have me watch Tommy with 'cha."

"Yeah. And Carter wants to come."

"Great."

"Are those hoops from the toilet?"

"Hm-hm. A little Dawny spiff that right up."

Shanice did pay for their meal. The two ladies spent the next thirty minutes discussing Shanice's car, the new TV, and of course, stupid things politicians had said. Only one thing wasn't said— "I'm sorry." Sure, Shanice said it. But Robin couldn't quite do it. She meant to, but she allowed Shanice to talk so she wouldn't have to say it. Her mom had to be proven right first. C. E. Proctor had to treat Robin like the adult she was, showing anyone can be accepted. Until then, Shanice's advice would be wishful thinking and therefore plan B.

Ding.

CATHERINE: *Hey, it's Catherine from work. I need to talk to you today if possible. I guess tomorrow will work too but let me know. I'll buy you coffee if you need lol.*

Oh goodness. More coffee? Robin sat in her car after her lunch. It had ended on a positive note. The only issue is that Shanice thought her daughter could easily implement her advice. Robin responded, hoping to postpone the conversation.

Andy Silvers

ROBIN: *Is it 911?*

CATHERINE: *It's about Carter.*

Oh no. Did he dump her?

ROBIN: *I'll be there. Tell me where.*

CATHERINE: *Alpine Supply on 4ᵗʰ. They have coffee for serious.*

A wood place? Was Catherine building an ark?

Alpine was largely known for construction tools. It was Lowe's but on a budget. The last time Robin had been there, Ray had been building a shelf for books and souvenirs (soon after their marriage). Robin had suggested buying a completed one, but he assured her he could do it. He proceeded to spend over $100 on tools and wood, only to fail miserably by smashing a vase and splitting a wood board in half. Suffice it to say, the wife won.

That reminded Robin to text her beloved.

ROBIN: *Talked with mom. It went well. I'm at Alpine with Catherine. Don't know why.*

She refused to mention Carter. It was better to investigate first, then report findings later.

CATHERINE: *I'm on aisle 5. Looking at nail guns.*

Goodness gracious. This lady had a life.

"Hey, Robin. That was fast."

"Yeah," Robin wheezed. She had run inside despite not needing to. "I was already out."

Catherine had a cart with wood boards, nails, paint, and a sponge. "Great. So, listen. I really wanted to talk to you since you're Carter's niece. He's been so wonderful but I'm a bit concerned."

"Well, I'm glad to hear he hasn't broken up with you."

"What? No, sweetheart. Nobody breaks up with Catherine Graham. *I* break up with you. Anyway—oh, I can't afford that

288

Hoop Drama

one—I wanted to thank you for what you did. Carter and I definitely didn't know what you were doing, but even when I figured it out, I still didn't believe it."

Robin had become somewhat discombobulated. Catherine spoke like a machine gun, and she was somehow buying random crap at the same time. "Okay. Um…what are you getting?"

"I'm building a dog house. I did this before but it was like a decade ago, so hopefully I do it right."

"Oh, you have a dog."

"No."

"…"

"So, anyway. That night, Carter and I obviously hit it off, but I didn't see romance. I just didn't see it. Oh, that drill is on sale. Yes, I can make it work. Anyway, he was cute and smart and nerdy, but I was like, 'Nah. Swipe left.' Then, I went home with him…"

"Oh, I know where this is going." Robin gave a telling wink.

"Um no. You don't. Get your head outta the gutter please and thank you. So, we go to my apartment, since I did sorta wanna show off my collection of Wes Kraven films and merch, but he said something that caught me by surprise."

Finally, she took a moment to breathe. Though she wasn't thirsty, she asked Catherine about the coffee.

"Oh yeah. They have that at the front near the registers. Weird, right? And it tastes better than Mary's. Sorry but not sorry. Anyway, Carter is telling me about his film collection and his signed what's it from Doug Jones when he starts talking about his future. He mentions that he loves monsters and ghosts, but he cares a lot about his work in the medical industry. He said that he wants to be able to share his life with his kids and that monsters would scare them. I asked if he has kids and he said 'no.' So, that means

Andy Silvers

he's like me. He wants kids. I—it's hard to explain."

It took Robin's brain several seconds to process that rapid fire monologue, but eventually she did. However, it didn't seem super special though. Many adults reference children when discussing their future. Then again, Robin remembered the photo on Catherine's desk. She wanted a family, and she found a man who wants the same. "Okay."

"So, he's passionate about healthcare and that's fine. He's good at his job, but I'm worried." Catherine stopped shopping to look at Robin. "I'm worried he won't leave his job for our kids."

"What?"

"I'm worried he won't leave his job for our kids. Robin, listen. He's a radiology technologist, and gets paid pretty well, I'm sure. But I love what I do. I could never leave marketing for a decade or more. I don't want to marry him or even spend another day thinking he's the one if he can't be my dream."

That was a lot. But she was beginning to understand. Catherine wanted someone like Ray who could stay home and be a father. Funny enough, Robin was actually wishing Ray would get a better job since the ad agency thing was proving to be too stressful. But Catherine was happy. It was hard to remember Carter ever saying that he didn't want a career, but she could remember him saying how much he wanted kids and that he wanted to be at home for the holidays.

"I'm gonna get some coffee," Robin said, sauntering off.

"Wait. I'll be done in a minute. We can get coffee then."

"No, I'm good. See you there."

She walked away, hoping Catherine wasn't hurt. She got a hot tea instead just because she was coffee'd out after lunch. In went one sugar and one cream. It was piping hot, so she watched a customer struggle with a massive pipe like a giant bendy straw until Catherine showed up.

Once Catherine found a self-check register, she motioned Robin over. "Help me scan."

"Uh…can't you just do regular check out? Half these things don't have codes."

"Robin, seriously. You have to help me."

"With the codes or with Carter?"

"Carter."

"I think he'd be happy to stay home with kids, but you should talk to him about it."

"I thought you'd say that. I will; don't worry. But I don't wanna waste time. Actually, can you arrange for me to talk to Raymond?"

Robin took a deep breath. This lady was a firecracker on heroin. "Okay. I'll see what I can do."

MONDAY, MAY 28TH

Pumpkin pie, but only because she was feeling generous. Oddly enough, her coworkers probably had forgotten she ever used to bring baked goods.

"Oh my gosh!" Kevin exclaimed. "I totally forgot you brought in baked goods. Is that apple pie?"

"Not quite. It's pumpkin and it's *not* just for you."

"Dang," Kevin snickered. "Sassy."

Catherine waited to clock in. "Oh hey. That looks good. She's right, Kevin. Save some for me…and Jacob."

Jacob was already there, doing his usual workout, keeping an eye on everyone like he was the school principal. Then, Robin got a message. She wouldn't have checked it so fast except that she thought it was a text message. Unfortunately, it was from Brody. She didn't hate Brody, but she really didn't have patience for this right now. If she blocked him, she'd miss the thrill of her former life, and at least he'd used her personal email this time. Before getting the chance to read it, Jacob piped in.

"All right, Chapel. You can watch *The Bachelor* later. Catherine, you can watch *Monsters Inside Me* later."

"I'm not even on my phone."

"I know. I just don't want Robin to feel singled out."

As if he ever cared about that before.

Hoop Drama

"Yeah. We still only have the Cavalry campaign right now," Kevin said, grabbing the brief. "I think we have one of these plates now. Hold on. I'll check the desk."

This awkward pause seemed like the perfect time to check that email which had been burning a hole in her cell.

Mrs. Robin Chapel:

I hope you don't mind a quick message using your private account, but I'm sure you are aware of the horrible Kenan Porter situation. Due to the increased frequency of events like that, we have asked him and his wife to speak on our campus on June 19th. The event will start at 8 a.m. to accommodate our civil rights speaker as well. Due to your work in civil rights at C. E. Proctor Creative, we felt that you should receive an invite. Furthermore, the images are wonderful and Tanya Kushall was a unique find. I've recommended some scholarships for her through our Action Network.

Hopefully, you can join us on June 19th. Feel free to let me know in your own time. Thank you for your service.

Dr. Brody Pearson, PhD

A lump got stuck in her throat while she tried to process that message. She was considered a civil rights activist? No, she was a pretender. And Tanya would receive scholarships? For a split moment, maybe Shanice had been right, but of course, Dexter would never let Robin leave. But she was going to try.

"See," Kevin barged into the room and Robin's thoughts. "It's rock solid, just like my abs."

"It's rock solid like your prostate." Jacob spoke quizzaciously as he got up to look at the plate. It was about a foot across and fifteen inches high. It curved slightly to make it easy to slip into a backpack. What civilian needed an armor plate for his backpack?

Andy Silvers

The police and the military were the only ones.

"Hey, guys. Could we market it to the military? Is that in the brief?" Robin tried to pitch in knowing she hated the product.

"I think this one's for civilian use, but we should check that."

"Already did," Jacob responded to Catherine with confidence in his voice. Oh, how Robin wished she could speak with such command. "They have quite a few military and law enforcement partners already. Their biggest customer last year was Bull Defenders, a private security company based out of Ohio. Private buyers don't create the biggest orders, but they compose 36% of total sales."

"Have you bought any yet?" Kevin asked.

"No. But maybe I will."

Gosh. Why would he need that? *Does he think deer carry Glocks?* Maybe it's so he can look cool at the gun range.

"See," Kevin held up the plate. It was a basic black color with the Justin Calvary logo in gray at the center. Robin took it. It was surprisingly light and it felt like stone more than metal.

"It's something." Robin was still somewhat peeved that Jacob would dismiss her idea too quickly, but if he was right that civilians made up less than half of sales, maybe the goal was to increase that percentage.

"I wished they had armored shoes or socks. That would've helped me for sure." Jacob threw his foot up on his chair, then pulled up his pantleg.

To Robin's shock, his foot was plastic. "Oh! Your—" She had spoken aloud when responding to her coworker's prosthetic foot. Jacob was an amputee.

"Wait," Catherine said. "You didn't know?"

Robin shook her head. She was still stunned, watching as Jacob removed his foot from a rough rounded leg. The skin on his

Hoop Drama

stub was raw and his rubber sock was full with sweat. She didn't know the terminology, but whatever it was must be a pain to maintain.

"I told her that Jacob wasn't all there, but she did not realize what I meant." Kevin laughed.

Jacob was more serious. "Yup. Iraq. 2003. I got shot twice by a fifty-Cal or something similar. My foot couldn't be recovered, especially not after losing a pint of blood. I'm just lucky the bastard had the aim of a drunk orangutan."

"Wow. I had no idea." His stub was so strange looking that Robin had to fight not to stare.

"Yeah. You should see the other guy."

Kevin joked, "Yeah. They're in a hole in the ground."

"Yup," Jacob responded. "Semper Fi."

Though his ability to work with others had yet to be fully seen, his work ethic was clear. Plus, now his morning workout made more sense. He hadn't quite earned Robin's affection, but he had earned some respect.

During a quiet moment when everyone had buckled down at their desks, Robin tried to respond to Brody's message. It would be an honor to go, but all she could type were a few words. She didn't want to reply that she'd try to go. Ideally just a yes or no. Finally, the stress mounted like a rocket ready to launch. She got up, ready to go to Dexter's office. On her way she saw Charles' office door. The door was shut like normal. It was impossible to tell if he was even there.

Downstairs, Dexter was standing behind his desk. He appeared to be looking for something. She really had come down there with no plan other than to ask if she could get the 19th off— just the morning.

It was all so surreal. It's like her mother's words of

Andy Silvers

encouragement led her to try the impossible. If she'd been asked whether she thought this would work, she'd say, "No way." But she banked on her mother's strength even knowing that Shanice was a coward. Inside, something told her not to be. "Looking for something?"

"Yeah." He seemed calm, like maybe he could understand that not everything was about him. Plus, he was being given plenty of notice. "I'm looking for a phone number. It's on a sticky note."

In order to help, she would have to wander around his desk and stare at his stuff. Instead of doing that, she waited while he rummaged through a pile of junk. He was just like every other man she'd met. Their desk was layered with weeks' worth of stuff, most of which needed to hit the trash can. Once he found the tiny yellow sticky note, he sat down, placing it onto his left-most monitor. "Can I help you?"

"Yes," Robin replied. Stress caused her to sit down first, followed by a deep breath. "I was notified of an event next month." She already felt manipulative. Not mentioning who notified her was a tactic to keep the discussion cordial as long as possible. If she claimed to just hear about the Juneteenth event online, it would make her attendance seem less necessary. Dr. Brody had to be mentioned, but when?

"Is this related to our current client?" Dexter stared at her like a confused parent.

It was unfair because in college, Robin had a professor who was the kindest person ever. His name was Wilkobe and he was plenty serious when students got out of line. At some point during the latter part of the spring, students began turning in assignments late and just asking him to accept it anyway. The next week, he used two minutes to firmly state that he would not accept assignments late without doxing 50%. There was a problem. Robin had also turned her assignment in late but for a legitimate reason. Her mother had asked her to help move stuff out so the house could be sold. Jesse had decided not to even return calls.

Shaking, she went to him after class to ask for leniency on the 2,000-word paper. With a cordial smile, he accepted her excuse and gave her another two days. What a guy! That was what a boss should be and Dexter could take notes.

"No. It's…related to Major Collins. They have an event on June 19th featuring Kenan Porter from the news. Since I worked on the campaign, I was invited to attend—just for the morning." Crap! She'd forgotten to check what date that was. It was probably during the work week since it was a university event, but perhaps not. It looked like Dexter was checking his calendar.

"That's a Tuesday. Who invited you to this event?"

Yikes. He was way too nosy. "One of the executives asked me personally and it would be an honor to be there."

Dexter shook his head. "If you mean Dr. Pearson, he's not an executive per say. He's part of the dean's office for the new business school. Plus, we agreed that you wouldn't talk to him behind our backs."

"I…he messaged me."

"Yes, because you spent months developing a relationship with him as though *you* were the agency. The answer is no. If you try to use PTO to hear a speaker, you will be fired since you already have two strikes. Trust me, I don't wanna do it—"

Yeah right!

"—but I will if I have to." Dexter pursed his lips. It was irritating because he treated her like an enemy. It would take an act of God to make him an ally.

She desperately wanted to mention that her attendance could be considered a collaboration with Proctor Creative; a follow-up

Andy Silvers

project. But of course, she didn't say any of that. Her career was too important. Maybe, in a few months, she could transfer to another ad agency and use Dr. Brody as a recommendation. Her spirit had been broken. "I understand, sir. I will let Mr. Pearson know I cannot attend. In the meantime, we will make Justin Cavalry a campaign they will love."

"That's what I want to hear."

Of course, it is. It's sanitized and useless. With little fanfare, she soldiered upstairs. Her broken spirit guided her into the elevator where she leaned against the wall like her balance was compromised. Charles' office was right there, but she didn't dare make Dexter even angrier. But he had made her angry for sure.

Dr. Brody Pearson,

It is with great sadness that I must inform you that I cannot attend the Juneteenth event. Much as I would like to, my work duties prevent me from going. I hope the event goes well as I know black voices are so rarely heard when it matters most. If the event is recorded, I do hope to listen to the inspiring words of Kenan and his wife. Thank you for your kindness and best wishes.

Mrs. Robin Chapel

Yeesh. That had been the hardest message to send ever! Dexter should want her to go to the event to show a business relationship between the two interested parties. But no! Brody had called her a civil rights leader at the company and she truly had felt like a pretender to the throne, but now, she felt like there was a shred of truth to that. Instead of crying about it, she took to social media.

On Twitter, she posted for the first time since February.

Hoop Drama

@robinchapel101 Mr. Kenan Porter was shot on Tuesday, May 22nd by a racist man with a gun. Kenan is scheduled to speak at MCU on Juneteenth, but his injuries are severe. Olivia and his kids shouldn't have to worry that their father won't come home because he visited the wrong house. #afatherlikeyou

She tagged Mr. Pearson who she forgot was her friend until then. It wasn't really a necessary post, not because it wasn't true, but because Robin had no voice. Still, her heart was heavy with the burden of knowledge. A quick search of the web confirmed her suspicions. He was back home thankfully, but a physical therapist had to visit him once a day to help him walk. He had to relearn basic motor functions in his right arm that had been so easy before. And what's worse, Todd's lawyers were actually trying to argue a case of self-defense.

Yes, Kenan was uninvited on the property, but he was unarmed and not actively threatening anyone. Plus, Todd hadn't opened the door before he shot. What the hell! If Todd knew someone was there, he likely knew what they looked like too. Did he think because Kenan was black that he must be a gangster thug or something? The story made Robin's skin crawl and it lived rent free in her mind until the end of her shift.

Because she had started working on actual work a bit late, she stayed an additional twenty minutes to catch up. It wasn't enough to finish everything, but she didn't want Ray to worry. She checked her phone to see if he had messaged her. Nothing yet.

On the way out the door, she did a double take. The spot where Kevin used to sit and eat was empty. She smiled at the wholesomeness. Hopefully, little Jon was enjoying his new home.

"People like your post," Ray noted while trying to empty out his soup bowl. His struggle was holding his phone in one hand

Andy Silvers

while cleaning with the other. "Wow."

The Tweet had completely left Robin's mind, though Kenan hadn't. She and Ray discussed it over dinner.

After checking the post, Robin's jaw popped open. She had amassed nearly four hundred likes and eight hundred views. There weren't too many comments, but Dr. Pearson wrote one of them.

@brodypearsonmcu Well said **@robinchapel101**. I'm hopeful justice will be served. #afatherlikeyou

"Robin, you on fire right now." Ray gave his wife a fist bump. It was definitely a guy reaction. Robin however, was tapping her feet with excitement. "Maybe you'll end up on Tommy Craven."

She giggled. Maybe if she reached a million likes. "I don't really have the hips for TV."

"What! You look like a goddess."

"Thanks." The couple kept refreshing the page with about twelve new likes every five minutes. Not bad for a woman with only 174 followers.

Then she noticed a familiar name in the comments.

@jacobabradley12 Proud of your courage Robin. #afatherlikeyou

What the heck! That couldn't be Jacob from work. A quick search of the account confirmed it was he. Why would he post that? He *despised* Robin.

TUESDAY, MAY 29TH

Jacob was a cynic. He didn't believe a word he said and now over 1,500 people had seen his comment. Ray thought it was great because he didn't understand who Jacob really was. His wife happily explained it to him.

"He sounds like he's changing." Ray said that while ironically changing shirts. His body was like a figurine at Target but with darker nipples. The way his pectoral jiggled under his skin had her mumbling.

"Do what?"

"Honey, I'm four feet away. I said that maybe he's changing."

She scoffed. "No. Guys like that don't change. It's obviously a ploy or trick or something. Either way, I won't mention it today. I just can't.

"You said he was missing a foot. That's a pretty big thing not to notice. I don't think you know him very well."

That was true but only because she didn't *want* to know him. "He always wears pants. That's not my fault."

Ray nodded. "It's up to you. Just don't get fired. I wanna get a massage chair."

Oh gosh. If only he knew. It hadn't seemed necessary to mention the meeting the day before. She only said that Brody offered for her to go to the event and she declined.

○ 301 ○

Andy Silvers

It hurt far more than she let on, but Ray wouldn't understand her pain. He'd think she was just emotional about every irritating life injustice. One time, a customer called Ray a 'douche bag' followed by writing an angry review on Google. The review suggested that Ray was mistreating customers even though he was merely following company policy. The thing is, Robin only found out about it from Carter since Ray hadn't thought to mention it. If the same had happened to her, she'd have reread the review twenty times before undergoing an existential crisis.

There were no treats today. Her morning conversation with Ray had lasted so long that he was in his car trying to pull away with Robin still talking. But he was a gentleman. He only rolled up his window after he was out of earshot.

Jacob seemed busy already. "We've got one more client, but it's small. Crazy small. I don't think we'll hardly be needed."

Kevin munched on a breakfast sandwich, took a hard gulp, then said, "Yeah. Dexter is not happy. He says we may have to have a company meeting this week."

Hopefully Charles would be there.

"I think we need a Skwad meeting right now...or at least, when Catherine shows up."

There he goes again. Acting like he's in charge and can coordinate meetings whenever he wants. Maybe he was a high-ranking sergeant or whatever the army hierarchy is.

"Robin, look." Kevin shoved his smartphone in Robin's face. "It's Jon sleeping on my belly. Guess the extra fat paid off. And here's him playing with the vacuum cord. So cute. Although, he won't stop drinking toilet water so I'm having to close the seat."

The pictures were precious, but the feeling of accomplishment was better. She had almost singlehandedly made Kevin's life better. Scientists had actually linked the sound of cats purring with

Hoop Drama

an increase of positive emotions. One day, he needed a roommate, but for now, he was satisfied.

Finally, ten minutes late, Catherine arrived with a large energy drink. It looked like an extra tall eighteen oz can. "Hello, everyone. Sorry I'm late, Carter wanted me to meet his coworkers."

Funny. Robin had done the same thing with Shanice's coworkers and that had not turned out well. Perhaps Catherine had a better experience. Then again, she seemed like a type-A personality who could throw shade harder than an oak tree.

Jacob waved his hands. Wonderful—the coveted impromptu meeting. "All right, Catherine. We're gonna have a quick meeting with just the Skwad. We have to acknowledge marketing tactics and success stories when they happen and *Robin* has achieved such a feat."

Wait. Did he say 'Robin'?

Jacob waved everyone to his computer screen. Indeed, her Tweet was pulled up and holy mother of Beyonce! She had amassed over 8,000 views and 1,800 likes. Wow! Just wow! She hadn't checked her post since early that morning and there were not nearly that many reactions. Upon checking her notifications, she discovered the secret to her success.

Dr. Pearson had shared her post. He had nearly 7,000 followers.

"Congrats, Robin." Catherine said before gulping down enough caffeine to kill a horse.

"Thanks."

"Yeah. Let's look at this." Jacob zoomed in the page to show the post clearly. "First off, she starts by stating what happened and to who. This grabs readers' attention by clarifying why they should read the post. Then she makes an emotional appeal. She clarifies a concern that many parents have and that the news amplifies. One way to make the post stronger would be a call to action, but I want to focus your attention to the end. The hashtag."

It was clear now. Jacob didn't actually think Robin was brave. He just thought she was a case study on viral marketing. It was still crazy that he was giving her credit, but not as crazy as before. However, he still turned her in to Dexter, so his ledger was stained red.

"It says 'a father like you'." He stood straight and tall with a finger pointed to his display. He reminded her of many college professors from Ohio University. "This is clever as it gives the post a summary of sorts, explaining why you should care. What is it about Mr. Porter's story that is so universal? It's the father connection. This post has nearly nineteen hundred likes in twenty-four hours. That's incredible, and I recommend we keep our eyes on this post for a few days to see how it goes. Why? Well, this is what Justin Cavalry wants and by extension every client we take: a quick, easy-to-read post that grabs your attention and stimulates your amygdala."

"Yes, and you are an expert on stimulating someone's amygdala, aren't you?" Kevin teased.

Catherine laughed. "Come on, Jake. Keep it family friendly."

Even Robin giggled.

"No promises, sweet pea. Also, it sounds like you got a boyfriend now. You better tell us about that soon." The meeting adjourned with everyone meandering to their desk.

"For sure," Kevin added. "We gotta know all the juicy details."

Jacob then took it too far. "Yeah. Do you prefer Trojan or Crown? Ha-ha!"

"*Thank you* for the compliments!" Robin had heard enough. She really doubted that Carter and her were doing anything too crazy given Catherine's trepidations, but she had forgotten that Jacob knew nothing about the arrangement.

"Anyway," Jacob concluded. "Congrats to Robin for reaching viral status. Let's get to work."

Before starting her work, she gazed upon the incredible Tweet from the day before. She desperately wanted to send it to her mom as a screenshot since Shanice didn't have Twitter. She had a Gmail, Myspace, and she used an IRC channel back in the early '90s to send pictures of Johnny Depp.

Then she noticed that Carter had replied to the post.

@carterchapil88 Agree, sis. See you Thursday.

Do what? Thursday? She immediately pulled out her phone to ask about that.

ROBIN: *Thank you for commenting. What are we doing Thursday? Remind me.*

While she waited, she checked out the small new campaign Jacob had mentioned. Apparently, it was a company called Digic-7 who made smartphone accessories inspired by classic tech from Apple, Xbox, Microsoft, and more. However, they only wanted some digital designs for a new product that Robin didn't understand. It claimed to be an adapter for the Sega Genesis to convert 8-bit to 16-bit, however that might as well be Japanese as it made no sense. Hopefully, Robin wouldn't be required to brainstorm ideas for it. Secretly, she wanted to know how much these campaigns cost, but Proctor Creative never put such information in their briefs.

Furthermore, she was conflicted about Jacob's recent attention. There was a warm fuzzy feeling in her heart that was thankful for the kindness but her brain wanted to stab it with a

Andy Silvers

butterfly knife. He hadn't actually earned her trust. Honestly, if the room were empty, she'd have asked about it immediately. Did he care about Kenan's safety? Did he recognize the threat to black lives in modern America? And did he understand the importance of equity?

"Hey, Robby?" Catherine rolled her seat next to her desk, happily observing Robin's work, which was mostly looking up keywords to add to the Justin Cavalry campaign.

"Please don't call me Robby." Wow. She said 'no' to someone. It came so naturally too. Maybe she could storm into Charles' office and demand one morning off.

Nope. Too scary.

"Sorry. I do think we need family nicknames though since we're so close and all. Anyway, have you been able to work out an arrangement for us?"

In order to process this oddly-phrased request, she had to stop her work to listen. "What arrangement?"

Catherine gulped the last of her energy drink then loudly crushed the can. "Me and Carter. We need to talk about serious issues before we can go out…like for real this time. But I can't just ask him about abandoning his career, can I? If you and maybe your husband help, we can get Carter to answer without anyone asking." She gave a telling wink. Gosh, where was this strange woman a month ago?

"Um…I don't know."

"You got us together at Friday Night Fright, so you have a sneaky side. Just work it out."

Now she was making demands. "I don't have anything arranged right now other than Thanksgiving. But I'll talk to Ray for you. Just be aware that he may not see things our way. He'll just want you to ask him yourself."

○ 306 ○

Hoop Drama

"Ray is your husband, right?"

"Yes."

"Fine." She rolled back to her desk.

Finally, she got work done, though even after weeks of working, it still never really felt like there was a definitive endgame or goal. She was only step two in a larger pipeline, and she never met with the clients (except when she broke the rules).

During lunch, she got the opportunity she had wanted but didn't feel prepared for. For some reason, Jacob had lunch downstairs in the conference room. It looked like someone was eating with him as their food was nearby, but no one else was in sight.

"Hi, Jacob. Thanks for the compliments." She stood in the doorway, unsure of how to begin what could become a heated discussion.

"Sure."

Short answer. Now her heartrate jumped up and she began to mouth breathe. She walked away but came to a grinding halt. She wanted answers badly.

But what could she say? Maybe mention that Kenan was a victim of racism. Maybe start by humbly stating that Mr. Pearson got her most of those likes. No easy answer, but she sat down at his table anyway while trying to hide her shaking hand. "I wasn't trying to go viral."

"Yeah, but there are skills you can learn to increase virality."

"What did you mean by your comment?" Realizing that was a stupid question, she flipped the words around. "Did you mean your comment?"

"Yes. I always say what I mean." He had a stoic face, perfect posture, and a strange meal that smelled of tuna.

A few weeks ago, he called diversity 'nonsense' so he must've

Andy Silvers

bumped his head on his headboard that morning. "Why did you turn me in to Dexter?"

That was it. The question that had to be asked.

"I didn't."

Another short answer. He refused to elaborate.

"You threatened me at my desk then Dexter called me to his office."

Jacob finally showed an emotion by staring in confusion. "I'm a gruff guy. That may seem threatening but it's not. Your computer made noises so I turned it off, then I saw the emails from Dr. Pearson. You can say I shouldn't have read them but I was worried about you. I knew you were new and that kind of stuff can get you fired. Remember, there's a ninety-day window where you can be fired for any reason."

That still wasn't a good excuse to read her emails. "So, you *didn't* tell Dexter?"

"No. You're in the Skwad. That's our team, and I don't rat out my team members."

"…"

"You used the company email address that he has access to. That's obviously how he found out." His stoic face returned.

"What about Kenan? Do you believe he was shot by a racist?"

"I do. I'm seeing more and more evidence that America has work to do, but I believe what I see."

"Do you think I'm a diversity hire?"

"What?"

Darn it! That was not a question for Jacob. Now she couldn't unsay it. "I'm sorry. Forget that question. I need to eat." She quickly popped open her lunchbox and scarfed down a ham and cheese sandwich.

"I'm not an expert of diversity or racial history or whatever.

I'm happy to led you lead on that. But I'm second amendment all the way and that ain't gonna change."

Let her lead? Really? Did that mean he'd embrace diverse voices in business? Would he see Tanya's interview in a new light? "If any American should have a firearm, it would be our brave servicemen."

Jacob nodded.

Then, Dexter walked in, shoving his phone in his pocket. "Sorry, Jacob. My client fell through. We're not where we need to be. Hello, Robin."

"Hi, sir."

Jacob responded, "So what's the worst-case scenario?"

"Um…that we have to go part-time for a few weeks. But I'm not too worried. Charles has some numbers to call and I trust his judgement."

A serpent of fear crawled up Robin's back and Dexter could tell. "Don't worry, Robin. We'd only be like that for a week at most. Let's deliver our best for Justin Cavalry and I bet we'll get jobs left and right."

Yeesh. Part time work meant cut hours. Ray worked full time so they could certainly manage, but it wasn't a comforting sign. The rest of her meal, Jacob and Dexter talked about sports and professional dune buggy racing; none of which Robin knew anything about. It was also too late to eat with Catherine.

Ding.

CARTER: *We're meeting at your place to watch Tommy Craven and talk gossip. 7 pm right?*

Now she remembered. When she was learning photography, she had promised Carter he could come. Now she felt awkward knowing this would be the first visit since Shanice had confessed her faults.

Andy Silvers

CARTER: *Maybe invite Catherine.*

Oh gosh. Robin knew what she had to do but she was screaming inside at doing it. "Catherine," she said at her desk.

"Yes."

She took a deep sigh. "I arranged for all of us to chat and have fun."

"See, you could do it."

"Sure, but my mom, Shanice, will be there too. Is that okay?"

"I think so. If she's nice like you, we'll get along great." Catherine was confident as usual.

It was still unclear what the plan was exactly. Funny enough, it would be pretty easy to get Shanice to mention children and then things would get awkward. Robin almost texted Carter directly to ask him if he would watch kids at home but there's truly no subtle way to ask that.

Plus, this was all so unnecessary anyway. They went to the mall, they ate at fancy restaurants, and Catherine was still wearing her shiny bracelet. They're basically already dating, but NO! It had to be official or it didn't count. Granted, it was pitiful for Carter not to actually ask her out, but still. They were an adult couple acting like goth preteens.

"If he's dad material, I'll ask him out, and if he's hubby material, I'll let you be my bridesmaid."

"Oh, goody gumdrops." At some point on Thursday, she was going to sneak out the door and drive to a military base where she'd be safe from the chaos.

THURSDAY, MAY 31ST

"Batton down the hatches, Raymond." Robin cleaned from the moment she got home. She literally couldn't recount her workday duties in the blur of her preparation.

"Relax. It'll be fun." Despite cooking and setting the table, Ray always managed to stay calm in everything.

"You don't get it. My mom, brother-in-law, work friend, and husband will all be here at my house tonight. And to make things crazier, Catherine wants me to probe Carter for secret intel like some special ops guy from *Rex Ryan*."

"What does Carter need to say exactly?"

Robin unlocked the front door. "I shouldn't say. That could jinx the whole thing. But I appreciate you asking me out like a real man."

"Oh, so you think Carter is too wuss to ask her out. I'll see what he does."

Ding-a-ling.

It was Shanice, who never let herself in even when the door was unlocked. After a few months, it was clear she wanted everyone to celebrate her entrance. "Hey, sweetie. It's been too long." She threw her arms up for a hug then tossed a teal trench coat on the 'stuff' chair. Why she wore clothes she'd inevitably take off was anyone's guess.

Andy Silvers

"Hey, Shanice," Ray hollered, unable to receive a hug. "You told Catherine the address, right dear?"

"Yes." Though maybe she'd grow to regret it. She tried to make the apartment look clean, but everywhere she looked she saw dirt. Plus, they had no idea what kind of food Catherine ate so they just made a healthy meal that Shanice would like.

"I've got grilled tilapia and greens coming up." Ray was a great cook and also proud. He could be black Emeril if he had a TV deal. Unfortunately, he didn't talk about work unless he was required to, so Robin would have to talk about her job and that could open up some wounds that needed to stay bandaged.

"We've got more guests coming, Mom." Robin kept an eye out for the couple lovingly named Catheter.

"Oh yeah. Carter is coming. I'm excited to see that boy. He gotta tell me all about his life."

"Yes, and his...um...not girlfriend is coming too." She bungled that up.

"Not what now? Girl, you talking in riddles."

"My work friend, Catherine will be joining us too. That's why we made extra."

"You could've just said that. Geesh, baby. I ain't raise you to be mysterious. What kinda greens you making, Ray?"

"You can choose between peas or green beans. I don't know what Catherine will want. Carter can shut up and eat what I got."

"Okay," Shanice said, sitting in her spot at the end of the table. "I'll take both, but not too much or nuthin' because I see you have dessert."

Ray had actually just bought cookie cake from Kasey Khel's but Robin put her baking skills to use by making peanut butter cookies. She hadn't planned on it, but it was a distraction from work and life in general.

○ 312 ○

Hoop Drama

Ding-a-ling.

"Oh, dear lord in heaven," Robin whispered.

Carter and Catherine were both out front as if they had arrived together, but they were not holding hands. Maybe things were off to a bad start. Also, had Carter not told his mother-in-law about his relationship? Hopefully, he was prepared for a surprise barrage of questions.

"Mrs. Baxter," Carter exclaimed. "Good to see you."

"You too, baby Chapel. You look good. And who is this lovely lady?"

Carter tried to answer but Catherine spoke first. "I'm Catherine Graham. I'm Robin's coworker at C. E. Proctor. Nice to meet you." She wore simple blue tennis shoes but her purse hung over her shoulder on a black chain that must've been painful. She had bold red nails and a perfume that smelled of ivory.

The Chapel's table for six easily served the small group. Shanice and her daughter sat opposite each other on the ends but interestingly, Carter sat next to Ray instead of his new chick. Speaking of her, she gave Robin a quick wink, prompting her to look at Carter with her lips mashed together.

"Oh, tasty," Catherine said, looking at Carter. "Do you have any of your brother's cooking talent?"

Carter acted bashful until he finally said, "I don't know. I guess I have some of it but my talent is definitely elsewhere."

Ray smiled while placing the last plate. "Yeah, he's great at basketball and breaking wind."

"Ray." Robin wanted to keep the guys from turning dinner into a competition to see who can say the grossest thing. Shanice went on to describe her car accident and the following insurance fiasco. Ray then mentioned a car accident he had back before he met Robin. He often did that—refusing to talk about recent events, preferring to discuss old stories with a thread of connection to the present.

But then Shanice asked about Robin's current job, probably hoping to hear good news about her social advocacy. "It's been fine. We got a new TV!" She pointed to the new TV.

Shanice nodded with approval. "Oh wow. Finally."

"Yeah, Carter. We're gonna give the other TV to you…and maybe Catherine." He was doing his part but in the clunkiest way possible.

"They can't share a TV, *Ray*. But I'll take it if you don't want it. Ha!"

"Sure," Carter said. "Be my guest."

Catherine waved her hand in agreement.

"Have you ever seen Tommy Craven?" Shanice leaned in to ask Catherine.

"No. Is he an actor?"

"I mean, he done acted a few times, but he's a TV star on late night. My family watch him every month. I bet he'll mention that terrible Kenan Porter story. Hm. That poor baby and his kids. I swear we never fix our problems. No sir."

She talked the same talk, but did she walk the same walk. If she could change, maybe Robin could too. She hesitantly asked a probing question that could shed light. "Mom, how did your coworkers react when you told them about it?"

With a somber expression, Shanice responded, "I ain't tell them about it, but we did discuss that thing, for sure. I told them that racism is in every corner of the country, and they said I don't understand."

If she had actually said that, maybe hope did persist. Before she could ask another question, Carter spoke up. "That man is crazy. He shoots through his door before Kenan had knocked. I'm pretty sure. That guy needs to be in jail until he dies."

Robin still had her mind set on Shanice's coworkers. "After they said you misunderstood—"

"He a crazy guy," Ray interrupted. "I know Tommy will tear him a new one tonight."

"So, Catherine," Shanice explained. "We watch Tommy together and he talk about news and life and stuff. He my favorite even though most people like that Kimmel guy. But I just like the way Tommy think, you know? He find the comedy in the crazy stuff like in Hollywood or Wall Street."

Now she wanted an answer even more. "Mom, what did you say to your coworkers then?"

"When, sweet pea?"

Damnit, Mom. "After they said you don't understand."

"She probably told them to screw off." Ray laughed. Robin gave him a death glare to shut the heck up.

Shanice giggled. "No, I don't talk to my coworkers like that. I just—"

Carter interrupted. "I honestly don't think Tommy will mention it tonight. I mean, it happened like a week ago."

"Damnit, *please* Carter." Robin probably seemed like a nut by now. She was acting as though the TV announcer was about to call out her winning lottery numbers, but it was similarly important. Did her mom do it? —stand up when everyone else sat down.

"I said there ain't much to not understand. The old guy shot a young man through the door. He could've died and his kids not have no father. Keith say I be watching too much CNN but he be watching too much *Fox News.*"

"Uh," Catherine grunted. "I just don't watch either. I get my news from Instagram and Google so I can ignore the spin."

"Me too," Carter said, giving Catherine a longing stare. They

Andy Silvers

had so much in common it was irritating for Catherine to expect Robin to tie the knot for them.

Just ask him if he'll watch your kids, Robin thought. It wasn't that hard and now Robin was going to develop and ulcer or worse. Out of pure desperation, she asked Carter a question that might reveal the needed info. "Would you watch our kids while we're working, Carter?"

Her question backfired completely. "You have kids now? That's news to me." He laughed hard enough to annoy the neighbors. Robin truly should never become a lawyer or TV presenter. Ray laughed too, acting as though his wife knew something he didn't.

"I'll watch your kids, baby," Shanice smiled like a proud grandmother. "But I'm gonna spank a little backtalker, just know that."

"I don't think I'd do that," Carter said. "Studies say it hurts them more than helps."

Yes! Carter was in the zone. Robin decided to push him along. "What about when your child screams 'no' at you and throws up their fist?"

"I'm not sure. I guess, I'd just try to talk to them or put them in time out if I can. Win them with love I guess."

Not good enough, Carter. Catherine, join in please.

Catherine asked, "What if they want to watch *Nightmare on Elm Street?*" She already knew the answer.

"I'd say 'no' to that. They gotta be at least thirteen or maybe twelve."

"You *better* say no," Shanice proclaimed. "That movie is scary, baby. Even I can't watch that. That's how me and Robin are the same."

She was right. They both hated horror films and pineapple

316

Hoop Drama

pizza. They also both enjoyed Tommy Craven, who was about to start in a few minutes. "Ray, help me clean up the dishes."

"Thank you for a great meal, Ray."

"Yes. Thank you. It was great."

Everyone handled their own dishes and then sat around the TV. As prepared as Robin was, she had forgotten to set up enough chairs for the broadcast. Carter grabbed his dinner chair to place in the living area. Robin sat in it as fast as possible to leave the sofa for the love birds.

Catherine sat down right where Robin wanted her. Carter *did* sit next to her. Thank goodness. He bought her a fancy bracelet *for crying out loud.* Catherine shot a quick smile. Ray took a seat next to his brother who showed him something on his phone, leaving Mom to sit alone on the recliner.

"Ray," Shanice called, lifting up an empty bottle. "Please clean up after yourself. You can't take care of my princess if you can't clean your castle."

"Yes, Mrs. Baxter." Ray spoke seriously but rolled his eyes. Shanice threw him the bottle. He handed it to Carter who handed it to Catherine who got up to throw it away.

"Children!"

Tommy started off with a monologue about the weather and his latest special with CBS. Nothing too interesting. As such, everyone checked their phones. Then, he began his first bit.

"Thank you, everyone. So, about a month ago, we asked several white people how many black people they knew…and it went about as well as you'd expect. But we're not gonna do that again today because if I really wanted to embarrass white people, I'd ask them to name *any* jazz singer. So…yeah. Instead, we're gonna play a memory game with tonight's guest, Winona Ryder, who's best known for playing the human Christmas tree in

○ 317 ○

Andy Silvers

Stranger Things. Give her a hand, ladies and gents!"

"Oh, yeah. I loved that." Catherine said.

"It was fun, but too predictable." Carter held the remote.

Shanice shrugged. "Is it on the internet or something?"

"Yes, Mom," Robin answered. It's on Netflix. It takes place during the '80s."

"Huh. Well, I don't know nothin' about that." Whenever Shanice didn't know what Tommy was talking about, she started random conversations until he got back to a topic that she found interesting. This was frustrating when the other two could relate but really...Shanice was the star of her own show and her kids just lived in it.

If Shanice had really told her coworkers all that stuff, maybe she'd earned an apology. Really, she deserved one a long time ago, but now Robin finally felt pressed to do it. "I'm sorry, Mom."

She hadn't heard her over Ray explaining something on his phone. "Robin!" he yelled. "Honey. Carter, mute it real quick. Look at this."

He passed her his phone which showed her infamous Tweet. Now though, it had over thirty thousand views and seven thousand likes. Wow again! "That's crazy. It looks like it's been shared several times."

"Is this from you?" Shanice had been made a Twitter account years ago, but she'd never touched it herself. To her, ten likes was an accomplishment.

"Yes. I'm shocked." Robin truly was. Her heart raced.

"Oh yeah. Jacob mentioned you yesterday. We'll definitely discuss this tomorrow. I think Dexter would be proud." Catherine pulled up the Tweet on her phone.

Yeah right. "Thanks." It was truly incredible. So many positive comments from people she'd never met. One even

Hoop Drama

appeared to be a celebrity with a blue checkmark next to her name.

@renemichelle25 Great point **@robinchapel101** It'll stop when we speak up. Some days, we have to speak louder! #afatherlikeyou

"Your hashtag has blown up, dear." Ray read as many comments as possible. "I wouldn't be surprised if Tommy has you on his show."

"Oh," Catherine noted. "If he does, be sure to mention the ad agency so we can get some work."

"You don't have any work?" Ray asked.

Robin froze, knowing she hadn't mentioned low sales to him. "No. We have plenty of work."

"If your hours are gonna be cut, you have to tell me."

Who told him? "No, I don't think that'll happen. It's—"

"Shush…everyone quiet." Carter unmuted the TV. Then he cranked the volume.

Tommy stood next to a large TV. "Now, we will do another BAE shoutout. This goes out to all the mamas, baby mamas, baby mama's mamas, and future baby mamas in the audience. If you want a chance to be mentioned next month, send in a picture of your BAE and a sweet caption to our Twitter page with the hashtag #tommysbae. Today, we picked five lucky couples."

"What about Robin's post?" Shanice asked. "Is anyone gonna show me how to read it on my phone?"

"Hold on, Shanice. Watch this." Carter gripped the remote like a toddler with a toy, then he leaned forward. Following his lead, Ray leaned forward too.

"First up," Tommy began. "Jonathan sent this picture in of his BAE in their apartment. Amazing. If *my* wife looked like that…well, let's just leave it there…"

319

Andy Silvers

Robin had a sneaking suspicion, just an inkling of a feeling what might happen. If he had somehow gotten Catherine on the Tommy Craven show, that'd be a miracle. But some kind of help is the help he didn't need. Catherine seemed disinterested, like this was a classroom assignment. If only she knew what Robin knew.

Two more photos passed by. "Next, Calvin sent in this lovely post of his boyfriend Jonah in what looks like a Build-A-BAE workshop. This looks like a special moment, but don't underestimate the manager in the background. She looks mighty unhappy. That's because the couple just asked her if the bears had accurate orifices."

Catherine chuckled.

"Finally, a young man named Carter sent in—"

NO WAY! NOT POSSIBLE!

Carter shot up in front of the sofa. Catherine's jaw dropped. Shanice simply whispered, "The hell?"

"—this picture of his BAE wearing a Morticia dress at a haunted mansion. If he doesn't propose soon, she may bite. That's all I'm saying. The text reads, 'Haunt me until we're old.' Wow, goth couples always scare me because they're the only ones who use real blood on Halloween. That's this month's BAE shoutout…"

Carter muted the TV. "So, if it isn't obvious, Catherine Graham, I'd like to go out with you."

Freaking finally!

Catherine looked stunned. "I don't know what to say."

"Don't worry," Carter said. "This isn't a proposal. Just let me know if the next time we go to Olive Garden, we can call it a date."

Robin was the only one not smiling. She wanted to, but if Catherine had meant what she said, this was the wrong order of operations.

"Carter," Catherine said. "I wanted to ask you out first, but I just really…"

"What?"

"I just really wanted to know if…" She looked at Robin. Robin nodded. *Just ask him.*

"…if you will raise our kids." The color in her skin faded. It's like she realized that now was the time to say 'yes,' and later was the time to ask questions.

"We're just dating, but yes, we'll raise our kids together."

"You got kids?" Shanice hollered.

"No, Shanice," Carter exclaimed without taking his eyes off Catherine.

"I mean…could you ever let me live my dream so we can live ours?"

"I don't quite follow."

Goodness gracious. Men are dense. "She's saying she wants you to stay home with the brats." Robin finally felt confident enough to help.

"Uh…yeah. Of course."

"But what about your job?"

"My job is making you happy—"

"Awesome." The love birds hugged each other long enough to glue themselves together. It was official, they were dating, and now Robin was free.

"Robin, help me pick kid's names tomorrow."

Oh, dear lord in heaven…

FRIDAY, JUNE 1ST

"Oh my gosh." Ray admired a batch of sugar cookies. "Are the hearts really necessary?"

"No, but Catherine will like them." She rose early to make custom cookies for work that day. They were heart-shaped to symbolize romance.

The Skwad liked the cookies, including Jacob.

"Thank you, Robin." He not only ate a cookie before meal break, but he appeared to be enjoying it.

Her face felt numb like she was waking from surgery or starring in an episode of *The Twilight Zone*. Jacob had seemingly changed overnight to being complementary, friendly, and thankful. In order to test his newfound kindness, she'd have to ask him about that day at the university where he had refused to interview students of color then completely ignored her concerns. There really was no good answer for that behavior. No excuse. The only positive spin would be to say that the old Jacob had died, replaced by a better version.

"Robin, stop," Catherine teased, face redder than a cherry. "This is unnecessary, but I love it."

"You're welcome." Robin enjoyed being popular. It was much easier to be Mrs. Cool in a small room of four adults than a college class of three dozen. But then...

Hoop Drama

"Hello...is there a birthday I didn't know about?" Dexter arrived with his gray tablet. He looked at the cookies but didn't eat one. The minor rejection hurt a little.

"No," Catherine said. "But I have a boyfriend officially. I know you've been married for a century or two so you're not excited, but at least pretend to be for me."

Gosh, if only Robin could joke like that with him.

"Wow, Catherine, I'm so excited for you. That's why I'm saying I'm excited for you." He spoke with a wide Joker-like smile and a monotone delivery as though he were nominated for most uncaring boss.

Kevin had been on the phone in what appeared to be a serious call, but he joined the group promptly. "Is your boyfriend going to visit us soon?"

"No," Dexter gladly answered. "We don't bring humans to the office for show-and-tell."

"What about your kids?" Jacob asked.

Dexter sighed like he deserved better. "That was a snow day, and I still regret letting them stay in my office."

The moment was relaxing. If only Robin could speak to Dexter exclusively in the company of her colleagues. When they were alone, it was like being interrogated by the CIA.

It also occurred to her how few of her coworkers had kids. Dexter did, and maybe some of the others did too. But she didn't, Catherine too, Jacob also, and certainly Kevin. It was odd that a room full of industry pros (and one newcomer) had so few kids among them. She knew that adults loved to talk about their kids at work. Shanice undoubtedly did.

"I don't want to break the happy thoughts, but we're low on clients. It's not uncommon at the start of summer to see lower sales, but this year's been particularly rough. And it's odd

Andy Silvers

considering the administration's great handling of the economy."

Really? The MAGA economy.

"If we absolutely have to—"

"Awe…"

"I know, but if we absolutely have to, we'll lower all creative team hours to twenty from June 11th through the 15th. Hopefully one week at most."

"What! That's like coming up quick! You can't be serious." Kevin spoke for the whole team.

Dexter crossed his arms. His facial hair was starting to grow back out and it made him seem more menacing somehow. "I know, but it's our only choice."

"Couldn't you just take a pay cut for the team?" Kevin mumbled the question through cookie bites. And yeesh. If Robin had asked that, Dexter would've slapped the black off her.

"Um…I'm salaried, so no. Plus, my paycheck isn't as huge as I'm sure you think it is."

"Wait," Jacob said, narrowing his eyebrows. "This is a real problem, though. Some—no, all of us got bills to pay. And rent. We can't go one month with hundreds of dollars less with a week of notice."

Good point.

Dexter's voice dropped an octave. "Yes, that's where PTO comes in. But *please* wait, guys. Let me confirm for positive that any of that is even necessary before we panic or call our credit card companies." He glared at everyone then left the room. Jacob was right. This wasn't a postponed exam; it was literally their livelihood.

Without any other ideas, Robin checked her Smartsheet account for work updates. Her task was to create a PDF with the elements needed for each digital ad. To start, she had to peruse the

324

major social media apps and a Google search page to figure out how each was formatted. On Instagram, she needed to add up to three pictures (to be taken promptly) and a quick line of text to grab people's attention.

She came up with something quick.

Got your back turned? No Problem! Use the new armor plate from Justin Cavalry to survive any attack.

Google seemed simple as the copy on the website did most of the work. Every time a person clicked a paid link, the host of the link got paid. Everything seemed pretty straight forward—just copy what has worked before. However, trying to determine what should be on the website was harder. The secret is that certain words must appear in the item page. Furthermore, even the HTML code itself must contain certain words that make the ad more discoverable. It was a nightmare since Robin had hardly studied anything like this in school. Yes, she had one class, but she made a B. "Oh, I think we should do that thing where when you hover over the image, it shows you the second image."

Catherine looked at her, then the other two did as well. "You mean on social media?"

"No. On the website. If you go to the online store, and you hover over the products, it should show you the next image for your convenience."

"Oh," Catherine said. "Yeah. That's a great idea. We've done that before with the UI. Right, Jacob?"

"Yes." His head was tilted down. "Good job, Robin."

For a split second, she thought he would say, "Good job, Catherine." Maybe he really had changed.

Upon searching for Facebook ads, she remembered her Tweet. She quickly checked for a status update and wow! It had amassed nearly 50,000 views and 10,000 likes. Holy salami! "Guys, check

Andy Silvers

it out. My post has gone way up."

Everyone immediately knew what she was referring to, but Jacob got to the post first. "Wow. Dang, Robin. That's incredible. That would drive traffic if it were an ad placement."

"Maybe we'll have Robin write all the copy," Kevin teased.

"No," she retorted. "I'll just do what I'm assigned."

"Maybe Dexter will assign you more stuff if you deliver the most results." Catherine spoke without knowledge of the behind-closed-doors shenanigans.

Robin didn't intend to sound harsh. "Dexter would never let me do that." It came across like an angry cry more than a joking statement. As such, the room got quiet as everyone interpreted her words. She could hear the HVAC system, prompting her to speak. "But maybe he could. I don't know."

She really didn't want to do more work for the same pay, but a great relationship with Dexter could certainly improve relations. The choices were conflicting. She really felt like advertising could be a career—but not there! Maybe she could transfer with a year or so of work to another agency. Hopefully, another agency would let her be a digital artist like she trained for. That would be amazing.

"By the way, guys," Catherine said, a wide smile breaking the symmetry of her face. "My boyfriend was on TV."

Robin smiled, remembering her 'Catheter' joke.

"Like on Dateline murders or something?" Kevin teased.

"Or *To Catch a Predator*?"

"Go to hell, Jacob." Catherine was a feisty one. "No! On Tommy Craven. I actually never watched it before, but Robin introduced me…and thank goodness because I was featured on it. Actually—yeah! But for real, they cropped Robin out! It's from Friday Night Fright."

Hoop Drama

"Oh," Jacob responded. "So, *you* were the murderer?"

Kevin and Jacob laughed. They were like highschoolers some days.

"No," Robin interjected. "She was pictured as Carter's BAE on social media. I guess he sent it in to the producers."

"BAE?" Kevin asked. "Is that like a metaphor?"

Jacob laughed at his joke before making it. "It stands for Big Ass Emo! Ha!"

"All right," Catherine agreed. "That's pretty funny."

Everything went fairly smoothly the rest of the day. It was great being on a team that valued every member. It was also great to work in peace and quiet. Without that, she had a lot of difficulty doing anything thoughtful. It was the same in college. If she didn't feel extremely confident in what she was doing, she'd get distracted by basically anything. Her phone was the number one culprit, but today, it was Xavier.

"Hey, fellas and *feller-ettes.*" He definitely had a Euro persona. "Good day, people. Is it afternoon? Yes. It is." Robin quickly realized that he answered his own questions a lot. "I got bored talking to the same weirdos for too long and decided to see how the Skwad was doing. Honestly, I hope to Mary and Joseph we don't lose pay." He motioned something akin to the Sign of the Cross, though he used his left hand, so he won't be greeted at the pearly gates.

"Awe, you heard about that," Kevin asked.

Robin really tried to keep working. She really tried.

"Yes." Xavier made himself comfortable in their office by grabbing a chair and sitting between Jacob and Kevin. "If we lose a whole week, I'm gonna blow."

Catherine paused. "Actually, he said it would be half a week, but yeah, I'm still pissed."

Xavier grabbed a stapler to use as a fidget toy. He opened it and closed it repeatedly, then removed the staples. "Yeah, whatever. I just haven't had that before. Like, he strikes me as a competent boss, but I don't know if he'll find the clients."

"Yup." Kevin had few words.

"I think it'll be fine. I know he's been in correspondence with Charles but I don't know what they said." Jacob seemed extremely confident. He even managed to work while he talked.

Robin gave up and scrolled through her emails. She did a thing she did in college where she pretended to be fully engrossed in her phone but actually, she was eavesdropping.

"Yeah, but they're not gonna prioritize us! Right? That's not how it works." Catherine knew how to see what others couldn't.

"What do you mean?" Jacob asked. "He and Charles—Chuck, whatever you wanna call him—they'll work it out."

"Really?" Catherine asserted. "You think he's gonna go to bat for us? You think he's in there vigorously trying to work out how we can be paid for that week? That's not Dexter, my dude. Charles would smash his Mercedes with a golf club before giving us paid time off."

"We're allowed PTO though," Xavier said, breaking a row of staples into tiny rows of staples.

"I know," Catherine insisted. "But I'm saying he'll demand we use PTO when *he* wants us to. That PTO is for vacation or sick days, not for bad company policy or low sales."

Xavier gave a lonely round of applause. Dexter had told Robin that she couldn't use PTO to go to the event. But it should be *her choice*! That's the whole point of it being protected.

"You think he could've gotten clients with more effort?" Jacob inquired.

"Yeah," Catherine said. "He's a pedantic son of a gun, and I

Hoop Drama

like the fella but he'll only take clients that he likes. We've never had certain clients before like…um…an LGBT ad or something."

That caught Robin's attention. She scrolled back to the top then tuned in.

"He don't like the gays," Jacob said, stretching in his rolling chair.

"I don't think he hates them, but it's not a coincidence that we've never done a rainbow ad."

"What about that one ad for Queen's Moon Advanced?"

Catherine was prepared for Kevin's question. "That was only a brief mention in a long website. The point is Dexter—and Charles too—could get more clients with a change in mindset."

"I won't disagree," Jacob noted, rising from his chair to take the stapler away from Xavier. Thank goodness. "In the military you win or die, so we just won every single time."

"Or did fifty pushups…" Kevin knew Jacob's whole backstory much like how Jacob knew Dexter.

Ping. An email appeared in Robin's personal email. It was a highly professional message that she assumed was from an online seller. She perused it very quickly until the word 'television' caught her eye and made its way into her conscious thought.

Mrs. Robin Chapel,

I'm contacting you from Channel 12 (KCC 12) on behalf of our morning anchor, Rene Michelle. Please refer to me as Grace Renolds in all further correspondence. We discovered your Twitter post hitting incredible marks this morning when it was brought to our attention by a friend, Dr. Brody Pearson. We'd like to have you on as a guest ASAP to discuss the post and the importance of black voices. If you are available tomorrow, Saturday, June 2nd, at 10:00 AM on the dot, we'd love to have you appear live on our television program. Please park out front in the lot

Andy Silvers

labeled 'Guest Parking.'

Please reply to this email to confirm your participation. You have until 5 PM today. If you have any questions, respond directly to this email thread, or call our offices before 5:00 PM EST.

Ms. Gracie Renolds, MFA

KCC 12 News

"…guys…" Robin spoke so quietly, a dog in a gymnasium would have trouble hearing her.

"Maybe he hasn't changed. I don't know." Catherine commanded attention when she wanted it. "I just don't think we're gonna pull a W out of this."

"Guys. Catherine…" Robin spoke up louder.

Catherine rolled over on her chair. "What's up?"

"Look," Robin pointed at her screen.

Catherine read the email. "Hey, Jacob. Kevin. I think the Pittsburg news just emailed our girl."

Everyone gathered around.

"Wow." Jacob read quickly. "I knew that message was gonna do something—but state news? That's crazy. You have to talk about C. E. Proctor Creative."

"Yeah," Kevin asserted. "You have to rep our company."

Robin began to mouth breathe. She wasn't worried about a scam or hoax, though she should've. She was worried about waking up with a different life. "Who says I should even go there?"

"What!" Catherine called out. "You have to. This is big for our company."

"They don't want me to talk about the company."

"Yeah, but do that anyway. We need clients."

Xavier pitched in. "And I need a new GPU so my PCIe slots won't be so lonely."

○ 330 ○

Hoop Drama

Catherine chided him with an audible hiss.

"Robin, this is what you believe in. Talk about that." Jacob was the surprise voice of reason.

Her heart pounded. 5 PM was just three hours away. That felt like three minutes in the mind of a lady who could never picture herself on TV.

"Hey," Jacob said. "I know that Brody guy. He works at Major Collins. I bet you he has connections everywhere."

"I bet it's her hashtag that's getting the attention."

"Probably."

She wanted to call Ray to ask him about it, but couldn't remotely begin to word her question properly. Plus, he worked Saturday morning, so he'd be unavailable to assist her. Gosh, that'd mean driving herself the hour trip. What if she had a stroke? What about appendicitis? It was too much stress, so she made the worst possible decision. "I'm gonna walk away and let you guys decide. Respond for me and I'll get coffee."

"Yes!" Catherine hollered. "We got this, Captain Chapel."

Oh, goodie gumdrops. Another nickname.

"Yes, girl. You just relax and let us handle this."

Robin got up, walking with a level of *jank* typically reserved for drunkards and former presidents. In the hall, her ears began to ring. Gosh, if she fainted, that'd be crazy embarrassing. Luckily, she made it to the employee lounge, where she grabbed onto the counter like a railing. She located the coffee pot, but neglected to insert the coffee filter. She decided on tea.

She pushed the hot water button, then leaned up against the counter. *What was Catherine doing? They probably signed her up for the interview. Did they mention Proctor Creative to the newsroom?* Yeesh.

ROBIN: *Ray, they're asking me to be on TV tomorrow at 10.*

331

Andy Silvers

No joke!!! I'm freaking out since you can't go. Please help.

Every moment took her breath away. She wasn't even sure what she was afraid of. Was it being on TV? Sure. But there was a sense that she wasn't ready for attention. Never one to demand attention (or even respect), Robin freaked out at the idea that the entire state (actually two) would listen to her opinion and guidance in a fraught political time. She was neither a civil rights leader nor did she know the Porter family. Plus, she wasn't a mother. Her hashtag, #afatherlikeyou, was directed at families, but she didn't have a family—meaning kids. It was a tornado of absurdity. The next day, she was going to go on national TV in front of hundreds of thousands of people and make an absolute fool of herself.

Crap. The hot water heater wasn't plugged in. No wonder it didn't boil. "I give up."

Catherine ran into the room. "Hey, Captain Chapel. We got it worked out. Come on back now so we can get you ready."

Everyone, and it was everyone, surrounded the poor black girl, happily spitting ideas at her like she was a rookie pitcher. But it was all noise. Catherine said something about mentioning the MCU campaign. Kevin said something about pretending to have a doctorate. And Jacob said something about putting a tiny earpiece in and letting him tell her what to say.

But it was all just noise. Blah. Blah. Blah.

SATURDAY, JUNE 2ND

"AH!" Robin shot up like a whack-a-mole at 7:15 AM. Her hands were shaking. Ray smiled at his beloved.

"You don't gotta get up right now. You can wait until like eight or maybe eight thirty to get up." His massive biceps weren't enough to distract her from absolute panic.

"You can't be serious. I can't sleep! How am I supposed to go on TV and talk about something I wasn't there for?" Her dreams were overtaken by thoughts of failure. She went on the show then started crying for no obvious reason. For a whole day, Twitter was a flood of hashtags referring to Robin's utter meltdown on live TV. Her heartrate increased until Ray gently placed his lips on her forehead.

"Baby…" He knew how to calm her down. "Did you write the Tweet?"

What Tweet? Oh, that one… "Yeah. So?"

"What did you mean?"

"I just meant that people of color have it rough sometimes because…you know, we often get mistreated despite all the progress since white pride still affects us today. That old man probably thought he could do whatever he wanted because that's how he grew up. Racism has to be untaught. People need to learn about black history and prejudice before they can unlearn it."

Andy Silvers

"And what about the hashtag?"

"Um…it's just me saying that anyone can be a victim. Any person of color can find themselves hurt by the system built in this country over two-hundred years ago. Kenan was a daddy just like Shanice is a mommy and Jesse is a father. It can be anyone and the scars that are left behind hurt the kids too. It hurts the whole family and—"

"Just say that."

"What?"

Ray walked out toward the kitchen. "I'll make a quick breakfast if you want it."

"Wait! But what if they ask a question that I don't know the answer to? And what about my coworkers, Ray? They want me to advertise or market or something…" He had left the conversation.

In the kitchen, he calmly made an omelet with toast.

"Did you hear me?" Robin asked, finally lowering her voice in fairness to the other tenants.

"Yes, madam."

"What about other questions? How are you so calm?" She flipped back a mess of box braids that had fallen in front of her eye.

He sighed, then smiled like he'd made a discovery. "Because your mom was right."

She took her plate with fresh food but paid it no attention. "Right? About what?"

"She believed in you and in your message. I know she hurt you, but she made it right. I've never been on TV either. Heck, I'd probably say something stupid. But that's not you. You're a warrior. Please eat your breakfast."

She plodded along to the table, using her meal as an excuse not to talk. Deep down, there was guilt. She knew she had the rare

Hoop Drama

chance to speak about important issues, to convey her lifetime of thoughts, but the messenger felt adrift.

Kenan and his wife had already been on TV several times talking about that day. Robin was a nobody marketer who posted one message on the internet. Speaking of which, she checked the message.

Wow! 70,000 views and 16,000 likes. It still wasn't a million, but apparently it was enough for TV. After getting dressed and applying mascara with military precision, she hit the road with a bag of dried raisins. And yes, she wore her emerald hoops.

She rocked out to her on-the-road playlist which was a great distraction from endless traffic. She had actually never been to Pittsburg or even Pennsylvania before, so the sights were completely new.

RAY HUBBY: *We're gonna play your video at the shop. Slay queen!*

Oh, please don't.

She found the correct address, parked in the front, and took a deep breath. "You've got this, girl. You've got this."

Nobody came out to greet her. She was on her own. The building looked small from the outside due to its irregular shape. It appeared to be a single story but parts of it were two.

A quick tug on the locked doors nearly broke her nails. "Oof." She located the buzzer to sign in. Inside the lobby was a central desk surrounded by many doors. One door clearly led behind the desk but the others were a mystery. For the moment, fear had been caged while curiosity and confusion took over.

"Hello, you said you were Mrs. Chapel?" The lady at the front desk appeared to be about forty, and her clothing matched her professional business location. Her makeup…was honestly a bit too harsh.

335

Andy Silvers

"Yes. I'm Mrs. Chapel."

"I'll tell them you're here."

It was 9:40 AM. Gosh, that meant only twenty minutes until showtime. Now her fear had returned. All of a sudden, a blond lady appeared from behind door number three. "Hey, Mrs. Chapel. Welcome." She was clearly in a hurry.

She followed her into the hallway. Everything was much brighter behind the door. The lobby almost felt like it suffered a power outage. It was a far cry from the bright C. E. Proctor lobby. "Hello. Thank you."

"All right, now you'll be on at 10:00 on the dot. Our host, Rene Michelle will announce her guest and then you'll be on air. Don't be nervous. No one has any expectations."

No one...except for Robin, Ray, Shanice, Jacob, Catherine, Kevin, Xavier, and likely Brody. "It's crazy that I'm even being interviewed for a Tweet with so few likes. I mean...Dr. Brody commented. That's probably it." She wasn't really explaining anything to Grace.

"He's not the *only* one. It's not that crazy. You'll only be on for five minutes. Maybe less."

Gulp. Five minutes? How the hell was a quiet restaurant manager going to talk for five minutes? Then she got a message.

MOM: *Good luck, baby. I got my team to watch you even if they don't want to. I texted Dad. I hope gone watch it.*

Yay. Another person to add to the list. The loud notification reminded her to put her phone on silent.

ROBIN: *Thanks, Mom. I love you.*

Twenty minutes turned to ten which turned to five. Grace returned. Robin followed the guiding hand to the stage. There were people everywhere. Many were wearing all black and half had bulky headphones. A large telescoping crane flew across the set of

336

Hoop Drama

the primary newsroom. It was clear Robin wouldn't sit at the desk with Rene, but she would sit in an adjacent room to have a virtual discussion using monitors. The second she sat down on the bland gray chair, her nerves shot up ten-fold. She began to mouth breathe and her mouth dried out. Luckily, the crew had seen it before and handed her a small water bottle.

The only way to hear the host was through a speaker placed below a monitor. The monitor showed a live readout of Rene at the desk. It was such a distant way of talking that could make someone feel isolated. Behind Robin was a large LED wall depicting an image of Pittsburg with the weather overlayed. She crossed then uncrossed her legs, completely unsure of how to sit or where exactly to look. Above her was a large microphone locked in place on a black metal stand. It was surreal to put it mildly.

She immediately pulled out her phone with only minutes to spare to check the infamous Tweet. It had roughly 78,000 views in less than a week. Impressive—yes. Newsworthy—not really.

"Okay, take a deep breath. If you don't know what to say first, just thank us for having you on."

She gave good advice but no 'You got this' or 'I believe in you.' Grace clearly wasn't a motivational speaker or therapist. The giant camera in front of her almost appeared like a weapon ready to strike. A large light glowed red to signal she wasn't on air. A screen in front of the camera that would normally feature a script displayed the time—9:58 EST.

For the first time, the heat got to her. She could feel her head becoming slightly wet. Hundreds of lights littered the ceiling and an unemotional man stood beside the camera ready to do his job.

Rene Michelle finished talking about the week's film news. "...if fans of the comics can have this much impact on the films being made, maybe Hollywood will start making projects based on

Andy Silvers

online chatter alone. I for one want a remake of the much-maligned film *Superman: The Quest for Peace*. Maybe one day. Okay. Joining us now is a young lady whose viral Tweet has—"

Oh no. I'm not ready. The pressure sent a horrid wave of bumps down her spine, causing her to shiver. In her panic, she yanked off her wedding band to fidget with.

"—embodied the feeling all of black America has this year when it comes to violence. This is West Virginia resident Robin Chapel. Good to have you on."

The light turned green! "Thank you for having me on..."

That was way too loud. Even the camera operator gave her a strange look.

"It's a pleasure to have you. Your Tweet, which was posted on May 28th, has garnered close to 80,000 views and 20,000 likes. It really speaks volumes about the current situation. You never knew the Porter family but you posted the hashtag a father like you. Tell us about that."

No time to think. "Okay...well I posted that in the afternoon. I was at work. I work at an ad agency called C. E Proctor Creative..."

All of a sudden it dawned on her how much she couldn't say. She couldn't mention the meeting with Dexter. That was private. The Justin Cavalry campaign was under NDA or something like it. Furthermore, her correspondence with Dr. Pearson was likely also secret. Her work with the MCU campaign was probably okay to mention but it was irrelevant to the story. And for certain she couldn't mention her meddling behind the scenes as that would result in immediate termination.

She started with something generic, hoping that time would fill her mind with great ideas. "...our whole staff had seen the Kenan Porter story and been troubled by it. The hashtag I guess

Hoop Drama

signifies the fact that shots don't just hurt one person. You know, they hurt a whole family."

"Wow. You mentioned that Mr. Porter will be attending an event on Juneteenth at Major Collins University. You worked with them to increase the volume of black voices but before we discuss that, we will play a quick clip to fill everyone in."

Suddenly, a news reel played, depicting the front door of Todd's house with the bullet hole still there. Then, they showed Mr. Porter surrounded by his family, opening cards from community members. The final image almost made Robin cry. Mr. Porter, with the help of a young nurse, gets up from a sofa using a crutch. His upper body strength was nearly gone and he had lost roughly thirty pounds. The only hope of not ruining the interview like in her dream was to face away. *Just don't look at it.*

"Mr. Porter and his wife have spoken out about the issue, calling on lawmakers to address gun violence in a serious way. But community members can show their support as well. Your work at the ad agency has helped promote marginalized voices using media. Please tell us how your team has answered the call."

If only she knew… "Our team at C. E. Proctor Creative is wonderful. We work well together and I'm so glad to have helped with that campaign. Um…the university really had an eye toward the future. That's why we used our platform to create a positive space for black voices. My—Our company is all about collaboration and I really took it upon myself to create copy and images that promote a positive message."

That was rough, but then things got rougher.

A screengrab from the website showed Robin on the MCU website wearing her hoops. "This is you on the website. We encourage our viewers to check it out to see the totality of your work, but the popular Tweet was posted outside of official

Andy Silvers

channels. Among the comments is one from Olivia Porter stating the following. 'Thank you for your honesty. People will not act until they see that Kenan was not special. He was just a father like so many.' How did you react to that comment?"

OH CRAP! YIKES! Robin had no idea that had been commented. She debated within a second whether to acknowledge that she hadn't seen it. The last thing she intended to do was lie on camera, but the guilt of admitting she didn't notice the victim's wife would be irreversible. "I believe that's a powerful message—more important than anything I could ever say. We at Proctor Creative support the Porter family wholeheartedly. Um…our words don't always come through—I mean here they did, but—that's why our actions are so important. Until America faces gun violence head on, nothing will change. But you can't change the country with news stories alone. You have to change the culture. More people see an ad than watch the news, so I am proud to create ads that tell stories that matter."

"Awesome. Do you have any kids of your own."

"No, but maybe one day, you know. And I want them to be safe."

"Likewise. Will you be in attendance on Juneteenth for Mr. Porter's MCU presentation?"

Oh gosh. She felt like a politician sweating bullets over having to answer questions about an ongoing scandal. "I definitely want to…um…my belief is that Mr. Proctor will open the door for me to attend that event…so…"

If he opened the proverbial door, that'd be a miracle. Unfortunately, now she had essentially pressured him into it…and she still hadn't met him!

"We hope you can attend."

Then she remembered what she needed to say. "I do want to

Hoop Drama

thank my mom. Shanice, I know you're watching. She's my rock. I don't claim to have all the answers, but I'm proud to have her guidance all these years. Without that, I'd not be on this show."

"Wow. Your mother sounds like an incredible woman. We have time for one more question. Do you have any advice for young women who want to make a difference but feel like their workplace or family wouldn't support their efforts."

Boy, did she? That question hit like a pile of bricks in light of the truth of C. E. Proctor Creative. They had to be tricked into supporting voices of color. But on live TV, she couldn't say that. She had laid the foundation that Dexter and Charles were altruistic like herself. And if she gave advice telling people to defy their peers, that would backfire on Monday for sure. It was truly the hardest question ever. And Robin was at fault for steering around the issues in her life, but what was she to do? —tell the country that her bosses were racist or bigoted? The hard thing to accept was that sometimes making a difference meant dragging one's enemies across the finish line kicking and screaming. If Dexter could just see the joy on people's faces at being seen, then perhaps he could change.

"So, it's not easy. I...I just see it like this. I will stand, even if I must stand alone."

"Wow. A powerful quote to end on. Thank you, Mrs. Chapel, for joining us on the show. We wish you the best with your work. Our thoughts and prayers remain with Kenan and his family. Thank you."

"Thank you." A weight like no other fell off the moment the little light turned back to red. Robin took a lengthy breath, then contemplated what she would do now that she'd spoken her truth so loudly that everyone could hear.

Grace waved her off. "Awesome job, Mrs. Chapel. Are you

sure you have no TV experience?"

Wow! Her Tweet had reached 120,000 views and 30,000 likes. Now, she was a superstar.

RAY HUBBY: *Amazing babe. I knew you could do it. Though you forgot to mention your sexy husband.*

MOM: *Wow sweetie. You're amazing. Thank you so much. You said what I never could. My coworkers felt uncomfortable just like they should.*

KEVIN: *Great job Robin. I hope Chuck feels the way you do about Juneteenth LOL.*

CATHERINE: *Thanks for mentioning us. If we don't get more clients, I'll eat a shoe. #afatherlikeyou*

TANYA: *I'm so proud of you. You're a legend.*

DEXTER: *We need to talk. Monday. 8 AM.*

MONDAY, JUNE 4TH

Time healed her wound...so to speak. The fear that had been racked up after seeing that text had diminished after two days. Still, she knew there was a double standard. The entire state of Pennsylvania was likely on her side, but somehow, she had gotten Dexter's attention in the worst way. By the time she clocked in, her mindset was hardened against fear, not due to bravery, but apathy. The only saving grace was that if she was fired, she could certainly attend the Juneteenth event.

"Oh, Robin. The rebel without a cause." Catherine opened the morning discussion with a sarcastic comment that lacked any nuance.

"I promise I have a cause."

Kevin was next with a pat on the back. "Amazing, Captain Chapel. You killed it."

She wanted to argue, but Ray had said the same thing. Yesterday, he had taken her out to eat (at Venue 45) to celebrate her quasi-celebrity status. She felt truly happy that day, but reality always won; her bosses may not appreciate being hurled under the bus. If only she had known about Mrs. Porter's comment. That was why politicians find out the questions beforehand. It's to prevent answers they will have to explain for the next four years.

The new and improved Jacob had his two cents. "I never

thought that contact with Dr. Pearson would pay off, but it really did." He grabbed his phone. "Look here."

Robin examined the comment from Mrs. Porter for the second time. She had missed it in the sea of thousands. "Yes. I saw that."

"How did you get Juneteenth off?" Kevin asked the burning question.

Dexter had explicitly stated that she'd be fired if she tried to attend, even with PTO. "I didn't."

Kevin laughed. That's all he had to say.

Speaking of the Devil, Dexter popped his head in. "Everyone! Idea Blitz now. You know where."

Everyone stared at each other for a few seconds. Jacob was first to leave, pushing his chair in and putting his monitor to sleep. In hindsight, it was obvious that he was ex-military.

The group led the way downstairs to the familiar meeting room. Melanie, Xavier, and Henry joined too. Today, Henry had an anime-inspired shirt. She saw Percy so rarely that she forgot he existed. Robin was too busy with her own work, but if time permitted, she'd sit in with the design team just to watch the process.

A piping hot cup of coffee became a fidget toy. Everyone was quieter than normal, likely owing to the stressful financial state of the agency. However, if Robin was fired, *her* financial state would be much worse.

"Okay, sit down. Kevin, what are you doing?"

"This is clearly a two-cup meeting." He waited for the coffee machine to spit out his second cup.

"Huh...so...today is going to be interesting—"

Hopefully that didn't mean firing her in front of a live audience. Dexter was cruel but not barbaric.

"We have had some developments over the weekend that I

Hoop Drama

must address." Dexter seemed adamant not to look at Robin, but he happily made eye contact with everyone else. "Due to our very own Robin Chapel, we have made great headway in terms of clients."

Catherine clapped.

Dexter continued. "Potential clients. So, over the weekend, I spoke with two companies that want the full package. I'll be meeting with some execs tomorrow and other execs this Friday, I think. We need to get the Justin Calvary campaign done in short order as our staff isn't quite big enough to cover three massive ongoing campaigns."

"I thought it was just two," Melanie noted.

"Well, there are two that are highly likely and one that is touch'n'go. The point is that we'll be very busy soon."

"Does that mean we'll do some hiring?" Catherine asked what Robin was thinking.

"Yes. I've spoken to Charles about opening up a new position or two. That's still undecided. What is decided is scheduling. So, we will have full time hours this week, however, the week of June 18th we will cut hours to twenty-four."

"Wait," Jacob said. "I thought it'd be June 11th through the 15th or that Friday."

"It was, but we wanted to give you more warning. Plus, we're not going down to twenty hours. We're going down to twenty-four. That means Tuesday and Thursday off. Consider it like a break from school."

Everyone had either fear or anger in their eyes. Robin honestly felt indifferent to the whole thing due to her concerns that Dexter would dropkick her after the meeting.

"Wait," Jacob said, voice raised with perfect pronunciation. "Will we be paid for those two days?"

345

Andy Silvers

"Yes, you will automatically be enrolled for PTO."

"Wasted. But this don't add up. If we have all these new clients, why are we taking this hit?"

Great question, Xavier.

Dexter sighed. "The thing is that we are looking forward to a great June month, but May wasn't so hot. We have to balance the record books for the month. It's not my decision. It comes from the top."

Jacob spoke again. "Can I talk to Chuck?"

"I won't stop you, but I suspect he's made his mind."

"Wait," Catherine said. "What did he say when you told him that was ridiculous?"

"I beg your pardon..."

"Charles. You told him that wouldn't work, right? We can't all be forced to leave for two days."

"You're gonna get paid. I can't stress that enough. Charles is the boss, so I just say *yes.*" He spoke very professionally as though he believed every word he said. No, he wasn't necessarily lying, but he seemed unfazed by dissent.

"Not always," Jacob added. "Remember when Charles wanted to make my position a part time position? You went in there with a spreadsheet or something and showed him the numbers. You fought for my job as a leader. I have plans for my PTO."

"Yes, Jacob. I get that it's irritating. But we truly need to cut the hours to balance things out. I fought then because part time jobs in this business are unnecessary. Life's hard, kids. Please email me any question you may have. In the meantime, let's talk creative."

It sounded like Robin might keep her job—and for the most unlikely of reasons. She had accidently brought business to the agency. Unfortunately, if they were anything like Rover Callum or Justin Cavalry, they'd be a pain to deal with. However, despite

Hoop Drama

feeling upset as well, she didn't dare to complain a single word. Jacob and Catherine could say the things she never could, freeing her to hide in the background.

"The primary company is Quin Nutrition. They make sleep supplements, but they're looking to expand rapidly to energy supplements and maybe other merch. They clearly want a website overhaul and a full campaign with videos and more. It's good news."

"That's good," Percy said, gulping down his hot tea. He seemed somewhat indifferent like Robin but likely for different reasons.

"Yes." Dexter retook the conversation. "We have much to celebrate."

Jacob pulled out his phone. "Yes. Like how Robin's post has boomed since her live interview. She's got 180,000 views and 40,000 likes right now. That's more than any post from our campaign so far as I know. I think we should embrace her techniques."

Dexter scowled at him. "You can't be serious."

"We want engagement. It's good for business."

Dexter looked down at the table as if looking inward at his soul. Presumably, he didn't like what he saw. "How's Justin Cavalry going?"

"Quite well," Xavier replied. "We got the new designs done and the website is great. The cookies will provide analytics for our client. Also, ad placement will encourage prospective buyers and Instagram is a primary target with its sizable gun and ammo fanbase. The ballistics reports have been formatted in a formal, design-friendly way that can be seen by clicking a link."

"Do we want to require a link click?"

"We don't have to, but our thinking was that it's a boring chart

Andy Silvers

to anyone who doesn't want that info."

"But people buying body armor want that info I would think."

"Um…ask the Skwad. It's their idea."

Dexter turned his eyes to the creative team. "Well…"

Jacob was prepared. "We can put the charts directly on the buyer page. You see, some sites have a separate info and buyer page. HP is an example, but it's clear that the whole website is an ecommerce platform designed to direct customers to add to cart. A chart would clutter the product page, and it requires several seconds or more to truly appreciate the info unlike the video of the bunny or the customer quotes."

"Okay. I'll trust your judgement."

The meeting went on far too long with everyone asking Dexter questions they likely already knew the answer to just to stall for time. Unfortunately, Robin's deep internal monologue about the implications of her Tweet and Jacob's comments left her alone with Dexter right as Kevin walked out.

"Robin…" Dexter could be terrifying. He had a coldness that could burrow through her new-found confidence.

"Yessir." She hated saying that at this point, but he was feared more than hated.

"You can go too."

Oh. Nothing crazy? She did not want to mention her cryptic message from Saturday, but she'd rather be fired now than later. Maybe he'd fire her on Twitter so the whole world could see it. Then again, she had made allies in the Skwad. They'd stand by her side, right?

"Okay."

"You got what you wanted."

NO! He spoke right as she was almost out the door. "Sir?"

"You've got Tuesday the nineteenth off. That's what you

Hoop Drama

wanted. Enjoy." He said 'enjoy' but he looked peeved or at least stressed. It was hard to tell since he switched his line of sight between her and his computer. Maybe he found out the IRS was auditing him.

"Okay." Robin left. She didn't want to say 'thank you' as he didn't give her the day off for fun. He did it out of necessity. However, the Skwad didn't feel the same way.

"It's bullshit! Plain and simple." Jacob was pissed. While everyone else sat at their desk, he stood. "I didn't think Dexter would do that."

"We're gonna get paid though," Kevin mentioned. "I know it's bad that we lose two days but some people have it worse."

Jacob smiled. It was odd. He seemed to be trying to communicate that he understood. "Yes, Kevin. I'm sorry. Let me explain. I can go without two days. That's not the issue."

"Oh?"

"The issue is Dexter and Charles. They can't be taking a huge hit from this, right? Even so, they're making *us* take the hit. I talked with Dexter on the phone, okay. He just…seems different."

"Wait," Kevin responded. "You think he got greedy?"

"No. It's weird. He always seemed to look out for us. Like a squad. He had high expectations but also high rewards. It's tough to explain."

"You saying he won't be winning employee of the month?" Catherine definitely spoke in jest as her eyes never left the screen.

"Do we *have* an employee of the month?" Robin had to know.

"No. I'd just win it every time." Jacob smiled and stood tall.

"Yeah right," Kevin teased. "You'd win sergeant of the month. Maybe."

"Or twat of the century." Catherine had the best jokes.

After everyone quieted down, she messaged Brody using her

349

Andy Silvers

private email.

Dr. Brody Pearson,
I would like to rescind my previous email stating that I cannot attend the Juneteenth event on Tuesday. Due to fortunate circumstances, I can attend after all. I am excited to see the campus once more and to see Mr. and Mrs. Porter. Thank you so much for the invite.
Your friend,
Mrs. Robin Chapel, B.A.

This email reminded her that she had actually declined the invitation twice. Crazy. But now she was destined to go. Even if she was fired or the schedule was altered, she would go. Come hell or high water. Hopefully, Charles would be a voice of reason.

Mrs. Robin Chapel:
Awesome. We'd love to have you. I know you're doing great at work (and TV), but if you'd like to get an online degree, Major Collins is the place to get it. Just let our academic prep team assist you after the event. Thank you.
Dr. Brody Pearson, PhD.

What a great salesman. Now Robin just needed to figure out what to do on Thursday. Luckily, Catherine helped out.

"*Psst.* Carter and I want to host an event on Thursday, June 21ˢᵗ. You're invited and all my coworkers. Well, not Dexter, but you get it. Bring Ray please."

"Sure. What's the occasion?"

Catherine looked at Jacob, then smiled. "We've decided to make you employee of the month."

○ 350 ○

TUESDAY, JUNE 5ᵀᴴ

"*You* are a saint." Kevin happily took a fresh raisin cookie before they were placed in the break room.

"I don't want to brag, *but…*" Robin felt at peace. Not with the job. With the Skwad. Even Jacob had miraculously changed. "Did Catherine mention a party to you?"

Kevin grinned. He knew. "Yeah. We're making you employee of the month."

"You really don't need to."

"It was Jacob's idea."

He left before she could comment on the details. Jacob? Wow. That guy must have been lobotomized right before the start of the month.

She knew he was there early working out, so she asked him directly. "Yup," he said. "Our sales are likely to go up considerably, so it's only fair."

"But there must be great sales before, right?"

"Sure. Some months are great, but if companies want the whole package, that's over $15,000 in a single month. That's why I'm so pissed. I know our sales vary a lot per month, but I signed up for forty hours, so Dexter and Charles need to figure it out."

She nodded. "Do you remember when we went to Major Collins last month?"

"My brain is like a sponge."

"Never mind…" She didn't want to seem pedantic. Perhaps bringing up the past would snap him back to his former self.

"You're good with Captain Chapel, right?" Catherine showed up with a giant energy drink.

"Um…it doesn't piss me off like Robby does, but it doesn't really fit."

"Oh no. You're basically the captain of the Skwad. You the leader."

Uh oh. Jacob might not like that.

"Hey, everyone." Kevin was late, but only by two minutes. "Guess what Jon did?"

"You got a new tenant?" Catherine inquired.

"Sort of. It's the kitty." He showed her a picture before showing Robin. "See. He climbed inside the vase. I honestly don't know how he squeezed himself inside that thing. Oh! And he's getting big. I have to stop feeding him treats."

"Adorable."

"No," Jacob said, sounding vaguely like his former self. "I could not clean cat crap every day. And they shed like crazy."

"I got me a fine metal brush to remove extra hair. He loves it."

"And why John. What's that from?"

"*You* know."

"Oh. Okay."

Robin still didn't know why he named the cat Jon but it was unimportant. Kevin was happy. "You ready for a real tenant?"

Kevin stared at her as though she asked him when he stopped beating his wife. "No."

Then Dexter came in. He did not look happy as though he had resigned himself to a life of misery. Robin had no sympathy for him, but it did inform her decision to stay at Proctor Creative as

Hoop Drama

long as possible. *Don't be a Dexter.*

"Alright, no more yacking. We have a large project. Quin Nutrition is up first. Luckily, they're giving us about a month to do everything and *we will need* it. They want a rebrand since their sales aren't quite what they wanted, but customers say they want a daytime supplement too." He laid the brief binder on the desk. "But there's more…"

Everyone got quiet. Robin noticed the emailed brief in her inbox. She took her hand off her mouse since Dexter appeared to be giving an important speech.

"So…the brief is unique. They want a focus on so-called DEI and that includes a diverse ad. What does skin color have to do with supplements that make you feel awake? No idea, but that's what they want."

"We got this," Jacob proudly proclaimed.

Robin could swear he was abducted by aliens and reprogrammed with new memories.

"Yeah," Dexter didn't seem confident. "It's part of brand image. Make the company appear good by showing their social bona fides. It used to be stuff like green compliance or military discounts but now it's 'Look, Hispanic people.' Anyway, let's make progress quickly. Use Smartsheet. Also, this Friday, another company will drop by so be aware. They sell roadside assistance, I think. They want an app. That's all I know for now."

Robin used to have to sneak over to the executives when they entered and tell them to think in terms of diversity. Now they just did it themselves. She chuckled. And thankfully, both companies weren't selling anything counter-cultural like guns or leftist tears mugs.

"Wait," Jacob said. "Are we gonna get some supplements to try?"

353

Andy Silvers

Kevin joked, "Yes. I'm ready to pop some pills."

Dexter simply said, "Yes." Then he left.

She bore a smile until she checked Smartsheet. The list of tasks for her alone was absurd. They needed a whole new website, social media campaign, a video, and product photos. Apparently, they were finally beginning to get their products in retail stores starting with CVS. But that's not what really stood out.

They wanted a focus on diverse groups. Robin quickly checked their social media. It was almost barren, but they did have a picture of Aaron Tash, the CEO. He was whiter than sour cream on a snowcapped mountain. But that was okay. The campaign specified shining a light on diverse customers. For instance, the video needed to feature three fake customers. One black female, one black male, and one white female. Given the population of WV, Robin nearly emailed them to ask to star in the ad.

Furthermore, they wanted to hire inclusive models and place a focus on parents, showcasing the importance of health and wellbeing for families. All of a sudden, Robin wanted to pop their pills. *See, reaching out to marginalized groups is good for business,* she thought so loud it echoed inside her head.

"Hey, Jacob," she said. "Are we gonna collaborate?"

"Oh yes. Let's all take thirty minutes or so then brainstorm together."

Awesome. She was more excited than she had been any day that month. Even being on live TV didn't compare with working with a team that values her—and *sees* her.

Wanting to be prepared, the employee of the month created a text document filled with ideas.

"All right," Jacob said, stretching to the point of shaking. "Over to the whiteboard." He brought the brief.

"I look forward to Captain Chapel modeling for us again."

Hoop Drama

Gosh, it's as though Catherine could read minds.

"Maybe."

"All right." Jacob said, clearing a mess of words from the board. "So, we need to come up with a brand image. I'm not a pills guy. I only take Advil if my head is pounding. Otherwise, I just don't."

"Hah," Kevin giggled. "I take every single pill ever."

"Yes, Kevin. We know you're a drug addict."

"Let me see the brief." Catherine received the binder from Jacob. "Here." She handed it to Robin who honestly preferred having two free hands.

Jacob gave Catherine a strange look. He seemed to be threatening her with his eyes.

"Actually," Robin suggested. "I'm happy to let Jacob take the lead on this. He has way more experience than me and I really don't want to hold this binder." She was dead serious. Jacob had proven that he liked to be in charge due to his work in the military (and being a guy). Was Robin qualified to direct the DEI initiatives? Perhaps so, but she never had any sort of goal to be in charge of a team or company. Creating amazing content that benefited marginalized groups was enough. If she wanted to keep her allies, taking the path of humility was the best way.

"By all means. You've got to start sometime." He was willing to let her lead, and that was the last piece of evidence she needed to bestow creative control.

"Nah. I'm happy to learn. What ideas do you have for the brand image?" Everyone glanced at her, but then accepting the change, they turned to Jacob.

He began to speak, and she grabbed her drawing pad, ready to use her art skills to support the team.

"Honestly, the DEI initiative stuff should be pretty easy. We

355

Andy Silvers

don't have to put any key words into the copy unless explicitly asked for. Instead, the diversity is subtle, just included in the images and videos without being distracting. The brief states they want to create a more holistic campaign that focuses less on technical jargon and more on real results."

"And I have some ideas for a pastel color scheme that will fit well with their goals." Robin pitched in with her pencil ready. She really needed to buy some colored pencils for work.

"Oh, really?" Jacob asked. "Let's make a new page for the visual elements they need." He quickly opened a new tab and labeled it THEME. "What'cha got?"

"Um…I was thinking we could create a different color scheme for each page or…um…each product category. So, I actually have the colors picked. We can do solid white and solid black followed by DFB9FF for purple. Then C9FFC3 for green and FAFF93 for yellow. The wake-up products will be yellow and the sleepy products will be purple leaving extra stuff like merch to be green."

"Wow," Catherine said. "Exact swatches."

"Yeah. I prepared. So—"

"Hold on," Jacob asserted. "I need to catch up."

After he finished writing what each color was, she continued. "So, I think they want a pastel color scheme based on the brief. They have an earthy quality to them without feeling harsh or overbearing. A white website is overall appropriate for this product line, but we want to change the page background color to separate off sections and to match product packaging."

"That means you're thinking pastels for all product packaging?"

"Yes," Robin spoke with confidence. "They don't have to be one solid color necessarily. They can be a splash of color like maybe just the bottle lid or just the bottom half."

Hoop Drama

"Okay." Jacob gave a quick smile. Then he switched back to the main page. "They have a current package design, but they want a complete overhaul. They're website is very scant and really doesn't lend itself to adding new elements."

"Yeah," Catherine added. "Their website is literally two pages. One overall page and one store page."

"Yes. What we will do is create an info page and a purchase page. It's a bit like Justin Cavalry. Customers who want all the details and lifestyle advice can check out the learn section, but customers who just want to buy can use the store section." Jacob saw a hand go up.

"Wait?" Kevin asked. "This is on the website, right?"

"Yes."

"Okay. Got it."

Catherine wrote a note on the board. "I think the bottle lids should have a petal-like shape to signify natural remedies."

"Robin, I need you to—actually, what do you want to do?"

"Um…" She had no idea exactly what to do.

Jacob continued. "I was gonna ask if you could research images we would need with exact poses and such. Like, I know we'll need several images of models holding the products and high key product shots for the store. You decide what we need."

"Copy, sir."

"Really?" Catherine gave a mean side eye.

"What?"

"Anyway, they're currently using some biodegradable paper stuff right now, but since it's more expensive to manufacture and since they're looking to enter retail stores, we'll need to help create packaging with the pastel themes. Also, they need a TV ad; one that really focuses on their inclusion at CVS."

Robin got excited. "We're making a TV ad?"

Andy Silvers

Jacob pressed his lips together before revealing the bad news. "No. We don't have the budget for that. If it's an actual TV ad, typically we outsource it to BVD Video nearby or someone else. Big agencies have inbuilt video studios but not us."

"Maybe that will be one of the next employees Charles hires."

"No way, Catherine." Jacob laughed but not snidely. "They would have to invest thousands of dollars into equipment alone and if they can't even give us five days a week, they won't be buying a Hollywood soundstage or lights anytime soon."

Catherine grinned. "I know. A girl can dream."

It was starting to hit Robin that they were looking to hire new employees, but not actually give the Skwad a full week. She looked forward to going to the Juneteenth event, giving her reason to be thankful, but her colleagues' feelings still mattered.

The day went well causing the normally timid girl to glow with confidence. Kevin showed her pictures of the new kitty before heading out early.

Later, Catherine texted Robin asking what kind of food she should make at the party.

ROBIN: *Wine. Lots of wine.*

CATHERINE: *Hey, my amazing boyfriend says we need to move the party to fit more people. Dexter said we can use the conference room since no one will be there. Still pissed that we can't work, but I'm excited. Bring Ray please. I wanna get to know my brother-in-law. ;)*

TUESDAY, JUNE 19TH

After two weeks, the agency was DIFFERENT.

Robin, now called Captain Chapel by all but Dexter, had successfully transformed the agency into something to be proud of. She still had no idea why Jacob had changed so fast, but it made him such a sweetheart. He even brought cookies last week (store bought, but he pretended he baked them).

Her colleagues were still pissed about missing two days, but Juneteenth had arrived and with it, the event that had eluded her for weeks. Mr. and Mrs. Porter would be speaking live at Major Collins University. Furthermore, her infamous post had now reached fully viral status with 300,000 views and 47,000 likes.

She arrived in style to the 9 o'clock event. She wore a stunning dashiki top and large hoops. There were no snacks, but people picked up university-branded waters. The civil rights leader from the Atlantic had already spoken. It was clear that a much bigger crowd was forming to see the famous man from the news. The room was huge despite it being the second biggest auditorium at the school.

The stage was at the end of a long room with theater seating. On it was a sofa and arm chair. It reminded Robin of the Tommy Craven show. The event was being filmed and nearly a dozen employees worked quickly to set up the stage for the next speaker.

Andy Silvers

Despite the nature of the event, Robin was one of only five or six black people in attendance. A group photo would look like a dalmatian with six spots. Nevertheless, everyone was cordial, giving Robin a quick smile or nod as she made her way near the front. She sat in the second row back, right near the middle. This gave her a clear view while also allowing her to rush to the restroom if needed. Dr. Brody was nowhere in sight. He better not send someone to sign her up for classes.

Despite the fact that the story had left the news, it was still insane to think that a young father had been shot directly through the door. Luckily, criminal charges had been filed, and Todd was looking at prison time for gross negligence involving a firearm.

Finally, the moderator, a forty-something looking woman with blonde hair and a blue blouse sauntered on stage. She could relax knowing that cameras hadn't yet recorded. Kenan poked his head around a corner backstage briefly enough to be seen. Robin became giddy as though she were at a Tori Kelly concert. She wasn't meeting a celebrity, but it felt that way.

After five minutes, the lady on stage introduced herself. "Good morning, everyone. Thank you for getting up earlier than my teenagers. I guess that's why students live on campus—they have no excuse to skip class just two minutes away."

She was going to be fun.

"My name is Allison Klement. I'm a professor of Cultural studies here including African American studies and Diaspora. I graduated with my B. A. from Stanford and a master's in speech communication from University of Arizona. Today we're here to celebrate the life of Kenan Porter but also to acknowledge the work that has yet to be done. If I can get everyone to stand up, let's give a warm West Virginia welcome to Kenan Porter and Olivia Porter."

Hoop Drama

Everyone got up to clap, but Robin was first. She knew that a tragedy like his could happen to anyone like her. The stars had aligned to save the life of a young father. Fate seemed to know who would be most important, thus Robin listened with full attention.

However, it was also odd seeing how small Kenan was. At about 5' 4", he wasn't even as tall as Allison, so the idea that anyone could find him threatening was odd to say the least.

Kenan seemed uncomfortable with the situation. He barely made eye contact with the audience and he kept his arms close to his body. His wife however, waved and gave a brief smile. A ray of hope in a dark situation was that Kenan had seemingly regained his weight from before the incident. A sign of healing.

"Good morning," Allison began. "We're sorry you're here."

The audience chuckled and eventually the couple smiled.

Allison took a quick peak at her notes written on a small five by seven set of cards. "This is not how I wanted to meet you, but here we are. I will assume for the sake of brevity that everyone here has heard your story—or rather, the story of your attempted murder." Allison sat back while crossing her legs. She was comfortable with leading live events. "On May 22nd, you walk up to Mr. Todd Vanheim's home near Moundsville, and you hear a bang—no, two bangs. The home owner had actually *shot you* through his door."

"Yes."

"Now, I should ask. Were you trying to sell him teddy bears laced with fentanyl or initiate him into the Gangster Disciples?"

The audience laughed quietly, but Kenan spoke without a smile. "No." It was easy to see he had missed the purpose of her rhetorical question.

"You've already stated it, but please tell us why you visited

361

Andy Silvers

the residence of a stranger that Tuesday afternoon."

Kenan paused before answering. He mumbled a few syllables before speaking clearly. "Um…that Tuesday I was supposed to pick up my kids, you know. And I can't pick 'em up at three when they get out since I work 'til then, so I gotta wait until about four. So, I parked at the end of the street because there wasn't really any place to park and I couldn't park in the line since it keeps moving, you know."

"Wait," Allison interrupted. "So, you were not in the school pickup line? You were on the street?"

"Yeah. I park somewhere on the street because I don't wanna be in the way of other parents or teachers or nothin'. So, I see this white dog on the sidewalk. I look at it, but it doesn't see me. I wanna ignore it and go get my kids who probably are ready by then. But the dog walks up to the front door of some house and starts scratching at the door. You know, he's barking and making a fuss. So, even though it's stupid, I get out and walk up to the sidewalk. The doggy turns around but then goes back to scratching or whatever. So, I walk up to the door, but I wasn't gonna open it. Okay, I really wasn't. I start calling out hoping the owner inside can hear me. But the dog runs off to I don't know where. That's when I knock like two times maybe. I hear two shots, but I'll be honest, I never heard gunshots up close. Then I feel numb like my stomach and right leg had disappeared or something. I don't remember much else, but I passed out. That's what they told me."

"Wow. Insane. Did you see the owner through his window or anything?"

"Nah., I didn't see anything, but maybe he could see me."

"Okay. How did your wife find out?"

"I'll let her answer here. I don't wanna misrepresent."

Olivia smiled cordially. "Yes. I was at my job working the last

Hoop Drama

hour of my shift when my manager hands me a phone saying it's a policeman or paramedic or something. They tell me my husband was shot and he's at the hospital. I nearly hit the floor; I was so scared. But my kids were my concern because I'd feared maybe they were hurt. So, I ask them and they say the only victim was a black male. I leave work to pick up my kids, but I can't tell them what happened, you know; I barely even know. The sad thing is…the first time they see their dad that day…he's unconscious on a hospital bed wrapped in bandages…" The confident woman broke into tears, but she regained composure after a loving hand held hers.

This kind of story broke Robin's heart. She wasn't the type to watch medical documentaries or court cases. She avoided severe trauma both in real and fictional forms. A deep breath kept her own tears at bay.

"Crazy. We're so glad you're alive. When it comes to gun violence and racism in this country," Allison began. "Few Americans really see the impact on families. But you are living proof of the bias that we see in neighborhoods all over the country."

"Sure. Um…I wanna say that I was raised by my great mama who passed away a year ago, but she raised me and my brother to treat everyone with respect. *Everyone.* No one was better or worse or less worthy of love. That just ain't right." Kenan's words prompted Olivia to nod in agreement. "So, I don't wanna hate Mr. Vanheim or his attorney. I just wanna be with my kids and my wife, honestly. If he goes to jail, you know, I hope he gets the help he needs."

Allison nodded while checking a note card. "Absolutely. Studies have shown that a new type of racism motivated by unconscious bias contributes to acts of violence or harassment in

363

Andy Silvers

the current decade. It's dangerous because it's so covert. It doesn't look like white robes or signs with racist slurs. It presents itself as disagreement or discontentment with the current system, but it's very sinister. It's been shown that people respond to black individuals in different ways than to whites. In the area of government assistance, blacks are often viewed as undeserving of that right due to a perception of laziness or poor work ethic."

Robin felt as though she should be taking notes. Not a surprise when a professor acts like a professor.

"I never heard that before. That's interesting." Kenan had a childlike curiosity that so many adults lacked. It was clear he wanted to learn and take feedback. "Yeah, I feel that. My family received government assistance when my son was born. Um…we just didn't have the money to pay for that and we definitely didn't expect a baby…so…I worked extra hours but it just wasn't enough. After a year, I left there to go where I am now. The company I work makes airbags and other safety technology. No, I don't engineer that. I test it. My wife works part time though since we got two kids now and they eat *a lot.*"

"I imagine so. How do your kids—let me rephrase—have you discussed the attack with them and how they may be seen growing up in America today?"

"Yes," Kenan responded. He looked to his wife who gestured for him to answer that question. "My wife told them first since I was knocked out. They cried a lot. My son, Raylan, was scared he was gonna lose his papa—"

Hold back the tears, Robin.

"They're both in elementary school so I worry that they'll be too scared to enjoy life, you know, but they're stronger than steel. For real, my son who's eight has been helping me with therapy and reminding me about my medicine." Kenan smiled for the first time

Hoop Drama

from telling his own story.

"He's a character," Olivia added.

"True that," Kenan continued. "We talked to them afterword. I said I was okay and that the doctors were gonna get me back to my old self. They asked me after school if Mr. Vanheim hated us. I said no, baby. Don't let anyone look down on you because you're young. You have to be the example to others with the way you speak and behave and love. That's how we end racism."

A brief pause was met with a round of applause. The clapping didn't boom with power but it lasted for nearly a minute.

"Your family is strong," Allison said, waiting for the crowd to settle. "We've seen time after time the resilience of black families burdened with violence or hate, but I think it's about time to stop saying 'sorry' and start saying 'never again.' You've been vocal about gun safety. Can you elaborate on that for us?"

Olivia led the response. "Sure. I'm not a gun expert and Kenan and I don't own any firearms, but no one should be shooting through their door. Seriously. I spoke with our state representatives about gun safety and how quick people are to pull a trigger when they're afraid. But they're slow to defend others. I support assault rifle bans for sure, but I also support gun owner competency. I'm not sure exactly how old Todd was—or is. But I don't think he was in a right state of mind and anyone like that shouldn't own a firearm."

"Okay. So, you support assault rifle bans across the United States?"

"Yes. I think it's necessary at this point."

"Okay. You mentioned that Todd was scared. We know that you didn't pose a threat and we know that you weren't trying to open the door or anything. But we've seen throughout history white Americans using fear of the unknown to justify

Andy Silvers

discrimination. For example, fear of Latin immigrants stealing jobs. Fear of Jews buying elections. And fear of the black community gaining real power in elections or education. Do you think Todd was scared of you—that you might shoot him maybe?"

Kenan seemed confused for the first time. "Are you talking about unconscious bias? Is that what it's called?"

"Certainly, that's one term that could be relevant here. I want to know if you feel that fear affected the actions of Mr. Vanheim."

"Um…I'm not sure…I…Listen, I have no clue who Mr. Vanheim is. I don't know what his politics are, so I don't wanna say he was scared, you know—"

"He shot you twice through a door…"

"Yeah. I didn't say he was good or smart. Um…I don't like change…like in politics. People that I know kinda just want things to stay the same. They don't wanna wake up and find out the world is totally different, you know. I voted for Obama though, because I felt that he wasn't a change so to speak, but like he was the next step…Does that make sense?"

"Are you saying he was inevitable?"

Olivia chimed in. "I think he's saying we voted for Obama because we wanted an America that could be race-hopeful. We were proud to be part of the next thing America was doing right. I think most Americans were happy to be part of it."

"Okay," Allison flipped to the next note card. "Let's talk about the recovery process. It's been a few weeks, but you're still doing therapy, correct?"

※※※

The event concluded with thunderous applause, Robin among them. Kenan and Olivia had remained professional and calm

Hoop Drama

throughout the entire event. Their story was inspiring, leading Robin to feel a sense of pride. If that man was shot, but still got up to tackle each day with joy, so could she with far less pain.

Suddenly, she remembered her friend, Tanya Kushall.

ROBIN: *Hey, just wanted to know if you're at the Kenan Porter event on campus. Say hi if you see me.*

"Excuse me," a voice called from over her shoulder. She had turned around to examine the audience, most of whom had gotten up to leave or chat.

"Yes," Robin turned around to Olivia and Kenan standing less than three feet away. Her mouth opened unconsciously but she closed it to avoid embarrassment. "Hi, Mr. Porter. Um…great presentation."

"Call me Kenan," Kenan said with a friendly and distinctly fatherly smile. "I don't know. I said 'you know' way too many times. Thanks though."

Robin fidgeted with her purse, unsure what to say next.

"I love your top," Olivia noted. "It's fabulous."

"Oh. Thank you." She couldn't help but ask, "Are your kids here. They seem really great."

Kenan gave a coy grin. "No. It wasn't a good idea to bring them. They like attention, but they just don't need to hear about Todd right now."

Olivia nodded. "Yeah, I wouldn't feel comfortable with them hearing the whole story rehashed in front of a crowd."

"…plus, they have camp."

"Okay," Robin said. She wanted to mention the infamous Tweet but didn't know how to say it. Luckily, Olivia did the heavy lifting.

"I saw your Tweet—and your interview, of course. You looked amazing."

Andy Silvers

"And you spoke so well," Kenan added.

"That too."

Really? They saw *her* as the celebrity? No way. "I was terrified...I could barely think straight."

"Well, you did a good job. I wouldn't have known you were scared. We just wanted to say thank you for your work. Yeah, without you, we wouldn't have been able to fund our hospital bills."

"Really?"

"Yeah. We got lots of support, but your post going viral got us the attention we needed for our crowdfunding campaign."

Kenan pulled out his phone. "See, $178,000 raised to date."

Robin was in a state of shock. She had done all that? It felt like just yesterday, she was a manager at a small diner and now, she was queen of social media and marketing. "Wow. That's incredible. I...had no idea."

"Yeah. We loved your quote," Olivia added. "That part where you said you'll stand even if you have to stand alone. Chills. I got chills."

Robin's eyes began to burn like she was about to cry. "Whoa. I need a cold drink."

"Hah. Go get that drink. Don't let us keep you. See you around."

Olivia joined her husband who was speaking with another attendee. "See you around."

In her shock, she forgot to respond. Wow. In less than sixty days, she found a career job, made new allies, appeared on a college website, changed the direction of her company, hooked up her brother-in-law, wrote a viral Tweet, went on live TV, met a local hero, and gave a lonely man new purpose. She was on fire. Boss Queen Robin.

Hoop Drama

For the first time in years, she puffed up her chest to walk outside. Starting that day, she'd never be afraid of anyone, not even Dexter. If she had the strength to sweep Ray off his feet, that'd be her first goal when she returned home.

TANYA: *Yes. It was great. Girl, you're going places. I can't wait to see you shine.*

WEDNESDAY, JUNE 20TH

"You look excited." Catherine gazed with heavy eyes at her Bibbidi Bobbidi coworker.

"Yeah," Robin replied. She wore the biggest hoops she could find knowing she was one of the Skwad. "Guess what I did on my day off?"

"Watched *Eat Pray Love* with a bottle of chardonnay and a heavy-set cat?"

"Um…no. I went to Major Collins—remember them? —to see Kenan Porter live. They answered questions and stuff."

Catherine popped open an energy drink. "Wow. That's right. I think you mentioned that."

"Yeah. And they thanked me afterword. Get this, their crowdfunding campaign had been boosted by my Tweet. The viral one. They raised like a hundred thousand off of it."

Catherine gave a quick side eye, then a long yawn. "Sweetie, they were so famous they could crowdfund anything for that whole week. They were being nice to you. But it's still cool that you met them."

She was right. They didn't need a viral Tweet from a nobody to raise funds. But it felt good anyway. "Sure. How's your new romance going?" Wink. Wink.

"Blossoming like a cactus," she said with a twinkle in the eye.

Hoop Drama

Robin and Ray had blossomed more like a night sky Petunia.

"Is that good?"

Catherine just stared at her. Then she did something incredible. She removed the now-dusty photo of the two children from her desk. The stock photo itself was balled up and trashed while the frame was shoved into her purse.

"Hey, Captain," Jacob arrived later than normal since he had brought a batch of 'homemade' cookies. Yet again, he had obviously just taken them out of a store package and stuck them on a plate. "Xavier saw your drawings on Smartsheet—loved them."

The new captain had drawn several designs for the website and the products. She had colored everything in with colored pencil and added shadow detail to about fifty percent of it. The final designs featured largely white bottles with pastel colors for the lid and font only. "Really?"

"Yeah. He says he'd love to have you on the design team."

Yeesh. "Yeah. I bet." Then she remembered a question. "Hey, Catherine. How'd you get Dexter to allow us to use the upstairs meeting room to party?"

She chuckled right as Kevin walked in. "I didn't. We're not even supposed to go upstairs."

Dexter had once said that Robin would never need to be in that room. But she didn't care anymore. Because even though she still couldn't hang out in there, she felt like she could. Like she deserved to. Dexter could take his opinions and shove them up his rear. And of course, Robin said all of that.

"Whoa," Kevin said. "Keep your voice down."

"I've kept my voice down long enough." Shy Robin was dead indeed.

"I can understand why he'd not be okay with food and drinks

Andy Silvers

all over the room." Jacob maintained his voice of reason. Everyone then calmed down to begin real work. After a few minutes, Jacob realized the cookies were sitting on his desk so he arose to put them in the break room. Robin followed him, hoping to finally ask the question lurking in her mind for days.

"You want a cookie right now, huh?" Jacob teased. "Okay. No one can resist my fresh homemade Walmart special."

She was right. Jacob probably couldn't make toast, much less cookies. "Uh…no. Later. Can I ask you something serious?" She had no hesitation in her voice or an unconscious need to breathe through her mouth. She was a captain speaking to her soldier.

He played it serious too, crossing his arms to signal engagement.

"I remember at Major Collins when you told me that we didn't need diverse voices for the campaign. Like…I asked about Miguel and Tanya and you shrugged me off. It's okay if you don't remember—"

"No. I'm sorry. I didn't treat you like a member of the team. I treated you like a secretary." His eyes told a deeper story. One of regret and maybe fear.

Robin's heart of gold knew no bounds. "I forgive you. We're a team."

He nodded.

She wanted to ask a follow-up, but it was clear everything necessary was already said. But before he left the room, he said one more thing.

"Look, Dexter doesn't really *believe* anything. I mean—I know he's Catholic or whatever, but he doesn't bring that to work. But *you*…you're always you. Just Robin."

Jacob returned to work. Whether shy or bold; feminine or masculine; annoyed or excited; Robin never wore a mask. Dexter, however, was a chameleon. He hid his religion like it was his darkest secret.

"Do you know about Carter's tattoo?" Catherine bore a sly grin when Robin returned.

"Yes."

"He said it was secret."

"It's secret from *most* people."

"Hey, Captain," Kevin inquired. "Can you check my work before I submit it. I don't want to sound inauthentic."

He had been charged with writing some of the copy for the website including DEI and related content. It took a good three minutes to read all of it. "It's pretty good. I'd just change this one sentence here to be more neutral. This sounds like you're saying that black families are unhealthy and need to use drugs to stay awake…"

"Kevin!" Catherine called. "You ain't some kinda racist, are you?"

Kevin blushed. "No! I just—I'll let Robin write it." He shoved himself back in his rolling chair.

"Don't worry, bro. I gotcha." Robin patched up the sentence in no time, delivering a product that the company could be proud of. Dexter wasn't in charge. Sure, he was in charge of her, but not the campaigns. Companies finally saw C. E. Proctor Creative for what it could be.

She checked her emails again, seeing something unusual in her work address. There was a strange message from Aaron Rafellow Creative LLC.

Mrs. Robin Chapel:

After reviewing your body of work for the past few months including a brave appearance on TV following a viral Tweet, we at ARC would like

Andy Silvers

to formally invite you to apply to our company. We understand that you live in West Virginia and that moving to Marietta would be a big move. However, we believe strongly in your message and have graciously decided to offer you this opportunity to work full time as a Graphic Designer FT starting in July. It pays a large salary with full benefits including dental.

No need to respond to this email. My name is Kiera Dublin. I'm the hiring manager here. If you are interested in interviewing, we can accommodate a digital face-to-face that'll take up to about thirty minutes. If you feel you are a fit for the role, click the link directly below and put Kiera Dublin under 'How did you hear about this job?' Openings fill up quickly, so be prompt. Thank you for your time.

Truly,

Ms. Kiera Dublin

Aaron Rafellow Creative, LLC

Goodness gracious. Could Robin's life get any more insane? Normally, she'd freak out about the email coming through her work account, but truly, she barely cared. No sweat to break. Knowing that she was caught up on her work, she actually clicked the link. It took her to the application page on the website. There was no indication of how much it paid, but the team was quite diverse. A tiny bit of stress did enter her psyche when she realized that while she had nothing to lose, she also had nothing to gain. She had only a few months of experience at Proctor Creative, a graphic design degree from a non-famous school, no leadership experience, no references since Dexter was a no go, and no interview charisma.

But for once she whispered, "To hell with all that." Her application was done by lunch break. She invited the Skwad (and Xavier) to pick up subs. They agreed and had a pleasant time

Hoop Drama

spreading gossip in the break room. The one thing she didn't mention was the interview. In an odd way, it felt like cheating on the team.

However, after lunch, she pulled out her phone in the stairwell to tell her husband all about it.

[Oh, gosh! Hi.]

Ray seemed concerned. And more curiously, his voice sounded far away from the phone, like he was on speaker.

"Hi. It's the woman you married. Are you okay?"

[Well, are you okay? You don't normally call in the middle of the day.]

Women can tell when something is up because men always act exactly the same. It's one of the constants women like so much. But Ray was nervous. Then she heard some distant chatter and what sounded like a shower curtain being drawn.

"Are you in the shower? I thought you had work—Wait! Our shower doesn't have a curtain! *Raymond Deon Chapel*, if you're in someone else's shower, Imma cut a bitch. I will!"

Finally, he had to talk. [No, it's not like that...honey. I'm in the hospital.]

"What! Oh, dear lord. Are you okay?"

[I'm fine. Lorenzo finally got his wish when the lift cables dropped the car with my hand still in the engine bay. I got a few stitches.]

Robin's jaw dropped below her waist. "Oh, dear lord in heaven. I'm coming there. Which hospital? Off Mountain Point I think..."

[No! I'm done. They're releasing me in like an hour. Just meet me at home. I love you.]

"Raymond, now is not the time for I love you." She had made it back to her desk where the Skwad heard her comment.

Andy Silvers

Jacob raised his eyebrows. "Uh oh. Is it the hubby?"

Robin didn't answer him, instead she debated her options. "Just tell me which hospital or I'll drive to all of them."

[Baby, I'm good. I don't want you to lose your job. Just stay there. I'll be home when you get done.]

Sadly, he had a point. While not afraid of her bosses, she certainly didn't want to test their patience. It's like how a man can be fearless around spiders, yet never chance it by placing one on his face. With a deep sigh she said, "Fine. But I'll bring medicine from the pharmacy. And if you can't drive, let me know now please."

[Thank you, pumpkin. I'm okay. I'll drive all right. See you tonight.]

"You better not think about building something in our apartment with your broken hand—" He hung up. "Ray? Ray! Unbelievable."

"Yikes," Catherine chuckled. "Is he gonna need a time out?"

"He's gonna need a wheelchair." Thankfully, Robin's coworkers were accommodating, allowing her to work as a partner.

"If we need to call off the party, we can," Kevin noted.

"No. Ray won't be joining us, but I'll go."

Robin left as early as she could get away with (four minutes), then bought several pain killers and bandages from the pharmacy.

※※※

"You're lucky I don't break your other hand." Robin pressed her lips together while handing Ray some meds.

"Whoa. When did you become nurse Ratchet?"

"I can't afford to see you hurt. Is that a water bottle?" She stared at a plastic bottle on the floor near her husband's chair. It

○ 376 ○

Hoop Drama

couldn't have been there before.

"Yes. I'm gonna clean it up. I just needed to rest."

"Then why aren't you in the bed?"

"I was trying to watch TV real quick."

Robin rolled her eyes. The second they get sick or hurt, men find time to do everything but the one thing they should do. Plus, the TV was off when she arrived home, meaning he must've heard the door and turned it off. Gosh, she had done something like that when she was in middle school. He was a grown man. "Do you work tomorrow?"

"About that…"

Oh, here he goes.

"I talked to my boss. He told me to just get better, but the problem is we can't have injured employees on the auto floor without a signed doctor's note. I'll still get paid the usual though. They said my hand can't be used to lift nothing until at least fourteen days."

Robin shook her head. "I guess we can manage that."

"I'm sorry, sweetie. Um…our insurance should cover most of it, but there's good news. The injury was an accident and not my fault so…"

"Huh. Did you say this was Lorenzo or something?"

Ray sighed. "Yeah. He's not too bright. We love him but I think he has a few screws loose. AH! Don't touch there!"

"Sorry."

"Anyway, we gotta lift the engine out of the compartment and it's a two-man job. I guess he didn't secure the engine correctly."

"He better be fired for this."

Ray frowned. "I don't want that, but that's probably what he'll do. I called you as soon as I could. I really did."

Nurse Robin finally began to relax. Her heart still raced, but

377

Andy Silvers

her mind was steady. She saw his hand. It had swelled to nearly double the thickness and was purple in many spots. The stitches were worse than he had described, numbering at least twelve. It seemed that something sharp and metal had ripped open the skin. "Well, you're gonna stay here tomorrow. I'm going to the team party, but I can take care of you in the morning. I may be home late."

"Yes, dear."

After returning his TV privileges, she made a simple dinner. They both watched football together without uttering a word. It was a Patriots game, but Robin wasn't really paying much attention and she suspected Ray wasn't either.

Monthly bills sat on the counter. Dirty dishes filled the sink.

Despite the sudden chaos, Robin relaxed by reminding herself of the good. Her coworkers loved her. Her boss tolerated her. Her career was on the right track. She could stand tall knowing she was making the world a better place. Here without all the noise, her coworkers, or her phone; she could just sit in silence. There she focused on what mattered most.

Regardless of what tomorrow would bring, she'd always have Ray. "Hey. I applied for a job today."

"Really? I thought you liked your job."

"I do, but I wanna keep my options open."

THURSDAY, JUNE 21ST

Early on Thursday morning, she received an email response to her application.

Mrs. Robin Chapel:

Thank you for submitting your application for the Graphic Designer FT position at AR Creative. At this point, we have decided to move your application forward to the interview phase. Please select one of the available times below to interview via web conference. You must select a time at least 24 hours in advance and you must cancel or reschedule with at least 12 hours' notice. Please be prepared for a minimum of twenty minutes and up to forty-five minutes for the interview. Be prepared with any questions you have after the interview concludes.

We will send you a link to the stream in a separate email.

Thank you. We look forward to meeting you.

Ms. Kiera Dublin

Aaron Rafellow Creative, LLC

Robin had difficulty breathing, and so did Ray. In order to get it over with as soon as possible, she scheduled her interview for that Saturday at 10 AM. She acted as house wife and nurse until 6 PM when she left for the group party.

Andy Silvers

※❀※

It was the weirdest journey. From being made fun of for her large hoop earrings to getting the employee of the month treatment (before any other employee), Robin found herself in a state of shock. Her friendships had proven that she could do anything she set her mind to, even in the face of repudiation.

She had planned on bringing cookies or something similar, but her husband's injury put a stop to that. Either way, the smell of food filled her nose upon arrival.

"Hey! Captain Chapel is in the house!" Jacob hollered to the young queen who was hoping not to be noticed so fast.

"Come get some wine, girl, before Kevin drinks it all." Catherine held out a glass with some red wine in it. Robin had actually been joking about bringing lots of wine as the last thing she needed was to be stopped for buzzed driving.

"I brought some muffins, Robin. I ate one to make sure it was safe." Kevin was dressed casually again. He really had skinny legs that made his rounder belly seem odd. He reminded her of Mr. Bobinsky from the animated *Coraline* film. That movie had scared the crap out of her as a girl, but now was a regular Halloween tradition.

Her heart fluttered seeing everyone there. The Skwad showed up, of course, and also Xavier, Melanie, Henry, and one other. Unsurprising, Dexter wasn't there. He probably had civil rights legislation to protest. It was odd that Mr. Proctor wasn't there though. Robin was still confident she'd meet the mystery man, even asking Percy about him while getting some grilled chicken.

"Uh…he was here earlier. I have no idea if he's still here."

"Gotcha," Robin said, not interested in pressing him on it. "How do you feel about the hours cut?"

Hoop Drama

"I'm upset, but I'll live. My wife told me to be happy since I'm still getting paid. She's right, as usual."

"Do you have kids?"

Percy's candor was refreshing. "Gosh. Too many. I got two boys and two girls, and one wants to go to private school. She can sing like an angel but creative arts school is expensive."

Wow. Another person with kids. Perhaps Robin truly didn't know her team too well. "Awesome. I wish I could sing."

"Yeah…"

Kevin stumbled over, though it was unclear if he had been drinking or just relaxing. "Hey, Purse. Don't flirt with this one. She's married."

Percy held up his middle finger. "At least I *am* married. Your pickup lines are so bad, single women have called congress to have you deported to Canada."

Ouch. Where was that craziness during the day?

"I guess I shouldn't have borrowed *yours!*"

"Whoa. Whoa. Whoa. You better not be picking on tonight's hero," Jacob said, putting his arm over Robin's shoulder. For the first time, his touch didn't elicit fear or loathing.

"Y'all still didn't need to do this for me." Robin maintained her humble spirit, recognizing that her mother would give her a speech for acting like a diva. That said, the attention was nice. It didn't serve to prove she was doing the right thing, but rather to prove her coworkers trusted her.

"Oh, we did," Jacob said. He gave a gentle push. "Come over here. He took her across the room to a young lady she recognized. "Hey, Lindsay. This is Captain Chapel. Tell her about June's finances."

Lindsay was a short lady with wide hips but a narrow waist. She had bold pink lipstick that complemented her blond hair. She

Andy Silvers

had no wedding band like so many C. E. Proctor Creative employees, but she spoke like she had practice. "Hello." She shook hands with the EOTM. "Yeah. We've had good sales. I mean, our June's tend to be a bit slower, but thus far, I've seen about twenty-four percent increase in gross sales. The biggest thing is the size and scope of our campaigns, not so much quantity."

"Yeah…so all that techno-nonsense to say that Robin has helped us reach big numbers." Jacob could truly be awesome when he picked a side.

Lindsay nodded cautiously. "I don't like to attribute growth to singular individuals without consistent observation, but I'm sure Robin has done a great job." Goodness, she sounded like an AI program designed to insult people with compliments.

"*Pfft.*" Jacob swatted at her. "That's BS. Robin's Tweet went viral and she was on TV. *National freaking* TV. That's why our sales went up." It was actually state TV.

"I'm sure that's a factor." Lindsay really didn't hold back. Even though Jacob was visibly irritated, Robin really just wanted to see Lindsay and Dexter duke it out. $100 on Lindsay, for sure.

"*Awe,* never mind. Let's go over here." Jacob guided Robin back into the conference room. To maximize space, they used the hallway to place food on folding tables, allowing everyone to gather and eat in the conference room. Though, filling it with nearly a dozen people did make it seem smaller.

"Hey, Catherine," Robin spoke to the young bachelorette who was sipping champaign and scrolling on her phone. "Sorry Ray couldn't be here. He broke his hand at work."

"Oh gosh. Are you sure you shouldn't be watching him?"

"I'm sure he's just watching TV. He'll be fine. But how about Mr. Carter. When you gonna get more than a bracelet?" She winked twice.

Hoop Drama

"Um…I hope soon. He's happy and I'm happy. No need to rush."

That didn't sound right. Catherine had wanted to put family on fast forward. "Do you have any wedding plans?"

For the next half hour, the two ladies sipped beverages and discussed romantic wedding ideas. Jacob occasionally popped in to make a funny remark, and Percy left early to put his kids to bed.

❄❄❄

"You don't have to go home but you can't stay here!" Jacob hollered across the room while throwing away paper plates in a large trash can. "Thank y'all for coming. Let's give one final round of applause for the first employee of the month." Everyone clapped but very quietly. It was nearly 9 PM and it was clear by everyone's droopy eyes.

"Thank you so much, Jacob. I'm proud of us." Robin personally thanked him and anyone leaving the event. Jacob threw everything he could find into the trash, then stretched his arms.

"I'm heading out. We'll clean this crap up tomorrow."

"Are you sure? Dexter will walk right through here to his office."

He yawned. His choice was clear. "Goodnight. Imma head out." He did just that, turning off the conference room light as he walked. With only the hallway light on, the office took on a spooky vibe. The narrow space became as cramped as a coffin.

"Goodnight." Robin felt a chill in her spine as soon as Jacob left. She was the only person there and she worried Dexter would make her clean everything up since the party was technically for her. She began to straighten the area. She paused to text her husband.

383

Andy Silvers

ROBIN: *The party is over. I'm cleaning up.*

She continued to put trash away as well as move furniture back to its proper location. Suddenly, a chill ran down her spine like a serpentine ghost. She was in the same office, but it took on a new life. Her mind kept busy by imagining Catherine's wedding. Perhaps she'd have it at the abandoned clinic where the movie was shown. And she could wear an all-black wedding dress. Robin wasn't the gothic type so she imagined black colors and large cylindrical earrings filling half the seats.

"Mrs. Robin Chapel..."

"Damnit!" She jumped, throwing a spoon onto the floor. She was in the hall, trying to fold up all the tables. "Don't sneak up on—"

There was a man standing there. A fluorescent light over his head left his eyes in shadow, making them appear as dark circles. There was only one possibility—that was Mr. Proctor himself.

"Mrs. Chapel. Please follow me upstairs."

His voice was gruff and deep like a country singer, but he had no twang. He wore a button-up shirt and black pants. His shoulders were broad and his hair was a sea of black and gray. His wedding band glimmered in the light. She followed him, dreading every moment. She wouldn't have been nervous at all if he'd actually talked to her before. But this was like speaking to a phantom. A ghost of a man.

Instead of taking the elevator as expected, the CEO trudged up the stairs, avoiding the railing by walking in the middle. His office door was wide open, so they both entered the room in complete silence.

His office was dark; only a few lamps lit the room. It was a large room indeed, but it felt small due to massive wooden shelves on all sides filled with books and binders. The smell of cedar was

Hoop Drama

strong. His desk stood ahead on the left, covered in documents and a single laptop. Mr. Proctor sat down and so did his employee.

Robin held her hands together as if at a funeral, she smiled slightly, hoping to remove the feeling of malaise. "Sorry you missed the party. I had no idea you were here."

He stared at her. He had a shaved face, no obvious tattoos, and a piercing stare that left her licking her lips just to feel something. "I know."

"Okay. Thank you for letting us have it here. It's nice to finally meet you."

He closed the lid of his laptop, removing the warm light hitting his face. Now, a single halogen bulb illuminated the right side of his face, making him appear almost skeleton-like. "Mrs. Chapel. I've heard about your job offer in Athens. You have an interview soon."

Yikes. He wasn't a fan of subtlety but it made sense that he'd know given his access to her company email. "Yes sir. I don't know if I will take it—I mean, that assumes I do well in the interview which is doubtful. I'm happy to work here as long as you need me." She never thought she'd actually get that job.

Another long silence brought the room's ambient sound to below 20dB. It was eerie, and truthfully, Robin was becoming more annoyed than afraid. Did this business professional really treat his clients like that?

"About that…" He sat so still it seemed he was paralyzed from the neck down. His head tilted some and he blinked in a regular rhythm, but he had a haunting persona for sure. "I think you should take it."

"The interview?"

"The job."

Wow. He didn't hide that he wanted her out. "Um…I might if

○ 385 ○

Andy Silvers

I do well in the interview."

"You should. I put in the good word for you—wrote an incredible letter with all the fancy words and positive affirmation."

Robin was speechless. *He did what? Why?* He couldn't possibly hate her, right? "Thank you, sir, but I may not get the job. My resume is close to empty, but I suppose my news thing will help. So…yeah."

"Yeah…I finally found you, or more accurately, someone like you. You had done good work there, and I was impressed."

"Work, sir. Here?"

"At the diner. Keep up, dear. I've been struggling for the past year, maybe two on what to do with my company. We hired you to do our part, to make the world better. I've been told at *every* conference in *every* state that my workforce is important. I try to take popular advice." His subtle smile lacked any warmth.

This guy would be great at riddles. "Okay. Thank you for recognizing my talent. I'm glad you did, Mr. Proctor."

"I don't feel like Mr. Proctor anymore." He flinched his shoulders as though feeling a sudden itch. "Our campaigns are being helmed by a waitress from a backwater college."

"Excuse me?" Robin had begun to resent his vagueness. And she knew an insult when she heard it. "Where did you go to school?"

"Duke. Anyway, I wrestled for months with the burden of knowledge because I too believed the hype. Hire a diverse workforce; get incredible results. But I'm not convinced that this corporate doctrine is for me. So, please. *Take* the job. They want you. Just be confident and say what you believe. Never lie about who you are." He spoke the last three sentences with a calmness fit for a Buddhist monk.

Finally, a point of agreement. Robin was willing to acquiesce,

Hoop Drama

just to get him to shut up. "Okay. If they pick me, I'll go. I see you want me to do new things and advance in my career. I'm happy to do graphic design. It's my dream."

"You will *never* do that here."

Maybe through his anger he could still see a path forward for her. "Really? Even with the new hiring?"

"No, Robin. You're fired."

Robin's jaw shook as she stuttered a few unidentifiable noises. He was petty. It was clear now. He hated her for some reason that he was too childish to say. And rest assured, Robin said all of that.

"I'm not petty, sweetheart. My company is *my* business and I've outsourced my morality to *you!*" For once he raised his voice. "No one can say I didn't try. No one can say I don't care about this country. Go. You *will be* successful. I know you have the talent."

"So...why fire me? Don't I at least get a report or investigation?" She was fully on the defensive.

He finally moved his arms to point at her employee file. "No. You've been here less than ninety days. The trial period is still ongoing. Please grab anything that belongs to you and be out by 9:30. Thank you."

Robin scoffed so he could hear. This guy was a moron. Or worse. A zealot. She leaned over his desk with an icy stare. "No *thank you!* You're insane. If I'm that talented—I mean—the profits have gone up like 25%. That's great!"

"I don't care about the money, Chapel. I choose the right side of history."

"Yeah right!" Robin stormed out, hitting the elevator button, then decided to grab her stuff after all. Her heart was racing and her lips were pursed together.

What the hell just happened?

Fired for being too talented? Fired for being too smart? What

Andy Silvers

an asshole. She took the stairs down as the elevator was too slow. She flew past the folded tables in a daze that lasted until she got home.

When she entered the apartment, only the TV illuminated her path. Robin dropped everything on the 'stuff' chair, looking toward heaven with a 1,000-yard stare.

Ray noticed her and muted the TV. "Babe. Hey, you're a bit late. How was the party?"

She said not a word. She crossed her arms to protect her heart then plodded over to the living room.

Ray got up instinctually. "Honey. What happened? Did you get hurt? Please speak to me." He caressed her cheek with his unbroken hand.

Finally, her mouth quivered and she shed many tears. Her moans were like weights that her husband happily carried for her. "Everyone hates me. I just make things worse. I always start with friends, but then eventually, they realize I'm obnoxious..." She bawled into his shoulder.

"Dear, lord. Sweetie, that's not true." She lowered herself to the floor where she sat in front of him. "You make every day better. Everyone loves you. What's wrong?"

"I...was fired." She tried to poise herself to no avail. The bulletproof Robin had taken too many rounds.

"Oh, good grief. That's not your fault. I know it."

"And now, I have no job. No family. No..."

"Baby. I'll always be here...until death do us part."

SATURDAY, JUNE 23ᴿᴰ

Friday came and went like a fever dream. The couple woke up on the floor, wrapped in each other's arms. By Saturday morning, Robin was prepared to tackle her interview. Ray made her an excellent breakfast to get her ready and insisted she drink lots of coffee. In her anger, she wanted to spite Mr. Proctor but had no way to do so. Reddit had recommended a wrongful termination suit, but that'd just motivate him to rescind his supposed letter of recommendation.

"Hey," he said with his trademark smile. "No matter what happens, we're gonna go back there and get your job. You were fired for nothing."

She nodded, though she had no investment in that place anymore. There were several texts from her coworkers asking where she was, but eventually the news got out and Catherine was quick to message her.

CATHERINE: *Damn girl; that's insane. I'm gonna talk to them for you because the employee of the month shouldn't be fired. I knew that Charles was controlling but my goodness.*

JACOB: *I'm pissed. You have no idea. I just talked to Charles for you. He's gonna lose me too if he can't make things right.*

Wow. Jacob was a soldier. He believed in her just like he said he did. But C.E. Proctor was in the past. The best decision, albeit

Andy Silvers

hard, was to do the interview confidently just like Charles wanted.

"It's nice of them to let you do the interview virtually." Ray dropped off a hot cup of tea. It soothed the throat.

"Yeah."

For some reason, she wanted this job more than anything. Sure, it would give Charles what he wanted, but it would also prove that Robin had made it—that she could stand on her own. Her job had not given her most of her accomplishments. Charles only lit the flame that she carried across the finish line.

She took a deep breath. A notification popped up, asking her to join the meeting. A gulp of tea preceded the click. Kiera Dublin sat on the right next to a black female with lovely dreads. They sat on rolling chairs in a brightly-lit conference room.

"Hello. Can you hear me?" Kiera led off the interview with a cordial smile. The bottom corner showed the other lady's name— Roxanne.

"Yes ma'am," Robin replied, an honest smile adorning her face. "Thank you for having me."

"Absolutely. Let's go ahead and get started today. My name is Kiera Dublin and my partner here is Mrs. Roxanne Tumble. We're gonna start by just explaining the job real quick for you."

"Awesome."

"So...the position is our full-time graphic design position. You will work in the creative team under Ms. Riley Zhao. Okay, so that's first. Your job will consist of working in the office Monday through Friday creating artwork and designs inspired by our research team. There're four other artists who you will meet and you will work under the lead designer. Any questions so far?"

"No, ma'am." She was loving it so far, but to seem more professional, she grabbed a sketchpad from work to take notes.

"Awesome. We are a deadline-based business so you will

Hoop Drama

have to work quick and fearless because we're pumping out content every week. Our clients range from food trucks to shoe brands, so that's just the workflow. Ms. Zhao will meet with the team and give you the necessary info to begin work. We use Adobe Creative Cloud and sometimes iPad apps. You will be provided Wacom tools and other stuff to complete assignments which will be documented in your employee log. That'll tell you what to do. Um…I'm gonna let Mrs. Tumble ask you a few questions real quick."

"Thank you. Yes, my name is Roxanne. Good morning."

"Good morning."

"So, at BL Media, we strive to always improve and deliver better results than last time. Can you describe an experience where you were asked to improve your workflow and how you did that?"

Oh gosh. Robin was admiring how professional and friendly the interview was compared to Charles' cold hatred, but an answer didn't spring to mind quickly. She smiled to buy time. "I remember creating copy for a website and typing up some ideas, but I collaborated with a colleague to improve my workflow. I drew stuff on my drawing pad and found ways to make it better so that I submitted something that had been read over several times."

"Okay. Nice. Can you describe a time when you were approaching a deadline and felt that you couldn't finish on time? What did you do to get the job done so that the team could work on the next project?"

"Oh my. I try to plan to avoid that by figuring out what tasks will be easiest, but I think that happened once. My job was to research product packaging and submit ideas. It was for a pill company—like a supplement type thing. I asked my friend for what to do and they recommended a few websites that aggregate designs and stuff that I used to prepare the PDF."

Andy Silvers

"Okay, so you collaborate?"

"Yes, ma'am. I do and I also create lists of sites that can make my job easier and allow me to finish on time."

"Okay. Great. If you work with a team—and I know you have—and you have a coworker who isn't really pulling their weight; they're getting behind. How do you handle that situation?"

Luckily that hadn't come up hardly ever at Proctor Creative, but she had to give a textbook answer anyway. "Okay. My coworkers have been great. They work really hard. When one of us gets behind, we are open and honest about it. We communicate and figure out how to coordinate the best solution. If they refuse to work, I guess I'd ask our supervisor to assist me with speaking to them. They may just be having a bad day. I try to focus on my work and get it done...yeah. I treat my coworkers with respect."

"Interesting. We get that."

She asked three more probing questions, and they were hard ones. She had never been in some of those situations and she knew they didn't want the real answer. They wanted the corporate answer that shows hard work and a competitive spirit. She was confident in her delivery, but inside a ball of anger formed.

The fact that Mr. Proctor would fire the only black employee there, she couldn't bring up. She couldn't mention Dexter's racist remarks or the way she altered campaigns without permission. Her true story—the one of a lonely woman fighting to be heard—she couldn't even mention. Her qualifications weren't her degree or her sketchbook drawings. They were her lived experience. Her bravery in the face of evil. For the latter half of the interview, she feared that generic answers would fail her yet again. Why would they hire the girl who didn't stand out? At the end of the interview, she brought up her TV appearance.

"Yes," Mrs. Tumble replied. "We saw that. That was

awesome. It's actually the reason you were on our radar."

"Sure," Kiera added. "That was big. We really appreciated your truthfulness and how you used your skill to bring attention to a just cause."

"Thank you. I met Mr. Porter and he thanked me personally for my Tweet?"

"Really. Well, how about that!"

"Yes. That man is the humblest person I've ever met. I hope to have forgiveness like that."

"For sure." Kiera put down a folder. "Thank you again for joining us. If you have any questions, please ask. We will be in touch with you probably within a week. Look out for an email.

"Yeah. Thank you, Mrs. Chapel. We hope to speak with you again."

"Awesome. Likewise." She shut her laptop's lid.

Ray prepared lunch in the kitchen. "Hey. How'd it go?"

"Awful." She wasn't being sarcastic. Despite being cheery and professional the whole time, her answers were mediocre at best and it was safe to say that unlike Proctor Creative, dozens of other qualified girls were waiting too. "I really want this job, but I know better."

"I bet you will. You sounded like you knew what you were doing. Hey, I know what you need. You need your mom's encouragement."

Yeesh. She hadn't told Shanice about the firing yet. The last thing she needed was an angry black lady storming into the agency screaming about racism. This wasn't a battle Robin needed to fight alone, yet it wasn't one she could share either. She could fight and kick and claw, but reality always found a way to push her back to the starting line. Everyone could agree she was mistreated, but only one person could agree she was right for the job. She texted

393

Andy Silvers

Jacob.

ROBIN: *Hey. Thank you for standing up for me today. I did an interview for a job in GA. Whatever happens, don't quit. I truly don't want to go back to Proctor C. I miss you.*

Finally, Kevin texted something.

KEVIN: *Hey, I'm sorry you were canned. I'm shocked Chuck would ever hire for DEI. Jon says hi.*

Robin reread that text three times. DEI? No. Whatever word salad Charles had spewed that night, there's no way he actually hired her to improve the racial makeup of the company.

ROBIN: *Tell Jon I said hi. Thanks for being there.*

"Babe. I've got it. Let's go there."

Robin tried to eat her first bite of chicken salad. "Huh?"

"Let's go to Georgia. Where is it? —Marietta. I'll get us packed."

"Whoa. Hold up, Mr. Chapel. We can't do that. It's like eight hours drive. Plus, you're injured."

"Nah. We'll fly. Come on. Our expenses haven't really changed but our income has. That means we have at least two grand to use for whatever. Hold on!"

He jumped like a kid back to the bedroom with their crummy laptop. He started scheduling a trip to the Atlanta airport. After she had finished her salad, he spoke up. "See, I got us tickets for tomorrow at 7 AM. It's like $700 for a round trip and we can rent a car probably."

Oh my. Anyone who said men and women were from the same planet were selling snake oil. "Honey, you didn't already buy anything. We gotta think about this."

"What! This'll show them you're serious. Plus, I can't go back to work for two weeks and you can't go back...ever!"

"Don't remind me."

○ 394 ○

Hoop Drama

"So, let's do it. A few hotel nights and it's like another $650 maybe. Plus, I'll let you share a bed with me." He gave a seductive wink.

"I just..."

"Too late! We're going. Tickets are non-refundable."

"You didn't. You know I can't hit you while you're injured." That man was a blessing and a curse. After putting up her bowl, he was in the bedroom packing up. "Do you really think I just wear bras and panties?"

"I haven't gotten to the other stuff yet."

After a long complicit sigh, she begun packing her suitcase herself. It was true. They had saved up hundreds of extra dollars other than their new TV purchase. Finally, she was excited. Every corner of Ohio had been visited in her childhood years, but Georgia was a mystery. Furthermore, she had only flown once before and it was a brief flight.

"Hey...Ray. Kevin said maybe Dexter hired me for DEI. Do you think that's possible?"

"Sounds good."

Did he hear me? "I was fired though."

"Don't think about the past right now. Let's look to the future. Heck, if you're done with Proctor Creative, maybe we'll move to Georgia anyway. There's a lot of work down there."

"Wherever you go, I go."

MONDAY, JULY 9TH

After two weeks, Robin was DIFFERENT.

She earned the job! She and Ray had found a small house to rent in the Marietta area, roughly thirty minutes from Robin's new job at the agency.

Shanice called to wish her well. [My baby. I'm so proud of you. You did what I never could. That's right.]

"Awe. Thanks, Mom. You still have my heart. Ray's at the house getting stuff ready. I'm about to walk in for my first day. I already know the receptionist and one of the finance people, so that'll help with the transition."

She could hear Shanice sniffling and inhaling on the other end. [True. My daughter's gonna be big. I'm so sorry. I should 'a had your back the whole way.]

"What? No, I don't remember what you're talking about. When I forgive; I forget. I'm excited about today."

[You're right. Hm...I can't wait to see what you do. You know, I remember a joke Tommy Craven made about that or something.]

"Uh, well I'll have to hear it later. I'm here."

[Oh okay. You do great, sweetie. Tell Ray not to mess nothing up.]

"All right, I will. Bye. Love you."

Hoop Drama

She took a deep sigh. Not because she was nervous, but because she was ready. She just needed some extra air.

She strutted up to the side door, but without a key card, employees can't enter there. Without losing a beat, she went right to the front entrance. "Hey, Ms. Thomas. I'm back."

The receptionist waved to her new friend, followed by a quick buzz to the hiring manager. The lobby was lovely. It had white tile flooring and beautiful oak accents. She could almost smell it. The ARC sign hung dead center on a glowing backboard amidst artificial vines. It was corporate, yet contemporary. Professional, yet personal.

"There's our newest Picasso." Kiera Dublin greeted Robin through the main entrance. While the lobby was quaint with a single-story design, the room right behind the wall impressed like a colosseum with nearly three stories of height. This was where the clients would *actually* go first. It was technically a hallway, as it led to every other part of the building, but it felt majestic in its own right. This was no midsized agency. This was a massive company whose building occupied four floors and whose parking lot was triple the size of Proctor Creative.

"Hey. Yeah, it's an honor to be here. Gosh, I never thought it'd be me."

Kiera smiled warmly. "Absolutely. Welcome aboard. Kevin—I think it was—said you had just gotten employee of the month."

Wait! Kevin? "How do you know Kevin?"

"I think it's Kevin. Your coworker in West Virginia?" Robin nodded. "Yeah. I had no idea the crap you went through until he called us; told us everything. I would've sued."

Robin froze like a statue. She was freaked out! How much did she know? Robin hadn't even hinted at that during her interview.

397

Andy Silvers

"Yeah. I wasn't treated the best. I'm still not sure why he gave me a recommendation, but I can assure you it's all true." For only ten seconds that day, she grew slightly nervous.

"Oh, sweetheart, don't you know? The crusty business types are all the same. They want your black skin but not your black voice. Let's go upstairs to where you'll work."

For the first time, she acknowledged the strange reality. Maybe she *was* a DEI hire. Perhaps Charles in his addled MAGA brain had really tried to give a black girl a chance only to rescind his graciousness the moment she spoke. Then, near the elevator, she noticed some busts. There were seven statues on Greckoroman stands placed symmetrically by the elevator. "What are these?"

"Ah. Those are busts of famous people. All people of color who have had an impact on our country. It was Aaron's idea."

Robin recognized the bust of Martin Luther King Jr., Barack Obama, Harriet Tubman, and Jackie Robinson. To her embarrassment, she couldn't quite identify the last few and there were no name plates. "I love the design."

"Yes. They're based on Roman and Greek designs. All throughout history, people of importance have been recognized with these marble busts. But you know, most were white. We understand that marble is white, but with modern technology, we can easily recognize the heroes of today. They're painted to accurately show the skin that's been ignored for decades. Oh, here's our ride."

"Wow." Even the elevator was fancy. There were doors on both sides and a two-tone finish of steel and Mahogony. The rear door opened on the third floor where a cascade of chatter enveloped the eardrums. People collaborated left and right. Down the hall, past several smiling faces was the design suite. A room marked clearly for the design lead was placed close to several rounded cubicles where designers worked on multi-monitor setups. One desk lay empty, promising a playground for the new artist.

Robin had only brought her sketchbook and purse, hoping that everything else would be provided. Kiera confirmed as much. "This is Corbin Wyobeih. And your other teammate is Alexandria Peirce, but she goes by Alex. The other two are probably making coffee."

"Awesome." Robin was greeted with a firm handshake from both and no rude comments about her hoop earrings.

Kiera continued. "Ms. Zhao, I think is in her office, but she's probably on a call since her door is shut. You'll definitely meet her before the day is out so don't worry. Your station is over there. I hope you know MACOS since that's all we got for the design team."

"I'll make it work."

"Great. And you know, Corbin is a tech wizard so he can help you if you have questions. He helps me a lot. That's for sure. Anyway, let me show you the restrooms. They're down this way to the left. We have men's and women's as well as non-binary for any who need that accommodation."

The floor was a light wooden finish that looked like the nicest kitchens at Ikea. Everyone dressed fairly casual (except Kiera) just like at her old job so that was a plus. Vaulted lighting fixtures gave the area a grand feeling. Despite there being only one window visible near the fire exit, the entire area was bright.

"This is the break room—"

"Oh, gosh!" It was enormous.

"You like it? It's got games and snacks and a pool table over there."

Andy Silvers

This room had windows. All the windows. "Would it be okay if I brought homemade cookies sometimes?"

"Girl, if you can cook, please bring whatever you want. We love celebrating our team's talents. For me, I play guitar, so sometimes I go to our room and strum a little tune."

"Awesome. I can't wait to hear that."

"Well, see we have two break rooms. One for our creative teams which includes you and another for the business team which includes me and the finances people. Don't worry though, you can visit us on your forty-five-minute lunch."

It was all incredible...at least on day one. A career job. Not a pay-the-rent job. This was the kind of place a girl could really shine. More importantly, this was the type of business that spotlighted everyone no matter what their background. Ads must reach the entire United States, but Proctor Creative only seemed to notice the Bible belt.

"Over here is our video suite. It's cool but I don't know how anything works." She pushed open a sliding door. Inside was the Proctor Creative suite on steroids. The video camera looked like it swallowed up an entire Radio Shack. "We film ads in here for the biggest brands. We occasionally have celebrities and athletes film stuff here. Like one time we had Bradley Beal with the Wizards here. He was filming an ad for some home security thing."

"Cool. That's that guy from Harry Potter."

Kiera giggled. "No. The basketball team. You know, the NBA?"

Robin clenched her hands in embarrassment. "Oh, sorry. I'm not a huge sports person."

"I can tell. Anyway, this is video stuff. Let me show you where I work."

Robin recalled her awkward relationship with Mr. Proctor and

Hoop Drama

thought she might want to meet the boss in person soon. "I would love to meet Mr. Rafellow if he's not too busy."

Kiera talked while she quickly led Robin back into the elevator. "I hope you mean Mr. Rafellow, not Mr. Rafellow. Aaron retired three years ago. His son, Augie, now runs things. We can see if he's available, but since I'm the HR person too, I wanna show you where to go to complain."

Funny. At Proctor Creative, she might've used that. It was strange to think that her former boss had no designated HR person. Perhaps it's because he knew he'd get too many complaints. On the second floor, she twisted and turned through a maze of hallways to reach the office of Ms. Kiera Dublin.

"Here it is. Yes, it's messy, but if I clean it, I'll never do anything again. I might be sorta ADHD. I just can't clean anything because then I'll just wanna clean everything, but if I start a project I can hardly eat until it's finished. Oh, it drives me nuts. Anyway, this is my office and the finances people are down there. Actually, you should go there now to sign some stuff, okay. Just knock on the door."

She met the finances guy, a short chubby man with thick glasses. He swung around to greet the new employee. Elton John blasted from a portable speaker, so he was probably fun.

"Hey, are you Rian?"

"No sir. Robin Chapel. It's nice to meet you." It was odd saying 'yes sir' again, but this time was different. Instead of being some kind of necessity brought about by fear or tradition, it was a kind gesture meant to start a happy career. In her mind, she saw herself with the window office. The man looked to be about sixty, but maybe she'd be his boss before he retired. Only time would tell, but at least there were no rooms she felt were off limits due to being 'too special.'

Andy Silvers

Ironically, she never did meet Mr. Rafellow that day, but her teammates proved to be grateful and kind. They helped her set up her new MAC and showed her how to use the drawing tools. Perhaps she wouldn't need her drawing pad ever again.

The day was boring truthfully, though she never felt weary. She signed the I9, setup her new credentials, and completed several training modules. This time, one included a 'Race and Inclusion' lesson, something her old boss would likely have imploded to see.

She left work at around six, knowing that life wouldn't always be easy, but it'd always pay off to stand tall, even if she had to stand alone.

❀❀❀

The new house was a showroom for the nicest cardboard and plastic the Chapels could afford. Carter and Catherine, lovingly called Catheter, helped the Chapels pack, but no one was there for the unpack, so dinner was on the living room floor and the mattress was on the bedroom floor.

"Carter's a sissy, you know." Ray slid his bottled water away from his bowl of microwavable pastrami.

"Yeah. Is this about the ring?"

"Yup. He bought that thing a week ago, but he's too scared to ask."

Robin nodded. "Give him time. His life will change completely. One day he'll be goofing off with his friends at the bar then he'll be finding missing Scooby Doo toys under the staircase."

Ray chuckled. "Yeah. Life does change quickly. Renters' insurance took a bite out of my check, but hopefully we'll have some cash to pay bills."

"I think we'll have lots of money with my new job."

Hoop Drama

Ray lit up like a boy on Christmas morning. "There's you thinking positive. Birdman money."

"Yup. You know, Catherine wants to move here…to be with family."

Ray's eyes narrowed. "She doesn't know about the ring, does she?"

"No. But she knows what's next, and she's excited. Me too."

Robin crossed her legs, finding her old position uncomfortable. The last thing she wanted was to feel unease at her new home right before her big announcement.

"Yeah. Maybe I'll get a job around here. I bet there's a lot of shops in the area. I think I could easily make eighteen an hour or more. At least it'd give me something to do."

Robin took a deep breath. She had her purse casually draped over her shoulder. Things were changing indeed. She had made her dream come true, only not to know what to do next. Maybe she'd love design and do that for decades, or maybe she'd decide management was the place for her. Her strategy to make allies at her old job had been fruitful, so perhaps the same thing could work in Georgia. The fight for equality had proven successful, so what was there to do once it had been reached? A run for president?

When everyone looked like her, how could she stand out? When everyone thought like her, how could she speak up? The cost of victory was that one day, everything would be conquered and there would be no new lands to traverse. The road not traveled became Main Street. That would be the challenge for tomorrow. Robin had one thing on her mind.

"About that." She pulled out a small box from her purse. "I've got a gift for you."

Ray scooched over with a grin. "I wondered why you were eating dinner with that bag on."

Andy Silvers

He removed a bright green bow from the small nine-inch box. It looked like a bracelet box, so Ray asked if it was. Robin shook her head. Ray trembled at the contents, seeing a famous double line that he'd only seen in movies. "Gosh, Robin. I can't breathe…"

She glowed brighter than the morning sun. With the setting sun came a new light. "Congrats, Raymond. You're gonna be a daddy."

ABOUT THE AUTHOR

Andy Silvers (Harvey Alter) is an author, filmmaker, and YouTuber who was born in Luga, Russia. His parents adopted him at the age of three and brought him to America where he required many surgeries to fix orthopedic issues including scoliosis, hip misalignment, and more. The Silvers also adopted four more kids from Russia in the early 2000s. Since his adoption, his father's work has moved him across the US including Illinois, North Carolina, South Carolina, and Virginia.

Since youth, he's always loved writing; starting with a never-to-be-released set of children's stories called Terra Menara. He once handwrote a book about the benefits of bees. After transferring credits from community college, he graduated Suma Cum Laude from Liberty University's Zaki Gordon Center. In 2021, he released an original short film entitled "Snapshot" that tackles oft-ignored themes of adoption and disability. As a person with a missing left arm, these ideas were close to his heart. This film won a newly-invented award in the Mozi Motion Int. Film Festival called "Accessibility."

Starting in 2020, Andy began writing novels and other books starting with *Red Sprites and Blue Jets*, a coming-of-age story for ages 8-12. Following this was a children's picture book called *The Very Colorful Caterpillar* inspired by the Eric Carle book. While wrapping up film school, he devised his first novella called *Solomon Grando vs the Jupiter Witch*; this book follows a vampire who must save the world during an epidemic outbreak while battling his greatest fear—witches. *Hoop Drama* represents his biggest undertaking being his first adult novel. This book was written while working a full-time job and creating YouTube videos about computers.

Printed in the USA
CPSIA information can be obtained
at www.ICGtesting.com
LVHW010112121024
793461LV00013B/567